D0090043

TIME AFTER TIME

"AN ADVENTURE YARN, A LOVE STORY, A HISTORY LESSON, A MORALITY PLAY—a smorgasbord served up in strong, admirable prose. Don't be surprised if you devour the whole thing in a single, gluttonous binge."
—Nicholas Proffitt, author of
Gardens of Stone

"MUCH FUN IS TO BE HAD IN THIS NOVEL: the action, the re-creation of Revolutionary Russia, several well-drawn and likeable characters, the various time-tricks. . . . This book should be read in a comfortable armchair, not far from a well-stocked refrigerator and a boiling samovar."
—*Best Sellers*

"A ROUSING STORY . . . high action, cossack attacks, and the changing of history."
—*Ocala Star Banner*

"VIVID . . . something of a historical novel, something of a science fiction novel, partly the story of a son's bitter relationship with his father, partly a romance . . . pleasingly balanced . . . with grace and skill."
—*The New York Times Book Review*

"MOVES AS QUICKLY AS AN EXPRESS TRAIN . . . Appel never lets things drag. Readers learn how a clever and knowledgeable novelist can be historically accurate, creating a fantasy that works without being ridiculous . . . a fascinating tangle of historical and personal coincidence."
—*Northwest* Magazine

QUANTITY SALES

Most Dell Books are available at special quantity discounts when purchased in bulk by corporations, organizations, and special-interest groups.
Custom imprinting or excerpting can also be done to fit special needs. For
details write: Dell Publishing Co., Inc., 1 Dag Hammarskjold Plaza, New
York, NY 10017, Attn.: Special Sales Dept., or phone: (212) 605-3319.

INDIVIDUAL SALES

Are there any Dell Books you want but cannot find in your local stores?
If so, you can order them directly from us. You can get any Dell book in
print. Simply include the book's title, author, and ISBN number, if you have
it, along with a check or money order (no cash can be accepted) for the full
retail price plus 75¢ per copy to cover shipping and handling. Mail to: Dell
Readers Service, Dept. FM, P.O. Box 1000, Pine Brook, NJ 07058.

TIME AFTER TIME

ALLEN APPEL

LAUREL

A LAUREL TRADE PAPERBACK
Published by
Dell Publishing Co., Inc.
1 Dag Hammarskjold Plaza
New York, New York 10017

Copyright © 1985 by Allen Appel

All rights reserved. No part of this book may be reproduced or transmitted in any form or by any means, electronic or mechanical, including photocopying, recording, or by any information storage and retrieval system, without the written permission of the Publisher, except where permitted by law. For information address: Carroll & Graf Publishers, New York, New York.

Laurel ® TM 674623, Dell Publishing Co., Inc.

ISBN: 0-440-59116-3

Reprinted by arrangement with Carroll & Graf Publishers

Printed in the United States of America

March 1987

10 9 8 7 6 5 4 3 2 1

W

Dedication

For my father, who always finds the things I need,
and my mother, who let me read at the dinner table
all those years.

Acknowledgements

I would like to thank my wife Sherry for reading, correcting, and offering always valuable suggestions, my son Allen for his confidence and high expectations and my little daughter Leah for taking long naps. Bill Garrison and Bhob Stewart helped when I most needed it, once again proving what good friends and fine writers they both are. And of course I would like to thank my friend Kent, the real Pastmaster.

"Reasons and opinions concerning acts are not history. Acts themselves are history."

William Blake

Chapter 1

THE HEADACHE WAS GONE. ALEX BALFOUR WAS LYING FACEDOWN in a shallow trench. The ground was cold and hard and smelled of clay and mold.

He had just enough time to lift his head up out of the dirt before the first shell slammed into the earth. A howling rush of air and then the explosion.

The sound, the feel, was like a locomotive falling from the sky. He was slapped up into the air then hammered back as thick clods of dirt thudded down. He tried to burrow into the earth, knowing instinctively that his only protection was to hide his soft body deep under the ground. All secondary thought processes were lost as the shells tracked in on a line that paralleled his trench. His heart was pounding. The terror drew small mewling sounds from him. His brain jammed, allowing only primary thoughts and functions; fear, confusion, survival.

Silence.

His ears rang with it. He flinched as a flare burst high in the air with a flat pop and drifted slowly down, hissing, casting a cold magnesium light that drenched his limited landscape, coloring it a pale, monochromatic blue.

There were other men lying in the trench with him. They were not moving. He risked a look over the edge and saw

1

nothing he recognized; flat fields, mounds of blasted earth, a roll of barbed wire in the distance. The air seemed to ripple for a second, then held clear and sharp. The pounding of his heart slowed, but he was still afraid. In the dim light he could see he was dressed in his usual cotton knit shirt and jeans. He was cold.

He pushed away a boot near his face. Part of the sole was missing and the ankle was wrapped in rags. No response. He crawled carefully over the man, trying not to touch him, stopping just long enough to look into a dirty bearded face with wide-open dead eyes. He crawled on. The ground scraped at him. His breath plumed into the air. The flare that had hung so long hit the ground and died, plunging the world back into darkness. He stopped and waited.

The shells. A high whine as they passed into the distance. A low tumbling roar if they were close; a tearing sound just before they hit, the sound of a giant cloth being ripped apart; then the unbelievable slamming crash as they exploded, each time more terrifying than the last.

He doubled up to protect his belly. He sucked in air, reflexively trying to supply his pounding heart and his brain with enough oxygen to keep from fainting.

Silence. The pop; the hiss of another flare.

Alex opened his eyes. The man beside him moved slightly. Alex could see that he was watching him, the whites of the man's eyes contrasting starkly with his dark, dirt-smeared face. Alex dragged himself closer. The trench was wider and deeper here, room for both of them to face each other. The man was half sitting, half lying against the dirt wall. His right arm was wrapped around an old rifle with a long, four-sided bayonet in a fixed position.

"Zdra stvuitye," the man said softly. Hello—Russian: Alex understood the words.

Another flare popped, and another. The scene was sharply lit. The man looked up at the flares then back at Alex. "They are being especially diligent tonight," he said, still in Russian. "The Germans are a meticulous people, you know." He smiled to show that he was joking.

Alex could see the huge stain on the front of the man's coat. It was black in the light of the flares. He pulled himself closer and reached for the buttons of the coat. Now he could

2

smell the fresh blood, the sharp coppery scent that was almost a taste.

"No," the Russian said, "leave it alone. It is almost finished."

"We need to stop the bleeding," Alex said, speaking Russian without thinking.

"There is little bleeding left to stop, my friend," the man said, laughing a little. "I am in God's hands."

The flares hit the ground and died; one, two, three.

"You know," the Russian said—he didn't seem to notice the sudden darkness—"for the first time in two years I am not hungry. Also, I am not cold. This dying is not altogether a bad thing."

Alex waited for the shells, but they did not come. His eyes grew accustomed to the dim starlight.

The crackle of sporadic rifle fire opened up along the trench. "My comrades shoot," the man said, motioning vaguely along the line, "to let the Germans know that we are still here, that we are alive. It is not important to hit anything; we are making a statement. You understand?"

"Yes," Alex said, though he understood little. "Where are we? What is the date?"

The man grunted. "Where? Who knows. I think we are near the Baltic. Sometimes in the morning, if the wind is right, I can smell salt in the air. As for the date, didn't you know? It's Easter." He smiled. "It is a holiday, my friend." He inhaled sharply. "You may have my rifle," he said through clenched teeth, "they are very rare these days." He exhaled a long, bubbling sigh and died.

Far off a shell hit, then another, and another. In the darkness around him the men stopped firing and began to sing; first one lone voice, then others. The shells marched toward them as the song was picked up along the line. It was a hymn. Alex recognized the slow church rhythm, like the solid, precise pacing of the human heart, imagined robed men marching down long church aisles. The words were distinct, twisting thinly into the cold night, punctuated by the approaching shells: "Christ is risen from the dead, conquering death by death."

Alex tightened himself into a knot and waited. The shells came.

Sunlight knifed in around the edges of the heavily curtained windows. Thin beams lit the floor in sharp oblong shapes, the strong light carrying motes of dust that floated slowly, rising, winking; bright tiny satellites in a miniature universe. Alex Balfour sat sleeping in a deep, old, soft plush easy chair. An empty George Dickel whiskey bottle sat on the floor near his feet.

Except for the thin blades of sunlight, the living room was dark. The wooden floors were covered with Oriental rugs in deep wines and reds. Heavy Victorian furniture lurked in the dim light; large humped shapes that crouched on carved feet, waiting to snare unsuspecting prey. Books filled the floor-to-ceiling shelves along three of the walls. There were old leather-bound volumes, whole sets of encyclopedias and atlases, modern hardbacks, novels, textbooks, several shelves of paperbacks. More books were piled on the floor. The fourth wall held a long, low bookshelf lined with the identical grey plastic cases of videocassette recordings, the identifying labels handwritten on the spines; old movies, vintage television shows.

Alex stirred in his chair. He sat up and rubbed his face, his whiskers scratching the palms of his hands; a small sandpaper noise in the dead-silent room. He squinted at the lines of bright sun. His mouth tasted like mice had nested there overnight. His head ached with a dull pounding that began in his heart and ended in his prefrontal lobes. He stood and stretched, feeling his muscles pull, painfully realigning themselves after a night of sleeping in a chair. He felt as if he'd been beaten.

He went slowly up the stairs to his dark bedroom, carefully keeping his mind blank, thinking only of the pain in his head. He kicked off his shoes and took off his shirt and jeans and threw them in a pile of dirty clothes. He did not look at them, did not see the clay stains on the knees of the jeans, the clumps of mud stuck in the waffle-patterned soles of the shoes. The woman who picked up his wash once a week would notice the dirty jeans and wonder how a grown man—a history professor, for goodness sake—could get as dirty as a little boy.

He went to the window and pulled back the side of the drawn shade. The sunlight cut into his eyes, making him wince. He squinted out the window. Nothing moved on the street. Early morning. In the background he could hear the ever-present murmur of New York. On his residential side street it was still quiet.

He leaned back against the wall and pressed his hands to his head, trying to squeeze the pain away. It didn't work. No, I will not think about it, not now; some other time, when my head doesn't hurt, I promise. Right now I will be normal and I will take a bath and get ready to teach my class and try to get rid of this hangover. It wasn't worth it; getting drunk didn't help any more, didn't stop the dreams.

He padded into the bathroom and turned the water on in the large old claw-footed tub. He avoided the mirror over the sink.

When he had bought his three-story brownstone, he had made no structural changes other than in the bathroom. He'd knocked out two of the original walls, installed a large window that looked out over the alley in the back, and positioned the old tub up on a low platform. He'd plugged up the overflow holes in the tub so he could fill it right up to the edge. The water steamed as it splashed against the cool porcelain.

He stretched again and found the pain easier to bear. He considered getting down on the floor and trying a few sit-ups or push-ups but rejected the idea. He ought to; he was carrying fifteen extra pounds around the middle that he would be glad to be rid of, but his hangover said no, not this morning. Tomorrow; he'd start tomorrow. Last week a woman in a bar had said he looked like a tall but chubby Robert Redford. Chubby. She'd meant it as a compliment even though the light in the bar had been dim and the woman more than a little drunk. She was referring to his unruly blond hair and his blue eyes. His blandly handsome midwestern face. And his spare tire. He sighed and checked the tub. The water had risen to the mark he'd made with a piece of waterproof tape. He turned off the taps. His body would now displace just enough water to bring the level an inch below the rim. If he lost any weight, he'd have to raise the mark.

He kicked off his underwear and climbed into the tub. He stretched out as the water rose to his chest and stopped at his chin. Relax. He had hours before he had to face his students.

The hot water would take away the pain, loosen the muscles. He closed his eyes. Eased down until the water covered everything except his eyes, his nose, his mouth. He was floating. It brought back the memory of the day before. He tried to push it away—tomorrow; worry about it tomorrow—but it came anyway. It was too much, two times in a row, last night following right on the heels of yesterday. Yesterday it had happened in the afternoon. He had been sitting in his chair, reading a magazine, when the headache began. It had never happened before during the day; they were dreams and dreams happen at night, not during the day, not while you're sitting in a chair, reading a magazine.

Reasons, explanations. He was working too hard: Obviously not true; he wasn't working particularly hard at all. He was staying up late watching too many rental movies, too many old Ernie Kovaks shows, too many Honeymooners and *I Love Lucy*'s. Too much *Twilight Zone*. True, but that was nothing new; that was an old habit that hadn't ever bothered him before. He was drinking too much: Also true, but he was drinking because he was having the dreams, because they were happening during the day, because they had gone beyond anything normal and were carrying him along and becoming more and more real, and lastly because, God help him, he had been enjoying them, the way one enjoys horror movies, finding them one hell of a lot more interesting than living alone in his three-story brownstone and going to teach a history class once a week and sitting around reading books and watching television.

He floated in the bathtub and let himself remember. To hell with it, let it come. Yesterday. He had been sitting in his chair, reading a magazine. The headache began; lights flickered in the corners of his eyes.

And then it was as if he were standing against the bare plaster wall of a basement room.

* * *

A single bulb hung from the center of the ceiling. There were men in the room, seated at rough wooden tables. They were dressed in varied shades of the same dull hues: ochre, khaki, sepia. Their clothing seemed to soak up the light, leaching what little colors there were into a uniform monochromatic stain.

An iron stove in the center of the room glowed red, melting the snow on the men's clothing into puddles of dirty water on the cement floor. The men closest to the stove steamed.

The room stank. He became aware of it with a jolt. This was new. Before this he could see and hear, but never before had he been able to smell. Wet oily wool, old sweat, dirt. The air was thick with it. Tobacco smoke, fumes from the burning coal, the humid effusion of wet concrete. It was real to him in a way that his waking reality seldom was, each odor separate and sharply defined, heightened to a point of razor-sharp awareness, as if he had acquired a totally new sense.

They were Russians. Low guttural talk, great drooping mustaches, broad Slavic faces. Siberians, Tartars, Balts, Uzheks. He was able to catalogue the nationalities the same way he understood the language, as if he had gained some innate knowledge when he'd entered their world.

The men were drinking. It looked pre-Revolution, like the photographs of such places he had seen in books. Workers, a few peasants.

He watched a man come down the steps into the room. There was a light dusting of snow on the man's shoulders and sheepskin hat. He stamped his feet, knocking off the snow packed onto his boots. He moved to a nearby table and greeted the men there. The conversation flared for a moment, rose to accommodate the new man, then settled back down.

Alex moved, or it was as if he were moving, walking unseen to the door and then up the stairs, outside. It was snowing; light, dry flakes that fell with a look of permanence, a winter condition rather than a storm. He knew that it was very cold, but he did not feel it. He had no body here. When the wind blew, it did not touch him.

He was on the sidewalk of a wide avenue that stretched away on either side into darkness. The snow-covered streets were lit by faint streetlights. The line of dark stone buildings that flanked the sidewalks formed two low cliffs with little detail. The snow perched on the ledges of these buildings. A sleigh drifted by, a troika, the runners hissing, the hooves crunching on the packed snow, the breath from the three horses streaming into the air, like smoke from the nostrils of comic-book dragons.

At the edge of his vision, turning onto the street, was a

7

pair of headlights and the low purr of an automobile. The falling snow filled the two cones of light as the car approached. It seemed to be having trouble, sliding back and forth, as if the driver were unused to the snow.

He could see into the lighted interior of the slowly moving car. In the front seat the driver peered intently out into the night. He wore a chauffeur's livery and a worried expression. In the backseat were two men. One of them was young and aristocratic, slight and pale in the yellow light. The man beside him was a direct contrast, dark and powerful. They were laughing.

The larger man was dressed in a blue peasant shirt. He had long dark hair, bushy eyebrows, and a full, unkempt beard. As the car passed, this man turned and looked at Alex. His eyes narrowed and he stopped laughing.

Alex felt a wave of shock, a quick spurt of adrenaline, as he realized that he'd been *seen*. And then another shock, a hot flush, as he realized he recognized the man in the car.

Rasputin. The pictures of the period had been unfaithful only in their inability to convey the power of the eyes. He had felt himself begin to tear away from the scene in a panic as his body back in another time struggled to wake up. He smelled the cold snowy night and at the same time the stale air in his living room, felt his eyes open and at the same time still watched those other eyes as they focused on his through the rear window of the car, felt the actual touch of the eyes the way one feels the heat from a torch, smells the stink of death.

*   *   *

Back in the tub his eyes snapped open. He sat up and took a long breath. He closed his eyes again, felt his racing heart begin to slow. He was in the tub, not in the chair, not in a trench, not on some snowy street somewhere . . . else.

The dirt on his hands had begun to dissolve, drifting up in thin veils. Sitting up had set up a current. The veils tore and swirled in the eddies, dispersed into the larger volume. He sighed. It was no use. It would not leave him, would not wait for tomorrow. What would he do?

He leaned back. The water sloshed to the edge of the tub and back, the waves breaking and circling the soft shoal of his body. He would wash; he would get dressed; he would

8

teach his class. Just like a normal person. But the question remained. He almost laughed at the craziness of it as he let the question form. Why was the bathwater so dirty? He knew; oh, yes, he knew, had been pushing it away, refusing to look. Now he held his hands up in front of him, looked at the backs of the hands, the torn fingernails, each one rimmed with black grime, cut and scratched from scrabbling in the hard clay ground. He put his hands back under the water and squeezed his eyes shut and wondered where he had been, what was next. He could see, hear, smell, be seen, talk and be heard; now what was next? What more was there?

Oh, Alex, where have you been? Where are you going?

Chapter 2

ALEX BALFOUR WAS THE END PRODUCT OF A LONG LINE OF PROFES-sional historians. The clan had emerged from a generally undistinguished and ordinary past when Alex's English great-great-grandfather, Henry Allen Balfour, broke the family tradition of agrarian poverty by becoming the first Balfour to actually attain a formal education. As a boy he had come to the notice of a local cleric. He was admitted to school, did well, and became a schoolmaster, as did his son.

Peter Balfour, Alex's grandfather, who was a university-educated man, found his own career opportunities hampered by his lack of upper-class forebears. He emigrated to the United States, found employment at Yale University, and had a long and distinguished career as a professor of history.

Alex's father began his own career as an assistant lecturer at a small midwestern school, worked his way up to head of the department, and then, departing from the family's schol-arly past, wrote a historical novel set in pioneer days; it became a best-seller. After that came a succession of books that guaranteed his father's fame and fortune. This streak of Balfour celebrity ended on a bright, clear morning when the light plane in which Alex's mother and father were flying went down in the north Atlantic, a hundred miles southeast of Nova Scotia. The loss of his father was mourned by a nation of historical novel readers bereft at the loss of their favorite author. The mother was mourned by her teenage son, who stood at the grave side on an appropriately gray misty day and watched the two empty caskets—the bodies were never found—being lowered into the ground.

Alex inherited the Balfour family's primary characteristic; a love of history and scholarship. He became a historian, had never considered anything else. If he had not studied biology and actually known better, he would have said that a professional history gene had somehow become a permanent link in the chain of Balfour DNA, passed down from generation to generation as a favorable characteristic that contributed to the general success of the Balfour species.

The hot bath had done its job of relaxing his cramped muscles, if not of easing his mind. On the way to school he decided to worry about everything later, which was his standard method of dealing with problems. Sometimes it worked and they went away. Sometimes they didn't.

He sat at his desk, waiting for his students to wander in.

His achievements in undergraduate and graduate school, while not overwhelmingly superior, were always adequate and often impressive. He found that he had a predilection for the 'small fact' rather than broad overviews, a gift for ferreting out interesting details that worked especially well in examinations. Even when inadequately prepared, he was able to give the impression that he knew what he was talking about. He received good grades and that, coupled with the Balfour name, had allowed him to choose a teaching job from a wide range of possibilities. He had chosen the New School in New York because of its relative freedom and the fact that it was in the city.

He taught, though there was no economic necessity, because it was a family tradition, because he liked teaching, and because it got him out of the house. Over the years he had become more and more of a recluse, involved in his books and his tapes, his studies, never making close friends that would intrude on his personal world. He was not sure why he was retreating this way, but he found it comfortable. But he also knew that he ran the danger of becoming a middle-aged eccentric, so he taught. It got him out of the house at least one day a week.

His room was small, with the seats banked up towards the back. It was a classroom like classrooms all over the world; the same wooden desks, the same classroom smells. The students were like students everywhere. Most of them signed up because they needed a history credit and they had heard that he was at least mildly amusing; a few of them attended for unknown reasons and would drop out or fail; and a few more enrolled because they possessed a genuine interest in Russia and her involvement in the First World War, which was the subject of the class.

They came in clusters, some of them nodding or saying hello but most of them just looking for empty seats near their friends. Alex checked his pocket watch, a heavy old gold timepiece that had belonged to his long-departed grandfather. He looked at his fingernails. They were spotless, clipped down almost to the quick. He had worked for fifteen minutes to get them that way. He would think about it later.

He checked the watch again. Show time. "All right," he said, standing, "does anyone have any questions about the reading they were supposed to do for this class? Did anyone do the reading for this week?" Nothing again; a few murmurs. He didn't really expect answers. He just wanted to get them warmed up a bit. He'd often thought that teachers needed warm-up acts to go on first to get the students' brains in gear and functioning before the main event.

A distinct flash of color caught his eye. A woman with bright red hair, a green shirt, and a grey tweed skirt came in the door, hesitated, then walked up the steps to the back of the classroom. He held his breath until she turned around. There was no real doubt in his mind, but his reasoning capacities were slow to accept what he was seeing. No, it can't be. But it was.

Oh, yes, no mistake; one ex-girlfriend, Molly Ellen Glenn, last seen ten years ago boarding a jet to San Francisco, rumored to have married shortly thereafter, and not heard from since, was now taking a seat in the back row of his Russian history class. He could almost feel the adrenaline as it hit his bloodstream. He tried to analyze the conflicting emotions that were beginning to tug at him: fear, pain, hope, denial, aggression, and a few others as yet unnamed.

He fixed his attention on a student in the middle of the room and calmed himself. Later, Alex, when there aren't thirty students staring at you.

"We were discussing Russia's losses during the period shortly before the actual revolution. As you remember, Russia had entered the war against the Germans three years before in a blaze of unified patriotic fervor. After great initial success in the field the Russian army began to feel the effects of the massive logistical problems that faced her. In a few short years Russia had moved from an agrarian-based economy to that of a major industrial power. This was the first of her revolutions—an industrial revolution much greater, much more profound than any that ever took place in Europe or America. The focus of this great mechanization was, of course, the production of war material. But Russia is an enormous country. The lines of supply . . ."

"Excuse me, Dr. Balfour . . ."

He ground to a halt, steadied himself.

"Yes, Ms. Glenn?"

"Pardon me for interrupting, but could you tell us about the Tsar?" She was smiling politely.

"The Tsar, Ms. Glenn? What about the Tsar? He certainly enters the picture, if that's what you mean."

"I guess I mean a little further along. I'd like to know about when the Bolsheviks killed the royal family." She still had a sweet little smile.

"We won't be there for at least three weeks, Ms. Glenn. We have to get through the rest of the war before tackling the Bolshevik Revolution." He consciously allowed just a tiny hint of exasperation into his voice. Who would have guessed that this woman was anything more than a pesky intruder who had wandered into his classroom? Who would ever guess that he had lived with this woman for two years, had come very close to marrying her.

"Oh," she said. "Three weeks? I'm sorry." The smile was gone. She pretended to look chastised.

"Wait a minute, Dr. Balfour," a boy in the front row said.

"Yes, Trent?" Alex said. Trent was his best student.

"Why can't we skip ahead a little? I'd like to hear about

that, too. Frankly, Dr. Balfour, I'm getting a little tired of hearing how many kilos of this and that weren't making it to the front lines and how many men the Russians were losing every day.'' The look in Alex's eyes stopped him for a minute. ''Not that it's boring or anything,'' he added quickly, ''but we can read about that for ourselves.''

Alex looked back up at Molly Glenn and back to Trent. They were both smiling. Mutiny. Right here in his Russian History 206 class. She sashays back into his life and in five minutes all discipline flies right out the window. She hadn't changed; she'd won over poor Trent and she wasn't even sitting near him. She'd always had that effect on men. Including him.

''Well . . .'' he said. She turned up the wattage on her smile. Why fight it?

He cleared his throat unnecessarily and began. He would throw a wet blanket of pedantry over the brush fire that was smouldering somewhere down in the region of his heart. Confusion would be banished by discipline and self-control.

''Tsar Nicolas, his wife, their five children, and four family retainers were all shot to death in Ekaterinburg, Russia, July 16th, 1918.'' He watched them settle back in their chairs. They liked it when he told history like a story. 'Once upon a time . . .' Out of nowhere the tag end of memory, the faint touch of the battlefield scene of the night before, the whisper of shells, wavered at the edge of his consciousness. He pushed it away. It was getting worse; last night was definitely the worst—the dreams, nightmares, hallucinations, whatever they were, creeping in around the edges of his mind even when he was awake. And now Molly Glenn.

''The difficulty,'' he went on, letting history crowd out memory, ''is placing events in the perspective of their own time. We tend to think of key events as happening one right after the other. The First World War begins; the Tsar is overthrown; the Bolsheviks take over the country; Russia goes Communist. One, two, three strikes, you're out. Unfortunately or fortunately, it doesn't happen that way. That sort of thinking is what invariably occurs when you study history as a succession of dates rather than as narrative.

''The time is early 1918. Russia is in chaos. The Bolsheviks have signed a peace treaty with the Germans. They can

14

now focus their military attention on conquering their own country. After months of growing insurrection the Tsar has abdicated and, along with the rest of his family, been arrested.

"Lenin and Trotsky have arrived back in Petrograd after years of exile, transported across Germany in a closed train, 'like a cargo of deadly bacillus,' as Winston Churchill so elegantly put it. They start hacking away at Kerensky and the Provisional Government until they pull it down around everybody's ears. Millions of Russian men had been killed in the First World War; most of the country was starving; no one knew who was in control from one day to the next.

"One of the things to remember is that while the government itself went to the Bolsheviks, the vast majority of Russians wanted to have nothing to do with them. The Reds were primarily a product of the cities and the industrial areas. Their political views were extreme and confusing. The Bolsheviks were holding the Tsar and his family in the town of Ekaterinburg in the Ural Mountains."

"I don't understand," interrupted a girl who usually didn't understand, "why they had to kill them all. I mean, maybe the King, but why did they have to kill his wife and children?"

Alex took the opportunity to look at Molly. She was writing in a notebook. Notes? She's taking notes? Usually it made him feel good when people took notes. This just made him nervous.

"He was called a tsar, not a king," Alex sighed. Where has this girl been all semester? "They were in the middle of a violent civil war," he continued. "Large armies were forming behind various leaders. The Whites, still loyal to the Tsar, controlled huge areas of the country. Various Cossack warlords took the opportunity to ransack, rape, and pillage. Fighting was taking place all over Russia, and in many parts of the country the Reds were losing. The Bolsheviks felt that any vestige of the royal family could be used as a rallying point for the opposition. The thing to remember is that critical confusion. Russia is the largest country in the world. Communications were primitive; no one knew just what was really happening at the other end of the telegraph line. Finally, someone, no one really knows who, decided that the smartest thing to do would be to kill them all and get it over with before something worse happened. Ekaterinburg, the

15

town where they were being held, is more than halfway across the country and was virtually surrounded by White forces. It was really the only thing to do under the circumstances. We have a tendency to think that large historical events were carefully planned, when in reality most events are simply reactions to other events."

"So they shot them all." Trent said.

"That's right," Alex said. "It was the middle of the night. The family and the few retainers that remained with them were all told to get out of bed and get dressed. They were taken to a ground-floor room where the Tsar, his son, and his wife were given chairs. A detachment of soldiers entered the room; the officer in charge told the Romanovs that they had been condemned to die. The soldiers opened fire. After the shooting stopped, they checked the bodies and found that they were all dead except Anastasia, who was then bayoneted to death. And that was the end of the Romanovs."

Maybe he should have left out the part about bayoneting Anastasia. They were looking at him as if he'd been the one to order the massacre. They didn't like it when their stories had unhappy endings. They waited for more explanation, something to make sense of it. They were used to TV endings, movie endings. Easy answers.

"Try," he said gently, "to think of it less in terms of good against evil and more in terms of people being manipulated by events. As an act of brutality it was a small thing compared to the torture and killing being committed by both sides. The Bolsheviks hated the Tsar, he was known as 'Bloody Nicholas.' The men who carried out the killings were soldiers who had been ordered to do so."

They just stared at him. Children, unhappy now that their fairy tale had turned sour.

"Lenin," he went on, realizing that it was hopeless but trying anyway, "was fond of quoting Napoleon: *'On s'engage, et puis—on voit.'* You commit yourself, and then—you see. Maybe people are more careful now, I don't know; we think that we could never do such things, but under the same circumstances, who can really say how they would react? As leaders or as soldiers."

"Are you saying," Trent asked, "that we, or rather you,

are capable of shooting a bunch of unarmed people in a little room, some of them kids?''

Alex shook his head, wondering if Molly was enjoying this. Alex, the killer of women and children. The two of them had marched in more antiwar demonstrations than he could remember. Comrades against the system.

"I don't think I'm capable of such a thing," Alex said. "I would hope not. But who's to really say what men are capable of?" This was beginning to sound like a sophomore dormitory bullshit session.

"I could never just shoot someone," Trent said stubbornly.

"Circumstances, Trent, circumstances. It's easy to say *never*." He'd lost them for now; he could see it on their faces. This was a generation who could never consider such things. Vietnam was before their time; Watergate, race riots, all of it was history to them. Fairy tales. People back then might do those things, but not us. They looked at him with expressions ranging from bored skepticism to anger. He would have to win their hearts and minds another time. By next week they would have forgotten all about it. Right now he had other problems.

"All right, it's early, but I'm going to let you go. Next week we're back to the stuff that Trent considers dull. Do your reading.

"Class dismissed.''

Chapter 3

ALEX STOOD LOOKING OUT THE WINDOW. THE GRAY SMOKED GLASS drained the color from the street outside. Traffic moved silently behind the unopenable windows. Yellow taxicabs nosed through lines of grid-locked cars like roaches seeking refuge.

He stood with his back to the classroom, staring out the window. He was aware that the pose was overly dramatic, but he needed the time to try and figure out how to play the coming scene. What do you say? Hi, Molly, long time no see? Hey, beautiful, been out of town? How's the husband?

"I'm sorry."

He turned.

He was surprised by the sudden flush of color after the gray window-world. Her coloring always surprised him, even when they were living together. Her hair was so red it hovered right on the edge of impossible. She was made up of the primary colors of the mythic heroines in Pre-Raphaelite paintings.

"I'm sorry," she said again.

"What for?" he asked. There were too many choices. Leaving all those years ago? Never letting him know what had happened to her? Walking back in on him like this?

"I'm sorry I asked that question and screwed up your

class. I guess I'm also a believer in the Lenin quote, 'Commit yourself, then see.''

"I seem to remember that." He turned away from her and sat on the corner of his desk, aware of the petulant tone in his own voice. He couldn't stop himself. It was as if some little boy had been waiting ten years to talk back. The little boy would not be denied. "I really don't know what to say to you, Molly. What is it you want?"

She sat down in one of the desks in the front row. "How about 'How have you been?' Or 'Nice to see you.' I'll have to admit, Alex, in my fantasies I never came up with a conversation like the one we're having. I know you're nervous; I'm nervous, too, but that doesn't mean you have to be so cold. It's as if you're still angry with me. This is incredible; we're ten years back in the past having the same argument we had then. Don't you remember?" He didn't answer. She sighed. "All right, here it is again. I left because I wanted to get married and you didn't. Sure, I walked out the door, but it was *your* choice." She looked at the ceiling. "Hasn't either of us changed at all?"

He went back to the window. The taxi-roaches were still nosing around, looking for escape.

She was right, it was incredible; he was acting crazy. Mr. Cool, no doubt about it: Old girlfriend walks back in; does it bother him?—no way, man, nothing to it. He just picks the same fight that he thought he had gotten over a long time ago. She was right about all of it. He *had* refused to get married, even though she had made it very clear that she would leave if he didn't. At the time he didn't know what he wanted. He still didn't know what he wanted. No, that wasn't true either. Why lie to himself? He knew what he wanted two minutes after she walked back in the door. He wanted her. It had been lying there in wait all these years, like a patient jungle animal lying in ambush, waiting for some luckless stoop to stumble by on the trail. Wham.

He turned back around. Begin again. "Hello, Molly, how are you? It's good to see you."

She smiled. Oh, God, what a smile. "That's nice. I'm fine; it's nice to see you, too."

19

"Want to go have a cup of coffee?" he asked. Start slow, right?

"I'd love to."

The coffee shop across the street from the school was just like nine million other coffee shops in New York. Salmon-colored booths, formica tables, run by any one of an infinite number of foreign nationalities. This particular one was Greek. Lots of hustle, lots of shouting back and forth between the waiters and the countermen. Lots of fluorescent lights. Alex was glad to see that Molly lost a little of her vibrancy under the fluorescence. Everything did.

He held up two fingers to the counterman who nodded. Molly glanced at the menu. He wondered if she felt the same way he did? It had never been easy to figure out what she was thinking. He looked at her hands on the menu. Normally, he didn't particularly care for redheads; they usually had funny skin. Molly's skin was healthy-looking, very few of the usual redhead freckles.

It wasn't as if he were particularly woman-hungry. Even though he was considered a very solitary man, he had more than normal success with women. He had never had to go out of his way or spend much time finding someone he liked. He had even found a few that he had thought he had loved, but never enough to take that last step.

The waiter banged down their coffee and tried to sell them a Danish. Alex considered it, then remembered the extra fifteen pounds he was carrying around on his gut. He rejected the Danish, sat up straighter, and sucked in his stomach.

"So, how's the coffee?" he asked.

She laughed and took a sip. "Just like it always is in these places. Who knows? It's dark brown and bitter; I guess that qualifies it as coffee. She stopped for a minute and tilted her head to the side. "You know, it's hard to believe, but you can get to miss things like New York coffee. The coffee is better in California, almost always fresh-ground, carefully prepared, but it never seems to give you the same kick this stuff does."

He considered running down California in general, one of his favorite topics, then decided against it. Bad move. But

20

now that he had decided to be a nice guy he couldn't think of anything to say.

"I've been in New York for two months," she said quickly. She was looking down at the table. She glanced at him and then back down. "My husband and I broke up three years ago. I've wanted to call you, but I couldn't decide if it would be fair. I thought you might be married or living with someone." She looked at him again and he shook his head no.

"Anyway, when this thing came up at work, it was so perfect I just had to do it. I called Maxwell Surrey first. He said you had moved to a real house. He gave me the address and telephone number." She stopped and fiddled nervously with her coffee cup.

"I've got a few questions," Alex said. "Work? Two months? This thing?"

She laughed. "I have a job at *The New York Times*. Reporting. They saw a series I did for the L.A. *Times* and made me an offer I would have been a fool to refuse. I've been living in an apartment in the eighties for a month. The first month I lived in a hotel. If you lean out my apartment window just to the point that you're in danger of falling, you can see the river. This thing. Well, that's a long story. It's a piece I've been working on, or at least I'm starting to work on." She stopped. "I'm babbling, aren't I?

"Oh, Alex." She reached out and touched his hand. He could almost see a little blue spark fly. His heart felt as if a medic had put the paddles on his chest, hollered 'stand back,' and shot him the juice.

"I took a cab by your house twice," she said. "I was terrified you would come out the door and see me."

He covered her hand with his. "That would have been great," he said. "I look out the window to see what the weather is and you ride by in a cab. Very weird."

They both just sat for a minute and looked at each other.

The waiter: "So, more coffee? Lunch? What's it going to be?" Molly laughed and Alex ordered a refill.

"Very romantic spot, huh?" he said.

She nodded. "Okay. The piece I'm working on." She sat back in the booth. "A book came into the *Book Review* section recently. There were some questions about it and eventually it ended up on my desk." She smiled wryly. "Probably

21

because no one else could figure out what to do with it rather than because of my reputation as a crack reporter. Give it to the new girl.

"Anyway, it's called *The File on the Tsar* and it's by two BBC reporters who are known in the business as respected investigative journalists. Not people who are easily taken in. The point of the book, to get to the point of my story, is that they've come up with new evidence that suggests rather strongly that the Romanovs weren't really killed by the Bolsheviks."

Alex snorted. "Where have they been? Living down in the South America?"

"Your initial skepticism is noted. To continue, the *Book Review* people thought it might be a hard-news story, so that's how it began its tortuous journey to my desk. I called up Maxwell Surrey. He remembered me and suggested I call you."

"I guess Max has heard of my historical prowess when it comes to the Russian Revolution. Really, Molly, there are other people in town who are a lot more knowledgeable than I am in this field; why not one of them?"

"Well," she said after a minute of silence, "this way I don't have to keep taking cabs by your house, wondering what's going on inside. Also, to put it bluntly, there's the matter of who you are. There's going to be a lot of name recognition."

"Oh." It was as if she had dropped a large rock on his foot. "You mean Alexander Balfour, son of the late Charles Ames Balfour."

Here it was again. Little Alex, son of the famous historical novelist.

"So you decided that your article would have a little extra pizzazz if you used me as your expert."

She gave him a long look. "Still the same old problem, huh? Somehow I thought you might have gotten over that by now." She shook her head. "Look, Alex, I'm a reporter" —she held up a forestalling hand—"please, no jokes, no snide remarks; just hold it for a minute. As such I'm paid to find stories and write stories. I try to do this in the most interesting and informative way possible. Right now I've been assigned a story about a famous controversial historical event and I just happen to know a historian who also is the son of a very famous historical novelist. I'd be a liar and a fool if I told you I wasn't going to try to work all these things together.

"In the old days you dealt with it differently, but it's still the same problem, isn't it? Back then you pretended that Charles Balfour never existed. Just as you used to pretend that you weren't rich, that you were just a regular guy struggling to get along. I've thought about it a lot since then. Don't you think it was pretty weird that we never talked about it?" She smiled ruefully at his stony gaze. "You don't want to talk about it now either, do you?" He didn't answer.

"I had this very weird experience four or five years ago," she went on. "I was in the library at the paper, researching a story, when I came across an old article in *Time* magazine about your father. There was this big picture. Your father with that mane of hair, looking very Hemingwayesque; your beautiful mother. And over at the side, sort of away from the two of them, was this sullen teenager. It was you, of course, but I could hardly recognize you from the picture.

"The story was all about how you traveled everywhere as a family. Back into the jungles or the deserts, everywhere that your father went to research his novels. Sitting there, reading it, I had the strangest feeling: I wanted to be you. I wanted that to be *my* family. You have to remember that I grew up in Ohio in the most normal midwestern family imaginable. Last year my dad retired and he and Mom moved to Florida. Perfect, huh?

"But your life sounded so adventurous, so glamorous, so exciting. It was like a fairy story about some fantastic Swiss Family Robinson, only real. When I finished the article, it suddenly occurred to me that I had actually lived with this person in the picture. The sullen-looking kid with the messed-up hair. We had lived together for two years, ate together, slept together, shared the same bathroom, *and I didn't know anything about this part of your life*. You talked a little about your mother; you talked a lot about Maxwell Surrey; but when your father came up, the lips were sealed and you got that stony look that you've got on your face right now." She watched him for a minute before going on.

"Back then I never said anything about it because I felt it

23

was something you had to work out on your own. Also, I guess I was a little afraid of you when you looked like that. But things are changed now, Alex. Or at least I've changed. I don't just let things go like I used to. And I'm not afraid of very much anymore." She laughed without humor. "You'd be surprised how one screwed-up marriage can change a person. If you want to hide things from yourself and refuse to confront issues"—she shrugged her shoulders—"that's all right for you. But don't expect me to pretend that real things that concern me don't exist; I don't work that way anymore."

She sighed and looked down at the table. She traced the patterns of green and blue triangles in the formica. "End of lecture. Look, Alex, aren't you even interested in the history involved in all of this? The mystery of what happened to the Romanovs?"

He waved his hand. "Of course I'm interested." He would go along with the change of subject. She was right; he didn't want to talk about his father.

"You know, it isn't the first time someone has come up with this theory," he said. "There are already quite a few books on the market, claiming various escapes for the Romanovs. While we're at it we can discuss whether or not Hitler is alive and living in the East Village. Hell, maybe they all live together, I don't know. See, professionally, I'm not very interested in big questions like that; I let that go to the big boys in the field. I'm more interested in things like what sort of underwear did they wear in the fifteenth century? Little things rather than the momentous events."

"You people going to buy some lunch or what?" It was the waiter. He was carrying more menus and a look of exasperation. "I got people waiting for this table. You want to talk, maybe you should talk outside. You want to stay here, you got to order something."

Alex looked at her and she shook her head. "No," he said, "we're on our way."

The waiter wrote up their check and tossed it on the table. Alex left him a reasonable tip and paid the bill at the register. Molly waited for him on the street.

"So?" she said when he joined her outside.

"So, maybe we should have dinner?"

She gave him a long, hard look. "You sure you want to do

24

this? You know as well as I do that there's a big chance that we're going to be up to our ears with each other if we start in again. I can find another historian to work with."

"I don't want you to find another historian. You know the address, right?"

She smiled crookedly. "Yes, I know the address."

"Seven o'clock," he said, turning away in the opposite direction.

"Wait a minute," she said. He turned back around. "What kind of underwear did they wear in the fifteenth century?"

"None," he said. "Underwear is a modern invention. Very recent." He smiled and headed toward home.

Chapter 4

ALEX HAD LEARNED TO COOK WHEN HE WAS SEVENTEEN YEARS OLD.
It was the summer after he'd graduated from high school,
right after his mother and father had died and he'd gone to
Princeton to live with Maxwell Surrey. The move to Princeton
was a natural one, as Surrey was a long-time friend of the
family, an honorary uncle who was as close as any blood
relative. Surrey had always been there, working with his
father on his books, living with his family during the summers, spending holidays with them.

Alex began cooking as a way of disguising the fact that he
took almost all of his meals alone and was, consequently,
lonely. Somehow the idea of the solitary gourmet was a
romantic enough notion to justify that loneliness.

Surrey would have been surprised to know how Alex felt.
A private man by nature, he let Alex do what he wanted with
little interference. He was fatherly, but he was also fifty
years older. They didn't have a lot in common to talk about
and Surrey cared little for eating beyond the small meals his
housekeeper fixed. At mealtime Surrey would be at school
teaching his history classes or in his study working. Alex
would be in the kitchen, struggling with a cookbook.

By the time he and Molly lived together, after graduate

school, he had given up culinary pursuits as being too effete. Molly did most of the cooking. Or they ate out.

After Molly left, he had gravitated back into the kitchen. Eating out by oneself in restaurants was boring and slightly embarrassing. So he stayed at home and cooked and got very good at it and enjoyed it. It also impressed the women he went out with.

Alex had spotted fresh chorizo sausage at the Italian market the day before and had had a paella in the back of his mind ever since, fresh chorizo sausage being the backbone of a good paella. The fish market had produced a half dozen jumbo shrimp and two Chesapeake Bay crabs. He opened himself a Yuengling porter, one of America's great unknown beers, and drank it while he put away the groceries and planned the dinner for Molly.

Molly. Molly naked. Ah, God, he couldn't help it; it had been lurking there in the back of his mind, so he let it out, conjured up the vision. So much for his raised consciousness. She was heavier now than she had been; her breasts and hips seemed rounder, more womanly. He could remember the feel of her skin, smooth; her long silken hair as it hung down and tickled his chest.

He stood up, sighed, and tossed the empty beer bottle into the small trash can in the corner. It clanked against the other empties already there. Time to clean up. The way to a woman's heart is through a clean living area. He opened up another beer, extricated the vacuum cleaner from the closet, plugged it in, and began threading his way through the stacks of books and around the curved feet of his old Victorian furniture.

Each piece that he negotiated, cleaned under and over, had a specific veneer of memories.

Alex's father had written five best-selling books, each concentrating on one pivotal historical moment and how it had affected the country involved and the world at large. They had all been enormously successful. His father had possessed a unique talent for making each period seem absolutely real. Each book had taken three years to complete, a year for research and two years to write. Alex's house was full of the memorabilia that went into the books, and all of it had to be cleaned or cleaned around.

27

The Victorian furniture was garnered from the family's year in England, researching *The Queen's Lover*; the shelves were spotted with carved wooden statues from Africa from *Isi, A Life*. The first book, *The Golden Land*, contributed the early American antiques. Fortunately, *Quest*, the book about Central America and his father's last effort, had added very little as their house in Connecticut had just about reached capacity. *Woman of the Sands*, the desert opus, had yielded nothing as the trunk with the camel saddles, bells, and beaten brass pots had gotten lost in transit. His father had liked having the objects around; he said he needed them while he was writing to give his work the proper feel.

Alex seldom cleaned, usually only when he was having over a woman he wanted to impress. The dust built up in small drifts in the intervals; cobwebs festooned the corners of the rooms; little tumbleweeds lay under the furniture. As Alex vacuumed he thought about packing all of the junk and giving it to the Goodwill. But he wouldn't. It seemed to be in the Balfour nature, perhaps because of their commitment to history, to save things. It gave their lives texture.

By six o'clock he had finished the cleaning, taken his bath, and was back in the kitchen.

He made his paellas in an old cast-iron pan that was extremely heavy and covered two burners on his stove but still heated evenly. He pricked the two long sausages with the tines of a fork and put them into the pan with a half an inch of water. While the sausages boiled, he washed six chicken thighs and dried them off. When the water on the sausages had boiled away, he sliced them up and fried them in a little olive oil, adding a chopped-up onion and a sliced red pepper. When the sausages were done, he removed everything from the pan and browned the chicken in what was left of the oil. He then put everything back in and added chicken broth, saffron, paprika, coriander, and a bay leaf, then covered the pan with a lid made out of a cookie sheet and put it on simmer for fifteen minutes.

He finished another beer as he peeled the fresh shrimp and chopped up the three tomatoes.

He sprinkled two cups of Italian rice onto the paella. While the rice began to swell, he shelled two cups of fresh green peas and opened a small can of garbanzo beans. All of it went into the now furiously bubbling mixture, along with the two fresh crabs. He stood back and watched it all work in a cloud of saffron-scented steam.

The doorbell rang.

She wore a cream-colored silk blouse and a deep green skirt. Her freshly washed hair gleamed with a reddish-gold tint. "It smells wonderful," she said, glancing around the living room.

"Balfour's Famous Paella," he said, taking her light jacket and hanging it in the closet. "It's a legacy from my father's Spanish period. While he was writing, he had to have his meals in the style of whatever country he was writing about. When I was a kid, I hated it. I wanted hamburgers like the other kids." Poor baby, he thought to himself, had to eat paella instead of hamburger.

"This is a nice room," she said, walking to the mantel over the fireplace. She touched an African carving made of smooth ironwood. With her pale skin and her bright hair she seemed to gather the light and glow. "It's nice to see real furniture. Most bachelors these days go in for the leather-and-metal-tubing school of decoration. Glass tables and white rugs. Brown walls. They think that it's seductive."

He raised his eyebrows questioningly. Maybe he should paint the walls brown?

"It isn't," she said. "Brown walls and tubular furniture. Seductive, I mean." She walked around the room. "Where did you find all of this stuff? It's beautiful, but somehow I can't see you crawling through antique shops ferreting it out. And you certainly didn't have it while we were living together."

"It belonged to my parents. It was in their house in Connecticut. I moved it in here when I sold their house."

"You mean that you had all of this stuff in an empty house in Connecticut when we were living in that crummy apartment in New Jersey? The place with one chair and the skinny mattress on the floor?"

"The Connecticut house was rented furnished at the time. Surrey took care of all of that. What was so bad about that apartment, anyway? It was very bohemian at the time to sleep on the floor."

"Sleep, eat, study; we did *everything* on the floor." She

29

laughed. She touched one of the plastic videocassette cases and glanced at the portable color television set and cassette player unit. "You must watch a lot of these things," she said. "What are they? Movies?"

"Movies and old TV shows. You remember that picture of the sulky teenager you mentioned this afternoon?" She nodded. "One of the reasons he was so surly-looking was because he was missing out on all of the artifacts of his popular culture. My father never allowed a television set in the house. And while I was out trekking through the boondocks, you and your friends, my peers, were at the movies." He gestured to the shelves of tapes. "So I've been catching up." A timer bell went off in the kitchen. "Someday I'll take you on a trip down memory lane, but right now I have to finish dinner."

"Go," she said. "And hurry it up; I'm hungry."

He threw a handful of ripe olives and tomatoes onto the paella and served it in the pan he had cooked it in. He opened a bottle of cabernet he had been saving and lit two candles on the table.

She worked her way through a giant portion, using her hands on the crab and sucking the meat from the claws. It reminded him of the eating scene in *Tom Jones*. Erotic. But then everything was beginning to remind him of something erotic.

"Enough!" she said, pushing her plate away. "God, look at this table." The cloth was covered with crab shell and chicken bones. "Did we make this mess? Have you lost all respect for me?"

"I like a woman who eats like a man," he said. "Umm, how can I put that so it won't sound quite so . . ."

"Never mind, I understand what you're trying to say. I'll accept it as a compliment. After this meal, however, I feel like I need a shower."

"That can be arranged."

"No, thank you; I think I'll just wash my hands."

He gave her directions to the bathroom on the second floor and began clearing the table.

"This is a huge house," she said when she came back. "What's on the third floor?"

He laughed. "Books, mostly. Along with those that I

inherited from my father I've got my own collection. Fortunately, I found this house a few years ago before the real estate boom priced everything out of reach."

"Do you need help?" she asked, gesturing to the pile of plates on the countertop.

"You can watch me do the dishes. I don't need help but I'd like the company." She climbed up on the kitchen stool and watched him work.

"Alex," she asked, her voice serious now, "will you help me with the article I'm working on?"

"Ah," he said, rinsing the dishes and placing them in the dishwasher. "This is the part I've been waiting for. Now we find out the real reason you've been humoring me."

"Be serious," she said. "You knew I didn't show up at your class today just for a refresher course in Russian history. I came for several reasons; one of them was I need help. I'm not qualified to decide whether or not this book they've given me has any validity. I want you to read it and tell me what you think."

He put the glasses into the rack, put soap in the holder, and closed the dishwasher door. "Why didn't you ask Maxwell Surrey to do it?" He pressed the start button. The water jetted into the machine.

She looked vaguely guilty. "I did. He said you'd be better equipped for the job. He speaks very highly of you, as he always has."

He lifted the heavy iron pan into the sink and began to fill it with water. He knew the real aficionado would simply scrape it out and oil it to protect the pan's seasoning. He washed it anyway. "I try to get out to see him as much as I can. He's so old now. It's hard watching your father grind slowly down like an old piece of machinery." He shook his head. "My father. Freudian slip."

She shrugged her shoulders. "It's certainly understandable. Even I know he was a real father to you."

"A real father," he said in disgust. "He wasn't a real father. Real fathers are not nearly so good. At least in my case."

"Here we go again," she sighed.

"Goddamnit," he snapped, "what do you know about it? What do you know about my father?"

31

"Not very much, that's for sure," she snapped back. "That's the way you've always wanted it. One thing I do know, though, is every time he comes up in the conversation you get very upset. Of course I don't know anything about your father. At least not beyond what I've read in the magazines. What is it that's eating at you, Alex? Why don't you just come out with it."

"All of this"—he waved one hand around the kitchen— "the house, the books, all the junk. Hell"—he laughed bitterly—"me, everything I am, is a part of *him*. I can't kick him. I know he's dead, but it's as if he's still around somewhere, watching me, getting ready to tell me how worthless I am and what a big man he is. I told you I hated him."

"No, you didn't. You might have thought it, but you never said it. It's more than obvious that you didn't like him, but hating your own father is an extreme position. I don't understand it and you can't expect me to. I can sympathize with you up to a point because I care about you, but you can't keep blaming me for not understanding what's going on inside you. Don't try to pin something on me that can't possibly be my fault."

He shut up for a minute and concentrated on slowing his breathing. Why did she have to be so obviously right? He crossed his arms and tried to smile at her. "I'm sorry I keep going on about this, but it's all tied up together. History, Maxwell Surrey, my father, me, what you want from me— it's all tangled up. It seems simple to you, but . . ."

"It doesn't seem simple to me; I never said that."

"All right, look, let's go in the living room and I'll tell you about my father and you can tell me what you want me to do. I'll tell you all about Charles Ames Balfour. You'll be the first to know what the great man was really like."

Chapter 5

THEY WERE IN THE TENT, HE AND HIS MOTHER. IT WAS A LARGE, old-fashioned safari tent; faded khaki canvas, a faint scent of mildew that never really disappeared. The three of them had lived in that tent all over the world. Alex's corner was blocked off from the larger part by blankets hung from a line. He was a little boy then, but he remembered it all very clearly.

His mother held him close, as she did when they both were afraid. His father hated it when she held him, called him a sissy, a momma's boy.

Outside the tent the hired African bearers drank their jugs of millet beer and tried to dance around the campfire. The men were clumsy and foolish, all of them drunk except his father. Their shadows, thrown there by the flames from the campfire, shuffled and bobbed on the canvas walls. His father would sit by the campfires, watching, patiently waiting for something that Alex never understood.

The night was cool under the huge trees of the forest. There were occasional howls from the monkeys and the night birds. Behind the tent, near the edge of the clearing, a man threw up, gagging, over and over.

Alex woke when his father pulled back the canvas door of the tent and stepped inside. He must have fallen asleep. His mother had put him on his bunk. He heard his father curse as he ran into the trunk near the foot of his mother's cot. The flames from the campfire had died down. The drums were silent. Cicadalike insects whirred in the trees, a sound like the rattles of angry snakes.

He heard his mother's muffled voice. His father's answers. And then the creak of the cot, the grinding of the wooden joints, the stretching of the canvas as his father added his weight. Night sounds; the creak of the cot, the slow rasping whirr of the insects.

"Where do you go when you drift off like that?" she asked.

"What? What do you mean?" Stall for time while he shook off the memory. He knew what she meant. Daydreams. It was as if the dreams and the memories were beginning to take over. How do you explain it? Without sounding crazy. Explain, confess; he felt the need rising in him.

She shrugged. "You've just been standing there, staring off into space."

She was sitting up on the turtle-back couch, with her shoes off and her legs drawn up under her. Two lamps in the living room created two low pools of light that overlapped near the center of the room, leaving the ceiling and the tops of the bookshelves in shadow. He stood at the mantel, touching the African fertility doll, a crouching figure with elongated features and a swollen round belly, pendulous breasts, and a wide-open mouth. His finger felt the smooth curve of the wood, the satiny finish.

"How . . . how long was I doing it?"

"Only a few seconds. It's just that you get a very funny look in your eyes. It's hard to explain it without making it sound too dramatic."

"You reporters notice everything." He smiled at her to show he was joking. "I was just thinking about something else." He ran his hand through his hair.

"I was telling you about my father."

"You weren't, but you were about to."

"Let's start with that picture of my family that they ran in

34

Time magazine. My handsome father with the mane of silvery hair, my beautiful mother with the American good looks and the blond hair piled on the top of her head. The sullen teenager at their side?''

She nodded.

''That was taken in Mexico right before we headed into the hills so my father could hang around with the Hueichle Indians. Sounds great, right?'' His smile felt tired. She said nothing; he didn't really expect an answer. ''Father had a peculiar method of working,'' he went on. ''We lived in an old farmhouse in Connecticut, but when he'd finally decided on a place to set his next book and on an era to frame it in, he'd leave home and come here to New York to start his research. We had an apartment here in the city, as well as the house. He'd come down here and just sink into it, reading everything he could get his hands on. Then he would gear up the expedition and we'd be off to whatever backwater he'd chosen for us.''

''Did you and your mother always go with him?'' Molly had settled lower into the couch.

''Always. God knows why. I never understood that. He didn't really need us. Or at least me. He couldn't stand me, but he insisted on it. We all had to go.'' Alex moved to a chair by the mantel and sat on the edge of the seat. He leaned forward and rested his elbows on his knees.

''My father met my mother when he taught at Ohio Weslyan. She was a graduate assistant in the history department. They got married the day she received her master's degree. They went on sabbatical and his first book came out three years after that. She was very beautiful but not very sophisticated. An Ohio girl. She never understood that she could have left him. She stayed with him all those years for my sake.''

''What makes you think she would have wanted to leave him?''

In the warm light of the lamps her skin was the color of thick Devonshire cream. He wanted to touch her. ''I'm getting to that. So we'd set off on the expeditions, strike off into the forest or the jungle or the desert or wherever father was taking us. He always had to get away from any civilized areas and drag us into the real outback. Three of his novels were set in absolute wilderness. We would be totally

35

isolated except for whatever natives were in the area, and they certainly didn't care. They were always interested in robbing us and in one case I think they were considering eating us. They always seemed to like my father, though. He had a way with them. Primitive. . . . Anyway, we'd get into an area suitably remote and we'd set up camp. After a time father would just . . . disappear. Take off into the bush, leaving us alone until he wandered back. Sometimes we'd wait as much as a month. And when he finally did come back, he'd be in terrible shape. Sometimes it took as much as another month to nurse him to the point we could get him out without killing him. Understand what I'm saying now. We would be left alone, usually with a few questionable natives that had been hired on, to fend for ourselves until he got whatever he had come for. He never asked if we'd been in any danger and never set up contingencies in case there was trouble. He just left.''

Alex laughed tonelessly as he looked down at his clenched hands. ''You don't know how many nights I lay there on that crappy canvas cot and prayed that he'd never make it back, that we'd wait until the food ran out and then pack up and leave him. But we didn't. Eventually he'd show up, just reappear without warning, to have us put him back together. Usually hurt and half-starved. He never told us where he'd been; he'd slap me if I asked, so I learned not to question him. It was as if he were deranged while we were on these trips. Insane.''

He stood up and moved to the other end of the couch. She moved up against the arm on her end so she was facing him.

''And then we'd go back to Connecticut and things would be pretty good for a while. He didn't pay much attention to me while he was writing. Usually Surrey would come and stay with us, especially if it was summer. Then the book would come out and he'd go off on a lecture tour. Those were the best times.

''When the lectures were over, he would be back home again and it would start to get bad. He'd wander around the house, sometimes all night, while he figured out what book he'd do next. Then he'd go to New York for his reading and we'd be back in the cycle.'' He looked up at the ceiling. He'd never told anyone these stories before. He wasn't sure why he was doing it now. Confess; tell it all. I'm mad; I have these dreams, hallucinations. It had curdled inside him for a long time. He realized suddenly that he was lonely, that he was tired of the way he lived, tired of his books, tired of teaching, tired of cooking up the little gourmet meals, tired of not having someone he could really talk to. Lonely.

She broke the silence. "I don't want to . . . diminish what you've told me, but doesn't that description of your father apply to any number of driven, successful men? I understand that it doesn't excuse them for their behavior, but . . ."

"You're right," he interrupted, "it doesn't excuse him. See, it was the lie as much as anything else. Everybody thought we were so perfect. Reporters"—he glanced at her and away—"have a way of seeing the surface quite clearly. Not you, maybe, but the ones that used to follow us around. The perfect family; Christ, he wasn't even there most of the time." He rubbed his face. There was a tiny tingling in his head, little sparkles at the corners of his eyes. Not now, he thought; Jesus Christ, not now.

"Maybe I'm too close to what you consider the opposition, but I find it hard to lay so much of the blame on reporters and . . . Alex? What's wrong." She leaned toward him and touched his face. "You're so pale."

The tingling sound turned into a low buzz. "For a long time I didn't think about him, but lately it's as if, I don't know . . ." A shell-burst of pain. He stood, pressing his hand to his head. "Goddamnit. It's like he's some sort of Lazarus lying in a cave, waiting." He laughed; a flat, rasping sound. "What do the scriptures say? 'And he that was dead came forth.' " He laughed again. The lights seemed brighter. "I'm . . ." he began. What could he tell her? Her face was twisted with a confusion of concern and the beginning of fear. "I'm not feeling well. I guess you'll have to go." He laughed again; not feeling well? That must be pretty obvious. She can't see this.

"Of course, but . . ." She frowned as she sat up and pulled on her shoes. "Is there anything I can do?"

"No," he said emphatically; he had to get her out of the house. He pushed the pain back, clamped down on it. "I'll be all right." He stood up, swayed as the room tilted slightly. She stood beside him, looked worriedly up into his face, and then went with him to the door. Jesus Christ, get out of here! "I'll call you tomorrow," he said, managing a small smile. "I'll be all right, really." He gritted his teeth, holding on.

"If you say so," she said, "but call me at the paper. Please?"

"I will, I promise." He closed the door and watched for a second as she walked down the steps. The room turned on its axis, like some giant record player. How had she come. Car? Cab? Subway? And her jacket. Molly! You forgot your jacket; come back, come back. Too late now, too late. His head ached. He made it back to the couch. He got one shoe off.

He stood on a broad expanse of lawn, a green swatch of beautifully manicured grass. The day was warm and the air smelled of spring and lilacs after a morning rain. He felt clean and light, the headache and the nausea gone. A breeze rustled the leaves of a small fruit tree. In the tall forest that backed the lawn a cuckoo called. He'd never heard a real cuckoo before.

A man and a boy were playing with a ball. The boy was around six years old, his voice high and shrill with excitement. "Throw it, Derevenko; throw me the ball, a high one this time." The man threw the red ball high into the air. The boy cheered and ran to where the ball thumped lightly to the ground.

The air was vibrantly clear. The two figures, the trees and ornamental shrubs on the wide lawn, the palace in the background, shimmered with brilliant color. In the park, to his right, Alex could see a red and yellow Chinese pagoda that gleamed bright, incongruous. It was a scene of intense beauty. He felt wonderful, light and clean. Free.

The man and the boy were dressed in identical sailor suits, white with blue piping around the collars, undershirts with wide blue and white stripes. The man had a large drooping mustache and a permanent air of concern that was focused on the boy.

"A long one, a long one, as far as you can," the boy cried, tossing the ball back.

The man reared back and threw, the ball flying for a moment into the sun and then beyond, a long, slow floating throw that hung in the sky before it fell and hit and rolled to a stop directly in front of Alex's feet.

The boy ran towards him, arms pumping, face twisted in concentration. He stopped, three feet away, looked at the ball and then straight up into Alex's eyes.

"Hello," the boy said shyly.

Alex felt his heart pound. "Hello," he said back. His Russian came, as it always did in the dreams, without thinking.

The boy's face was open and pleasant. His light brown hair was combed across his forehead and his eyes were dark blue. "My ball?" he asked. "May I have my ball?"

"Of course," Alex said, bending and picking it up. The ball was made of soft red cloth, lightly weighted. He tossed it to the boy.

"It's not a proper ball, is it?" the boy asked with a small frown. "They say a real one might hit me and start the bleeding." He tossed the ball back and forth in his hands. "Why are you wearing only one shoe?" he asked, pointing at Alex's feet.

Alex looked down. One shoe. Suddenly he felt the cool ground, the grass beneath his sock. "I don't know," he said. "I guess I was in a big hurry this morning and just forgot to put the other one on."

The boy nodded, his face serious. In the near distance Alex could see the sailor standing with one hand on his hip and the other shading his eyes from the brilliant sun. "Alexis!" the man called. "What are you doing?"

"What's your name?" the boy asked as he turned and waved at the man.

"Alex."

"Really? That's my name, too. Alexis Nikoleaivitch. We live in that house."

The man began walking toward them. "Alexis!" he called again. "Is anything wrong?"

"Go on, Alexis," Alex said, motioning toward the man who had now begun to trot toward them. "Go on; he's worried."

The boy ran to the man and then stopped, talking excitedly. The man glanced in the direction the boy was pointing and shook his head. He knelt down and looked closely at the boy. He stood and motioned toward the palace. The boy ran off, tossing the ball into the air and catching it. The man followed. The boy waved good-bye to Alex. Alex waved back. He turned and studied a leaf of the small tree beside him. The leaf was a deep green with serrated edges. A light wind touched the branches. Alex inhaled deeply. He walked towards the nearby woods. He would look for the cuckoo. He had never seen such a bird.

He woke up on the couch. The lights were still on in the room. He sat up. The house was dead quiet. The air was close, still, thick with the odors of cooking, himself, cars from the street outside. He pulled out his watch: four A.M. He thought about Molly Glenn, the little boy with the red ball. He looked down at his feet. He was still wearing only one shoe. He looked at his sock. It was grass-stained. He pulled his foot up onto his knee. There were little twigs sticking to the sock. Blades of dead grass. He brushed the sock clean and stood.

He went to lie on his empty bed.

Chapter 6

HE WOKE UP AT NINE O'CLOCK. AS HE SAT UP HE REALIZED THAT AT least he was spared his usual morning hangover. He stood up, stretched, and thought about the evening before and how he'd sent Molly off into the night as he'd lurched around holding his head, quoting scripture, raving about his father. The dream, the little boy, he had seen him, had talked to him, it had been so clear . . . the air had been so clean. He felt a sense of distinct loss.

He called Molly at work from his bathtub.

When he'd remodeled the house, he'd decided that if he was going to spend a lot of time in the bathtub, he should have all the necessities, including a telephone. Up to this point he'd not yet dropped the receiver into the tub, but it worried him. Would he be electrocuted?

"Where are you?" she asked. "You sound funny. Are you still sick?"

"I'm in the bathtub, and I'm no longer ill." He splashed a little with his foot for veracity.

"God, this sounds like one of those Paco Rabanne ads," she said. "What happened to you last night? Was that a normal occurrence, or did it have something to do with my company?"

"Rest assured that it had nothing to do with you. I was

41

very unhappy when I felt it coming on. It's a sort of migraine; I've had them since I was a kid. When they start, the only thing I can do is to lie down until it passes."

"I don't remember you having migraines."

"It's a fairly recent reoccurrence."

"Don't you take anything for it?"

"Whiskey, generally. But that doesn't always help. Nothing else does much good."

"Ever see a doctor about this?" she asked. In the background he could hear people talking and phones ringing.

"I don't believe in them." He changed the subject. "Look, if you want me to read that book, you're going to have to get me a copy."

"Great, you can have mine. I'll send it over by messenger."

"Wait a minute; it's time I got out of here anyway. I'm starting to wrinkle. Why don't I come over there and you can take me to lunch on your *New York Times* expense account. You can just hand the book to me, though I know how you reporters love sending messengers around the city."

"Let me check something." He heard her talking to someone in the background. He noticed there was no sound of typewriters. Computers had taken over the newspapers. The romance of the battered old Royal was gone.

"Okay," she said into the phone, "you're on. I'll meet you outside at twelve-thirty."

He hung up and leaned back in the tub. He thought about Molly curled up at the end of his couch. Then he thought about the headache and the dream.

Alex arrived early and spent his time waiting, watching the tide of young women on the sidewalk outside the *New York Times* building. Even though he'd lived in and around New York City for most of his life, the women always amazed him. Right now the style was punk; purple hair, crew cuts, sweat shirts for dresses. He had gotten used to it on his students—one gets used to anything on students—but he had forgotten that the rest of New York's women took up whatever fashions were extant. With a vengeance. Bank tellers with purple hair, secretaries with Mohawks. Somehow, though, in New York it didn't look bad.

42

Molly, he was glad to see, had not glued her hair into spikes or painted her lips black.

"Where are you taking me?" he asked as he took her hand. It felt natural.

"Mexican all right with you?"

"*Si.*"

"Then we're here," she said, turning in under a marquee announcing they were entering Manuel's.

The interior was white stucco with exposed beams. A maitre d' dressed in a black suit and a pink shirt with ruffles down the front bowed to her and led them to a table. The clientele was uptown New York, which made him wish he'd thought about it and dressed up a bit. No purple hair here. He was in his usual outfit; long-sleeve white dress shirt with the sleeves rolled up, reasonably new blue jeans, and white running shoes. Would he ever grow up? "Is that Manuel?" he asked as the maitre d' left them with two menus. "I love his shirt," Alex said.

"Shut up and look at the menu. I'm sure they make them dress that way. He probably has a house in the Village and dresses just like you when he goes home in the evening."

"God, I hope not. What's good here?"

"The usual. Mexican Whatever. Really, I just brought you here to pay you for reading *The File on the Tsar*. It's not really a very good restaurant." She opened her large bag and handed him a book.

"Great," he said, taking it. "But then it's probably not a very good book, so we'll be even. Do you treat all your sources this way?"

"Only the ones who are difficult." The waiter came and took their order. Molly had the chicken enchiladas with sour cream sauce and Alex ordered some shrimp combo that he didn't really understand but that cost a lot.

The waiter brought Carta Blanca beers for both of them.

"Did you know," he said to her, holding up his beer bottle, "that the Carta Blanca people used to make indentations in the bottom of the bottles that fit perfectly over the cap of another Carta Blanca bottle. This was in the early days of twist-off caps. When you finished one beer, you used the empty bottle to open the next. I've always considered that one of the most civilized pieces of technology I've ever come in contact with.''

"Very interesting, Alex. Still a fount of odd facts and curious happenstances, huh?''

"Well, I read a lot. I also drink a lot of beer.''

"Speaking of reading, what made you decide to read this book and help me out?''

He hefted the book and looked at the cover: black with red title, pictures of Lenin, the Tsar and his family, a gun. "It's not because I think I'm going to believe this thing.'' He put the book on the table and poured some beer in his glass. "It's because I want to see you. This way you can't run away again.''

He watched her flush. He smiled. She got even redder.

"You know,'' she said, "I don't know how many times I have to say it, but I didn't run away, I . . .''

He held up a hand. "Kidding. Just kidding.''

The waiter brought their food. Molly began to eat while Alex tried to figure out how to eat his. The shrimp were sauteed a bright pink and set atop a pile of pinto beans. Scoop it all up together? He took an experimental bite; curiously enough, it was good.

"I'm going to read the book, don't worry, but just exactly what is the 'Dramatic New Evidence' they've announced on the cover?''

She slid the book back to her side of the table and leafed through it while she ate. "You already know all about this stuff, right?'' she said, not looking up from the book.

"Let's just say I know all about what the professionals say occurred. It's called history. As opposed to journalism.''

She looked at him and gave him a twisted smile. "And of course that means that all the information you know is correct and everything else that comes up is wrong. That's what I like in our educators, an open mind.''

He let it go. He wasn't like that. Was he?

"Do you know who a guy named Solokov is? Or was.'' She asked.

"You mean Sokolov. It's easy to get the letters backwards. Sure, Nikolai Sokolov, last of the monarchist investigators in the enquiry. He was on the White side, as opposed to the Reds. He wrote a book named *Judicial Enquiry Into the Assassination of the Russian Imperial Family.*''

She looked at him respectfully. "Not bad. How do remember all that stuff?''

"I don't know; I guess I inherited it. Anyway, it's not really all that impressive; anybody that researches the period ends up with Sokolov's book. It's the definitive text on what happened.''

She nodded. "Well, the guys who wrote *The File on the Tsar*, even though they're only journalists,'' she added, with a tilt of her head, "say that they tracked down a bunch of unpublished stuff by Sokolov that casts a different light on the matter. The definitive text is no longer definitive, as far as they're concerned.''

Alex frowned. She took that as encouragement and went on.

"Also, and this is sort of weird,'' she picked up the book and found the place on the page, "I'll paraphrase since you're going to read this, but one day, this is in 1936, a man—no name; just says that he's a foreigner—who seemed to have something wrong with one of his legs, walks, or rather limps, into a place called the Tower Building of the Hoover Institute on War, Revolution, and Peace, at Stanford University, and hands over a black cloth bag with the top sewn shut. The guy wants to donate the material to the archives but only on the condition that it stays unopened for fifty years.''

Alex finished off the last of his beans and sat back. 1936; nothing significant about the date as far as he knew. The Hoover Institute still existed. They waited while the waiter cleared off the plates and took their order for coffee.

"The guy was probably a White Russian afraid that the Communists were out to get him.'' He shrugged. "Maybe they were. Expatriate monarchist Russians always thought the Commies were trying to kill them. In some cases they were. And did.''

"Right,'' she went on. "Anyway, the bag gets kind of lost for a while, and then in 1976 someone who didn't bother to honor the fifty-year injunction opens it up and finds these files, uh, let's see''—she ran her finger down the page until she found the name—"these files written by a guy named

Nikander Mirolyubov. Ever heard of *him*?'' She looked up from the book.

"Nope.''

"That's a relief. He was a professor of criminology who had been public prosecutor at Kazan, and I assume that's a place, which administered the Ekaterinburg area.'' She closed the book. "Which was, as we know from your fascinating lecture of the other day, where the Romanovs were all assassinated. Or weren't assassinated, depending on who you believe has the definitive answers.''

The coffee came. They had ordered expresso. He twisted the small slice of lemon peel over the cup and put it on the saucer.

"I always just drop the peel into the cup,'' she said, picking up hers and looking at it.

"I spent time in Mexico; remember my father's last book? You twist the peel over the cup so that the lemon oil sprays out onto the top of the coffee. If you put the whole peel in, it gets too lemony.''

"Gee, what a guy. Wait till I tell the girls back at the office. All these years I've been doing it wrong. How embarrassing.''

"Look,'' Alex said, "to get back to the book, what was in the files that's so important?''

Molly looked vaguely embarrassed. "That's a little unclear,'' she said. "I've only been through this one time. But I did call this Hoover Institute and they're getting me a copy of everything that was in the bag. It should be here tomorrow or the day after.''

"Ah, the investigative journalist at work. Okay, give me the book. I'll read it this afternoon and give you a call.'' The waiter came up to the table and handed Alex the check. He handed it to Molly. "Leave a big tip,'' he said. "Manuel might need a few more pink shirts.''

He glanced through the book while she filled out the credit card sheet. Outside they walked the one block to the *Times* building.

"How about tonight? It's Friday; we have the whole weekend,'' he said. He was holding her hand. "I promise I won't get a headache.''

She lifted his hand in hers and looked at it. "We escaped

this dangerous trap last night," she said, looking at him. "Are you sure you want to chance it again? You weren't sure once before."

"You're right, I wasn't. That was a long time ago; can't we forget it? Don't condemn me to repeat the past. I'm sure, Molly."

She nodded and pressed his hand to her lips. "But I can't see you tonight. I have to work."

The little airplane of hope he'd been piloting crashed into the trees. He felt disappointment and pain as he slammed into the instrument panel.

"But I can see you tomorrow night," she said, touching his lip. "Isn't this the part where you're supposed to kiss me?" she asked.

"Yes," he said solemnly. And did.

New York. Near them, on the sidewalk, a large crowd stood watching a young man with a collapsible table and a brisk three-card monte game. Five feet away another kid with a blaring boom-box spun on his head on a piece of brown cardboard. People bought slices of pizza from tiny streetfront pizzerias. No one looked twice at their sidewalk embrace.

Chapter 7

HE SPENT THE REST OF THE AFTERNOON AT THE STRAND, LAST OF NEW York's great used bookstores. The Russian section yielded a hefty pile of oversize picture books spanning a period of sixty years. He caught a cab, stopped at two markets and the liquor store, and was back in the kitchen for his evening ruminations.

He ran the knife under the skin of a chicken breast, pulled it out at the top, then stripped the breast down. He severed the small tendon at the top of the meat, ran his thumb into the pocket between the two fillets, and cut the large one free. With two more quick cuts he removed the small fillet. He put the meat on a plate and the excess bones and skin into the bag he kept in the freezer. When he had accumulated enough scraps, he made broth.

It was the asparagus he had found that decided it. Fresh asparagus, chicken breasts with white wine over rice.

Cooking freed his mind. It required just enough mental energy to keep him from dwelling on specifics but not enough to tie his brain down. In the past he'd found if he could get far enough above a problem, or a set of problems, he could make out enough of the shape of the thing to come to an understanding of it. He'd once read the same sort of thinking described in relation to scientific discovery: It was said that there were four places or activities that seemed to be especially conducive to creative problem solving; these were known as the four B's of creative thinking—Bed, Bath, Bus, and Beach. For Alex the four B's were Broiling, Boiling, Baking, and Basting.

He put a cup of rice in a pan and added a cup and a half of chicken broth and a half a cup of the white wine he would use in the sauce and ultimately drink with the finished meal. He brought the mixture to a boil, let it bubble for a minute, then covered it and turned it to simmer. He now had exactly seventeen minutes to finish the rest of the meal. He sat on the stool and stared at the stove.

His mind drifted. He thought of the terrifying bombardment where he had talked with the dying Russian soldier, of seeing Rasputin in the backseat of the car, of the pleasant game of toss with the little boy on the grounds of the vast estate. He had come back with physical manifestations: dirt under his fingernails from the one, the grass-stained sock from the other.

The dreams had begun twenty-some years ago. Sometimes only flickers of scenes, seen in a half-light between sleep and waking; sometimes full-blown scenarios, complete with action and dialogue. In his boyhood his mother had discounted them, which didn't really surprise him. Adults discount most of the stories of children. He stopped telling her about them. But it was only recently that he had begun to *participate* in the action, as if it were somehow a function of age; that he was progressing along a preordained path that drew him deeper and deeper into a fantasy where all things were real, even the dreams. He had seen Rasputin; he had talked to the Russian soldier; he had talked to the little boy. They had answered.

He turned on the fire under an iron skillet and put in a tablespoon of butter and a couple of tablespoons of olive oil. He floured the breasts and placed them gently in the pan when the oil and the butter stopped foaming. He filled a pot with water for the asparagus.

It was time to stop dancing around the central issue and admit, always allowing the caveat that he might be stark raving insane, that he seemed to have an ability to appear, at least in his mind, in his dreams, in various situations and

49

participate in those situations. And that these situations were, in some way that he did not yet understand, real.

He was ninety-percent certain that the events that occurred in the dreams were real. The bombardment was circa World War I, he was sure, and he would make certain of the second event shortly after he ate. He was dreaming backwards in time. By waking up with dirt all over him, it now appeared he was actually, physically participating. And here was a good question: What was sitting in the chair, lying in the bed, *here*, when he was back *there*?

He turned over the chicken. A brown crust had formed. He pressed down on the thickest part of the breast with his fork. The meat should have exactly the same feel as the fleshy part of his hand at the base of his thumb.

So now what? Now that he accepted what was happening, or at least put it into cold, hard words, what would he do about it? Was there anything he could do about it? He had to admit that he didn't want to change it. That he enjoyed it. All three times had been exciting; all three times he had felt more alive than he ever did while he was awake. The problem was not the dreams; the problem was believing, accepting what was happening to him.

The chicken was done. He put it on an ovenproof plate and put it into the warm oven. He tossed the asparagus into the pan of rapidly boiling water. Into the pan in which he had fried the chicken, he put a half a cup of white wine and a half a cup of chicken broth. He turned up the fire, scraping the pan as the liquid foamed.

And now Molly. Could he tell her any or all of it? Would she believe it? Why should she? But if they were going to be together again, he had to tell her, could think of no way not to. He'd just have to take his chances on whether she believed him.

When the wine and the chicken broth had been reduced to around half, he took the asparagus out of their pan and put them into the sauce. He checked the rice. Done. He put the rice on a serving dish, added the chicken from the oven, then poured the wine sauce with the asparagus over the whole thing. It steamed, the odors mingling as he breathed deeply. He put it on the table and went back to the kitchen for a plate and silverware.

And what would happen next? Where was it leading? It seemed to be intensifying. Were all of the parts connected, part of a larger whole that he would eventually recognize?

He cut off a piece of the chicken, scooped up a bit of rice with it, and ate. He tried the asparagus. Once again it had worked just as it was supposed to. The perfect, no-fail meal. Oh, if the rest of his life could be so easy.

After putting the dishes in the dishwasher, he settled down in his chair with the pile of books he had culled from the Strand.

He picked out the one he was most interested in, *The Romanov Family Album*. He poured himself some more wine and balanced the glass on the arm of the chair.

He opened the book and leafed through the pages. Almost none of the pictures had been taken by a professional. These pictures were essentially snapshots, showing the Tsar and the rest of his family in attitudes of relaxed openness. They looked, even in the photographs where they were surrounded by men in uniform, friendly and happy. Except at the end. The last few pictures showed the family in captivity, and there the serious faces seemed to understand their inevitable end.

The Tsar remained remarkably consistent throughout. His pointed thick beard and broad mustache were always perfectly trimmed and neat. His small dark eyes were the only element that ever changed, usually smiling but often wary, sad, or resigned. He was a short man, with the compact body and stature of a man who would always be trying to appear taller than he really was.

The Tsarina seldom smiled. Her mouth was one of those with thin lips that tended to purse, that would turn down at the corners as she aged. She had the permanent look of one who, when questioned, would answer no, whatever the question. She wore her hair up on her head, pulled straight back with little attempt at style. Her eyes were strained, melancholy.

The five children looked like normal children with one major exception; they were aware of their station and the distinctions that separated them from other children and the rest of the world. Of the four girls, it was Anastasia who stood out the most, bright and tomboyish to the very end.

The other girls tended to meld together in the photographs, each becoming only a slightly different version of the other. The little boy, Alexis, was obviously the crown jewel of the family, heir to the throne and at the same time slightly twisted, literally and figuratively, by the hemophilia that had plagued him throughout his fourteen years. He had a round head, dark hair, and eyes that flickered between innocence, arrogance, and pain.

He was the little boy in the dream; there was no question. Towards the front of the book Alex found several photos of the estate in the dream: Tsarskoe Selo, the royal compound outside of Petersburg. And there was the clincher, a blurry shot of the Chinese pagoda. There was no way he would have known about the pagoda. He'd never read about it or seen a picture of it. He remembered it, bright red with gold trim. Oh, yes, he had been there.

He began the book that Molly had given him, *The File on the Tsar*. Originally skeptical, he quickly found himself caught up. The two authors built their case patiently and meticulously. The amount of research was impressive. They began with a history of the period, recounted the deaths of the royal family in the accepted version, and then slowly tore that version to shreds. While he was not sure that their conclusions were correct, he was convinced by the book that the official explanation was untrue. Something had happened that night, but it was not what history said it was. People had died, yes; but who?

He pulled out his watch. Two A.M. He'd finished the bottle of wine without really noticing. He thought about calling Molly to tell her that he thought the book was definitely a story. Get her out of bed. He had a moment's pang of jealousy. What if she was in bed with someone? Did she say she had to work? Maybe she had a date.

He didn't want to think about that possibility. He would go to bed. He stood up and tossed the book onto the chair.

Lenin stared at him from the cover. The Tsar leaned on a snow shovel. The little boy looked up at the photographer. Alex remembered the sound of the cuckoo, the smell of the clear air.

Chapter 8

He slept eight hours. He woke, feeling fragments of a dream slip away. No Russians. He and Molly had been riding a cable car in San Francisco when they'd been attacked by a giant squid. He fought valiantly. Her reward to him was just and wonderful. He saw it as an omen: seafood for dinner. For a minute he thought about just having a steak but then rejected the idea. You don't go against an omen.

He peered out the window from behind the blind. It was a beautiful day. Several of his neighbors were out beavering away on their tiny front yards.

Fish. Sliced tomato, maybe just a touch of fresh basil on each slice. And a little chunk of mozzarella cheese just to balance the plate. A fresh vegetable.

He dressed. A walk to the fish market would clear away the mist. Giant squids?

In a way he was relieved not to have spent the night flitting around somewhere back in the Dark Ages. He wondered what the factor was that decided whether he would dream regular dreams or his time-travel numbers. He needed to find that particular switch, that on/off button.

But even though he was relieved to have spent the night with Molly on a cable car, he felt a note of disappointment. As if some part of him were afraid that it was over. Had he become so used to it that after one night without it he was afraid that it wouldn't happen again? He felt a little like a junkie must feel. After one night of regular sleep he missed his fix, his dream, his . . . whatever it was. He pushed it around a little further, prying at the edges of it, and found that what emerged was the fear that he would lose the ability. Was his life so boring that the only intriguing moments occurred while he was asleep? Evidently.

He'd trained himself for years for a particular task, in this case the study and teaching of history, and only after he had attained proficiency could he see that it was a relatively empty, or at least boring, way to be spending his life. Except on a purely intellectual level, he was fairly useless. And his personal life had been honed down to little more than a series of relationships with machines and objects: TV, VCR, his kitchen, his bathtub and a long series of casual affairs with pleasant but nonthreatening women. These were not pleasant thoughts.

But the dreams were exciting. Especially now that he had admitted to himself that they were real. It felt like learning to fly an airplane or a helicopter. Release, a sense of freedom, danger. Even if it was only in his head. A regular Walter Mitty, he thought.

He bought a two-pound bluefish that had been caught only hours before. It was so fresh that the big clear eyes still held a look of surprise. He also got a good deal on a pound of tiny bay scallops. He hit an Italian produce market for green beans and a fresh anise stalk and two ripe tomatoes.

He put the food away and decided that it was time to do what he had always done when he had questions that he couldn't answer. Ask Surrey.

He caught the train to Princeton.

Maxwell Surrey's house would forever remind him of his college years. The pain and uncertainty and loneliness after his parents' death had merged in his mind with old wood-paneled rooms and dark hallways, coalescing into an emotion without name. The house had become as much a feeling to him as a place.

"Come, eat," Surrey called from the dining room. The housekeeper was off for the day. Alex thought Surrey had made lunch just to prove that he could actually do it.

"This is an old man's lunch, Alex," Surrey said as they sat down. "Or maybe a child's lunch." They were having grilled cheese sandwiches, tomato soup, and tall glasses of milk. "When you get to be my age, there's not much difference. I was ninety this year and I've started to notice that time is beginning to run backwards." He waved his spoon at Alex for emphasis. "I'm getting smaller. Shrinking. My clothes are all too big for me. As if I'm waiting to grow into them next year. Hah!

"And I'm not as smart as I used to be. I can't remember as well. I'm regressing. I find that I prefer simple things." He held up his sandwich as an example. "Soon I'll be a helpless little baby and then I'll be dead." He slurped his soup.

"You're exaggerating, Max," Alex said as he ate his sandwich. He'd forgotten how good grilled cheese sandwiches were. "There's a story about Einstein. Someone asked him his telephone number, and he had to go to the phone book and look it up. He said that he refused to clutter up his brain with information that he could always find if he looked it up. You're just clearing out the clutter."

Alex knew that the story would hit home with Surrey. As the old man had aged, he had more and more come to resemble the elder Albert Einstein. He had seized on the resemblance and exploited it shamelessly. He had let his white hair grow long and cultivated a bushy mustache and a benign expression.

"Einstein?" Surrey said to his bowl of soup. "I knew Einstein. A very nice man. Played the violin."

"Max," Alex said, trying to figure out just exactly what it was that he wanted to ask him. Or at least how to ask the questions without sounding crazy. "You got a phone call last week from an old friend of mine. Molly Glenn. Do you remember?"

Surrey gave him an offended look. "Do I remember last week? Yes, Alex, I do. Does that surprise you? I also remember Miss Glenn. She is, or at least was, quite beautiful. Red hair, correct?"

Alex nodded. Surrey put down his spoon and pushed his bowl back.

"I always liked that one. You should have married her. Let's see now, she called with some trumped-up nonsense about me reviewing a book for her, some Russian thing."

"That's right," Alex said. "Two English guys wrote it.

They've done a lot of research and come up with the theory that the Tsar was killed at Ekaterinburg but the rest of the family, at least the female members, escaped."

Surrey nodded but didn't reply.

Alex had expected more of a reaction than a simple nod. "You go along with this?" he asked.

Surrey gave an elaborate shrug. The old man was enjoying his own performance.

"So?" Surrey asked.

"You believe it?" Alex had come all the way out here for, among other things, Surrey to point out where the book was wrong. He wasn't getting what he expected.

Surrey shrugged again and smiled. "I might believe it. I haven't read the book."

"Max," Alex said incredulously, "this is History we're talking about. With a capital H. Accepted History."

"History." Surrey gave a little wheeze. "So what? Maybe somebody made a mistake? You forget your own education. Don't you remember Napoleon's definition? 'Agreed fiction.' "

"For Christ's sake, Surrey. A mistake? That's a pretty big mistake, isn't it? And yes, I remember my Napoleon." He hadn't, but he hated it when Surrey did that to him. "Come on, you were in Russia; is it possible?"

Surrey gave a theatrical sigh. "Calm yourself, Alex. I'm very old; I try not to get too excited.

"I was there, yes. Is it possible? Possibly." He smiled at Alex's look of exasperation. "I was not where they were shooting Romanovs; I was in St. Petersburg." He nodded to himself as if he were remembering.

"You know your history, Alex, I taught you much of it. But over the years you are beginning to solidify. You spend too much time alone. You're turning into an old man. You now believe what you know, or what you think you know, which is a mistake—and not just in matters of history. Andrew Jackson once said, 'I have nothing but pity for the man who knows only one way to spell a word.' I like that; it's a good way to think. It's only fashion that says we must spell a word a particular way. For a long time people spelled things anyway they felt like it; it just wasn't important. And these were not stupid people."

"Are you saying that it's not important that we know

exactly how a historical event occurred? Then what's the point of all our research?''

Surrey shook his head. "What I am saying is only that we must be open to possibilities. Events did happen in only one way. It is our interpretation of these events that is interesting. And the search to find what we think happened. The journey rather than the destination.''

Surrey picked up their plates and carried them into the kitchen. Alex watched Surrey roll up his sleeves and run hot water into the sink. Ah, Christ, the old man's arms are like old sticks. Someday he will die. It hurt him to think it. He'd never questioned Surrey's mortality, he'd always been there, always would be there. He could not remember a time when there was no Surrey.

"Tell me about my father,'' Alex asked, going into the kitchen. He had no real idea what he wanted from Surrey. He was looking for definitions rather than answers.

"Your father,'' Surrey said. He did not look at Alex but slowly washed the dishes. "What is it you wish to know?''

"We never talked about it when I lived here. Or before or since. I want to know why you were his friend.''

"Why is one man another man's friend? There are no answers to questions like that, Alex. I worked with your father on his books. We were collaborators to an extent. Your father was a wonderful researcher, but his writing style was not particularly good. I helped him with that. He paid me well. He trusted me with his work.''

And that is not an answer. Those are not attributes of friendship. There was more to it. Surrey had always been there. During the summers he often lived at their house. There was not a time that Alex could remember when Surrey was not at least on the periphery of their lives. A thought suddenly occurred to Alex. It came so suddenly that he said the words aloud before he had a chance to think it out. "My mother?''

Surrey rinsed the last dish, dried his hands, and turned slowly to Alex. "Your mother,'' the old man said, his head nodding. "Yes, there was your mother.''

Was that it? Was it as simple as that? The concept was too large to be digested all at once, but it would explain why Surrey had been around so much.

"But . . ."

Surrey held up his hand. "Stop, Your mother loved your father. She and I were friends. Do not let your imagination run away with you. These are things that do not concern you."

Alex shut up. The old man still had strength when he wanted it.

"You are thinking in absolutes again, Alex." His voice was gentle now. "Your questions: my father, my mother, Russia, history. These are complicated things. Stop trying to put them in little boxes so you can take them out and hold them up to the light and say, 'Aha! Now I understand.' Open up your mind and eventually things will become clear."

"Max, there are things happening to me right now that I don't understand. I don't ask you these things out of simple curiosity. There are reasons."

The upraised palm stopped him again.

"Eventually you will understand," Surrey said. Now he sounded tired. "I can see you are having difficulties, but I cannot help you. There are reasons for me as well. Trust me. Open yourself; remember the journey." His hand dropped to his side.

Surrey suddenly looked his age. "I'm sorry," Alex said, feeling guilty. Great, why don't I hang around and badger him until he's completely exhausted? "I've got to go, anyway. Why don't you lie down for a while?"

Surrey nodded and smiled faintly. "Yes, time for the baby's nap."

Alex looked at his watch. There was time to catch the train and be home to make dinner. He would come back.

They walked to the front door. Alex opened the heavy oak door and looked out over the university campus in the middle distance. He wondered if the little train that ran to the Junction was still called the 'dinky,' as it had been when he'd lived here. "I'll send you a copy of the book, Max. You can see if these guys are really changing history."

The old man smiled and shook his head. "You never change history, Alex. History simply is. Each man writes his own version of it. Go, Alex. Good luck."

Alex turned at the end of the walk and looked back at the man still standing in the doorway. He was so old.

Chapter 9

HE CLEANED THE FISH AND PUT THE HEAD AND TAIL INTO A BAG to save for fish soup. He stood for a moment, looking into his freezer. There must have been ten little freezer bags of scraps saved for various reasons. Christ, he thought, I'm turning into an old woman.

He pulled the strings from the beans, chopped up the anise root, sliced the tomatoes, and thought about Molly. By the time he'd finished his chopping and slicing he'd worked himself up into a mild fit of desire.

An image popped into his head. When he was a kid, he'd once endured a fire safety lecture. Grade school. The lecturing fireman had said that sometimes a fire will start in a closed-up part of the house, say a spare bedroom, without the knowledge of the occupants. The fire will burn at a low level until it exhausts all the oxygen in the room. The flames will go out, but it will still burn. Embers, like those on a log in the fireplace when the flame has gone out. Alex had imagined such a room: four-poster bed, chest of drawers, an easy chair, an oval rug on the floor. All of it built of glowing embers like little red Christmas lights embedded in the wood. Tremendous heat, no air, all of it deathly still.

Open the door, the fireman said, and it goes off like a bomb. The oxygen hits the fire and the room explodes.

Wham. Always feel a closed door if you suspect something. If it's hot, don't open the door.

For weeks afterward he'd gone around the house feeling all the doors before he opened them.

This is like that, he thought, putting his hand on his chest. It's very warm in there.

When the doorbell rang, he led her into the kitchen and sat her up on a stool. She handed him a thick brown envelope, which he put on the countertop without looking at it.

"So, Mr. Balfour, what's new?" she asked. She had on pale blue jeans that looked as if they'd been washed a million times. They fit her very well. A fancy soft-looking T-shirt, plum-colored. Very white sneakers.

She tilted her head and looked at him with a small smile. "Alex?"

"Did you know," he said, his voice tight, "that the male inhabitants of certain parts of Malaysia and Thailand occasionally experience the mass conviction that their penises are shrinking?"

"Is that so?" Her smile faded.

"Yes." He walked slowly to her. "The rumor usually starts with some specific cause. In 1976, it was thought that Thai oranges were the culprits. The story spread like wildfire."

He put his hands on the small of her back. He was beginning to breathe a little too quickly. "I'm about an hour ahead of you," he said. "I know you're probably hungry; so am I, but I think it's too late."

She looked down at him. "I see you haven't been eating any Thai oranges," she said. She shook her hair back. She slid forward on the stool until she had moved against him. Her arms curled around his shoulders as she arched her back. "We'll eat dinner later," she said.

At the side of the bed was a pool of blue jeans. The blinds were pulled, but the evening light came in around the edges. He lay on the bed.

She had disentangled herself from him and placed a finger on his lips.

"One minute," she whispered.

He watched her, reflected in the full-length mirror on the inside of the partially open bathroom door. She had picked up her purse from the floor. He saw her bend over the sink. Her round bottom formed a heart shape; lovely. She put her hands to her eyes. Contacts. She was taking out contact lenses. He had forgotten she wore them. This simple gesture, domestic in a way that he had not been part of for so long, pointed up the loneliness of his life. He felt it wash over him. She straightened up and turned. She saw him watching her in the mirror. She faced him and stood, waiting, letting him look. Her breasts were round and full, the nipples dark against her cream-colored skin. Her waist was slim and taut, the hips a languid curve. She waited and then she smiled. The loneliness faded away. She came to him.

They were back in the kitchen. She was up on the stool.

"Hungry?" he asked.

She burst out laughing. "Are you kidding?" she said. "I'm starving."

She brushed her hair. It floated round her head, charged with a reddish-gold electricity. There were spots of high color on her cheekbones and her eyes looked as deep and clear as a spring-fed well.

He put the fish with a few pats of butter and a sprinkle of fresh dill under the broiler and threw the beans into the boiling water. Usually he put them in very carefully so the water stayed at an even boil, but tonight he was beyond such niceties. Cooking seemed a small act compared to the performance he'd just participated in. He felt clean, as if all his anxieties and questions had been washed away. It wasn't as if they'd been answered, simply removed from the center of his being where they'd been coiled for the last week or so. He felt free of doubt. Alive. Whatever happened would happen.

He'd left the door of the oven open a little, and the smell of the broiling fish began to fill the room.

"You really are very good at this, you know," she said.

"Good at what?" he asked as he checked the beans.

She blushed. "Good at many things," she answered. "But also good at cooking and setting the table and taking care of things. You seem to have it figured out. Most men are self-conscious when they do things like this. Sort of proud of themselves; showy. You just do it. You didn't use to be this way."

He shrugged. He took the sliced anise root out of the refrigerator and put it in to cook with the beans. "I've been doing it for a long time. I like it. I like being good at it."

"I can see that. Does that mean you like being alone?"

He stopped and looked at her. She was serious, and he could see what she was getting at. "I don't mind being alone. I'm able to do it without worrying about it. But I don't prefer it, if that's what you mean; at least not now. I'll go out on a limb and say that I'd much prefer being with you for as long as you want to be here to being alone. Does that sound stupid?"

"No." She shook her head. "Because I feel the same way. Does that mean we're in love again? After ten years of not seeing each other it just comes back all at once?"

He thought about the silently burning room. Had it been there all those years? Unconsciously he touched his chest. "I guess it does. It has for me. I think one of the problems we're having is that we don't have any words for what's happened. We're both used to putting emotions into language."

"Explain," she said.

"Well, we have the phrase 'love at first sight.' Everybody understands that. It's a recognized phenomenon." He peered into the oven. The fish was done. He got down a large fish-shaped platter.

"English is a very imprecise language. Especially the American brand of English. I once heard a Welsh word, I don't know how to spell it, but it sounded like *grefenwendenvent*, or something like that. It was explained to me that what it meant was if you woke up in the middle of the night, heard a burglar downstairs and went down in the dark and shot him and it turned out to be your mother who had gotten up for a drink of water, what you felt was *grefenwendenvent*. A very complex set of emotions summed up in one word.

"The point of all this," he said as he carried the fish on the platter to the table, "is that we don't have any words for what has happened. We were lovers when we were young; we separated for ten years; we get back together and fall instantly back in love. A very complicated set of events with no name. Because we can't put a name to it, we're afraid of it." He stood by the table watching her.

"Then let's agree to not be afraid," she said.

"Yes," he said. "I'm not afraid. Not anymore."

She admired the fish, the beans with anise root, and the tomatoes. She admired the way he was able to grow purple basil in a pot on the windowsill and cut it up on the tomatoes. She admired the meal and ate a very considerable portion of it. He figured that she was so taken with him at the moment that if he was ever going to tell her about his time-dreams, now was the time to do it.

The only way to do it was just to tell her. He went to the kitchen and picked up the pot of coffee he had put on during dinner. Along with two cups, two small glasses, and a bottle of George Dickel whiskey. He put everything—cups, coffee, glasses, whiskey—on the table and sat back down. He had not said a word during this operation and neither had she. He poured them cups and glasses of both.

"All right." He took a sip of the whiskey. "From the beginning."

He told her about the dreams as a child, about the way he'd learned to keep quiet about them when no one understood. About how they'd increased in intensity until recently, when they'd turned into something more than dreams. About the little boy and the dirt on his clothes from the bombardment and seeing Rasputin.

They'd each had two cups of coffee and an equal number of whiskeys. She hadn't said much during his recitation, had just sat and looked at him.

He ran his hands through his hair and looked up from his glass to her. "So what do you think?" he asked.

She fiddled with her coffee cup, not looking at him. "Well, first of all, I don't think you're crazy. . . ."

"That's a relief," he said cynically.

"Don't interrupt," she said. "I think that if I'd gone to bed with a crazy man, I'd be able to tell." She held up her hand to forestall him. "But that doesn't mean I don't think you might need some help with this thing. Headaches, hallucinations, those are not your everyday symptoms. I think you should see a doctor to rule out any physical causes."

63

"You mean like a brain tumor or an exploded blood vein in my brain or some other horrendous disease."

She gave him an exasperated look. "I don't know, Alex; maybe it's something as simple as not eating right, or maybe you're allergic to something. Why are men always so silly about going to see doctors? I'm just saying, and it's a pretty obvious suggestion, that you have some rather striking symptoms that should be looked at by a professional."

He had a mental image of himself flat on his back, rolling into one of those doughnut-shaped machines that does brain scans. Doctors peering at X rays while he sat in the background waiting for the verdict. No, thank you. "All right, just for now let's say that we've ruled out any physical causes."

She poured herself another half inch of whiskey and sat back. "There has to be some explanation for it. I mean other than that you're stark raving mad. I would think that the most probable is the one you mentioned—that your research, your involvement in each historical period, in some way programs you to dream, very realistically, about that particular period."

"So then how am I able to know things that are impossible for me to know? Like what the Tsar's estate, Tsarskoe Selo looked like. Believe me, it was the same as the picture in the book. The red Chinese pagoda, everything."

"You must have seen the picture sometime and forgotten about it. You know that the mind can drag up things we never knew we knew."

That answer had already occurred to him as the logical one, but he knew it wasn't right. The experiences were too perfect. There was no way they could feel so right to him. And there was also no way he could explain it to her. Just saying that it felt real was not enough.

"Maybe," he said, realizing that it was futile to keep beating away at it. At least he'd tried and gotten this far. Sooner or later he would come up with something concrete so she couldn't dismiss it.

"Let's let it go for now," he went on. "I don't want you to forget about it and I'm not taking any of it back. A few days ago you told me not to expect you to pretend that real things don't exist. Well, to me, this is real. But I wanted to tell you. Just keep an open mind, will you?"

She gave a little laugh. "It'll be as open as it can be under the circumstances, but I'm not used to men telling me that they're able to dream themselves back into time."

He nodded. "Let's go in the other room," he said, standing and picking up the whiskey bottle.

She stood up and stretched and put her arm around him as they walked into the living room. She settled down in her spot on the couch, looking like she belonged. He sat beside her.

"By the way," she said, "that envelope I gave you when I came in was the photocopy of the report from the Hoover Institite. The one in the book about the murder of the Tsar. You seemed to have other things on your mind when I handed it to you. I believe you left it in the kitchen."

He had an image of the brown envelope sitting on the countertop. Oh, Christ. She was looking at him oddly. He put his hand to his head. There were little lights beginning to twinkle in the corners of his eyes. "No," he said.

She leaned forward. "What's wrong?"

"Goddamnit," he said, rubbing both temples. The pain began.

"You're having one of your headaches?"

He nodded. It was already building. He felt his stomach turn queasy. "I'm sorry." He leaned back on the couch and closed his eyes. He tried to smile but couldn't manage it.

She put her hand on his head. "You're hot," she said. "I'll get a washcloth." She stood up and walked toward the kitchen. He didn't want her to see him like this, but he wasn't going to send her away. They were about to find out what happened to him here when he went there.

He doubled forward as the room began to turn. He saw her come back, saw the look on her face as he looked up at her, saw the room turn, go black.

Chapter 10

HE WAS FREEZING. HE WAS LEANING AGAINST A STONE WALL ON A snow-covered street. It was night. He moved away from the wall, rolled down the sleeves of his shirt and folded his arms over his chest. It did not help.

A few snowflakes drifted in the air. He looked both ways along the street. He was in a residential section. The houses were huge, more like palaces than homes. It was very quiet, obviously late at night. There was no traffic of any kind on the street. He stamped his feet. He could feel the moisture on the inside of his nose and on his lips begin to stiffen. He was wearing running shoes, blue jeans, and a long-sleeved dress shirt. He had to do something or he would die of the cold.

There was no way to decide which direction to go, so he walked straight ahead. If he didn't see anyone soon, he would go to one of the houses and pound on the door. There was nothing else to do.

He assumed he was in Russia. The only thing he really knew was that it was winter. A very small thing to know. That and the fact that he was freezing. He wondered briefly if he could actually die, or if he were somehow immortal in this other time. The cold convinced him that it was indeed possible for him to die. And soon, if he did not get somewhere warm. He thought briefly of Molly, but the coldness was his reality. Molly was the dream.

The house behind the stone wall beside him was the biggest and most impressive on the street. It looked like an art museum. It was painted a creamy yellow with white trim, and unlike the others, there were lights burning in most of the rooms that faced the street. In the dead silence he thought he could hear music coming from the house.

He came to a gate. He stopped and listened. He could hear a record playing in the house, hear it faintly but clearly. "Pop Goes the Weasel." "Pop Goes the Weasel"? The record stopped and then began again. Same tune.

He could now see that he wasn't even at the front of the house but at the side. The street entrance was wide enough to accommodate a car, but just barely. There were no guards. The wrought-iron gate stood open onto a courtyard that was lit by an outdoor light. Snowflakes fell steadily through the pool of white light. The air was so dry and still that they floated down in straight lines, like fake snow in an opera. There was a doorway in the side of the house facing him. He hesitated a moment and walked through the gate toward the house.

At that moment the door was flung open. It slapped against the wall of the house with a noise that stopped Alex dead. A man, silhouetted against the light inside the house, stumbled in the doorway, steadied himself, then lurched forward. The man stopped, stood swaying, in the pool of light outside the door. He was thirty yards from Alex and his thick black hair and beard gave him a wild, inhuman look. He stumbled forward. His head was thrown back, his lips twisted, teeth bared.

In those few quick seconds Alex felt a surge of pure terror unlike anything he'd ever felt before. It flashed over him, seeming to start at his feet and wash up over his entire body like a wave of heat lightning. He felt his chest tighten and then a flush on his face like an instant sunburn. And then it was gone. The second it left him he felt completely clean. It was as if the fear had been burnt from him, leaving him clean.

The stumbling man's eyes were open and Alex knew who

he was, where he was, and when it was. The crazed eyes, hypnotic under normal circumstances, smouldered with a look of fear, pain, and hatred. A dangerous animal that had been mortally wounded, gut shot, bleeding, but not yet killed. There was the knowledge of death and the white heat of pure hate.

Another figure appeared in the doorway. A tall man with a very large pistol raised and held in both hands. Alex flung himself down as the pistol went off with a flat report that reverberated around the walls of the courtyard. The running man plunged forward, facedown, into the light snow as if he'd been kicked in the back. He slid forward and stopped directly in front of Alex. There was a moment of quiet that was so intense that Alex's breath seemed to be the only sound in the world.

Alex scrambled to his feet and looked at the man in the doorway. He was still holding the pistol out in front of him. "Don't move," the man said. His voice was high-pitched and trembling. Alex raised his empty hands. He felt the snow begin to melt and run down his wrists. He shivered. He was very cold. "Don't move," the man said again in the same voice and began to walk toward them. He stopped near the feet of the prone man and lowered the gun. There was a look of disgust on the man's face as he looked at the body. He looked at Alex and commanded, "Turn him over. See if he's finally dead."

Alex knelt and put both hands on the dead man's shoulders. He was heavy, thick-bodied. After a struggle Alex got him over onto his back. Alex looked down at the snow-encrusted face.

Suddenly the eyes snapped open and Alex felt his wrist grasped in an iron clutch. The standing man cried out, a wordless squall of fear. The eyes of the man at his feet looked straight up into Alex's terror-stricken soul. The hand on his wrist tightened. "Why . . ." the man hissed. He tried to raise himself; the cords of his neck were stretched taut, the eyes wide with rage. "Why? . . ."

The gun went off two feet from Alex's ear. For an instant the sound and the sudden flame from the barrel blanked out everything. As the bullet slammed into the prone body, Alex felt a tremor like a jolt of electricity. The grip on his wrist tightened spasmodically and then opened. Alex jerked back. The bones in his wrist felt as if they'd been crushed. He could hear nothing. The man with the gun was saying something; his lips were moving, but there was only a loud whine in Alex's ears, a sound that he knew came from inside rather than outside.

The man with the gun turned. Another man strode toward them from the house. He was tall and wrapped in a black greatcoat. He had on a thick fur hat. A muffler hid the lower part of his face. The only part that showed was the eyes. The man with the gun seemed to shrink back at the other's approach. They spoke. Alex could barely hear the sound of voices. The two men glanced at him; the eyes of the man in black narrowed. The man with the gun held it out to the other man, who took it and put it into the pocket of the coat. Alex could hear them now, almost make out the words. The man in the coat was giving the assassin orders; the tone of the voice was imperious.

The man in black glanced at Alex again and then walked toward the gate. He stopped just outside the pool of light from the house and Alex could feel him watching him for a moment. The man turned and walked away, a shadow slipping around a corner. The first man tugged on his sleeve.

"We must get him inside," the man said. The voice sounded faraway, but the words were identifiable. "Help me."

They each took one of the arms and pulled the body toward the house. They tried to lift the body over the doorway, but it was too heavy. The head thumped as it slid over the jamb. They dragged him inside to a small room near the door that seemed to Alex to be filled with boots. "There's blood," the man said to him. "Go outside and cover it with snow." Alex nodded and went outside.

He would go along with things at least for the time being. No matter what happened, it beat freezing to death outside in the snow. Besides, he knew where he was: The man who had just been shot to death was Rasputin.

There was a path from the courtyard to the door where they had dragged the body, but there was little blood. Alex began to scuff up the snow where it had been smoothed out.

The murder of Rasputin. December, 1917; St. Petersburg,

Russia. The man with the gun was Count Felix Yussapov, scion of the greatest royal family in Russia. What he had seen was historical fact. The events had been recorded in some detail, down to the record of "Pop Goes the Weasel", which someone had finally turned off.

An historical event, no question. And he had just seen it occur. He had been part of it. He felt almost drunk on the excitement but at the same time clear and aware, as if a high pure note had been struck somewhere inside his body.

"You," a voice from the gate commanded. From the street a large man in a bulky gray overcoat walked toward him. "What are you doing?"

Alex could think of nothing to say. The man was obviously an official of some sort. Behind him he heard a low curse. "What is it, officer?" The first man, the murderer, Yussapov, came up and stood beside Alex.

"I was asking this man what he was doing, Your Highness. And may I ask you the same question? I heard a shot."

"Yes," Yussapov said. His voice was firm. He spoke like a man who was used to speaking to those below him. "We were having a party here; the men were drinking. One of the fools shot my dog." He nodded at the few speckles of blood.

They all looked down at the snow. The policeman pushed at a bloody spot with his boot. He looked at them in disbelief. Alex couldn't tell if he actually thought that Yussapov was lying or that he couldn't believe that there were such aristocratic idiots.

"I must report this. The shot was heard by others."

Yussapov nodded. "Of course, officer, as you see fit. But really, there's no need for you to bother about it." The last words were a clear dismissal. The policeman nodded in return, looked at the bloody spot again, and turned and walked out the gate. Yussapov took Alex's arm and led him back in the house.

They stood in the room with the boots. They looked down at the body. Rasputin lay faceup, his blue silk shirt and black velvet pants wet with melted snow and blood. The puddles of water on the floor were tinged pink. "God, I thought he'd never die," Yussapov said. He looked at Alex. "And now there is the problem of you. Who are you?"

Alex hesitated as he tried to decide what tack to take.

Simply going along seemed the best course of action. He had no idea how long he would be where he was; to cause any kind of trouble would be stupid and dangerous. "My name is Alexander Balfour, Your Highness."

The other man grimaced and waved his hand. "Call me Yussapov. This is neither the time nor the place for formality. I assume you know who this man is?"

They both looked at the body. For the first time Alex felt a stirring of nausea. The air in the room was overheated and thick with the coppery smell of blood. He nodded. "Rasputin. And I know why you have killed him. For the good of Russia."

"Let us hope that it is not too late for Russia," Yussapov muttered. "So you have a choice. Because of circumstance you are involved in this. Are you for us or against us? I cannot simply let you leave; surely you can see that."

"Yes, I understand, I would rather not have been a part of it, but it's too late now. I know you did what you did because you thought it was best for your country. You have nothing to fear from me. I won't betray you."

"You are a foreigner?" He looked pointedly at Alex's clothes.

"American."

"Then we must trust you to understand. If you were Russian, I could be sure of it, but . . . I haven't the stomach to kill two men in one night. We must go downstairs to the others. I'll have my man wrap the body and clean up the mess. Just go down those stairs; I'll join you in a moment."

Alex went to where Yussapov pointed, glad to get out of the small room. The stairs led down to a basement apartment.

As Alex came down the stairs three men who sat at a table in the center of the room fell silent. "Yussapov will be down in a moment," Alex said. The men just stared at him. One of them, a fat man in a chauffeur's uniform, looked as if he might faint. The others simply stared.

The room had a low vaulted ceiling with gray stone walls and a granite floor covered by a Persian carpet and, by the fireplace, a brown bearskin rug. Alex had never actually seen a real bearskin rug. The table where the men were sitting was covered with plates of little cakes and several bottles of liquor. There was a fire in the fireplace. Alex walked toward

71

it and looked at the elaborate crystal and silver crucifix that sat on the mantel. The silence in the room was as heavy as the heated air. Still Yussapov did not come. Alex felt as if the fat man would surely faint if something did not happen. The others continued to stare at him; he could guess what they must be thinking. Here they had conspired and successfully killed perhaps the most powerful man in the country, outside of royalty, and suddenly a stranger walks in on them.

Finally Yussapov came down the steps. He looked at all of them, pulled out a chair, and dropped into it. "Gentlemen, this is Alexander Balfour, an Englishman," he said, nodding at Alex. "He was a witness to the last minutes of the late Gregory Efimovitch Rasputin. He has assured me that he can be trusted, and unless one of you has sufficient nerve to kill him, I suggest we take him at his word. I have given the pistol to Charonsky, so any more assassination is beyond me." He smiled thinly at them. Alex stood very still as they made up their minds.

A youngish man with a thick handlebar moustache shrugged his shoulders. "It seems we have little choice."

The others nodded. "Yes," Yussapov said. "He of course knows who I am; that was unavoidable, but the rest of you will remain nameless." He gestured to Alex. "Come join us, Mr. Balfour. We will drink to the success of our scheme."

Alex sat at the table. Yussapov poured him a drink. Alex hesitated, which brought forth a short laugh from Yussapov. "Do not worry"—he took a sip from his own glass—"this particular bottle has not been poisoned."

"Tell us, Yussapov," the fat man said. "What happened? Why did it take so long? My God, I thought I would die when he came up the steps."

The man with the moustache shook his head in disgust. "He fainted upstairs," he said, gesturing to the fat man. "He has no nerve."

"No nerve!" the fat man blustered. "I drove him here in the car. I prepared the poison cakes. It is you who have done nothing."

"I have a job for him," Yussapov said. "The body must be disposed of as we planned. He will do it."

The man nodded. "I will do it." He looked at Alex. "But I will need help. I will take the foreigner; that will assure his complicity."

Alex nodded in return. He could see no way out of it. He had nowhere else to go. It was very cold outside.

"Tell us!" the fat man demanded.

"I could not believe it," Yussapov said. The brandy they were drinking had put color back into his cheeks. "When he came in, I offered him some of the cakes, but he refused. Then he changed his mind and ate two of them. I waited for him to fall down, but nothing happened."

"There was enough cyanide in those cakes to kill ten men," the fat man interjected. The man with the moustache snorted and the fat man turned to him. "I'm a doctor; I know these things!" Seeing his mistake, he glanced at Alex to see if he had caught it. Alex pretended he had not noticed the man refer to himself as a doctor.

Yussapov held up his hand. "Please, there's no time for arguing. Anyway," he went on, "he just sat there. I gave him the Madeira; he drank two glasses of it and still he sat there. Nothing. He asked me to sing. I got my guitar and sang Gypsy songs until I thought I would lose my mind. He sat and drank and grinned at me like a fool. The man was inhuman. He should have been dead twenty times. I sang for two and a half hours." He stopped and took a drink and filled his glass again. "That's when I went upstairs for the gun. Charonsky was waiting; he gave it to me.

"I came back downstairs and suggested to Rasputin that he look at the crucifix on the mantelpiece. As a supposed man of God he would, I knew, be interested. He stood up and looked at it. He said he liked the cabinet better as a work of art. I said to him, 'Gregory Efimovich, you'd far better look at the crucifix and say a prayer,' and then I shot him in the back. He fell there"—he gestured to the bearskin rug in front of the fireplace. Alex glanced at the rug and saw a small bloody spot on the thick brown fur. Yussapov paused for a moment and then went on. "His eyes were closed. I knelt down to see if he was still breathing. Suddenly one eye popped open and then the other. I felt my heart stop. He looked at me with such hatred as I have never seen before. I jumped up and so did he; he grabbed me by the throat. I thought he would kill me." Yussapov's voice was harsher now; he was breathing heavily. "I broke away and ran up the stairs. I hid in the boot room. I heard him come up the stairs, throw open the door, go outside. I knew that I must finish it; he was getting away. He would tell the Empress and then we would all be dead men. I went out in the courtyard and shot him. Mr. Balfour was standing there; he saw me do it.

"And still he was not dead." Yussapov thumped his fist on the table. "I shot him again in the chest." He sagged back in his chair. "And now he is dead."

They were quiet for a moment, and then, as if the same thought had occurred to all of them at the same time, they looked at the doorway at the top of the steps.

"No!" shouted the fat man. "He is *dead*! There was no pulse; I checked."

"Please," Yussapov said. "We are all nervous. I suggest that we finish it and you should all go home. You will use my car," he said to Alex and the man with the moustache.

They stood. The sound of the scraping chairs seemed very loud in the small room. Upstairs Alex took Yussapov aside as the others were putting on their coats. "I have no coat," he said. "Can you lend me something?"

Yussapov looked at him, suddenly realizing that Alex had never had a coat, not even when he had first seen him outside. He went to a rack and took down a heavy cloth coat with a fur collar. He held it out. "It was his," he said, gesturing to the sheet-wrapped body on the floor. "He won't be needing it anymore."

Alex shrugged and put on the coat. If wearing a dead man's coat was supposed to frighten him, it didn't work. It was too cold out to worry about ghosts.

The others left and Yussapov went through a door into another part of the house after conferring with the man with the moustache. The man left the house, telling Alex to wait there.

Alex stood, beginning to sweat in the overheated room and the heavy coat. The body on the floor wasn't helping things either. Blood was beginning to leak through the sheet he'd been wrapped in. Alex tried to ignore the body, but even in death Rasputin demanded attention.

The man was back at the door. Alex could see the car outside. They picked up the body at either end and half carried, half dragged it to the car. They loaded it into the backseat and sat in the front.

"My name is Sukhotin," the man said. He took his hand off the wheel and held it out to Alex. Alex shook it. "I have done what I have done because I felt that my country would be destroyed if I didn't. Do you understand that?" Alex nodded. "I am not afraid that you know my name and I am not ashamed of what I have done. Now let us finish it." He put the car in gear and drove through the gate.

It must have been near dawn, but the sky was still black. Alex could see a sprinkling of stars. The snow had stopped. They drove through deserted streets for at least twenty minutes. The stuffy car and the drink started to get to him. He began to nod off.

"Here," Sukhotin said. He parked the car at the bottom of an embankment. Alex could see a dark bridge against the stars in the sky, the broad, pale expanse of frozen water in front of them.

They dragged the body out of the car and down onto the ice. They slid it toward a black hole near the pilings under the bridge.

"I was here this morning," Sukhotin said. "I found this hole then. The ice is very thick here; one of the pilings must have collapsed and made the hole."

They slid the body out onto the dark area. It just lay there, seemingly suspended in midair. "It has frozen over," Sukhotin said. He cursed for a moment and then went back to the bank. Alex glanced back at the body.

Rasputin was up on his knees. The sheet was still wound around him. The lower half of his body was wet with blood, shiny and black in the moonlight. Alex tried to speak but could only manage a low *uhhh, uhhh* sound.

The body began to move inside the sheet, struggling, a worm inside a chrysalis, struggling to be born.

Alex fought the urge to run, to flee this thing. He looked at Sukhotin.

Sukhotin, a long pole held javelin-fashion in his hand, stared at Rasputin. The sheet loosened. The figure inside began to writhe. The sheet fell away from the head. Rasputin's eyes gleamed, focused on Alex. Alex suddenly regretted very deeply the fact that he was wearing Rasputin's coat.

Sukhotin ran to the ice and began to chip away around the body. He stopped for a moment and brought the pole up,

75

then down on Rasputin's head with a sharp crack that sounded to Alex as loud and final as the crack of doom. Rasputin fell to the ice but continued to move. Weakly.

Sukhotin chipped frantically. The pole went through the ice. Rasputin flopped over on his back.

Sukhotin pried at the ice until there was another crack; then a straining sound from the ice, and Rasputin began to slowly slide toward the widening gap. At the last moment the arms came free and the hands scrabbled at the edge of the ice. The current caught him and pulled him under. Silence. The sound of escaping air, a gurgling, and beneath it the whisper of the river.

Sukhotin turned to Alex and the look of horror on the man's face was imprinted forever on Alex's mind.

Pain. A twinkling in the corners of his eyes. Sukhotin's eyes widened even further. Alex fell to his knees.

Blackness.

Chapter 11

THE AIR CLEARED. THE VEIL OF NIGHT DISSOLVED. HE WAS STANDING in his living room. The room was in darkness, lit only by a weak glow from the curtained windows. In the corner he could just make out Molly curled up in one of the big overstuffed chairs. The house was silent. He could hear her breathing.

He walked across the room and looked down at her. She had her hands beneath her cheek. He leaned down and accidentally knocked over a pile of books. Her eyes opened and she looked at him.

She screamed.

"It's all right," he said quickly. "It's me—Alex." He reached for her arms. She pushed herself further back in the chair.

She stayed pressed back in the chair. He went to a lamp and turned it on.

He saw her body relax. She rubbed her face and looked at him. "Alex?" she asked.

"Yes. Don't be afraid." He sat down on the couch.

She swung her legs down and rubbed her face again. "You frightened me. You looked so huge and dark standing there. I didn't know who it was. I'm still half asleep. Excuse me a minute."

She left the room. He heard the water running in the bathroom and then she was back. Her eyes were wide-awake now. "It's the coat," she said. "You look so big in it. I'd never seen you in it before; I didn't know who it was."

He was suddenly aware that he was still wearing Rasputin's coat. He took it off. "I'm sorry I frightened you. What time is it?"

She looked at her watch. "Almost six in the morning. Can we have some coffee?"

He took her hand and they went to the kitchen. The warm smell of coffee helped restore at least a semblance of balance between them. She still seemed wary. She was up on the stool and he was warming up some Irish soda bread he'd made several days before.

"I don't think I've ever been so frightened," she said. He handed her a cup of the coffee.

"I didn't mean to wake you like that. It was those damn books."

"Not then," she said, shaking her head. "When you went away. I've never seen anything like it." She gave a small laugh. "I don't imagine anybody has seen anything like it. You were there, holding your head in your hands, and then you just started to fade. You just disappeared."

"I'm sorry. I have no control over it. Did you sleep in the chair all night?"

"All night? I was up for most of it, but I guess I finally fell asleep."

He took her in his arms. The great comforter, he thought as he rubbed her back.

Suddenly she pushed him away. "Alex, where the hell have you been?"

He smiled as he looked down at her flushed face. This looked more like the Molly he remembered. He took the soda bread out of the oven and grabbed the coffeepot. "Bring your cup," he said, going into the dining room.

They'd reduced the slab of soda bread to crumbs. She'd sat quietly while he told her. Every once in a while her eyes had widened and glanced away in disbelief.

"I guess I have to believe you," she said when he had

78

finished. "If I hadn't seen your Incredible Disappearing Act, I never would have, but that part I saw with my own eyes."

"And then there's the coat," he said.

"Yes, there's the coat. Go get it; I want to see it."

He went to the living room and got the heavy coat. She put it on her láp and stroked the collar. "This is black sable," she said. She opened it to the inside. "Good God, the inside is lined in sable. Do you know how much it must be worth?"

"Besides the fact that it's a genuine historical relic? Rasputin the Mad Monk's coat. I can tell you quite sincerely that there at the end I was wishing I'd never laid eyes on this thing. I was waiting for him to point his finger at me and say something about the fact that I'd had more than a small part of putting him in the position he was currently in. Namely, shot several times, poisoned, and on the edge of drowning. And on top of it all, I'd stolen his fully lined black sable topcoat."

She gave him a small smile. "How about the rest of it? Is this tale in the history books?"

"Yep. You can check it if you want, but I can assure you that it matches up pretty well. I don't remember any mention of the guy in the black coat and muffler, but they never did find the gun."

"So what do we do now? Do you have any explanation for it?"

"Still nothing solid." He thought for a minute. "Surrey used to have a lecture that he would give to his graduate students. He used the image of history as a series of whirlpools. He applied the image to people who study events and how they're drawn to specific periods, but I think he may be more right than he knows. What if history is made up of events that act as whirlpools. Events that are so important that they tend to exert an actual force?

"Certain people, historians, other people who have an extraordinary interest in the past, maybe they can become so close to these events that they somehow are affected by this force. Maybe some of them, like me, are particularly susceptible and are pulled back in time."

She shook her head. "You say people. If it happens to other people, how come we never hear about it?"

"How would you hear about it?" He laughed. "Who'd

believe it? Maybe other people have tried to tell it and now they're locked up somewhere. I know I'm not going to go out and shout it on the streets.''

"Well, I guess it doesn't really matter how it happens. She looked at him. Her jaw was set in a stubborn line. "Now what, Alex?''

He looked at the table. "I don't know.''

"Oh, Alex, can't you see? You don't want to stop it. It's written all over your face. When you talk about it, you get all excited and lit up. You want to go back there, wherever the hell there is.'' He could see tears in her eyes.

"I know,'' he said quietly. Guilty, no question about it. He did want to go back. "I wish I could explain it so you could understand. When I'm there, I feel different, really alive: I feel as if I've got some purpose.'' He could see that his words were hurting her. He reached across the table and took her hand. "I don't want to leave you. But I can't stop it. It doesn't have anything to do with the way I feel about you. I don't know when it will happen or how long I'll be gone, but I feel like it will be soon and I think I'll be gone for a long time. It's like I have to be there for a reason. That it's important.''

She shook her head and sniffed. She wiped her cheeks with her napkin. She couldn't look at him, but she held onto his hand. "What if something happens to you back there? I'll never know. How long am I supposed to wait?''

He just looked at her. He had no answers.

They tried to plan for it, but there wasn't much that seemed very practical.

The episode with the overcoat seemed to mean that he could go back and forth with whatever he carried on his body. He had never arrived naked. But he couldn't think of anything that he could take to make it easier. Any Russian money he could get hold of would be different than what they used back then.

"Take a Swiss army knife,'' she suggested. They'd been talking about it all afternoon and by now he couldn't tell if she was serious or not.

"I'm not going camping, Molly. At least I don't think I

80

am. I don't even know if I'll go back to any of the same times I've been to before."

"Wherever you're going, there's a good chance you could use a Swiss army knife," she said firmly. She got her purse and rummaged around in it for a minute before coming up with a thick red knife. "Here," she said, handing it to him. "I'll donate mine. I'm a great believer in them."

He shook his head, but he pushed the knife into his pocket. "Jesus, it must have at least fifty blades," he said. "I feel as if I've got most of the Swiss army in my pocket."

He was slumped down in his reading chair.

"Maybe I ought to take a gun," he said glumly.

"What do you know about guns?" she asked. She was curled up in her usual spot on the couch.

"Actually," he said, standing and stretching, "I know a lot. My father taught me how to use them on our expeditions. I guess I was supposed to guard my mother from the natives. Anyway, he taught me to shoot rifles and handguns."

They were in the desert. He could feel the heat radiating up from the sand, baking down from above. They had set up a line of cans and bottles. A row of Bedouins squatted behind them. His father paced back and forth, ordering him. Madness. "You must point the gun just as you point your finger!" His father's hair was disheveled, his face flushed. "Don't think! Point, squeeze. Point, squeeze. Remember"—he was standing over him, shouting now—"you must not stop to think; you must act, react: when you point the gun, you are the wrath of God!" Alex pointed, fired. The row of bottles exploded, one by one, as fast as he could pull the trigger. His father's madness entered him. He fired until the gun was empty.

"My advice is to stick with the Swiss army knife," she was saying. "It's a lot less dangerous if someone takes it away from you." She watched him moving restlessly around the living room. "I feel as if I'm sending you off to war or something," she said. There had been no more tears. "I keep wanting to tell you to be careful, but it sounds so stupid."

By evening they'd both gotten tired of talking about it. He made them a huge Italian omelette with prosciutto ham and Parmesan cheese. They drank a bottle of wine between them and went to bed.

After an hour of exploring each other they were ready to go to sleep. They were both exhausted, but sleep would not come. He lay there waiting to go back into the past and she lay there waiting for him to disappear. After several hours of waiting they drifted off to sleep.

The next day she went to work and he went to his class.

The next several days became an odd sort of torture. It was as if Alex were scheduled to go away on a business trip, but the airport was snowed in. She really didn't want him to go, but the waiting was getting on their nerves. She began to feel that if he was going to do this thing, then he should get on with it.

Alex himself had conflicting emotions. At times he couldn't remember why he wanted to go; then he would remember the exhilaration of it. Then the delay and uncertainty would chafe until his nerves were scraped raw.

He read voraciously. He decided that his only real asset was going to be his memory. He read histories and economic books and memoirs and political references. He looked at picture after picture, implanting the likenesses of the famous men of the time into his memory.

He and Molly spent every evening and night together. Even though they knew why they were doing it, they began to snap at each other. The tension filled the house with an electrical field that had them circling each other like oppositely charged particles, sometimes bouncing apart, sometimes coming together with such force it astounded both of them.

On Wednesday morning she called to check on him, but he didn't answer. Early that morning, after she had gone to work, he had seen the blinking lights and felt the pain. He was dressed and in the bathroom brushing his teeth.

He heard the phone ring.

He was gone.

Chapter 12

THE MAN WAS SELLING SUNFLOWER SEEDS. ALEX WATCHED HIM
from a small alcove in the long wall that ran the width of the
room. The man had a tray of the black and white striped
seeds slung around his neck on a strap. Occasionally he
would scoop a measure of seeds into a cone of rolled-up
newspaper and sell it for a single coin to one of the crowd in
the huge room.

"Seeds," the man shouted, his voice carrying above the
chaos that surrounded him: chuffing trains; men, women, and
children all talking and shouting in dozens of languages.
"Seeds--very good, very healthy, very cheap. Help an old
soldier. Help our fighting men. Buy these delicious seeds."

When Alex emerged, he was crouched in a small snowdrift behind a line of railway cars. The cold hit him with
his first breath. He realized that once again he'd come
through into winter. He had on a long-sleeved white shirt,
blue jeans, and running shoes. And his toothbrush. He looked
at it. He was holding it in his hand. He had been brushing his
teeth when the headache had come. Terrific. He might freeze
to death, but at least he'd have clean teeth. He stuck it in his
pocket and thought longingly of Rasputin's overcoat eighty
years away in a closet in New York.

He felt the snow beginning to melt down into his sneakers

when he stood up and stamped his feet. There was no one around except a few workers a hundred yards or so down the tracks. He looked around the railroad yard. It was a flat open area surrounded by blocks of low buildings. There was a huge ornate railroad station across the yard. Obviously Russian. He'd returned to where he'd been before. He wondered briefly what the mechanism was that was sending him back to this particular time and place. Too cold for questions that had no answers. He trotted toward the station, clumsily leaping the intervening tracks and snowdrifts.

The stench and noise inside the building seemed almost solid; heavy and wet with fumes of drying damp wool and sweat and dirt. The smell of a hundred wet dogs slowly drying in front of a hundred coal stoves. And people, acres of them, dressed in black, grey, and olive drab. Here and there flashed patches of brilliant color; clustered families from far-off regions where travel meant you wore your finest clothing.

"Seeds. Seeds. Very good. Very healthy." The seed seller was wearing a heavy wool army greatcoat; worn, muddy felt boots; pants that seemed to be made of rags wound round his legs. His smile was continuous, like the smile of a beauty queen or an entertainer. Or a salesman. "Very fresh, very good, very healthy."

Alex leaned back against the wall and closed his eyes for a moment, consciously slowing his breathing and trying to calm his pounding heart. It was not so much his dash across the yard outside but more the sheer immediacy of everything, the color and stink and noise and the fear. He could almost taste the adrenaline as it splashed into his bloodstream.

He went through his pockets, taking inventory of his possessions. A few coins. his wallet, his pocket watch, the toothbrush, and the Swiss army knife that Molly had given him. The touch of the knife reminded him of her and for a second he wondered if she knew by now that he was gone.

He walked to a newspaper kiosk and searched the front pages for dates: January 3, 1917. Only a few days since the murder of Rasputin. The newspaper seller eyed him suspiciously. Alex moved on.

"Seeds, sir? Would the gentleman like some fresh seeds?"

"I have no money," Alex said. It was not the way he had

wanted to start, but it just came out. The fact that his Russian simply came as always without thinking rattled him and made him forget what he had thought to say.

"No money? No money at all?" The man's smile grew even wider. "Seldom do I meet a man who has even less than I. Thank you, sir, thank you. You have made me rich by comparison. No money at all, think of it. I, Yuri the seed seller, at least have a little money, a few coins. Not much, granted, but more than none at all. Suddenly I am wealthy."

The constant grin and mad speech made Alex wonder if he had picked a lunatic as his first contact. He considered trying someone else but decided to stick with Yuri the seed seller.

"I'm a foreigner," Alex said, gesturing to his clothing. "Can you tell me where I could find a pawnbroker? Someone who deals in secondhand articles?" He wasn't sure that he knew the right words for what he wanted.

"Of course," the man replied without hesitation. "I myself deal with these merchants. This area boasts many such establishments; they seem to gather around railway stations. Perhaps like vultures." He pointed a grimy finger across the room. "The exit at the other side opens onto Michialava Street, where you will find what you are looking for. Try the proprietor at number 27, he is the least likely to pick your bones clean." He looked Alex up and down. "You seem to have little enough to sell."

"Thank you," Alex nodded, not wishing to get into a discussion of his few possessions. He started to walk away but was stopped by the man's hand on his arm. The man's smile was very white against his dark skin.

"Here; some seeds." He thrust the packet into Alex's hand.

Alex nodded his thanks and pushed into the crowd.

He hesitated by the huge wooden doors. The air blasted into the room as the crowds came and left. Alex fumbled open his cone of sunflower seeds and ate several, spitting the shells onto the floor as he had seen others doing. He felt as if he were poised at the open door of an airplane, parachute strapped to his back, about to leap out into the void. He stepped in behind a fat man with a wooly hat and pushed through the door.

The street outside was about as wide as a New York street.

The snow was packed and there was a blend of cars, trucks, and horse-drawn sleighs of all kinds. The foot traffic was light, consisting mainly of people entering and departing from the station. He paused only a moment as the cold drew tight around him. He turned left on a guess and started down the street, the snow crunching lightly under his sneakers.

It was primarily a residential section with a few shops; a bakery with empty shelves, a stationery store, shoe repair, all in narrow storefronts with small signs over the windows. He found with some relief that he was headed in the right direction. Number 27 was in the next block.

He stepped into a vestibule and searched the list of names posted by the door. He found a Levinovitch with a small three-ball sign drawn in after the name. Fourth floor. He'd found his pawnbroker.

The walls inside were painted a bilious green, the color of welfare offices and police stations. The steps were wooden and well-worn; the dank hallway smelled of cooked cabbage. He climbed the stairs.

Memory nagged at him. Climbing stairs to a pawnbrokers? It broke over him like a soft wave. Raskolnikov, Dostoyevski's *Crime and Punishment*; Raskolnikov mounting the stairs in utter fear on his way to murder the lady pawnbroker, driven to his desperate act by his grinding need for money. He reached the fourth floor and found the name on one of the two doors. He knocked.

There was silence and then a shuffling behind the door. "Who's there?" a voice asked, muffled by the heavy oak door.

"Raskolnikov," Alex blurted out the only Russian name that came to mind. There was a long silence as Alex wondered whether saying anything more would just make it worse.

"Very humorous," the voice behind the door said. "What do you want?"

"I'm a customer," Alex said. "I have something to sell."

The door opened a crack and Alex looked but saw no one. Then he looked down and saw an eye peering up at him. "Raskolnikov, is it?" the man said, his voice clearer. "And I suppose you've come to smash in my head with an axe?"

86

"No. I'm sorry I said that. It was just something I was thinking."

The door opened and the small man stepped back. "Come in," he said, gesturing into the room. "You are not the first, you know, to appear at my door with that poor joke. Dostoyevski was very familiar with pawnbrokers because he was always in debt to them."

Alex followed the man down a long, dark hallway into a brightly lit room. Broad, high windows looked out onto the street. The bright sun, reflecting from the snow outside and the lemon-yellow wallpaper, made the room glow. The furniture was worn but comfortable-looking. Alex glanced around, half expecting shelves full of pawned cameras, radios, and electric guitars. Switchblade knives for sale. Another time, another place.

"Well, what is it you have to sell? Not much from the looks of you."

The pawnbroker was a very short man. He was dressed in black pants and shoes, a white shirt and a black vest. He had a graying goatee and a black skullcap perched on the bald area of his head. His expression was pugnacious, but there seemed to be little real rancor behind the look. More like a professional expression, part of the job.

"A watch," Alex said, pulling his father's heavy pocket watch out by the chain. He unclipped the chain and handed it to the pawnbroker. "My name is Balfour. Alex Balfour."

The pawnbroker merely grunted. He went to a writing desk and took a jeweler's loupe out of the center drawer. He screwed it over his eye and opened the watch.

Alex wondered if he should be giving some sort of a sales talk. In his whole life he'd never pawned anything, never had the need. While he hated losing the watch, he assumed that the rules of pawning were the same here as they were in his own time. The three-ball sign after the man's name indicated that. Three balls, taken from the coat of arms of the Medicis, Europe's first pawnbrokers. Of course the Medicis' operation was on a larger scale, but the essentials were the same. If you pawn something, you have a certain amount of time to buy it back before it was sold to someone else. "It's gold," he said a little nervously. It's my first time, he felt like adding. Be gentle.

The pawnbroker eyed him through the jeweler's loupe. "Of course, it's gold," the pawnbroker said, his expression and the loupe giving him the look of a slightly exasperated one-eyed frog. "One hundred rubles."

A hundred rubles? Ten dollars. Before he'd left his own time, he'd looked up the exchange rate for this time period. A ruble was worth about a dime. The problem was he didn't know what a room, a meal, clothing, anything, was going to cost him. But he knew he should ask for more. This was a pawnbroker, right? You were supposed to argue. "But it's gold; it's worth more than that."

The man waved his hand. "One hundred ten. Absolutely the best I can do."

"But it's worth more."

The pawnbroker went back to the watch, then eyed Alex again. "There is a flaw," the pawnbroker said triumphantly, as if he were playing a trump card that he had been carefully hoarding. "You're lucky I give you that much." He motioned for Alex to come over where the light beamed straight through the window. He held the watch into the light and pointed to the inside of the open case. "There. Read. What does it say?"

Alex bent down. The script was flowing, elegant, thin but readable. "Bulova. Twenty-four carat gold. Eighteen jewels. Bulova Manufacturing Corp. Albany, New York. 1937." He straightened up, looking down at the little man's beaming face. "So?"

"1937!" the pawnbroker crowed, pointing at the case. "It is a misprint. They must have meant 1907. A flaw."

Alex felt the room seem to shift an inch or so under him as the discontinuity shook him. He felt a shaft of fear, as if the man had found him out and would now call the police. Arrest this man! He is a spy, an impostor! "Well," he said, giving himself a second to regroup, "that just makes it more valuable. Like a stamp that's printed upside down."

The pawnbroker frowned as he took that in. It made sense; stamps were more valuable if flawed. "This is not a stamp," he said, holding the watch up. He turned it slowly, catching the light and reflecting it around the room; a gold spot flashed along the walls. "This is a watch." His expression showed he would listen to no more nonsense. "A hundred twenty, and that is absolutely my last offer!"

"Sold," Alex said, almost giddy with the transaction. He held down a burst of laughter as he looked down at the little man holding the watch in the air and the jeweler's loupe forgotten in his eye. What did he know? Maybe it was a lot of money. The pawnbroker lowered the watch and took out the loupe. He looked a little disappointed, as if he had hoped for a stiffer resistance to overcome.

"Anything else?" the man asked hopefully.

Alex put his hand in his pocket and felt the Swiss army knife. Worth about fifty dollars new in an outdoors store. But first he needed information. "Can you tell me how much a room might cost me? In this area." He gestured toward the windows. The pawnbroker's frown deepened. "I'm a foreigner," Alex added. The man walked to the window and looked out as if he were unsure of what area Alex was talking about.

"A room? If you want just a room, nothing fancy mind you, you might find something for ten rubles a night. It would be more with meals." He shrugged.

He could last a couple of weeks on the watch, but only if he ate nothing. Besides which he needed clothing and other supplies. Hairbrush, soap, necessities. The pawnbroker's answer was reassuring, though, at least intellectually. He now realized that if he didn't know something, he could simply ask. He might appear stupid, but no one was going to think he was the mysterious man from the future just because he asked dumb questions. His own perception of things was unique; he was being silly to keep operating under the constant assumption that everyone around him was suspicious. He would play the naive foreigner. After all, that's what he really was; he was just from a little further away than anyone might guess. But he still needed more money.

The pawnbroker held up his hand in a forestalling gesture as if he had read Alex's thoughts. "The price stays the same. I have more gold watches than I know what to do with; everyone is getting rid of their watches, their jewelry. These are difficult times; you would do well to take my offer."

Alex pulled the knife from his pocket and held it out. "Genuine Swiss army knife," he said, wondering if there

89

even was a Swiss army in 1917. He let the question pass as he felt himself gripped by the goofy scene he was now playing. "Absolutely genuine; I doubt if there is another in all of Russia." A stab in the dark, but probably very true nonetheless.

The pawnbroker took the knife and turned it in his hand. He looked up at Alex and then back to the knife. Alex took the knife back and opened one of the blades, then another. He paused for effect, then opened up the tiny scissors, waited, and with a small flourish, pulled out the ivory toothpick secreted in the handle. The pawnbroker's eyes widened as he took back the knife. "Fabergé?" he asked, watching Alex closely and at the same time staring at the wonder in his hand.

"L.L. Bean," Alex said mysteriously. The pawnbroker nodded solemnly.

"Five hundred," the pawnbroker said. "And call me Levinovitch."

"Five?" Alex said, amazed at the sum. It was twice as much as he thought he was going to get.

"All right, all right," Levinovitch said impatiently. "Six. But that is absolutely my last offer. That's it. Six." He opened up another blade, the fish scaler, and nearly gasped in astonishment.

"Done!" Alex said, laughing at the look of naked greed on the pawnbroker's face.

Levinovitch laughed briefly himself, proud of the coup he had just pulled off. God in heaven, the look in his eyes said, send me more foolish foreigners. He closed all the blades and slid the heavy knife into his pocket. "You have two weeks to redeem your goods," he said, hoping inwardly that this man's tastes would run in the same directions that a Christian's usually did. Vodka and whores.

"Two weeks. After that the goods are mine."

Alex nodded. If the plan that was slowly forming in his mind worked out, that should give him just enough time to earn the money to get everything out of hock. "And now I need clothing," he said. "I need a coat, pants, and a shirt"—he gestured to himself—"everything. Can you tell me where I can get these things?"

Levinovitch eyed him professionally. This foreigner was

certainly an odd man, traveling without even clothing. No coat? A criminal? German spy? Not his problem. "Clothing? Balfour, wasn't it?" Alex nodded. "An Englishman. I get very few Englishmen here. You speak excellent Russian; you have almost no accent." Flattery, yes; but true nonetheless.

Good point, Alex thought. In all the dreams he'd been able to speak Russian without even thinking about it. The ability seemed to come with the territory.

"Let's see. . . ." The pawnbroker appeared to be measuring Alex, his fingers rubbed together in unconscious expectation of the money he was about to make back. "Excuse me for just a moment while I look in the back room. I believe I have just the very thing. You are tall, but not too tall; broad, but . . ." He waggled his hands back in forth in the air, as if to say that Alex's size would be no problem. He turned quickly and left the room. Alex could hear him hurrying down the wooden floor of the long hallway.

He walked around the room once, then sat down in an overstuffed armchair to wait. The light had dulled in the room, the sun having dropped below the buildings that surrounded them. It would get dark here early, Alex realized, well before evening, at this latitude. He looked out the window. The buildings across the street appeared twisted through the two layers of thick, imperfect glass. The pawnbroker bustled back into the room, carrying a stack of clothing. He dropped it onto a backless sofa that looked like a classic psychiatrist's couch.

"Clothing," he announced, waving his hand at the stack. "Only the finest, straight from the backs of noblemen. As I said before, these are precarious times." He leaned forward conspiratorily and lowered his voice. "You are a foreigner; you may not know it, but we are due for a change here in Petrograd, and it will not be long before it comes." That's right, Alex thought, they call it Petrograd now instead of St. Petersburg. The original name sounded too German. St. Petersburg, Petrograd, Leningrad. Yes, you are due for a change.

The pawnbroker glanced around as if expecting a policeman to leap out of the corner of the room. "The Bolsheviks, and I am not one of them but many Jews are, will be heard from, and soon. The Tsar is at the front and his wife rules in his absence. The war has drained us; there is no bread, no

91

coal; the people are freezing and they are hungry. Not me, perhaps, but I have eyes; I see what is happening." He gestured again at the pile of clothing. "It is as if the young men sense what will come. They gamble and they whore until their money is gone and their families refuse them more. Then they come to me. 'Take this, Levinovitch,' they say, tossing me their coats, extra shoes, whatever they have. As if there were no tomorrow." He shrugged. "I take it and I give them a little money and they go out and throw it away. It is not my problem, but it cannot last." He looked down at the floor and then around the room again, looking for hidden policemen come to arrest the old Jew for seditious talk.

Alex stood and picked up a heavy wool coat. He tried it on. It fit perfectly. The pawnbroker nodded his head and smiled and gestured at the other clothes. "I will leave you alone to try these on," he said, backing toward the door. "Just say my name when you are ready and we will complete our transaction."

Alex stood on the street outside number 27, dressed in his new wool coat and a fur hat on his head. He had always wanted one of these hats and now he had it. The pawnbroker had sold him the hat, a suit coat and pants, two plain white shirts, and a pair of shoes that fit fairly well, for two hundred fifty. Alex had felt that he was probably being taken advantage of, but he didn't really mind. He was now warm, reasonably well-off, and confident after having achieved his first major transaction. The sun had gone down, but the streetlights had not yet come on. The sky was a clear deep indigo, just beginning to show a few stars. The air was clean, sharp with cold that made his nose crackle. Next a room. Then food. And then he must make his plans.

Chapter 13

ALEX JAMMED HIS HANDS INTO HIS POCKETS AND FOUND A SURPRISE. Gloves. A pair of leather fur-lined gloves. Alex held them to his face, smelling the leather and feeling the smooth softness of the high-quality hide; imagining the former owner, some dissolute younger member of the *pridvorny* who had pawned his coat before heading off to an evening of vodka, women, wild Gypsy singing, and then later perhaps flinging himself off one of the many bridges of the city onto the frozen Neva. Alex sighed for his imaginary doomed young Russian as he slipped on the gloves. They fit like a glove.

The electric streetlights flickered on, casting a pale yellow halo onto the snow. Beyond the circles of light the snow appeared palely phosphorescent. Alex turned back toward the train station.

After half a block he stopped in front of a store that advertised stationery and school supplies. He peered into the small window at the front of the shop. The window was layered with ice, but he could see light in the shop and a shadowy form staring back at him. A bell tinkled as he opened the door. A gloomy young man behind the counter greeted him perfunctorily and then sold him the schoolboy's notebook and several pencils that Alex had found for himself on the mostly empty shelves. There were no Bic pens, no spiral-bound notebooks with *Star Wars* pictures on the front, and no racks of amusing greeting cards.

The man counted out his change, ninety-five kopeks, gave him a desultory *spassibo* (thanks) and went back to staring out the frosted-over window. Perhaps he was only looking at his own blurred reflection.

Alex was disappointed. The seed seller was gone from the station. In the brief time he'd been in the past he'd come to almost think of the man as a friend, the station as home. Ridiculous. He shrugged it off and decided to walk around the neighborhood before asking help from anyone else.

The streets leading away from the station were wider and less residential-looking than where he'd been. He walked several blocks until he came to a very wide street that bordered the great expanse of a river. The Neva, the great river that flowed through Petrograd. He could see the lights of the other sections of the city as he stood leaning against the parapet. The Neva was a great, white, silent expanse that stretched away on either side. He shivered as a thin wind off the frozen river cut into him, blasting a spray of hard ice crystals from the frozen surface against the skin of his exposed face. His eyes began to tear. He turned back toward the station.

On the walk back he realized he was very hungry. He hadn't eaten anything since the night before, back in the present. No wonder he was hungry; he hadn't eaten for sixty-five years.

He found what looked like a place that served food. There was a sign hanging over the door that he translated as We Eat Nobody. We Eat Nobody? But it was cold and he was hungry.

It was warm and humid inside, thick with the smell of cooked cabbage. It resembled a crude version of a New York take-out; a counter where you ordered and rough, high wooden tables where you stood and ate. For one brief mindspinning second he envisioned a huge slice of pizza, thick with cheese and pepperoni.

There was one other customer, an old man furtively spooning up a thick soup. The woman behind the counter was very fat and not very clean. Strands of stringy hair hung limply out of the edges of her tightly bound scarf. She was wearing an apron bearing the remains of many meals and was holding a large wooden spoon like some sort of culinary weapon. She watched him distrustfully. He nodded to her; she nodded back. He looked around for some sort of menu and found none. There was a large black coal stove with a large black pot on the top; he surmised that whatever there was to eat was cooking. Taking his cue from the other patron, he asked for soup and waited to see what would happen. The woman nodded again, put down her spoon, and came up with a ladle and a large white bowl. She took the top off the pot, cabbage steam wafting into the air, and ladled out a bowlful. This she placed in front of Alex with a spoon that she rubbed clean with her thumb. "Fifty kopeks," she said accusingly. Her hand stayed on the bowl until she saw him bring out a handful of coins. He handed her the money and said *spassibo* with as much sarcasm as he could put into it. He took his bowl to the table furthest away from the counter.

The smell from the soup was not a particularly good one. Alex studied the bowl, pretending he was waiting for it to cool rather than deciding if he could stomach it. There was a thin broth with a smear of grease on the top and a pale green wad of cabbage sunk at the bottom. His stomach growled, sensing the nearness of food. He steeled himself and lifted a spoonful. It tasted better than it smelled, and it was hot. He spooned up a chunk of the cabbage and ate it. Not a hell of a lot of taste when you got right down to it but not really bad.

The old man had finished his own bowl and was silently eyeing Alex. Finally he built up his nerve and shuffled over. "Good, eh?" he said with a sly smile. Alex nodded and kept on eating. It wasn't near what he would call actually good, but he wasn't going to argue. "You think this is good, you should eat the cabbage my Galina used to make." The old man shook his head. "That was cabbage the way it should be eaten." He shook his head again. Alex nodded, not knowing what his exact response was supposed to be.

On closer inspection the old man was not as seedy as he'd first appeared. He was a little man, wrapped up in several layers of coats and scarfs that looked old but well cared for. His eyes were clear and bright. Big bushy eyebrows and moustache. He had perhaps the most wrinkled face that Alex had ever seen. He looked like a prune. A friendly prune.

"Why," Alex asked around a spoonful of soup, "do they call this place We Eat Nobody?"

The old man glanced at the cook who was trying to eavesdrop on their conversation. "They're vegetarians. Some sort of religion. They don't eat any meat at all." He gave a short snort of laughter. "Not that there's any meat to eat anyway. I haven't had any meat this winter. It's all going to the soldiers, or at least that's what they say."

Alex nodded and scraped up what little of the broth that remained in the bowl. He was still hungry. "What else do they serve in here?" he asked.

The old man snorted again. "Cabbage, cabbage, and cabbage. That's all there is, and most are thankful to get that. There's been very little bread. She can make you some tea if you want it."

Tea for dessert didn't sound great, but the thought of pushing off back into what was now a very cold night didn't appeal much to him either. Besides, he'd made a new friend, a possible source of information. "Can I get you a cup?" The man nodded, so Alex went back to the counter and ordered two teas. The look on the fat woman's face had softened a little with his purchases, but it hadn't yet approached looking friendly. He carried the thick white cups back to their table.

"God be with you," the old man said in thanks. He sucked in his tea noisily, like a wine taster. Alex waited for him to put a cube of sugar between his teeth and drink the tea the way he'd read about in Russian novels. He looked around; no cubes of sugar on the tables.

"I'm looking for a room to rent," Alex said, sipping quietly at his own tea. "My name is Alex Balfour." I'm a stranger here in town, he added silently.

"English?" the man asked. He'd finished up his tea. Alex wondered how he could have downed it so fast without burning his mouth.

"American," Alex said.

"Vassili Vassiliovitch Chizov," the man said. "At your service. I live in a building not far from here. Ever since my Galina died, God rest her soul. There is a room there that you might rent; actually there are several. I will introduce you to the *dvornik* who you will find to be a peevish, suspicious old busybody, as are all his kind. He will tell you that there are no rooms or he will try to cheat you on the price. But in the end you will have a room if you want it. He only runs the building; he does not own it, no matter what he tells you. So, offer him half of what he asks. In the end he will accept it.''

"Thank you," Alex said. He pushed his empty cup back. He felt, if not exactly full, at least warm inside. Suddenly he was very tired. The prospect of the room beckoned.

It had not been easy getting the two old men out of the room. Voyiokov, the *dvornik*, turned out to be a concierge just like concierges everywhere else in the world. Voluble, once the negotiations had been completed. They had haggled about the price, but Alex had remained firm.

The doorman was the janitor, the building super, the local gossip, and, if Vassili was to be believed, also a police informant, which seemed to be part of a *dvornik's* regular job. The police informant part reminded Alex he'd better come up with a story pretty quickly. A stray American with next to no luggage was going to draw attention.

He sat down on the bed and looked around the room. The bedsprings squeaked and settled under him. The room was lit by a dim single bulb that hung on a frayed cord in the center of the ceiling, casting a harsh and yet curiously feeble light. There was a table with a drawer that he could use as a desk, a spindly straight-backed chair pulled up to the table, a cheap dresser with a round mirror that appeared to have leprosy, a matching wardrobe to hang his clothes in, and a reading chair that looked awful but turned out to be comfortable. And the bed. Alex bounced a little, setting off the springs once again. The wall was papered in faded rose halfway down to a wainscoting of dark wood that ran the rest of the way to the wooden floor. There was a small, thin carpet next to the bed.

The dreariness of the room should have depressed him, but it didn't. Simply to have a room, clothing, and money seemed an accomplishment. Traveling into the past had turned out to be not much different from traveling to a slightly backward country in his own time. He'd stayed in places in Mexico that were ten times worse than the room he was now in. This one was at least clean.

He got up, took off his coat and hung it in the wardrobe. He took off his suit coat and hung it next to the overcoat. Even though there was a coal shortage, according to the *dvornik*, the room was warm. He reached into his pocket to check the time and then stopped himself as he realized that his watch was hostage to the pawnbroker. It had been dark for some time, but he knew it was still early. Vassili told him that darkness fell around three in the afternoon and the streetlights were turned off at 9:15. He glanced out the one window in the room and saw that it was at least earlier than 9:15.

He got his notebook and pencils out of his coat pocket and laid them on the table. Fortunately the pencils already had a point, as he now had no knife. Already he missed his few possessions. There was a kerosene lamp on the table and a pack of matches. He lit it and after a bit of experimenting got it going with a minimum of smoke. He turned off the overhead bulb and found that the lamp gave off plenty of light. The orange color of the flame made the room seem much more pleasant as most of it was in shadow and the rest was now softer and warmer-looking.

He opened the notebook to the first page and wrote 1916-17 at the top, then sat back to think. After a few minutes he began to write.

Somewhere in the building the heat went off and a chill immediately began to creep in. He got his coat and wrapped it around himself. He stared at the notebook for a while longer, until his head began to nod. To hell with it. He went to bed.

* * *

"As I told you this morning," Vassili said, "I worked as a railroad man for many years. All over Russia. I was born in Smolensk, not far from Moscow, and began my career there. My father worked for the railroad; I worked for the railroad."

All the livelong day Alex hummed as he stamped his feet. The fancy dress shoes that the pawnbroker had sold him went well with his suit but were only marginally better at keeping out the cold than his running shoes would have been.

They were waiting in front of the Finland Station for the *isvoshchiks*, the drivers of the taxi/sleighs, to sort out who

98

was first in line for the fare. Even though they were standing in brilliant sunshine, the temperature was still well below freezing. No one else seemed to notice the cold, but then they all had boots. High boots, low boots, fleece-trimmed, leather, felt boots. A nation of sensible boots. Their breath frosted into the air. Vassili's large moustache was rimmed with frozen mist.

"From Smolensk I went to Moscow; from Moscow I came here to Petrograd. I have worked in many of the stations in this city; consequently I know my way around. You are in good hands, Alex, my friend. Soon you too will know the city as if you had been born here. If you are to write about us, you must know our most beautiful city." He smiled, his face crinkling, the road map of wrinkles radiating out and upward.

Vassili had roused him out in the morning with a cup of hot tea and the offer of a guided tour of Petrograd. Alex had taken him up on both.

"We are presently in the Vyborg district. We will be going to Vasilievsky Island, and there we will walk across the bridge. It is a sight that will astound you." He waved his hand in a flourish, obviously happy with his role. Finally one burly fellow snapped the reins of his sled and maneuvered his horse to where they stood. The driver was a shapeless mass the size and shape of a mattress stuffed into a heavy black coat.

"In the summer we could have taken the trolley," Vassili said. "It's much cheaper. But the snow . . ." He waved his hand again to indicate the broad expanse of white that covered everything. He argued with the *izvoshchik* for a minute and then motioned that Alex should climb in. Once seated, he pulled a woolen cover up over their legs as the sled started off.

There was a fair amount of sled traffic. The pedestrians were men in uniform and civilian men and women. Everyone was wrapped in coats, capes, blankets, hats, and scarfs.

"The *Nevka*," Vassili said, motioning to the river. They started up a small incline and then crossed over onto a bridge. The wind off the river cut into them. As they came down the other side, Alex could see the walls and domes of the Fortress of St. Peter and St. Paul, originally Peter the

Great's fortress against all of Europe and now the Tsar's prison.

Alex was struck by the sheer size of everything. And that feeling that he'd never been able to explain to Molly, the correctness, the absolute immediacy of it all. The smell of the clean air, the sting of the blown snow, the jingle of the bells on the horse's harness. He realized what a small pale thing his profession really was. He studied not the past but what books told him the past was. There was a difference. The map was definitely not the territory.

They were moving along beside a canal that ran behind the fortress. The traffic, both foot and sled, had begun to pick up. Now there were occasional cars and crude trucks in the streets. They came out from behind the fortress and crossed another bridge.

"The Little Neva," Vassili said and pointed to the end of the bridge. "And that is Vasilievsky Island; we are moving up in the world." The streets were wider now, even the thickening traffic moving, seemingly at random, unable to fill the open spaces.

Vassili shouted up to the driver and the sled pulled to the side and stopped. Alex put his hand in his pocket for his money, but Vassili had already handed the man a few kopeks. They stood stamping their feet for a moment to get the blood moving. Alex crossed the wide street, like crossing a football field filled with motorcars and long sleds with goods piled high. He stood at the chest-high marble railing and looked out over the broad expanse of the river and the monumental city that lay beyond it.

"Did I not warn you, my friend?" he asked. "Have you ever seen anything like this in your country?"

Alex shook his head. They were standing between two huge Egyptian sphinxes, probably looted in some far-off Russian campaign. The statues were incongruous and inscrutable, staring blankly into each other's eyes, far away from their desert home. Beyond them, across the frozen river, Petrograd's great monuments and palaces lined the marble banks. The buildings, painted various pastel shades and trimmed in gold, were luminous in the keen air.

Vassili tugged at his arm and nodded toward the long

bridge before them. They joined the swelling crowds walking along the sides toward the city at the other end.

The wide streets were lined with elegant shops. The Nevsky Prospect: Fabergé, banks from every country in the world, hotels, restaurants, the Summer Palace, the Winter Palace. They bought hot chestnuts from a vendor. They wandered along like a pair of tourists just in from the hinterlands. Even Vassili, the world-weary railroad man, was awed by the sheer opulence of it all. The men and women in furs, the fine troikas with uniformed drivers lining the walks, the foreign shops. And on the other side of the river the workers stood in line for hours to get a loaf of thick stale bread.

In the late afternoon they hired another *izvoschik* to drive them back to the boarding house. Alex was cold and tired, but a bowl of *schli*, sauerkraut soup, purchased from the caretaker's wife, filled him with warmth and fresh energy. He was back in the cabbage district.

He lit his kerosene lamp. Vassili had told him that, unlike many of the other buildings, they had a good stock of wood and coal for the stoves and kerosene for the lamps.

He got out his notebook with its several pages of scrawled notes. He read them over, writing additional notes along the margins of the pages.

He had the rough outline of a plan. The morality of it, even the workability of it, was still hazy, but the direction was clear.

He had very little money. The only thing of value that he possessed was his knowledge of the future. He knew what was going to happen. All children, and most adults, have dreamed the dream of being in this position. He knew.

He had worked out what to use and how to use it. The only real question left was . . . should he?

Granting that it was even possible to change things, that history was susceptible to tampering, the moral factors on top of the bare survival questions were enough to make him hesitate. What gave him the right to manipulate events for his own benefit? What would happen if he changed something that really mattered, that had an effect fifty years down the line? What if *anything* he did made a difference?

To hell with it. He was tired of worrying about it. He

could go on and on with the permutations until he tied himself into knots. He would be careful. He had planned it so that he would influence nothing that wasn't going to happen, at least as far as he was able to know. Beyond that he was just howling in the dark.

Chapter 14

HE WASHED HIMSELF IN THE BUCKET OF HOT WATER THE CARETAKER'S wife had brought him. He'd tried to make friends with the fat old woman, but she wasn't interested. She announced the price of services such as hot water in the bucket and that was it. Hot water, hot tea, linens, cabbage soup, and sometimes bread were all available but for a price. "That will be two kopeks, Alexander Balfourovitch," she would say to him. "Put it on my bill," he would respond.

He had borrowed Vassili's thin bar of soap, and as he stood drying himself with the old man's meager spare towel, he vowed to buy himself supplies no matter how low it brought his cash reserve. He put on his good white shirt and got his pants out of the bed and pulled them on. Tips for Travelers: Place pants between mattress and board over springs and have wrinkle-free trousers in the morning.

Socks. He was still wearing his modern ones and they were beginning to show the use. He had found that in general the people of this time didn't seem to notice the sights and smells that would later become anathema to civilized society. But his socks were getting stiff. He had never in his life, even when camping with his father, had to wear dirty socks. He had grown used to his oversized bathtub over the years. His comforts. He wanted a hot bath, total immersion type;

clean, thick towels; a full change of fresh underwear. It was amazing how many things he took for granted to the point that he no longer even noticed them. Clean socks, underwear, a toothbrush, they all fit into the category of items so casually purchased that they no longer were seen as basic needs. Until you needed them and they weren't available.

Once when he'd been in Italy, he'd sat in a bar in Rome talking with an Italian Communist. He had asked the man what the goal of the revolution in his country would be. The answer had been simple: The workers would be the bosses and the bosses would be the workers. At the time he'd thought just how stupidly simple that concept was. Now maybe he was beginning to understand it.

He shook his head as he saw himself, the rich child becoming the rich man, whining at what he saw as his miserable childhood, growing up in what would be absolute luxury to ninety-eight percent of the rest of the world. His bathroom that was larger than many people's homes. It embarrassed him, not so much because he was a distinct have in a have-not world, but that this new social conscience was based on such minor deprivations.

A knock on the door. Vassili with the morning tea. Alex realized that if they were to enact this ritual two mornings in a row, it would then have become a tradition. The old man was lonely and had seized on Alex as a companion, someone to talk to. Alex didn't mind; he liked the old man and found him a useful and unthreatening source of information on the practical aspects of life in Petrograd, circa 1917. Alex opened the door and smiled as Vassili put the pot and the two cups on the table.

"I found a copy of *Vechernee Vremya* downstairs." He waved a newspaper at Alex. "It is last night's, of course, but we will have the news. I used to buy the newspaper all the time," he said with a frown, "but now there is no one to read it to." His face switched to its habitual smile as he pulled out the straight-back chair and sat down. "Newspapers are not very interesting unless there is someone to comment on the articles with you." He opened the paper to the front page and spread it on the table. He looked up and noticed that Alex was dressed in his best clothing. "You are going out, then?" he asked.

"Yes. I have to do some business. I need to go to the bank."

Vassili nodded sagely. Banks were serious business. "I'll loan you my tie. I used to wear it to church. If you are going to a bank, you will need a tie." He turned back to the newspaper.

Alex went to the table and peered over Vassili's shoulder as he poured them both a cup of tea. The print was very small and there were no pictures. The stories were set in long columns. Vassili put his finger on a column and moved his lips as he read to himself.

"According to the government, we are winning the war," he said after a moment. "Hah! If you believe what they say, we would have already won it several years ago. According to their figures, we have killed more Germans than exist in all of Germany. They also say that there is no true shortage of bread and coal. Tell that to the man on the street. And yet over here is a story of a fight in a breadline, women beating each other over the head with their shopping baskets after waiting in line for seven hours and then finding there was no bread when the bakery opened. If you ask me, they were beating the wrong people over the head." Alex sat down in the reading chair and sipped at his tea. It was hot and tasted of smoky peat. Reading the newspapers in 1917 didn't seem to be much different than reading the newspapers in 1985. It was a matter of deciphering government propaganda and reading between the lines.

"The police are still looking for the killers of the devil Rasputin; no luck there yet, they say, but they expect to arrest someone at any moment. They are still searching for clues on the Petrovsky bridge. Very wise; it's only been a week since they found the body; there are probably many clues still on the bridge." He snorted. "Police. They couldn't find their own *poopkas* with two hands and a lantern."

Alex laughed even though the mention of Rasputin had given him a mild twinge. "Are there any suspects?" he asked. His voice sounded high and thin to him. Guilty. Definitely a guilty voice.

Vassili did not seem to notice. "Suspects? Only most of the populace of Petrograd. The only people who might *not* have killed him are the Tsarina and her family and the leeches who lived off the man."

"I take it then that the general public was not all that unhappy when he turned up under the ice?"

Vassili laughed. "The day it was reported in the papers people came out and danced in the streets. I thought we had won the war." He put down the paper and turned to Alex. "As a foreigner you would not know of this man. There are many who say that all our problems began with him. They say that the Tsar and the Tsarina were under his complete control, that he gave the Tsar drugs and that he slept with the Tsarina. I myself do not believe these stories, but I do know that he had much power in the government and that the Tsarina did his bidding in most things. He was evil; he drank and whored and did not care who knew it." He looked down at his hands, clasped in his lap. They were old and lined like his face, workman's hands. "As a Russian I am ashamed of him. And yet"—he looked back up—"the peasants, the *muziks*, felt that he was a holy man, that his death was one more example of the rich killing the poor. I am glad he is dead, but I think it is too late to save my country." He shrugged, embarrassed at his own words.

"What do you think will happen?" Alex asked, wondering what would become of this one old man in the months to come.

"Everyone says there will be a revolution. Everyone talks about it. When is the revolution? they ask, as if it were a party that was not yet scheduled. I think that it must happen, but what the result will be I do not know. The poor—I am not really one of them, there are many who are worse off than I—must have some sort of relief. The rich are too rich, that is certain. How these two inequities can be resolved is beyond me. I'm a railway man, not a politician." He handed the paper to Alex. "Would you like to look at it?"

Alex opened up the paper while Vassili poured them both more tea. Most of the stories dealt with the war news and the political questions. There were reviews and notices of operas and dance troupes. Chaliapan was singing; Pavlova was dancing.

In the center of the paper was the Russian equivalent of want ads. A few were for lodgings, but most seemed to be selling numbers. These numbers were outlined in small boxes with boldface headlines: Stops the Most Stubborn Discharge—606. Guaranteed—914. "What are these?" Alex asked, turning the paper so Vasili could see the ads. There were hundreds of them.

The old man's leathery, lined face began to flush. "Those? You do not have them in your papers?"

Alex shook his head, trying to remember if the American world of 1917 would have had anything comparable. Numbers for sale?

"They are for people who have . . . who are sick." He seemed at a loss. "The numbers refer to specific cures. You order them at the pharmacy by number. You can also send for them through the mail. You don't have that problem in America?"

Comprehension dawned. Stubborn Discharges? "Uh, yes, we do." Three pages of ads for venereal disease medicine? Order by number? It seemed a very curious aspect of Russian modesty.

Vassili was still watching him, but Alex couldn't think of a thing to say to add to that particular conversation. "Could I borrow that tie?" he asked.

Vassili seemed just as anxious as he to change the subject. "Of course. Stop at my room on your way out, and I'll give it to you." He stood up and gathered up his teapot and cups. "I will leave you to your business. I will be in my room."

He hesitated on the steps. He'd gotten this far, all the way to the marble-faced bank of the Nevsky Prospect. The Merchants Bank of London was inscribed on the bronze plaque to the side of the large oaken doors. But now he hesitated. He'd managed to get himself to the bank without any problem. Now all he had to do was go inside and bluff himself into a position where he could tamper with the course of history. Nothing to it.

He mounted the three broad steps and pushed open the heavy doors. The heat was immediately stifling. He unbuttoned his coat and looked around. It looked like a regular bank. Tellers behind a waist-high counter and a row of desks off to the side.

"May I be of service, sir?" A young man in a three-piece suit with a high shirt-collar. Small moustache like William

Powell. He smelled lightly of some sort of cologne. The odor told Alex that he was in the presence of a loftier class than his own. Somehow it annoyed him.

"I'd like to see the manager," he said. He actually wanted to see the bank's president, but realistically he thought he should start a little lower.

"May I inquire your purpose?"

"Yes. My name is Balfour." Solid English name, he thought to himself. "I'd like to open an account."

"I'm sure one of our other officers can help you; could you just step this way?" The man stepped back and held out his arm in the general direction of the row of desks.

"This will be a special account," Alex said, keeping his voice firm but polite. "Prince Yussapov suggested that I speak directly with your manager."

The dropped name thudded obviously into the conversation, but it had the desired effect. The man's eyes narrowed briefly, hesitated in decision, and then the head nodded. "Very well, sir. Could you wait here for a moment? I'll just go and see."

The manager's name was Mr. Hartweight. He was a short man with a red face and tufts of white hair that rimmed the bald area of his head. Icebergs circling a miniature pink sea. He resembled caricatures Alex remembered from *Punch* cartoons. Alex understood that the bank manager was probably a bit more shrewd and calculating than the avuncular manner he affected.

"Balfour?" the stout Englishman asked as he approached Alex across the wood-paneled office. "No relation to the prime minister, I don't suppose?"

"I'm an American Balfour," Alex said. "We left the motherland quite a few years ago." He left it at that, hoping that the implication would be that his was the American branch of the illustrious English Balfours. And perhaps I am, he thought, having never really looked into it.

"Quite right," Hartweight said, apropos of nothing Alex could think of. "And how can we help you, Mr. Balfour? Young Leighton mentioned opening an account. I'm sure we'd be glad to. Quite simple, actually."

"Mr. Hartweight . . ." Alex looked around for something to do with his coat and finally laid it across the arm of a chair. If the Russians were running short of coal, you'd never know it from the heat in the English bank. "I know this is a bit unusual, but I really think I'd better speak to your superior. It's a confidential matter, and while I don't for a moment doubt your integrity, I've been told that it might be better for all of us if we did it my way."

"Leighton mentioned Prince Yussapov. May I take it that it was he who sent you to us?"

"That's right; Yussapov suggested it. You may call him if you like."

Alex had just played one of his minor cards. He was virtually certain that this particular personage was too lowly placed to actually call the prince of Russia's richest family and also virtually certain that the man would never admit that he couldn't. The president of the bank was another matter, but he would deal with that problem when it came up.

"I see." The man frowned and rocked up onto his toes, thinking. "It's really rather unusual. . . ." He rocked back and forth, but Alex could see that it was all show. He couldn't afford to send away a friend of the Prince's. "I'll have to see if Sir William will make an exception; yes, Prince Yussapov, quite a different matter. All right then, perhaps you might take a seat, Mr. Balfour. Could I get you some tea? No? I'll just be a moment."

Alex sat down and watched the man go to a door at the back of the office and tap lightly, wait a moment, and then enter.

He looked around the room at the dark wooden paneling and the marble floors. The ceilings were painted with scenes of historic battles. He was too far away to see who was battling whom. He pulled Vassili's tie up a notch under his collar, aware that his black pants and coat did not quite fit him as well as they might. Definitely off the rack.

Mr. Hartweight appeared through the door just as silently as he had disappeared. He was smiling. "Yes, if you could come this way, Mr. Balfour, Sir William will see you now." He stood back and opened the door and gestured Alex through.

Sir William was younger than Alex had guessed he would be. He had expected something more along the lines of Mr. Hartweight, only a little more upper class. The man behind the desk was younger, leaner, and not nearly as avuncular.

But still decidedly British. He had a long, horsey English face and ruddy skin. Sir William appeared mildly put out that his day had been disrupted and his quick appraisal of Alex seemed to do little to alleviate the impression.

"Sir William Smith-Carrendon," Hartweight murmured as he gave a short bow and exited.

"Yes, Balfour, is it?" he asked. He stood up and held out his hand, which Alex took and gave a hearty squeeze. "Why don't you sit down while I call Yussapov? You don't mind, do you?" A small smile. The tone of voice and manner were brusque and businesslike.

Alex was aware that the man was watching him closely. Sir William wore a pair of rimless glasses that magnified his eyes and the look of suspicion Alex saw there. He understood that this threat to call Yussapov was supposed to frighten him if he was bluffing. He played his second card.

"Certainly, Sir William." He sat back in the leather-covered chair across the desk from the other man. "Although I must say that the Prince is probably busy with more pressing matters at the moment."

Sir William had picked up the spindly black receiver but did not lift it to his ear. "I see. And just what might occupy the Prince so completely, Mr. Balfour? It will only take a second to verify you; I'm sure he wouldn't mind. We do quite a bit of business with the Prince and his family. I've always found him an accommodating man."

"And so have I," Alex said evenly, not responding to the pressure the man was applying. "In a word, Sir William: . . . Rasputin."

The other man watched him silently and then matter-of-factly replaced the telephone on its cradle. "So you know about that? In that case, perhaps we hadn't better bother the prince." He sat back in his chair and put his elbows on the desk and clasped his hands. "Just what is it you want, Mr. Balfour? Who are you? Why are you here? What, exactly, is the point of all this?"

Chapter 15

Sir William sat silently, his eyes, magnified through the rimless glasses, as suspicious as they were colorless. Not blue. Colorless. He seemed willing to wait. Now that he had allowed the interruption he would attend to it. No matter how tiresome. Very British.

"I have," Alex began his mentally rehearsed speech, which came out sounding stilted even to him, "information which I think you, as a bank official and an Englishman, will find important."

"Are you a spy, Mr. Balfour?" It was a very dry question. The inflection made it clear that he did not like spies.

"No. If anything, I am, like yourself, a patriot. Or at least I assume you are. But my motives aren't important. I have information which your country can use, as well as your bank. I'm not selling you this information but rather offering it to you with the proviso that you allow me to profit by it along with your bank and your country. I'm offering you a deal, Sir William. As a banker you must be used to this sort of thing."

The banker leaned back in his chair. The room was quiet but for the sigh of the leather cushions being compressed. Air leaking out around sewn seams. The man's eyes had not changed. Suspicious. Flat with dislike.

"As the president of the Russian branch of the Merchants Bank, Mr. Balfour, I do not 'deal' as you put it. I assume that word is an Americanism that assumes a contract between two parties. The selling of information as you are describing it, at least in my country, is the province of spies, though you obviously reject at least the appellation. But you require profit, and to me that says spy rather than patriot. I do not like spies; I do not 'deal' in espionage." He leaned forward, his hand near a row of buttons on a speaker-box on his desk.

Bluff, Alex thought. Nicely done; just the proper amount of scorn. My turn.

"Rasputin was murdered in premeditated cold blood by Yussapov and a group of other upper-class Russians. He was killed at the Prince's palace. The fact that Rasputin needed murdering does not lessen the criminality of it. By any standards of law, Yussapov is guilty. Of murder." Alex's flat statement had the desired effect. The banker's hand hesitated, hovering over the button of the intercom. Invoking the name of Rasputin had stopped him now for the second time.

The outstretched hand withdrew. "Mr. Balfour"—his voice was now tinged with a weary sarcasm—"This piece of information you possess is relatively common knowledge among the Russian royal hierarchy. I heard it myself the day after the monk was murdered. Yussapov told everyone that he'd done it. Even the police are aware of it. Of course the man is guilty; everyone knows that. Perhaps in your country or in England justice might prevail, but here, you can rest assured, there will be little in the way of punishment. To the noble classes Yussapov is guilty of little more than killing a rat or a wolf. One does not go to jail in Russia for ridding the countryside of pests. What is unusual, though, is that a man of your background"—he gestured here at Alex's suit—"should be privy to this information. Unusual but certainly not impossible. If you are trying to sell me this tidbit, I can tell you right now that I would not want it even if I did not already possess it. Now if there's nothing else?" The polite question and the raised eyebrows did little to cover the real meaning: beat it, get out, screw-off, forget it.

For the first time since he had reached adulthood Alex felt the unconcealed scorn of the upper for the lower class. The faint sneer of the businessman to the bum. I guess my suit doesn't fit quite as well as it seemed, he thought, trying to push back the anger building in him. And after I bothered to press the pants under the mattress. The man was acting like a pompous asshole. It was the attitude that was grating at him. And the inference of his own inferiority.

"Your country is losing the war, Sir William." He hadn't planned it this way, but any milder or cleverer course now seemed obviously ridiculous. He was no longer playing his cards; he was throwing them in the man's face. "The German submarines have sunk enough merchant shipping to push England to the brink. You have virtually no reserves of raw materials left. Your government does not acknowledge this, in fact not only denies it but publishes evidence to the contrary. Without help, you have at most three months before Germany crosses the Channel. Is this a well-known piece of information? Or perhaps you're not senior enough to be privy to this level of knowledge. England is losing the war. To put it crudely, soon the Kaiser will have his heavy German boot on your upper-class throats and his hordes will have their way with your women." Easy; keep the cynicism to a minimum. This is an Englishman you're talking to.

"Your supposition that we are losing the war and that the Germans are poised at the Channel are statements of opinion. There are other views."

Alex looked at him with unconcealed scorn. "The other views are propaganda." He stared hard. "I really didn't expect you to be a fool." He sighed heavily. "Shall I go on, Sir William, or should I slink silently out of your magnificent bank and leave you to your little games?" He borrowed the other man's tone of superiority. "I'll take my information elsewhere; you're obviously not interested." Alex stood up.

The bankers eyes remained impassive.

"Just who are you, Mr. Balfour? We have reached an impasse of sorts here. I'll admit that you are at least well-informed, if, indeed, a bit crude in your presentation. More than that I'm not at liberty to say, at least as far as the accuracy of your information is concerned.

"Let us say that I might be interested in what you are proposing. You sound like a spy, but you say you are not.

You profess to some sort of patriotism, but to whom? Your clothing is of high quality, but it does not fit you. You are an enigma, Mr. Balfour, and Englishmen do not care for enigmas. We prefer our friends, and our enemies, to be straightforward. Which are you? What are you?'' He gestured to the chair Alex had been sitting in. "And do sit down. We'll both have to stop this meaningless posturing if we're to get anywhere.'' He reached back to the intercom and held down one of the buttons. After a moment he said, "Tea, Hartweight.''

Alex sat back down, grateful that the first round was over. He'd won it, he was sure of that, but the next part would be more difficult.

"I'm an American. I am not a spy. Try to think of me simply as a man with information, certain resources that I am offering to you. I could offer them to others, the Russians or the Germans, but I won't. Even if you do not accept what I'm proposing, I won't go to them. My sympathies lie entirely with the Allied cause and particularly with the English.''

Alex felt rather than heard the door open behind them. There was a movement in the air and then a very large servant in livery was putting a tray with tea things on the desk between them. Sir William nodded at the deliverer, who silently disappeared. A fat man who moved very lightly on his feet, the way fat men are always said to and seldom do. Sir William poured them both a cup and handed Alex his with none of the particular English tea formality that Alex somehow expected. Vassili did not suck his tea through a sugar cube and this man did not fuss. So much for his knowledge of the tea ceremony in various cultures. Sir William put cream into his cup and nodded for Alex to continue.

Alex sipped politely at his tea. "What I am proposing is fairly simple and yet at the same time entails a complicated acceptance procedure. I'm not aware of your communications facilities here, but much of what I propose hinges on your being able to work quickly. I assume you will need clearance from your home office.''

"We have our own phone lines, Mr. Balfour, and then there is the telegraph. We are not exactly cut off from civilization. If what you are eventually going to propose depends on speedy communications, you have little to fear. We keep in quite close touch with our central office as well

114

as our government. What we do as a bank often has consequences that extend beyond simple finance; provisions for that have been made."

Alex was aware that this was a mildly roundabout way of letting him know that the bank's role could be diplomatic as well as economic and that intelligence-gathering was not unknown. All European financial concerns acted in some ways as conduits for information; to expect otherwise was foolish. It was why he had come there in the first place. A simple visit to the local English ambassador would have probably gotten him nowhere and possibly expelled from the country. He was a man who was traveling with no letters of credit, introduction, or safe passage, with no papers of any kind. In this situation one does not approach the standard sources of government officialdom. Only bankers and thieves understood that information was often closely connected with money, and money, profit, was their business. The Rothschilds had proven the value of intelligence with a network of spies and a homing pigeon communications setup in the last century. It was a lesson that Alex knew had not been forgotten by the rest of Europe's bankers.

"What I would like to do," Alex continued, "is offer you a piece of information that will be valuable, I think, to your country, in particular to your secret service. It should produce results quickly and should establish my credibility. I will then offer you something with much larger consequences, something that will profit both England and the bank. As you no doubt are aware, it is not necessarily knowledge that ensures victory but knowledge that is timely."

"And what do you get out of all this?" The banker had finished his tea and now sat with his hands clasped in his lap. While his manner was no longer outwardly hostile, there was still a polite coolness.

"The first piece of information is free. If it proves useful to you, I would like a retainer, part of which I would like you to invest for me in whatever direction you take as a direct response to the next piece of information. As you are no doubt aware, this city is filled with agents, all of them trying to get the government to buy arms from their respective countries. This is only a suggestion, but any nation—England, for example—with advance information of a military nature would certainly have an advantage over the competition. You see, if you make money, then I will too. If it doesn't work, then you haven't lost much as far as cash is concerned."

Alex finished his tea and put it on the tray. He wished there had been something to eat with it. He was beginning to feel as if he were living only on liquids: tea and soup. One of the reasons his suit didn't fit was that he'd already lost weight in the few days he'd been there. If he didn't get a real meal pretty soon, he was going to be in trouble.

Sir William got up and moved the tray across the room to a sideboard. Alex assumed he did it to give himself time to make his decision. He had suggested the second hand in the game they'd been playing; now it was up to the banker to accept the game or reject it.

"All right," Sir William said, his back to Alex. He turned and moved back to his desk. He sat in his chair. "The way I understand it is you will give me something whose value I can ascertain for myself, something that is immediately verifiable. No strings attached. That's the correct phrase, isn't it?" Alex nodded. "Right. Now what is it?"

Now we will see if history is vulnerable, Alex thought. "There is a woman in Paris, a well-known woman, a dancer. She is a spy for the Germans." The banker did not move or respond. Alex went on. "Her name is Gertrude Margarete Zelle. She is known as Mata Hari. She should be easy to locate; she is not in hiding."

Sir William lifted his right hand. "That's it?" he asked. His voice was neutral.

"That's it," Alex said. "If you get that to your people, they should be able to check it out quickly. If what I say is true, then you should have a bit more confidence in me. Then we'll get on to the next part." Somehow he didn't feel very good about what he'd just done, even though he knew that Mata Hari was due to be arrested any day now. He'd once read a biography of her, was sure of his dates, but he still felt like a stool pigeon. Sir William didn't look as though he had similar thoughts, but to him the idea of German spies was more real than it was to Alex. Alex thought of the photographs of Mata Hari he had seen in the book; dressed in belly-dancer costume, dressed in furs and a hat. Her greatest act had been to dance nude. She had never been either a first-rate dancer or a first-rate spy.

History, Alex thought, names and dates, places, figures and statistics. Old photographs. Mata Hari, French dancer, tried, convicted, and executed. Did I just pull the trigger or would it have happened anyway? Or am I here in this time to cause things to happen?

Sir William was back to the buttons on the intercom. "Mr. Hartweight will see you out," he said to Alex. "I'd like to see you back here at six o'clock."

"That fast?" Alex asked. The most he'd hoped for was at least a day.

"Possibly," Sir William said, unwilling to commit himself as usual. Alex suspected, not for the first time, that Sir William was more than just your ordinary branch bank president. And that Sir William suspected that he was more than your ordinary information peddler.

He found an old lady selling hard-boiled eggs. He felt like he could eat the whole tray of them, but he held himself back. The memory of an old videotape movie he had seen recently came over him. Paul Newman as a prisoner on a southern work farm. "I can eat fifty eggs." And then he did. Barely. Alex bought two, shelled them, and ate them.

The main street, the Nevsky Prospect, was mostly business with a few very fancy-looking restaurants, dress shops, and jewelry stores. The people who were out and about were well-dressed and only descended from their elegant troikas and single-horsed sleds to climb down and go straight into whatever shop or business they had drawn up in front of. In places the snow had been swept clean and Alex noticed that the whole street was paved with long wooden boards so carefully joined as to be almost seamless. The marvels of technology, 1917.

There were a few lone men walking the streets like himself, but there were none of the poorer-looking people that he had found in his own district. There were also policemen who gave him hard stares as he walked along eating his eggs. He tried to look as if he belonged in this part of town, but the facade that he had once had so much faith in was beginning to offer less and less comfort. He had all afternoon to kill and

117

did not feel like going back to his room or to a Russian police station to explain who he was. I know this is hard to believe, officer, but I come to you from the far future.

The streets behind the Nevsky Prospect were significantly less splendid. There were no sidewalks and the snow had not been removed. As he wandered along, the houses became smaller, linked buildings, like townhouses in most inner cities. He was surprised to see single cows in many of the yards behind the houses. On a back street he came across a man hurrying along, carrying a bundle of leaflets. As the man passed, he glanced around and then thrust one of the leaflets into Alex's hand.

Alex stopped and looked after the man who hurried on down the street. He looked at the leaflet, half expecting an advertisement for Madame X, palm reader.

"Brother Workers!" Red type across the top of the page. "There is no bread, no fuel, no peace. We must act! The Military Industrial Committee urges you to act *Now*! The message must be given; The People will no longer bow to the will of the Rich. Come to the meeting of the Vyborg workers of the Novyi Lessner Steel Works. All work will stop! Our demands must be met! Peace! Bread! Freedom!" Alex now knew why the man who had given him the leaflet looked so nervous. He pushed the paper into his pocket and headed back to the main street.

A large clock on a lamppost told him it was approximately one o'clock and he still had five hours to kill before his meeting back at the bank. On impulse he found an empty *iszvoshchiki* and climbed into the seat. "Vyborg," he told the driver. "Novyi Steel Works."

Alex paid off the driver when the sled could go no further. The narrow streets were jammed with people. He got out and walked the last few blocks, immediately surrounded and absorbed into the throng that shouted and sang scraps of song as they marched. The happy mood of the people contrasted sharply with the banners and signs many of them carried: All the Land to the People, Down With the Capitalist Ministers; Peace to the Whole World; and one he recognized that sent a quiver through him, All Power to the People! Again he felt the time-fabric stretch as events in his future were recalled by his present, the past. All Power to the People. Right on, brother.

He was caught up in the mood as quickly as he'd been caught up in the crowd. After two blocks he was chanting along with the rest of them. Down With the Autocracy! The feeling of belonging to something seemed to cover them all with a protective net, a security that he accepted willingly.

The marchers began to sing a song and soon Alex had picked it up and was singing along with them: "Bravely, Comrades, We March, Our Spirit Strengthened by Battle." It wasn't exactly "We Shall Overcome," but then these people weren't exactly pacifists.

The march slowed. The front ranks began to funnel down as they squeezed through the gates of the factory. Things speeded up again after a group of men simply removed the gates altogether. A knot of factory guards and city policemen watched as the gates came down and the crowd pushed through.

They trotted across a large open yard toward a huge shed which stood in the center of the clustered factory buildings. They jumped across train tracks and pushed carts and empty sledges out of their way, a steady flow of people that curled around large obstructions and carried away smaller ones. The mood now was not quite so carefree, was more concentrated and purposeful. They filtered into the shed through huge doors that ringed the perimeter of the building.

The shed was half full of standing people when he came through the doors. He made a quick decision and broke away from the others, moving to the left where there was only the back wall of the room and stacks of construction materials. The room was warmer than it had been outside, already beginning to hold the heat from the throng. The noise, a vast steady single sound, echoed from the stone floors and sheet-metal ceilings, becoming a presence that hovered, almost like the pall of tobacco smoke from the crowd, in the air above the amassed marchers. The room filled.

Alex found himself being pushed against a partially built steam locomotive that loomed up in the gloom like the bones of a strange metal dinosaur. As the crowd pressed him against a giant wheel, he decided that the only place to go was up. He hoisted himself up on the spokes and climbed carefully along the ribs of the superstructure. Crawling now, he came to the front of the machine. Directly in front of him was another locomotive, this one in a more finished condition. He moved down to the end of it and found himself now quite near the center of the room, although more than ten feet above the floor. He straddled the curved plate that ended in what would eventually become a headlight. The height and the surging crowd all around gave him a moment of giddiness, but he quickly forgot it, caught by the spectacle before him.

He'd been in protests this large before, but never inside a building. It gave everything an odd twist, as if the crowd had come to witness some titanic sporting event, giant wrestlers who would fling themselves around while the onlookers smoked and cheered. There was even a platform in the center of the room, though the floor of it was wooden rather than canvas and the people there were sitting on a rough bench. There were five men, all talking and gesticulating among themselves. The skylights in the roof of the building gave the only light and it was centered primarily on the stage. The light was blue with smoke, broken into shafts that cut like spotlights. One of the men rose from the bench and walked to the front of the platform. He raised both of his arms into the air.

The crowd began to quiet as those nearest the center of the room stopped talking and turned to watch the man with the upraised arms. A wave of hushing noises rippled outward.

Alex dimly felt men climbing behind him on the locomotive, but he was drawn only to the man on the stage. Upraised arms, caught in a shaft of cold sunlight that seemed to isolate him from the rest of the world. He spoke.

Chapter 16

"*Khleba!*" THE MAN RAISED HIS FISTS HIGHER. THE SINGLE WORD cut through the crowd and twisted them in his direction. His voice boomed, amplified by the natural acoustics of the huge shed. "*Khleba! . . . Khleba! . . . Khleba!*"

There was a moment of gathering, then fifteen thousand voices chanted the word back to the speaker, "Bread! Bread! Bread!"

Alex perched atop the locomotive and felt the massive iron structure beneath him tremble with the chant, the metal bones resonating in sympathy. The sound rolled around the perimeter of the building, bounced between the metal roof and the concrete floor.

"Comrades! *Da Sdrastvooyet International!*"

They shouted it back at him, "Long Live the International!"

The speaker lowered his hands. The words floated up to Alex over the heads of the others like the smoke from the thousands of cigarettes that glowed in the crowd.

"The Military Industrial Committee has called this meeting to show the bosses the solidarity of the people. The Revolution is not an abstract concept. It is Alive. *We are the Revolution!*"

The speaker's hands were up again, palms out to stop the

shout that was gathering. His disheveled hair seemed to bristle with the energy that flowed to him.

"These men here"—he gestured behind him to the men on the platform—"will speak to you, will tell you what must be done. You will listen to them." He paused and stared out, turning his head slowly back and forth as he took them all in. "Bread!" The answer rolled back at him like a wave smashing into a cliff. "Bread! . . ."

"Peace!"

"Peace!"

Another pause. "Long Live the Revolution!"

This time it massed and rose into the air and echoed back from the ceilings and shook the floor: "Long . . . Live . . . the Revolution!"

Alex held on to the steel rods on both sides of his legs as the roar surrounded him. The man on the stage held his position for a moment and then went back to the bench, slumping down as if drained.

The crowd cheered and jumped up and down and applauded themselves. Alex felt himself drenched in sweat beneath his heavy coat.

Then came two hours of incredibly boring speeches from three of the speakers on the stage. No one seemed to mind the dull parts; they just didn't pay much attention, using the time to talk and argue among themselves. It was as if they were hungry not just for bread but for talk. They shouted and waved their hands and moved and rolled with it: talk, everywhere at once, passionate, demanding. At times the noise from the crowd completely submerged the drone from the stage.

First there was the representative of the Collective Peasants of the Rural Republics: "I am only a simple peasant, ignorant of your city ways." He was received politely. Then an ex-university professor who had been fired from his teaching position and jailed for two years by the Tsar's secret police expounded on the theoretical basis of the economic factors that precipitated all revolutions. Last was a bureaucrat who read off lengthy lists of painstakingly precise figures showing the assembled masses that they were indeed poor and hungry. He retired amid a scattering of applause and a few hoots from the people directly around the stage who actually heard what he had been saying.

The man who had introduced the speakers rose again and stood quietly on the stage. His person—spiky red hair, rimless glasses, pale complexion, bushy moustache—seemed to draw attention like a sponge or a magnet. Individuals noticed him, nudged their neighbors until the crowd was again quiet and facing him.

"Comrades." Someone knocked a tool onto the concrete floor. It rang like a bell. "Our last speaker is a member of the Bolshevik party who comes to you with a short speech from a comrade far away, driven from our country by the oppressive forces of the government in the person of the secret police. Comrade Lenin has been forced into exile several times over the years but has remained faithful to the ideals of the Revolution through all his many hardships. His representative here, whom some of you may recognize as Comrade Gorky, one of our finest writers, will present Comrade Lenin's views."

Maxim Gorky stood up and approached the front of the stage. Alex watched him and felt a pulse of excitement as he recognized him from photographs he had seen. This was the first time since he had arrived that he had felt that he was actually seeing a man that he knew about, a real historical figure who would live forever. This was myth made real, flesh and blood instead of paper and ink.

He looked just like his pictures.

"Comrades." He began in the same low key as he had been introduced. "I bring you greetings from our comrades in exile. They are with us in spirit, working from without for the good of the proletariat everywhere. These brothers and sisters are the mind of the revolution while we are the body." He looked around and raised his voice. "We Are One."

The crowd rustled and murmured as if readying themselves. An animal hulking down into a crouch, bunching its muscles, ready to spring.

Alex felt himself slip into a semihypnotic state, lulled by the repetitive phrases as they rolled over the crowd, carried by the intensity of the speech rather than by any logic in it.

"Workers! Take the factories! . . . Comrade peasants! Take the land from your enemies the landlords. . . . Comrade soldiers! Stop the war. . . . Seize the wealth! . . ." His voice carried as it ranged from a shout to a whisper. "We have fought and died in this war that the ruling classes have inflicted on us, a war that has brought our country to its knees, a war that cannot be won."

The words washed over the crowd. Alex was conscious of only the peaks; it was like seeing a mountain range from above, projecting through a layer of clouds. "Peasants . . . Workers . . . Landlords . . . the rich . . . the poor . . . Russia . . . Russia . . . Russia . . .

"How . . . much . . . longer?"

The voice lashed at them, waking them up.

"Steal what has been stolen!"

"Down with all war!"

"Long life to the social revolution!"

Two heartbeats passed, three, there was no sound; breath held by fifteen thousand people, waiting. It came.

"Long Live the International!"

"LONG LIVE THE INTERNATIONAL!"

The locomotive rocked as the crowd leaned against it, began to sing, swaying, one voice. Alex held on, heart pounding. No more dull speeches; oh, no, this was the real thing, no college kids marching along with their earnest signs and their undergraduate philosophies.

"Rise up, children, for your country. . . ."

Two lights outside the bank lit the marble facade and the steps leading up to the door. Walking up those steps, Alex felt the full force of the schizophrenic nature of the day. From the walnut-paneled office in the bank to the steel works and then back again. It was almost as disorienting as shifting from the present to the past. Or the future to now.

He was tired. The bank was closed for the day. He pressed a button by the wooden door and waited. It opened slightly while he was being identified and then opened wider and admitted him. The same young man who had first spoken to him on his earlier visit nodded in recognition and motioned him in the direction of the president's office. The short heavy assistant, Mr. Hartweight, was not in evidence. Home to his comfortably warm apartment, safe in the arms of the English community, Alex supposed. The bank itself was dark, empty of the clerks and customers that had been there earlier.

Sir William glanced up at them as they entered, then went back to the sheet of paper he was reading. Alex took off his coat and handed it to the man who had brought him in. He sat down in the chair facing the desk.

"Did you have an interesting afternoon, Mr. Balfour?" Sir William asked, peering at Alex over the top of the paper.

"Yes," Alex said shortly. It didn't seem necessary to report in. Somehow he didn't think that the Englishman would have approved of his afternoon.

"So it seems," Sir William said, nodding, "so it seems." He laid down the paper and folded his hands over it. The lights in the room glinted off his glasses, giving his eyes a blank look.

He'd been followed. The report was already in. Very quick work. It made him feel odd, as if he'd been tricked or cheated or robbed. Very clever, Sir William, yes, you certainly have the resources here; no flies on you, Sir William.

"I believe this meeting had another purpose, Sir William. I assume that you've gotten through to your masters or whomever it is that you report to. My activities have nothing to do with my proposition. Was my information accepted? Are you interested in hearing more?"

"I'm interested. It's the price that's bothering me."

Alex allowed himself a theatrical sigh. If they were going to turn him down, he wouldn't still be sitting here. Sir William's self-righteousness was beginning to wear thin.

Alex crossed his arms and gave the man his toughest stare. He put the weight of history behind it: Remember *our* Revolutionary War; we beat you people once—don't make me do it again.

"Really, Sir William," Alex said, his voice edged with sarcasm, "aren't you getting a bit tired of sitting up there on that high horse? How long does this have to go on? Your country is the one who's got the most to lose. Can you really afford this holier-than-thou attitude? It's beginning to piss me off. Do you know that expression, Sir William, piss me off?"

Sir William sat for a few more seconds under the gun and

125

then gave it up. He leaned back with an almost normal expression.

"I suppose there's no real point to it, is there?"

Alex shook his head.

"Right. Well, let's get on with it then, shall we?"

Alex nodded again.

"As you have no doubt correctly surmised, I've got on to our people in London. They've given me the go-ahead on your little proposition. We're ready for the second piece of information. I'm prepared to advance you a modest amount of money, in rubles of course, and to invest a small percentage of any transaction the bank itself makes while acting directly on any information you provide. They've asked me once again to ask you if you will reveal the source of your information."

"No," Alex said.

"I thought not. All right then, we have a deal, as you put it."

"Good," Alex said. He had been ninety-eight percent sure they would go for it, but the last two percent had been bothering him considerably.

"I would like to point out, though," Sir William went on, "purely from a standpoint of national pride if nothing else, that your information was not new to our people. The dancer, the one they call Mata Hari, has been under observation by our people for several years. The French are also aware that she is a German spy. She'll be brought in quite soon, merely a matter of the right moment. You didn't actually turn her in, though you may have influenced the timing a bit."

And that's that, Alex thought. It was a comfort to hear it, even though he'd hoped it would be true. His actions, at least so far, wouldn't have changed anything significantly. The timing shouldn't be crucial as long as the end result remained the same. Mata Hari would be caught, put on trial, and shot. Just like in real life. Bang, you're dead.

"The second piece of information, Mr. Balfour?"

Alex thought about it but couldn't come up with any real reasons to stall. His offer had been accepted; now it was up to him to fulfill his side of the bargain.

"In the next several weeks, I'm not sure of the exact date"—he was sure, but to reveal it would give away more

126

than he could afford—"the German foreign office will radio their ambassador in Mexico City. I assume that the Allies monitor all radio communications out of Germany?" He knew they did. Sir William nodded. "This particular communication will be of major importance."

Sir William leaned forward. "And how will we recognize it? Nothing is sent out unless in code. What will differentiate this particular message from all others. And how will we decipher it if we do come up with it?"

Alex knew that by this point in the First World War England was regularly intercepting all communications coming out of Germany. Books in his time on the English code-breakers were constant best-sellers. He'd read a few of them, but it was Barbara Tuchman's work that had given him his primary information. Most historians read Tuchman's books. They read them with envy, but they read them and read them carefully. Alex admired her. According to Tuchman, the message would be sent and would be intercepted and would be one of the pivotal moments of the period. It had happened; he would change nothing. The Zimmerman telegram was fact. History.

"Sir William, I can only tell you what I know." Or rather what I can allow you to know, he thought. No matter how high up this Englishman was in his country's secret service, he wouldn't know about his compatriots' code-breaking capabilities. Very few did. "I don't know the exact contents of the message but you must tell your people to look for passages that contain references to an alliance with Mexico against America and in particular the information that Germany will resume unrestricted submarine warfare on all shipping bound for you and your allies. That includes American merchant shipping. That's all I can tell you."

"Good God, man, what do you mean that's all you can tell me?" Sir William was tightly erect in his chair. His face showed his indignation. "Don't you know what this means?"

Alex certainly did know what it meant. But he couldn't give the man anything more. "I'm not a crystal-gazer; I can't see into the future. I understand the implications of the message, but that's really all I can tell you."

"But an alliance with Mexico? Of course it's been suggested many times, although usually it's the Japanese who are seen as the instigators. It's possible, there's no doubt about it, but actual proof is something else. And if the Germans begin torpedoing American ships, you understand what that means?"

Alex nodded but let the other man say it.

"America will come into the war on our side. President Wilson will have to throw in his lot with us. It's what we've been waiting for." He had been talking almost to himself. He suddenly became acutely aware of Alex. "You're sure of this?"

Alex shrugged. "I've told you everything I know. It really won't do you any good to pump me for something that isn't there."

Sir William frowned and then nodded once. "All right, I'll take your word for it." He pressed one of the buttons on his intercom and said to Alex, "If you'll wait outside, I'll be with you in a moment." The young man entered carrying Alex's coat.

Alex stood up to leave and felt himself begin to fade out. For a moment he thought that he was going to shift back into his own time, and he was filled with fear; it wasn't time, not yet. The room whirled once, then held. He stayed where he was. He wiped his hand down his face.

"I say, are you all right?" There was a note of actual concern in Sir William's voice. Alex supposed the man was worried that the goose that had just laid the golden egg was about to drop dead on him.

"Yes, I'll be okay."

"When was the last time you had something to eat?" Sir William asked. Alex thought about it and couldn't really remember. Beyond the hard-boiled eggs earlier that day he remembered nothing but vague smells and tastes of watery cabbage. The thought that he was weak from hunger for the first time in his life struck him as ironic. I am one with the starving masses, he thought. The rich man hungry at last.

"Wait outside. As soon as I'm done here, we'll go to dinner."

Alex nodded and allowed himself to be led outside. As long as it isn't cabbage, he thought. Bread maybe. Possibly some other vegetable. But no more cabbage.

Chapter 17

I<small>T</small> <small>WAS EIGHT O'CLOCK, DARK, AND BITTERLY COLD WHEN THEY</small> came out of the bank. The winds that blew in from the Baltic had dropped, leaving the air crystalline, clear and dry. It felt as if the world—stone, skin, clothing, all of it—had been dipped in liquid nitrogen, capable of shattering at the flick of a finger.

Sir William had outlined their restaurant choices: The Bear, Cubat, the Café de Paris, Ernest, the Astoria, all within reasonable distance of the bank. It seemed that while the lower classes would have to line up at three A.M. in minus-forty degree weather to shop for bread, he and Sir William could pick and choose where and what they wanted to eat. Alex chose the Astoria Hotel. It was one of those names from the past that rang in his mind, like the Raffles of Rangoon, hotels and restaurants long departed into legend.

His feet had gone through the first several stages of freez-ing, pain and then an alarming numbness, by the time they walked into the hotel. He had to make an effort not to limp as they stood in the huge marble lobby removing their coats. Sir William had wound himself in a long scarf and topped it off with a sable fur hat before leaving the bank. He eyed Alex's overcoat and hat as they handed them to the servant at the door.

"I'd suggest a few more garments if you're to be in this climate for very long, Mr. Balfour. Winter in Russia is a bit of a chiller if you're not properly set up for it."

The observation was made not unkindly. After an hour shut up alone in his office with his telegraph and telephone he'd seemed to have developed a friendlier attitude. Whatever instructions he'd received had obviously included orders not to antagonize the new man.

The lobby was ringed by large rooms that led off the main area. They entered an alcove that led to the restaurant. Alex stopped at the door, amazed at the acres of damask tablecloths, shining silver, and well-dressed people. There was the soft hum of conversation punctuated by the light touch of a woman's laughter, the clink of silver against porcelain, the sounds of upper-class civilization. The room was warm with the colors of old wood and burgundy carpets, the smells of rich food.

The headwaiter greeted Sir William with a short bow. "Ah, yes, Joseph," Sir William responded. "This is Mr. Balfour, an American who's new to Petrograd." The waiter gave Alex a short nod. "We'd like a table away from the thick of it, if you would."

They were led to a quiet table toward the back of the room, where they could keep an eye on the rest of the room but would not be disturbed.

"Joseph's an Italian," Sir William said as they opened the menus. "Best damn headwaiter in the city."

The menu was in French.

"I expected something a little more Russian," Alex said. "Seeing how we're in Russia."

Sir William gave a short laugh. "You'll have to get used to it. The Russian upper classes don't have much to do with indigenous fare. Actually, they're quite mad about anything that has to do with England. Nice for us English. You can buy Pears soap and tinned biscuits in the shops. In the summer people wear football jerseys from Oxford and Cambridge. You won't believe this, but most of the noble families send their laundry to Paris to have it done. It seems they've heard that the French do the best job, so there you are. Quite a fad. They've also picked up a few things from you Yanks. Poker and bridge parties are the current rage."

He laughed again. "If you're looking for samovars and sauerkraut, you won't find them in the better homes. Too common by far."

Alex's stomach gave a growl. Now that it was actually near food it was becoming impatient. They ordered wine from the steward. Even though alcohol had been prohibited at the start of the war, the prohibition didn't seem to include the Astoria Hotel. Sir William put down his menu and motioned to the headwaiter.

"I say, Joseph, my American friend would like to try some of your Russian specialties. Wouldn't mind it myself, to tell you the truth. One gets a bit tired of the usual. Would that be possible?"

The Italian gave them a short bow. Alex had seen more of the top of the man's head than he had of his face since they came in. Not only would it be possible, they would be delighted to serve them something authentic. The chef was, of course, French, but he had made Russian fare something of a private specialty.

Their waiter poured them each a glass of wine and disappeared on little cat feet, leaving them on a small island of quiet amid the other diners. Some of the others had glanced at them and Sir William had fielded a few waves from the assembled, but otherwise no overt notice was taken of them.

Sir William was eyeing him over the rim of his wineglass. "Quite a distance from the Novyi Steel Works, wouldn't you say?" He gestured to the room around them.

"Yes," Alex said without emotion. "Whomever you had follow me must have reported back quickly enough. I wouldn't have thought he'd have had time to type up the report before I got back."

"He didn't stay for the speeches. We've heard them before. Death to the Autocracy; Stop the War. The usual sort of thing." He shrugged.

"Demonstrations are the usual sort of thing, then?"

Sir William nodded. "Unfortunately, yes. And becoming more usual all the time. The government seems to take no notice of them and then suddenly cracks down with a regiment of mounted Cossacks with whips. There's no real policy from above; only vigorous application of the knout, that sort of thing. No attempt to address the real problems."

131

"Which are?"

Sir William didn't answer. Alex could see that he was coming to some sort of decision. While he had been ordered to do nothing to antagonize Alex, he was still unsure whether or not to trust him.

"Do you really want to hear it?"

Alex nodded. "Yes, I'd like to. No matter what you think of me, I'm very interested. I'm an historian, so there's a natural desire there, but even more I'm personally interested. I'm here, I'm involved in it. I've come a long way. I'd go so far as to say that this time in history may be one of the most important in the last hundred years. And perhaps in the next hundred."

Sir William protruded a lower lip and tugged at it. Alex could see a faint nod of acceptance. "All right," Sir William said. "But don't forget you asked for it."

Alex sat back and took a sip of the wine. It was very good.

"Interesting what you said just then about it being historically important. I believe you're quite right, but we're in a minority I'm afraid. It's this damned war. England sees Russia only as someone to keep the pressure on the Germans in the East. They don't really care about her, not really. The Tsar's the King's cousin and yet very few in Parliament have any real idea what goes on here. Did you know that no one in the foreign office speaks Russian? Quite amazing really. That's how I got mixed up in it; I speak Russian. Always good in languages. They had to bring me in a few times to straighten things out diplomatically simply because of their inability to speak the language.

"Speaking of which, there's a funny story about it. Our man here, Sir George Buchanan—a very good man, by the way—doesn't speak a word of Russian. An excellent ambassador, but as a linguist he's a dead loss. They had a trip on where George was to go to Vologda to accept some sort of award for something or other having to do with being staunch allies. Bolster morale, beat the drums a bit. It was decided that Sir George should show his appreciation by saying 'thank you' in Russian. Doesn't sound like much, but for George it turned out to be damn near impossible. They prepped him for weeks on that one word. So there they are, up on the stage with his huge crowd of Ivans in front of him, and George gets a little rattled. They'd given him this loving cup kind of thing, so George holds it up over his head and gives it his all and what comes out is not 'thank you' but the Russian word that means 'for beer.' There he was, waving around the damn cup shouting about how he was going to use it for beer. It went over better than you might imagine—the Ivans thought that it was a pretty smart thing to do with the cup. No one ever told old George what he'd done. He was quite pleased with the reception. Wanted to learn a few more words, but they talked him out of it. Fortunately he forgot what he thought he knew."

They were interrupted by the waiter bringing them each a bowl of borscht, thick with sour cream. Alex stirred his, watching the curling pink eddies form patterns like the end-papers of old books. He tasted it. It was tart and at the same time sweet with the earthy taste of beets.

The story reminded Alex of one of his own. "Ever been to Germany?" he asked. He had to be careful here; no slips about the future.

"Through it a few times. I don't speak the lingo."

Alex nodded. "We had an American politician, very high up. He went to Germany—this was years ago—to express some American solidarity with the Germans. Hard to imagine with the present war on, but alliances change. Anyway, this politician decided to open his speech with a real grabber: '*Ich bin ein Berliner!*' I am a Berliner. He gets up on the stage, shouts out his one line of German, and the crowd goes crazy. Cheers, applause, on and on. The American press reports it as a great success." He stopped to eat some of the soup.

"I'm afraid I don't get it," Sir William said politely.

"Neither did the Americans. Not till years later. It turns out that the word in Berlin for doughnut is *Berliner*. Our politician had gotten up and shouted 'I am a doughnut.' The Germans thought it was hilarious."

They both meditated for a moment on the foolishness of politicians and diplomats.

"So there's nothing the English can do about the political situation here?" Alex asked, getting them back on track. Sir William took a sip of his soup and then put the spoon down. Sir William didn't really look like the borscht type.

"What are we to do? Tolstoy's famous question: '*Tak chto*

133

nam delat?' You ask what the English can do and I'm afraid that the answer is nothing at all. You should know that; you're the one who pointed out how precarious our own situation is. These poor buggers are even worse off than we are. Not for public consumption of course, but the figures are quite bad. The Russians have sustained losses averaging 300,000 men per month over the last three years. Their soldiers have run out of rifles at the front. Fight with anything they can get their hands on; clubs, pitchforks, anything. When one of their number gets killed, there's a long line waiting for the rifle.

"Magnificent fighting men, absolutely fearless. But they've nothing to fight with. Most of the artillery units have fewer than ten shells between them. Have you heard about the gas masks? No, of course you wouldn't. They try to keep these things quiet, but people find out about them anyway. It seems that there's damn few gas masks at the front. So the men have this idea that if there's a gas attack, the thing to do is piss on a handkerchief and tie it over their faces. Doesn't work, of course.

"The real tragedy is that there's plenty of gas masks here in Petrograd, just sitting in railway cars on sidings. Problem being that more than twelve hundred locomotives are broken down because the boilers have frozen and split. Can't get supplies to the front from the city and they can't get supplies to the city from the country. There's food for everyone; they just can't get it here." He shook his head and looked up as one waiter cleared the bowls and another put a plate of stuffed pastries on the table.

"Piroshki," the waiter said.

Alex picked up one of the kasha piroshki. He bit into it and found the hot buckwheat inside lightly herbed. He felt a mild pang of guilt, talking about the misfortune of others while he was stuffing himself, but he could think of nothing constructive to do about it. It seemed to bother Sir William, too. The other man sat staring morosely at the plate of piroshki. But then maybe he just didn't like piroshki.

"The laborers in this city work ten and a half hours a day. They've performed economic miracles for this country, and what do they get? The wages have gone up one hundred percent in the last three years and the prices have gone up *five hundred percent*. Boots are fifty to a hundred rubles; butter, when you can find it, more than a ruble a pound. I'm no Socialist, never would be, but, by God, something has got to change in this country before . . . well, maybe it's already too late. Strikes, Socialists, Bolsheviks, you can't really blame them. God knows, we've tried to get the message through to the Emperor, but it doesn't do any good. He's at the front and the Empress sits out at that great damned palace, holding seances trying to get in touch with that bloody Rasputin."

The pastry pies disappeared to be replaced by a large whole fish on a silver platter. It was perhaps the ugliest fish Alex had ever seen. It had the snout of a bulldog fringed with catfishlike whiskers. "*Som*," their Russian waiter announced. "Fish. Very good." He then filleted one whole side of the fish. Sir William stared at the exposed white flesh for a moment, then looked away.

"Good Lord, I can't eat something that looks like that. You must be starving. Have Joseph send me a meat pie," he said to their waiter.

Alex spooned a piece of the fish onto his plate. He added some of the garnish, hard-boiled eggs, sauteed mushrooms, slices of lemon, and sprigs of parsley. He lifted the lid of a little boat and found a tureen of Bernaise sauce redolent with tarragon. He spooned a little of the sauce over the fish and ate a piece. The flesh was thick, like a swordfish, with the clean taste of the ocean. It was wonderful.

"But what about the upper classes?" Alex asked. He'd seen the workers since he'd arrived, understood at least at a distance their problems. Historically he was aware that the upper classes were unable to effect any change in the situation, but he had never seen any real reasons why.

Sir William waved a hand at the room around them. "That's why. God knows, we've class differences in England, but nothing to compare with these people." Alex looked around at the diners at the other tables. He'd eaten enough by now so that his inner self allowed him some thought beyond simple feeding.

The tables were filled with all physical types of people with one common characteristic: They were dressed in the most elaborate clothing Alex had seen outside of a costume party. There were many military men, most of them in different uniforms, brilliant scarlets with reds with miles of gold braid and uncountable gold buttons. Many of them wore leather pants so tight that Alex could see the outlines of their private parts quite clearly. The women wore intricate, bustled dresses that were cut low to the nipples in the front. Everyone seemed extraordinarily happy, or possibly simply drunk.

"There isn't a thought in their heads beyond eating, drinking, dancing, and sleeping with each other's wives. Everyone is making simply tons of money off the war. If there's anything that unites them it's contempt for the Empress and disgust with Nicholas. There are more plots among the nobles to topple dear Nicky off his throne than there are anywhere among the Socialists. Alexandra is a German and they can't forget that. Some of them accuse her of being a spy, while the rest understand that she's simply empty-headed. Nicholas is too weak to deny her anything. She put that idiot Protopopov in as Minister of the Interior and no one can get him out."

Their waiter slid Sir William's meat pie in front of him. "Meat pie," the man said. He took away what was left of the fish.

"So what is there to do?" Alex asked. He sat back in his chair with his glass of wine. For the first time since he had arrived he was not hungry. The waiter arrived with the next course. More?

"Roast duck," the waiter said, putting down a cripsy brown duck on a white porcelain platter with a frieze of wildflowers. "Rice. Apples. Beans," he said as he put down separate platters for each. "Cucumber salad," he added. He smiled at Alex to show that he understood that he, Alex, was indeed a real man and that the Englishman with his meat pie was a barbarian. Alex smiled thinly and watched the waiter carve the duck. From across the room Joseph the headwaiter beamed at them.

"No one seems to have an answer. Some of them become terrorists and make bombs. Our agents tell us that there've been six thousand incidents over the last five years. At least according to the police files. Three thousand people have died both as a result of the incidents and the executions afterward. So far that's been the answer from Globachov, the head of the secret police. The Okhrana. A very extensive organization." He put his fork down and pushed back the meat pie that he'd only toyed with.

"I don't know how you can eat all of that," he said, watching Alex with a mixed look of admiration and disgust.

"It's a matter of national pride at this point," Alex said. "I asked for a Russian meal and now I've got to show I can eat it. Even if it kills me." The irony of the outlandish meal was beginning to get to him. It was all so incongruous. Reality was softening at the edges.

Unaccountably, a memory touched him. He'd once been in a small town, Missoula, Montana. He'd gone there to visit a friend. He was alone, in a bar called the Chicken Shack, with a red plastic basket of fried chicken and a mug of Olympia beer. He was sitting at the formica bar, just going to work on his chicken, when he heard it. Out from the kitchen, which he could just glimpse through the slot where the food passed out into the bar, came the strains from the aria, "*Mon coeur s'ouvre a ta voix*," from Saint-Saëns', *Samson and Delilah*. Beautifully sung, obviously live, over the background of deep-fat frying and clanking dishes. There was no mistaking it; it was his favorite aria in all of opera, perhaps the most beautiful piece of music ever written. He'd sat with his piece of greasy chicken in his hand, his hunger lost in the wonder of it. The aria ended; someone punched up a song on the jukebox. He'd paid his tab, leaving his chicken and beer behind, and left. He'd wanted to ask the obvious questions, but then he decided that he'd rather not know. The moment would only be lessened by the explanation. It had no reality beyond itself. It was a cultural discontinuity, a rent in the social fabric.

This whole day was becoming like that moment. Only not beautiful, just incongruous. The time travel was almost beside the point: the ricocheting back and forth between upper-class and lower-class Russia had by now become stranger than going between two times.

He could eat no more. He gestured to their waiter who was hovering in the background and came forward and began cleaning up the plates.

"Everyone says it will end in revolution, and I see no

reason to doubt it." Sir William had not noticed Alex's brief excursion back to Montana. "It all depends on the army, of course. They've had a bellyful of the war, there's no doubt about that. It's not really our concern, beyond keeping them in the war. At least as far as the foreign office is concerned. And if what you told me this afternoon works out the way we think it will, then maybe even that won't matter. You Americans will be in it for bloody sure and that ought to turn the tide against the Kaiser." Both of them looked up as the waiter appeared again.

"Bombe surprise," he said putting two plates of ice cream in front of them. The ice cream was shaped into an inverted cone.

"Tell Joseph that this will be quite enough. Have him put it on my bill and thank him for us." He picked up his spoon and made a dent in the side of the ice cream. "And what do you think, Mr. Balfour? I've done all the talking this evening. You're the mystery man with the advance information. What will happen to Russia?"

Alex scooped out a spoonful of the ice cream. The center was filled with shredded chocolate. What will happen to Russia? All this will end. The image that came to Alex's mind was one of those slow-motion films of a dummy in a test car as it slams into a brick wall, the dummy moving inexorably forward to smash against the steering wheel, ricochet upward, and begin its slow journey through the windshield, glass flying into the camera as the viewer's stomach turns in time with the dummy's flight. Is there anyone who does not feel that they are the dummy in those films?

"What will happen, Sir William?" He finished his ice cream and pushed it away. "I really couldn't say."

To a Russian, brandy is the best protection one can have against the cold. You drink it in quantities that are in direct relation to the weather outside. It was very cold that night when they left the restaurant and they were well-protected.

At the door, after having struggled into their coats but before plunging out for the dash to the sleigh that had been brought up for them, Sir William had slipped him a thick bundle of rubles. "For services rendered," Sir William had said drunkenly. "Buy yourself a pair of boots." Alex had stuffed the money into his coat pocket without counting it, feeling, just for a second but nonetheless bitterly, like a whore.

It was snowing again, although Alex would have thought it was simply too cold to snow. He had never felt cold like this, and yet there was their driver sitting up on the high seat in front of them. He had not spent the last several hours in an elegant restaurant, drinking brandy to fortify himself against the cold.

Sir William got out at the bank, mumbling that he had a motorcar that would drive him home. They lived in opposite directions in more than one way. Sir William gave him a brief wave and started up the steps to the bank. The driver pulled away quickly, clicking to the horse and shaking the reins, showing movement only in the hands and arms attached to the mound of heavy coats and blankets that indicated the man somewhere deep inside.

The falling snow slanted in the wind and stung Alex's cheeks. He burrowed down into the pile of furs that covered him. The wind blurred tears into his eyes, giving everything an impressionistic look, the lights on the street and in the homes along the way flaring as he blinked to clear his vision.

Chapter 18

THEY CROSSED THE FIRST OF THE THREE BRIDGES. THE RIVER BENEATH them seemed to glow, its coating of snow and ice gathering the pallid light from the obscured moon and holding it, a pale swath that ran flat and true into the darkness. He twisted around to look at the city they had just left. The lights sparkled like faraway stars through the snow. He turned back and settled down beneath the furs. By now his body heat had warmed up a burrow in the pile. When the wind shifted around to their back and no longer blew the snow into his face, he found himself enjoying the ride. The hiss of the runners, the clop of the horse's hooves, the creak of the springs beneath the sleigh.

He added it up. He was not hungry. He had some money. He had a few acquaintances who were almost friends. He was living right in the middle of one of the most exciting periods of history. He was happy. For the first time he felt like he belonged where he was, even though intellectually he understood he was still just a visitor. But, as he was becoming increasingly aware, things of the intellect were not necessarily true barometers of reality.

For the first time since the whole thing began he wondered if it were possible that he was here to stay, trapped in the past, unable to shift away just as he had been unable to consciously shift here. He probed the thought, searching for soft spots and pain, but found little to disturb him. Except for a lingering longing for Molly, he didn't really care that he was not back in the present. He liked the excitement, the satisfaction of overcoming problems as they arose.

Another sleigh going the other direction passed them. There were bells on the other horse's harness, jingling in time with the horse's trotting. For a second he felt like he was living in one of those crystal balls you see at Christmas, the kind you turn upside down to make the snow fall. A souvenir of Tsarist Russia. Welcome to Petrograd.

They hissed up over the approach and crossed the next bridge.

The succession of people who had inhabited his early dreams flitted through his memory. He thought now that those early dreams had been only partial journeys back into the past, imperfect practice runs readying him for the real thing the way pregnant women have practice contractions months before the real birth. The dying soldier, that must have been a year or so ago. Somewhere on the western front where Russians and Germans were dug into miles of wandering trenches.

Rasputin.

He brought out the dream of playing ball with the Tsar's son to push away the memory of Rasputin and the murder. That one had been pleasant. He'd liked the boy. He thought about the child's eventual end, shot with the rest of the family and dumped down an empty mine shaft. Now it was no longer pleasant. Would it happen? Where was the truth?

Truth. He shook his head. Truth, history, reality—he should have learned by now that words like that looked different and meant different things from your physical vantage point. From here, from there; it was not the same.

He noticed the great bulk of the Peter and Paul Fortress on his right as they curved along behind it.

And then turned into it.

The sled slewed to the left as the driver slapped the reins and pulled the horse in a tight right turn. The snow blew back off the blue netting that covered the horse's back, blinding him for a moment. Alex wiped at his face with his gloved hand as the sleigh passed through a large open gate in the wall and into a courtyard. He turned around in time to see the gate swing heavily shut, pushed by a man in a uniform with a rifle slung over his back. The sled cut across an inner courtyard and then drew up in front of a low square stone building. "What's going on?" Alex shouted up at the driver. The man did not move, a silent mountain of fur coats, mufflers, and hat. The door in the building opened and two men came out, moving quickly. One of them pulled back the fur covering and grabbed Alex by the arm. They dragged him out of the sled. He struggled briefly before getting his legs under him so he wouldn't fall. Both of the men were bigger than he was and obviously knew what they were doing.

"What the hell's going on?" he demanded. They pulled him through the doorway into a small bare room with a low wooden bench around the walls. One of the men slammed the door and he was pulled forward, through another series of doors and into a long hall. It was very dim, the only lights being low wattage bulbs screwed into the ceiling at long intervals. The walls and floors were all cut from the same gray stone. They looked damp, dirty, cold.

He started to protest again.

"Zamolchite," one of the men growled with a sidelong glance at him. He was being told to shut up. Alex could smell the sauerkraut and garlic on the man's breath. All right, he would shut up until he understood where he was going or what was happening. Not that he had any choice. The three of them continued down the long hall. They seemed to be in the actual walls of the fortress. They passed a succession of heavy wooden doors with thick cross-braces.

They stopped. One of the men fumbled out a key while the other held him from behind and searched him clumsily. Alex submitted, had no intention of resisting, wouldn't know where to run to if he could get away. He was breathing heavily; they all were. He was afraid, felt the fear whirling in his brain trying to find release. He clamped down on it. Simply being afraid would do him no good.

The door opened. In the light from the hall he had a glimpse of the interior; the same gray stone, a cot against the wall. They pushed him inside and slammed the door behind him. He stumbled forward and fell to his knees. It was dark, the only sound the rasp of his own breath.

He stood up. He waved his hands in front of him as he shuffled forward to where he had seen the cot. He banged his knees against it at the same time his hands touched the damp rock wall. He felt the cot; it was a wooden slab with a thin rough blanket thrown on it. He sat down and tried to slow his breathing.

Gradually his eyes adjusted to the dark. Dim light came from a small window high up on the wall at his back. Alex twisted around to look up at it but couldn't actually see anything beyond the pale rectangle that showed where the window was. There were thick bars over the window. He slumped back against the wall.

The fortress was the jail where political prisoners were kept, he knew that. The Russian Secret Service, the Okhrana, used it as their headquarters. He was obviously a prisoner. His mind veered from outrage to panic, rattling around on the edge of control. He almost laughed: obviously a prisoner. Yes, he thought, reaching back and touching the rough stone wall, you might say that. Now what? What was he going to do, complain to the American embassy? Would he get to make a call to his lawyer? Demand his rights as an American citizen? Let me out! They didn't read me my Miranda rights!

He pulled the blanket around him. It was cold, not as cold as it was outside but cold enough. The blanket was stiff and stank of sweat and other substances he didn't want to think of.

By now he could see his hand in front of his face. Across from him the wooden door showed the light from the hallway outside around the edges and through the imperfectly joined boards. Down at the lower right corner he could see more light where the door had a piece chipped away. As he watched that opening, he felt his gorge rise as a large rat sniffed up to the hole and then scraped through. It blended neatly into the gray darkness and disappeared, heading, as far as he could tell, directly toward where he was sitting.

He heard himself make a little whiney noise as his mind began to ping-pong around again. He heard the rat scratch close to his feet, then felt the touch of a tiny nose with whiskers as it pressed against his ankle.

143

Chapter 19

A long time ago in a galaxy far, far away . . .

MOLLY READ THE WORDS AS THEY SCROLLED UP THE TV SCREEN. SHE
forced herself to pay attention.

She knew that seeing a *Star Wars* movie was supposed to
be something of an event, but she just couldn't get interested.
She had never seen this one, the first of the series. She
had never seen any of them. She knew that she was perhaps
the last person on earth never to have seen one. Deep down
inside she took a perverse satisfaction in her ignorance, but
she supposed that since the films had become cultural phe-
nomena, she really ought to see them. She was a newspaper
reporter and newspaper reporters were supposed to stay on
top of things. It was part of the business. Right?

She focused her attention back on the television set. The
character she knew to be Luke Skywalker was wandering
around on some desert planet. He seemed to be wearing
pajamas.

It was Alex's TV set. There was also a VCR, but she
didn't know how to hook it up or what she would do with it if
it was hooked up. She plugged the set in, and after a few
seconds of electronic hissing and popping it came on.

Her own TV set back at the apartment was a nine-inch black-and-white she'd bought back when she and Alex lived together. She'd paid eighty-nine dollars for it back then and had been waiting for it to break ever since. But it hadn't. The antenna had fallen off and was replaced by a coat hanger. The knobs had come off more times than she could remember. For a while she changed channels with a set of pliers until an obliging date glued the knob back on. The channel marker had no real relationship to the actual channel, the numbers indicating nothing in particular with reference to the stations. But it still worked, so she couldn't buy a new one. Her husband had hated it, thought it a leftover from her early days, which it was. He was strictly state-of-the-art as far as electronics went. She only watched the news, anyway.

At least she used to watch only the news. Now she found herself looking at Alex's set for hours. Not that she paid much attention to what was actually on, but she spent hours in front of it.

There was Alec Guinness looking like Alec Guinness wearing a blanket and needing a shave. He looked old.

She had called from work the morning Alex disappeared. She knew that when he hadn't answered by the fourth ring, he was gone. He'd been afraid to leave the house, so he always answered by the fourth ring. She sat and listened to the burr of it in her ear until she finally had to put the receiver down. She told herself that he was probably at the store, but in her heart she knew he had left. To wherever it was he went: Russia, the past, wherever it was. But he was gone; she did not doubt that.

It had given her a sick, surprisingly empty feeling. On top of the other emotions banging around in her: fear that he'd be hurt, worry that he'd never come back, uncertainty, jealousy, wounded feelings (how could he just leave after they'd finally gotten back together?), and above all, an aching sense of loss.

She went to his house after work. She had to make sure. She walked up on the porch and looked through the bars on the little window in the door. It was dark inside. She rang the bell. No answer. She tried the knob; it turned. She pushed the door open. This is New York, Alex; how could you have left the front door open? With a small jolt of guilt she realized that she'd probably forgotten to lock it behind her when she left for work that morning.

She felt like a character in one of Alex's old movies. The door opened up easily, stood open while she peered down the hallway inside. What if she went in and he was laying there dead, victim of some junkie on a money-raising expedition? What if he'd had some sort of heart attack? What if a monster was waiting in the dark, quiet house, waiting for her to come on in? "Don't go in there, lady; don't go in!" the audience shouted from their seats.

She went in. She did not have a very high tolerance for fear of the unknown, inaction because of uncertainty or old movies.

The house was empty. Everything looked perfectly normal except there was no Alex. In the bedroom she found his house keys on the dresser. He must have just been dressing when it took him. She pulled the coverlet up on the bed, over the rumpled sheets. She missed him already.

She left the empty house, pulled the door shut behind her, and locked it with his keys. She thought of putting the keys through the mail slot, but in the end she took them with her.

That had been a month ago. At first she simply called each day, several times, called and waited while the phone rang. After a week of that she started going by the house in the evening. Then she began spending the weekends there.

In the beginning it bothered her to be alone in his house, but that quickly wore off. She was used to apartments, used to moving from one area of necessity—bedroom, bathroom, kitchen—to another with only a few steps in-between. Here she had to go up the stairs to go to bed, up the stairs and down the hall to take a bath in Alex's monster bathtub with the griffin feet. But she got used to it and would have liked it if Alex had been there to be in the room she had just left or there in the room she was going to or just there in general. But all she had was the house that held the artifacts of Alex, the expectation of Alex. So she sat and read his books or watched his TV.

There were occasional logistical problems to occupy her, but she was good at such things and soon had everything under control. Alex's school had called and wondered why he had missed class. She made up a wonderful story of a rare disease that had demanded his immediate flight to a special medical center in Tucson, leaving her behind to contact the school. In the worry of it all, she told them, she had forgotten to call; she was sorry; no, it was not a life-threatening disease, not if promptly attended to, but there was no way to predict when he would return; yes, they should hire a substitute for the rest of the semester; yes, Alex would get in touch with them just as soon as he was able to function well enough to use the telephone. Very sorry. Unavoidable.

She paid the electricity and gas bills. She paid the phone bill and a couple of magazine subscriptions.

It had been more than a month now; thirty-six days. It was another Saturday night in front of Alex's color television with her feet up and a beer in her hand. This was the extent of her social life these days, but she didn't care. What was she supposed to do, date? She could have some wonderful conversations: "Well, my real boyfriend isn't around at the moment; he's a time-traveler and he's in Russia right now, probably fighting the Revolution or something; but when he gets back, we'll be getting back together again, so don't get your hopes up or anything."

She was wearing a pair of shorts and one of Alex's T-shirts. Luke Skywalker had acquired a girlfriend that she knew was Princess Leia. Princess Leia's hair looked like she had two cheese Danish stuck to the side of her head. It was amazing how she knew most of the characters without ever having seen any of the movies. The story had become such a part of everyday life that the characters existed beyond the fictional frames. She really ought to be paying attention. When Reagan had announced his support of a Star Wars defense system, she felt her lack of information had moved from the personal sector of her life into the business sector. So she would watch the silly movie. So far it looked like a lot of little boys dressed up in funny costumes and having a lot of fights. Fighting in spaceships, fighting with flashlights that emitted some sort of beam. Fighting. Big deal. She yawned. Her thoughts wandered back to Alex. She was never very far from thoughts of Alex.

The two of them getting together at college had been a natural. They were both good-looking and knew it but would never flaunt it. They were both interested in the same things, had a few history courses in common and a mutual appetite for the ways of the flesh.

Alex was funny and very smart. After a semester of dating they had moved in together. It had worked well as long as they were wrapped in the cocoon of college life, but once reality began to move in, the relationship had begun to fray at the edges. There was something about Alex that took her a long time to become aware of, an emptiness at the center, a lack of purpose that came out in a lot of little ways but never was big enough to be obvious. To either of them. He had so many good qualities that they tended to obscure anything negative.

After they both graduated, they had kicked around at a few do-nothing jobs, and gone to Europe. She had a degree in journalism and finally got a job on the *Village Voice*. Alex did research part-time for a textbook publishing house. After a year at the *Voice* her boss had moved on to the L.A. *Times* and offered to take her with him as part of his staff.

She had known Alex would never go. Even though both his parents were dead and he had no physical ties to New York, he wouldn't leave. He said he hated California, but what she saw was that he was afraid that leaving New York where it was busy and dirty and loud and rude and exciting would mean that he would have to sit back and take stock, figure out a life for himself that was based on something besides Living in New York City.

The thing about getting married was the same. Yes, she'd given him the choice, but again she knew from the first he would turn her down. It wasn't that he didn't love her—she knew he did—but it was that lack inside him. He wouldn't commit himself because he was unsure of what there was to commit. She'd tried to talk to him about it, but she couldn't get through because she didn't know what was wrong any more than he did. They were both too young. Now she knew it had to do with his father, with Alex's life growing up, and in some way with this ability of his to . . . do whatever it was that he did.

So she'd left. It was the only way. He would only see what was missing if he lost something because of it. But the communications had broken down, and then there'd been the job and then Steve and then the damned marriage that she hoped would fill the hole that was now inside her after they split up. Finally she'd said to hell with it and come back. It had taken ten long years. She didn't know where he was or what he was doing, but she came back anyway. Working for the *Times* was all the excuse she needed. She'd come back to find him and she had, and things were looking just right when all of it came apart. All of that in a few days. Incredible.

Where was he right now? When would he be back? She didn't suppose that what he was doing was dictated by some timetable, like a chartered tour of the Holy Land or a bargain trip across all of Europe in one week. But just how long was she supposed to wait for him? A little voice inside her gave her the answer to that one: as long as it takes. She'd come too far to give up easily. She hadn't been back with him long enough to know if time had filled in the empty spot in Alex, but she didn't care. She'd been given a second chance. All of it—the love, the caring—all of it had come back in on them ten times stronger than before. She felt welded to him, linked, tied, bound, connected in a way she had never felt with anyone else.

She would wait.

Her eyes wandered to the rows of books along the walls. So many of them. To Alex they were the friends he didn't seem to have. She looked at the row of his father's novels. And there was something else. She was beginning to think she had figured out how Charles Ames Balfour had come up with all his realistic characters and settings.

The television caught her attention. The guy that breathed funny was on, Darth Vader. Mr. Bad. Great costume. She sighed. Maybe if she turned on the sound, it would be more interesting.

Chapter 20

OH, THE GODDAMN INDIGNITY OF IT ALL. MAXWELL SURREY FELT tears flood his eyes. He blinked them back and leaned down. His back hurt. Fine, let it hurt; hurting he could deal with. It was doing—or rather, not doing—that was getting to him. By the time he got himself bent over far enough to tie his shoes his fingers would not cooperate. They would not, could not, perform the delicate task of tying the laces.

He sat back up with a grunt. He pushed the offending shoes from his feet and went to his closet. To hell with them, I'll wear the loafers. I'd rather wear the loafers anyway. If I cannot physically conquer, then I will overcome. He found the loafers and pulled them out with his feet. He slipped them on. Downstairs he heard the housekeeper bustling around in the kitchen, making his breakfast. One piece of toast made from heavy German bread and a cup of coffee strong enough to take the enamel off your teeth.

He went downstairs, slowly, and shuffled into the kitchen. He answered the housekeeper's cheery greeting with a grunt and accepted his breakfast. He took it to his study, where he always ate it, at his desk, surrounded by his books.

The rough bread was imbedded with seeds. He chewed it slowly, thankful as always that he still had most of his own teeth. He sipped the coffee. It was hot and strong. What was the old Mae West line? "I like my coffee just like I like my men, hot and strong?" Or was it "strong and black"? He decided he was mixing it up with the punch line from a racist joke he'd dredged up out of the past.

The past. Alex. Alex must be there by now.

Over the years he'd wondered how and when he was going to tell Alex about the past, but he'd never figured out the right way to go about it. In the end he'd decided to just wait and let it happen and then tell him about it. Besides, up until it actually happened, the boy would never have believed him. No, best to let the past, history, take care of itself. Then figure it out.

Alex must be there by now. He hadn't called in a week and he would have if he'd been home.

He pushed away the empty plate and drained the last of the coffee. Yes, sir, Alex was going to have some questions for him when he got back. He tried to remember that early time together . . . it was so long ago.

The Revolution. People running and screaming through the streets. Gunfire. He'd been so young.

Those were some times, those few days when they turned the world upside down. Later it all fell apart, but then, then it was a dream: truth, justice, liberty. Of course, at the end they had really pulled it off. Too bad no one knew.

Pain. He looked at his left hand as if it belonged to someone else. The echo of the stabbing hurt that had run down his arm like some internal lightning lingered in his palm, drawing his fingers up into a claw. What is this? Surrey rubbed at the hand, seeing it old, knobby, age-spotted, rough. He clenched his fist. He raised it to shoulder height. Down with the Tsar! All power to the people! He laughed at himself. He might be old, but he still had the stuff. Up the Revolution!

Maybe he should call that girl and see if she knew where Alex was. Just to make sure. After all, he could have simply gone on vacation without letting him know. No, he always let him know when he went out of town. Alex saw him as a father. How would he see him now? It had been difficult all those years, looking at the boy growing up and knowing. Besides, the letter was written. If anything happened to him, there was always the letter.

151

The shaft of pain ripped down the inside of his arm. This time it did not stop. It went on hurting as he tried to stand, tried to make some noise beyond the almost inaudible *ahhh* sound that whispered from between his clenched teeth. He felt it tear at his chest, squeeze the breath out of him. The room blackened around the edges, began to recede. He fell forward onto the desk.

He smelled the old wood beneath his face, saw scraps of paper tremble in the last of his breath. Look out! Hold on! Here comes Surrey. Oh, God, into the past, the long lost past. His eyes closed.

Chapter 21

ALEX LAY ON HIS SIDE ON THE WOODEN BOARD THAT WAS HIS BED and watched the family of rats as they squeezed through the hole in the door and scurried into the room. It was too dark to see anything once they were inside, but he could hear them. Was there food somewhere in the cell? Sometimes they made noises as if they were fighting among themselves; harsh squeaks, scratching, tiny tumbling noises as they rolled around the floor. Maybe they were playing. He lost count of them: momma rats, daddy rats, little baby rats.

He did not sleep. He was wrapped in the filthy blanket. He had lost his hat in the struggle outside.

Nothing to do but keep away from the rats. And think.

Big surprise. What did he expect? No papers, no money, no friends, no reason to be in the country. Look a little suspicious?

Fucking rats. He leaned over the edge of the board and listened. Were they chewing on the leg of the bunk? Could rats climb?

You bet they can.

He'd been set up. Sir William was the obvious candidate. Had he decided that Alex was too dangerous to roam free, that he was some sort of double agent, a German spy?

Then there was his trip to the steel works. If Sir William

had had him followed, then anyone could have. There must have been Okhrana agents in that crowd. The secret police wouldn't pass a chance to see the opposition in action. Alex pictured himself marching along, singing and chanting slogans. At one with the people. Death to the Tsar. Stupid.

Now that he thought about it, he'd acted pretty stupid since he'd arrived. Did he really think it was going to be that easy? That he could just appear out of thin air in one of the most paranoid countries in the world in the middle of a world war and set himself up without anyone noticing?

Obviously not.

He must have dozed off because when he looked around, he realized that he could actually see all four walls of the cell. While there was no direct light through his window, there was enough to see by. He sat up, first checking to see that the rats had gone. They had. He swung his feet to the floor.

The cell looked just as bad as it had the night before. He got up and stretched, trying to loosen his cramped muscles. His clothes were wrinkled and stiff. He had always hated sleeping in his clothes. He took off his overcoat and laid it on the bunk. Somehow the light coming through the barred window made the cell seem warmer.

The cell was approximately fifteen by twenty feet. He paced it off. His bunk was on the long wall opposite the door. He walked over and touched the door. It was like a typical grade-B movie dungeon door. Heavy rough beams crisscrossing thick planks. Inset at face height was a small door with a peephole and a ledge underneath.

On the wall to his left was a small table that had been bolted to the wall. On the table was a wide-mouthed earthenware jug that on closer inspection was found to hold water. He picked up the jug and sloshed it, listening to the heavy lipping sound of the water. Suddenly he was very thirsty.

He put the heavy jug to his lips and drank. Immediately his mouth filled with water and a variety of objects, hair, small sticks, and a slimy substance. He gagged and spat the water onto the floor. He stood for a moment trying to control his heaving stomach. He carried the jug over to the window and looked inside. His sloshing had stirred up thick algae along with other floating foreign material. Prison Lesson Number

One: If you're actually going to drink out of the jug, and he was not sure he'd be able to now, don't slosh it around first. He put the jug back on the table.

As he walked to the boundary of his cell, he found the last amenity. A slit-shaped depression and a foul smell: the toilet. Inventory time. Clothes: shoes, socks, shirt, pants, tie, suit coat, overcoat, aging underwear. His wad of money they hadn't bothered to take away. Nothing else. Dead end. His only plus in the inventory department was that he probably wouldn't actually freeze to death. Unless they took away his clothes.

He tried to form a plan. Nothing. What the hell kind of plan could he come up with, anyway? He was in a fifteen by twenty cell with virtually no resources. He hadn't the slightest idea what was going to happen to him. His great store of future information wasn't going to do him a bit of good if they simply took him out and shot him. Or pulled out his fingernails or smashed his kneecaps or electrocuted his testicles. His mind wandered off onto various tortures he'd read about. He pulled away from that train of thought. He got up and did a few deep knee bends and walked the perimeter of his world.

He was standing in front of the door when the judas hole snicked open. The small sound startled him. An eye stared at him for a moment and then the inset door swung open. A short tray appeared, settled on the ledge on Alex's side of the door. The door slapped shut. The whole operation had taken only seconds.

There was a dirty bowl and a rough wooden spoon on the tray. Alex picked them both up and went back to the bunk. The rim of the bowl was encrusted with old food. He sat down, listening to his stomach growl. He smelled the liquid in the bowl, leery after his encounter with the water jug. It didn't smell like anything.

It was yellow, slightly cloudy, with a few free floating bits of vegetable matter. He tasted it. It was cold. Virtually tasteless with an underflavor of boiled grass. His stomach heaved slightly. Reject. He tried it again; he really was hungry. His stomach roiled even more. Reject. He put the bowl on the bunk and sighed. Maybe there'd be hamburgers for lunch. He thought about a thick bacon cheeseburger. Or sausage sand-

155

wiches, the kind you buy on the street in New York. His stomach growled a foolish assent. Christ, he thought, it's like having a trained dog in my gut. Listen, stomach, no breakfast, no cheeseburgers, no hot cup of coffee. This is a Tsarist prison, for God's sake. He suddenly wondered if he'd already gone mad. One night in a cell and he was talking to his stomach.

Time must have passed, though he couldn't have proved it. He was already bored with trying to figure out who had set him up. He couldn't come up with anything to think about that didn't bore him. The trick seemed to be not to think about anything if you could help it. He paced the cell and sang every Beatles tune he could remember.

Lunch was served the same as breakfast once he learned to put the morning bowl of slop up on the tray inside the door. The door opened, whisked away the bowl and deposited a chunk of what appeared to be bread. It was black, dry, and had all the taste of the wooden shelf he had slept on. He tried to break it up into smaller pieces. He ended up chewing it the way a dog chews a bone. Softening the edges until it flaked away in his mouth. It was not good, but he knew that he would have to eat to stay alive. It took some time, but he eventually got it all down.

In the brigher light he made a discovery. The walls were covered with shallow scratches. Graffiti. His mind seized on the find. He began to read as if he'd come across the Rosetta Stone. Messages from the past, advice to the prison-weary, a code of conduct, sex, love, and death; it was all there. For the first few minutes he realized that if he didn't slow down he would finish the whole cell in one day. He needed to stretch it out. Already he had felt the ominous drifting of his thought processes.

He started on the top left as far up as he could see. The light was brightest there.

He was surprised to find that most of it was the same sort of graffiti you would find in bus stations back in his own time, sex being the predominant theme ranging from the crudest drawings to elegant renderings that must have taken days to produce. Most of it was heterosexual but there were plenty of homosexual yearnings.

Many of the areas were divided up into segments that were

organized around a particular admonition, statement, or judgment that would elicit comments from others; written suns around which a variety of planetary comments circled.

A political sector was organized around the advice, carved in block letters with thick lines: "Never confess." Scattered around these two words were the thoughts of others. "Resist!" "Courage!" "Good advice!" And longer statements. "I confessed; now they will shoot me." "Confession is useless; death to the Tsarist pigs!"

Alex thought it over. Among all the prisoners who had occupied this cell he was unique. He couldn't confess if he wanted to. No one would ever believe him. Was he guilty? Innocent? Just exactly what was the crime?

His fingers traced more of the faint letters. "Yuri, I'm sorry I turned you in. You were the best pal a man ever had."

"Two years down, five to go."

"Boris Ivanovitch—a lonely man."

"Lena. I will fuck you."

"God save us all."

And then they came for him.

He was sitting in a wooden chair in front of a wooden desk behind which was another wooden chair. Over the desk, low, was a hanging lamp with a shade just like the ones that trendy young couples were buying a few years ago. Green metal shade, bare bulb, hung on a cord. High tech.

It was a small room with the usual gray stone walls. No windows. What was the line from the old song? "Stone walls and bars a prison do not make." Obviously written by a man who had never been to prison.

The light from the hanging bulb was bright, directed downward onto the desk, reflecting only dimly into the room around him.

Everything looked as if it had been bought straight from the special-effects-prison-movie catalogue, Hollywood, 1920. He wondered if there was a standard prison architecture that had come down through the ages, unchanged, modified only slightly by generations of prison officials. This particular prison had originally been designed as a fortress, Peter the

Great's bastion against the hordes of Europe, but the functions were essentially the same. As a fortress, the purpose was to keep people out; as a prison, it was to keep people in. A simple shift in direction.

They had taken away his belt, shoelaces, and tie. He supposed this was to prevent him from strangling himself. When they led him out of the cell, he'd had to shuffle along in his tieless shoes, holding up his pants at the waistband. The two who'd searched him had also taken his wad of rubles that he had never even bothered to count.

They had put him in the room and left him. He hadn't any idea how long he'd been there. An hour? Two? He supposed it was to soften him up. If that was the purpose, it was working. There was no time, no sound, only his own breathing. He waited, alternating between mind-numbing boredom and heart-thumping fear.

The scrape of the door woke him. He was slumped down in the chair, sleeping soundly. He sat up quickly, feeling like he'd been caught at some petty, embarrassing crime; shoplifting, peeking through windows at night.

He sat facing forward, unwilling to twist in his seat to see who had come in. A small gesture of pride; oh, yes, one very tough *hombre*. He heard the door close, the rasp of a key in the lock. Footsteps circled the desk.

A man in uniform entered the pool of light. Or at least the lower two-thirds of a man stood by the wooden chair across from him. The rest of the man was lost in the shadows above. Alex supposed that this was part of the standard prison scenario: strong light to dazzle the eye, the disembodied voice from above.

"Having a nice rest, Mr. Balfour? Good, good. We wouldn't want you missing any sleep." The man pulled out the chair and sat, loomed forward into the light.

A long, angular face. Very pale with a flaky pink rash across the forehead. Close-cropped iron-gray hair. For one giddy second Alex fought back a laugh. The man looked like the commissar in the old "Rocky the Flying Squirrel" cartoons. All he needed was the monocle screwed into the right eye. The irony of it all.

"I am to be your interrogator. I am Litenov, Gregor Passlovich Litenov. I hope that our collaboration will be a fruitful one, that you will trust me. I hope this because it is easier for both of us that way. If you, on the other hand, wish to be stubborn, then it will simply take a bit longer, though in the end the result will be the same."

"What result is that?" He had to clear his throat. He tried to keep his voice calm.

"The end result is that you will tell me everything that I wish to know. It is very simple."

"And what if there is nothing to tell?"

Litenov smiled. His lips contrasted with the bony face; they were soft, feminine. He smiled like a man who had to read the directions first: To smile, pull up on corners of the mouth. Alex felt a cold hand settle around his bowels and give a gentle squeeze.

"Nothing to tell? Really, Mr. Balfour, there is always something to tell. Your well-being depends on it." The puppeteer pulled the strings a little tighter and raised the corners of the lips higher. "If you insist on thinking you have nothing to tell, well . . . You wish to live, I assume, like all mortals. So let that be your primary goal, to live and to answer my questions. Other things along the way—pain, fear, all the rest—will be merely transitory. Keep that in mind; it may be of some solace to you."

Alex nodded, unable to think of any snappy comeback to that one. His whole body felt weak. Any resemblance of the interrogator to a cartoon character had fled. Maybe I'll shift back, he let himself think. He hadn't meant to hope that so soon. He'd been saving it until things got really bad. Things were getting really bad.

"Your name?"

"Alexander Balfour."

"Where are you from?"

"New York City, United States of America."

"Good. See how easy this is? What is your reason for being in Petrograd at this time?"

"I am writing a book about your country. I'm an historian."

"Wonderful, a book about Russia. And who is to publish this book?"

What? "Viking Press." It was the first publisher that he thought of. What difference would it make?

159

"Then you have some sort of contract or letters with this Viking Press that you can show me? Just to verify, of course."

"All my papers were stolen after I got to Petrograd. At the train station." Lame. Very lame. He'd thought about it and couldn't come up with anything better.

A theatrical sigh. "Really, Mr. Balfour, even you must see how ridiculous such an explanation must look. Do you take me for a fool?" The chair creaked as he leaned back.

"No," Alex said. There wasn't anything to add.

"Have we come to this point already? Surely you can explain your position in a bit more detail. What I need to know from you, Mr. Balfour"—he leaned back into the pool of light—"is who you are, what you are doing here, who you work for, and what your purposes are. Simple, is it not?"

Alex remained silent.

The sigh was longer this time. "All right, I will give you time to consider. Perhaps you are not a man who makes decisions quickly. You may return to your cell and we will talk tomorrow. We have much time, Mr. Balfour. The length of the process is up to you." He stood and went to the door and knocked once.

The key scraped in the lock and the door opened. The two men who had brought him stepped in. This time Alex couldn't help himself; he twisted around so he could see them, vaguely relieved that they were the same two. These men had not harmed him.

"Take Mr. Balfour back to his cell. You may bring him back in the morning after he has had his breakfast." He stepped back to allow the others in. Alex stood, wondering at how he was getting off so easily. No beatings? No slivers under the fingernails?

"Oh, and"—Litenov was almost out the door, but he stopped as if a thought had just occurred to him—"remove his overcoat and leave it here. He can have it back tomorrow. Perhaps."

At first it was not too bad. The light was gone from the small window, but it was not pitch-dark, as it would be later. Evidently he had missed the evening meal or they had decided not to give it to him. He felt a childish anger at this, as if they were cheating. They had taken away his coat as his

160

punishment, the interrogator had said nothing about taking his food. No fair, no fair.

He drank a little of the water and got it down. If you lifted it carefully, the slime stayed at the bottom. He remembered how he'd once read about clever lifers who could make a cup of hot coffee in a paper cup in a cell with no cooking facilities. You put a spoonful of instant in the paper cup, filled the cup with water, then floated it in the toilet on a raft of wadded up toilet paper. You set the toilet paper on fire and allowed it to burn just to the point where the cup began to sink. Rescue the cup and you had a cup of hot coffee. Unfortunately he had none of the makings for a hot cup of coffee. Not even a toilet.

He lay on the bunk, wrapped in the thin blanket. It was getting colder.

Since he had not slept much the night before, he thought he'd be able to sleep and get through the night. But he was wide-awake. He lay in the darkness feeling his nerves sing with energy that coursed through him, building up a charge of nervous anxiety that could have no release. His brain raced over the events of the last day, touching here and there but unable to concentrate on anything in depth. He felt like leaping to his feet and doing a thousand jumping jacks or push-ups until he collapsed, but he was too tired, the floor too cold. He envisioned doing a push-up in the dark and coming down on a rat.

He wrapped the blanket tighter, but he'd squeezed all possible warmth out of it. He shivered uncontrollably. He tried to relax his clenched muscles.

Shivering is an automatic response to cold. First you get goose bumps, the skin trying to fluff up the body hair, which the human animal no longer has enough to do any good, to trap a layer of warm air. The next response was to shiver. The muscles trembled, warming the body with the effort. Counterproductive in the long run, though, as it tired the body out and made it even more susceptible to the cold. Japanese skin divers train themselves to disconnect the shivering response. Unfortunately, he was not a Japanese skin diver.

Goddamnit, he was cold. It had reached his bones and soaked in to the point where he couldn't find a warm spot on his body. Under his arms, between his legs, it was all the same. He rolled off the bunk and staggered to his feet.

He walked the perimeter of the cell. After a few circuits he found he was able to turn automatically before touching a wall. It wasn't actually any warmer once he was up and moving, but his body wasn't able to clench up the way it did when he was lying down. He walked. Around and around like a hamster in a wheel.

He never even noticed the light. The door snapping open and the appearance of the bowl of yellow liquid brought him out of the walking trance. He stopped his circling, swayed dizzily while his body accommodated itself. He picked up the bowl and drank down the broth, tasting nothing. He felt the small warmth of it and was insanely grateful. Tears ran down his cheeks. He sat down on the bunk, still holding the empty bowl in his hands, crying. He wondered what he would do when they really decided to hurt him.

Chapter 22

YOU SEE IT IN THE MOVIES OR ON TELEVISION OR READ ABOUT IT IN books. It doesn't look so hard, or at least that's the way it's always played. As long as they aren't hooking your testicles up to a wall socket.

Reality is, as always, much different. You're afraid; you're bored; you're uncomfortable; you itch because you need a bath; your breath stinks because you haven't brushed your teeth; the chair is hard; you're so tired you can hardly keep your head up and on and on and through it all you have to talk until you're so sick of hearing your own voice you want to scream. And through it all, underneath, like the hairy pad beneath a rug, the fear.

You talk. Alex Balfour: the early years. Schooling; Mom and Dad, the sanitized version; life as a teacher. Omitting only dates and time references which would confuse the issue. You're trying to think on three or four levels at once, give information, not give information, and it's very hard and tiring and you slip and make mistakes and that's the purpose of it all.

"Tell me about the English bank manager. He is your friend, is he not?"

"No, I'd only just met him."

"Then he is your employer. What is the work you do for him?"

"I don't work for him." Alex felt his eyelids droop, his head nod.

"No, no," Litenov says almost gently. "You are not here to sleep. We give you time to rest. You are to sleep in your cell. Here you will answer my questions. Now once again, what is the work you are doing for the English? You visited his office several times; you went to dinner with him. Do not lie to me."

"I told you, I don't work for them. I met with him on a business deal, nothing more."

"Business." Litenov nods, as if to himself. "Spy business. You know the Englishman is a spy; don't lie."

"For God's sake," Alex said, his nerves grating under the continual, accusing voice. He touched his neck where the skin had been worn raw by the rough worn blanket clutched tightly. His head hurt; the goddamn light was too bright. "You're both on the same side, remember? Russia and England are allies. What if he is a spy, and I'm not saying he is. If I did work for him, which I don't, that would then mean that I was also working for you. It would put you and I, Litenov, on the same side. Allies."

"Russia has no allies," Litenov said, brushing away Alex's argument. "The rest of them—England, France—care nothing for us. They are interested only in having us engage the Kaiser on the western front to relieve them. That is all. Again, what work do you do for the English? You have admitted that the Englishman is a spy."

I did? He tried to remember. Couldn't, "I don't work for the English."

"Do not lie. You are a spy. Admit it."

"I'm not a spy." He felt everything—body, sanity—eroding, wearing away under the steady rain.

"You are a spy."

On and on.

"What revolutionary faction do you belong to, Mr. Balfour?"

"I am part of no faction. I am not a revolutionary."

"You attend a rally whose purpose was the overthrow of the Tsar, do you deny that?"

"I don't deny that I attended the rally. I did not intend to overthrow the Tsar." He didn't bother to keep the sarcasm

164

out of his voice. He sat up straighter in his chair. There were moments when a kind of strength returned to him.

"Surely you are something? Menshevik? Bolshevik? Socialist? Social Democrat? Kadet? We are familiar with all of them."

"I generally vote Democrat. If you've got a good Independent, I might go with him if I agree with the platform, but usually I'm a Democrat."

"Democrat?"

"Yeah. You've heard of democracy, haven't you?"

The head edged into the light. The hard eyes were flat with professional distaste. The rash on the forehead was worse. It gave Alex, that rash, a small tic of satisfaction.

"You are making a joke, Mr. Balfour. I do not like that."

"What are you going to do, take away my shoes?" He didn't much care anymore. That was one of the things he was learning about fear; after a certain amount of time you didn't actually get used to it, but it just didn't matter so much. He figured he couldn't get any colder than he was last night. "Take them. But I'd watch out for the socks if I were you. They must be killers by now."

Stand. Knock on the door. Take him away.

"Oh, Mr. Balfour? Do they give you enough water?" Pause. Litenov was not finished.

The relief of being taken back, the simple question, confused him. Water? He thought about the thick jug. "Yes, they give me water."

"Good," the interrogator nodded. "Make sure he has water," he said to the two guards.

Back in the cell they pushed him down on the bunk. One of the guards picked up the heavy jug and dumped the contents over his head.

"We'll bring you more tonight," one of the them said, gesturing with the now empty jug.

After a while his clothes began to dry to the point that he wasn't constantly aware of them chafing him. He got his bread for lunch and had spent at least an hour worrying the stale loaf, chewing at it as much for recreation and solace as for sustenance.

He spent the rest of the afternoon reading the walls. His

damp clothes kept him awake, that and the fact that every time he slumped down on the bunk and closed his eyes the guard opened the small inset door and yelled at him to wake up. He'd get up then and walk the cell, running his hand along the stone walls, feeling the hundreds of incised words.

He remembered reading, as a boy, a book about the pioneers and how on their way west, in Idaho, there was a rock where they carved their names. It was a tradition, a good-luck talisman, to carve your name, your wife's name, your children's, into this huge rock covered with the names of others who had successfully made it that far. The rock had survived, the way rocks do, bringing from the past the reminder of men and women who had padded that way. The walls of the cell were like that, reminders of men who had been imprisoned, made their small marks in the stone, and then gone on. It was a tie, a line of succession that connected the past with the present so that in this enclosed space there was little difference between the two. The circumstances were the same for all the men who carved words into the wall; the cell reduced them to a common denominator; the prison scraped away unimportant differences until they became a separate but unique species. *Homo prisoner.*

There was a section that seemed to be devoted to self-pity. As if certain types of individuals naturally gravitated to the same spot, drawn by the pain of others like themselves. "Vladimir is lonely." "I'm sorry." And etched deeply, over and over, by what must have been a succession of hands, that last cry of the doomed: "Mother."

More bread for dinner. Soup that tasted vaguely of fish. He gulped the hot liquid down and wiped the inside of the bowl with the bread. Part of him seemed to sit aside and watch himself eat, amazed at the man he had become in such a short time. Here was the gourmet chef, effete cooker of exotic foods, wolfing down watery fish soup as if it were life itself. Fuck it, he thought. He was hungry. It was neither good nor bad, distinctions that were too fine to exist here. He ate because he was hungry.

The same two brought the water as the light in the cell faded away. He backed into the corner. They came at him. He fought them, but it didn't do any good; they held him, dumped the whole jug over him, careful not to waste any.

166

He felt hot tears of impotence as they left. He sat in a puddle on the wooden bunk, trying to think of something to do to keep from freezing to death.

He wondered abstractly how much body heat he would lose through the wet clothing, if there was enough reserve to carry him through the night. It was probably a question of medical physics: If body A retained a core temperature of X degrees in an environment of XY degrees, how much temperature could this body maintain if subjected to the wicking effect of wet clothing against skin. He didn't have an answer, but he knew he was going to find out.

He removed each article of clothing, one by one, wringing it out over and over until he'd removed as much of the water as possible. The effect of it kept him moderately warm, or at least as warm as he could get under the circumstances. The water had taken away some of the bone-numbing fatigue that he had been feeling. But as he sat cross-legged on the bunk, it began to catch up with him.

At first he tried to sit so as little of his body as possible was touching the surface of the wall or the bunk. That way the damp clothing didn't actually press against him. The touch of the wet cloth was beginning to rub raw patches on his skin. But finally the effort of just sitting up got to be too much. He lay down. He lay with his head against the rough wet wood, feeling the raised grain against his cheek, distancing himself from his body by concentrating on a simple flaming red ball of energy. He spent his time putting his tormenters into the pulsating ball—the guards, Litenov —one by one and watching them scream in agony as the flames consumed them. He basked in the heat.

Sometime in the night the fever came; this was the heat of his dreams, and he was at last warm.

It woke him up. He tried to sit up but didn't make it. He lay back on the bunk in surprise. His throat hurt and it was hard to breathe. He felt a shock as he realized that he was sick. He had not thought it possible to feel worse than he had felt earlier.

His eyes were dry and grainy. He needed water, but he didn't think he could get to the jug. He almost laughed. The jug. All the water in it had been dumped on him. A chill shook him. Fever, chills. Pneumonia; it had to be. He'd had

167

viral pneumonia when he was a child and remembered the feeling as his lungs filled with fluid. Amazing how fast it occurred; in a matter of hours you were drowning in your own phlegm. His joints ached.

How clear and calm his mind was. Or at least he thought it was. He thought about shouting for help, even tried an experimental croak, but gave it up. He didn't care much. He understood that there was a very good chance he was going to die. He still didn't care much.

He'd come a long way in a very short time.

The sickness seemed to detach his mind from his tormented body, allowing him to consider things in the abstract.

He'd fucked up. Failed. He cast back over his whole life. Is this the dying man's response? Seeing his life flash before his eyes. There wasn't much there to comfort him. He hadn't done anything really bad, but then, he hadn't done much good either. He'd got good grades in school and that was about it. He visualized his tombstone: He Got Good Grades. Hell of an epitaph.

He started to cough, a wet racking sound that he couldn't control.

A childhood of repressed hatred toward his father. Parents die. Loses Molly the first time. Ten years of putting in his time. Finds Molly for a couple of days. Into the past. Can't even get through a few days of interrogation without becoming seriously ill. Pneumonia. Dies.

Nothing much there. Not too impressive. Not even a life of desperation. There wasn't anything to him. If you held his life up to the light, there was so little there you could read a book through it. What the hell, is this it? Is this the way everybody else is? Where's the joy, the passion, the peaks; goddamnit, where's the life?

Very slowly he forced himself into a sitting position. The fluid gathering in his lungs sank to the bottom, giving him more room to breath. He was chilled again. He wrapped his arms around his legs and tried to keep from coughing.

The worst part was he seemed right on the edge of changing things. Molly was back; he was involved in a very strange but exciting event. The travel into the past had to be important. There was something here, something to fill up the empty hole in the center of him, something to do, for Christ

168

sake, that might make a difference. That was it. Nothing he had ever done had ever made a difference. Live, die; no difference. Even his deathbed response was banal, ordinary.

When he was a child, he used to make promises to the Lord. He tried not to do it often, as even his imperfect theology told him that you could easily wear it out. Dear Lord, he would pray, if you help me pass the math test tomorrow, I swear I will be good. Dear Lord, if you let me get to first base with Mary Ann Hays, I swear I will be a good person. Not that he ever really believed, but there was always a chance.

Dear . . . Whoever (he would give it a try): If you get me through this one spot here, this sickness, I swear I will . . . what? . . . What could he promise that would mean anything? He didn't have anything to trade. The only thing he had was himself. There was no one to blame, no one to ask for help. Just Alex sitting here, drowning in his own juices. Burning up with it and still cold on the outside, like the shell of an egg; it was surrounding him, freezing him. Hungry and at the same time repelled by the thought of food. Afraid. Christ, in his whole adult life he'd never had much worse than a bad cold. He'd never hurt like this.

Where was he? Brain beginning to drift. A difference. If he was going to make a difference, he was going to do it on his own. He prayed. Dear Alex. Get your self together and get your own ass out of the hole it's in.

He was panting like a dog. Not much room left in the old lungs. Too bad these deathbed revelations always came on the deathbed. Doesn't leave much time.

He felt himself fall over. Not on the floor, he thought, not on the floor. Rats.

When he woke up, he was in a large, high-ceilinged room. A woman hove into view beside him, dressed in white, wearing a tall mitered headdress that looked like some of the Catholic Church's more ridiculous headgear. A red cross on the front of the crisp white bosom of the dress proclaimed her Nurse. He knew where he probably was, but he asked the obvious question anyway.

"Where am I?"

"In the prison infirmary," she answered, tucking the bed-clothes tighter around him.

"How long have I been here?" There were barred windows. He could see light coming through.

"Three days."

He'd lived through the night and then some. He tested the feel of his body, moving his extremities, tried to breath and found himself filled with Elmers glue. All in all, it wasn't too bad. He felt like hammered shit, but at least he wasn't cold.

"You'll be all right. You need rest; that's about all we can do for you." Her tone was exasperated, with an underlying sympathy and frustration. "I don't know why you do it," she went on, "why don't you just tell them what they want to know? It's not worth it, whatever it is; in the end they'll kill you for it."

He looked up at her, floating there above him, a look of worry and concern on her face and in her hands as she smoothed the sheets around him. It felt very good to be warm again. He drifted away. He tried to remember: not much in the way of antibiotic in this time. Must have been the body deciding not to die. Rest.

"Why don't you just tell them?" She was far away.

"Ah," he said, looking one last time before he went; the hat was so tall he was afraid she would topple over onto him, bending there above. "If I only could."

They left him there for ten days. He stretched it out as long as he could; the food was much better than he got in his cell. He could feel his body healing itself. He could breathe again. Eventually they sent him back.

It was a new cell. Alex found he had a moment's nostalgia, a sense of loss for the old one, as if it had somehow become home. A terrible home, perhaps, like an evil orphanage to a lonely child, but a place that he knew, a place that would not have changed while he was gone, a place where he knew what to expect. At least to some degree.

The new cell was not all that different. He checked the walls immediately after being left alone. He was relieved to find the same myriad tracings etched into the stone. Probably every cell in the prison had the writings. Perhaps this was some sort of basic definition of man: an animal who, when

170

left alone, makes marks. Not all of it was writing, many of the men incarcerated here would have been incapable of that. They were the ones that drew the pictures or simply made scratches, each one representing another day in prison.

For a moment he was struck by the concept of the building as a giant book, the walls of the cells constituting its pages. If he was back in his own time, he could probably apply for a grant from someone to transcribe all the graffiti and then organize it in a scholarly way. Break it down into categories, reduce it to scholarship, bleed away its power. You needed to touch it to understand it, feel it to interpret the emotions and ideas that the words represented. He touched one, carved deeply: "Innocent!!" He understood.

This cell was larger than the last. The window was lower, though still a foot above his head. It was round, the window, actually two half-moon shapes with a stone centerpiece. Beyond the bars he could see blue cloudless sky. The only other difference in the cell was that there was an extra wooden bunk.

The food seemed better. Maybe it was a change in him, but he seemed to have adapted to it, found it nourishing. Every once in a while there was even a chunk of meat in the broth.

They left him alone. The only other human he saw was the face of the man who brought the food. Alex found himself looking forward to food time, waiting by the little door for the glimpse of the man's face. He felt so much better he invented an exercise program for himself. He'd pared off any excess fat a long time ago. He started slow and built it up: sit-ups, push-ups, your standard regimen. No Nautilus machines.

He fantasized a whole program he could institute back in his own time. The Prison Diet and Workout Program. Cabbage soup and black bread. Interrogation every couple of days: "Have you been sneaking food, Jones? Don't lie! Confess!" Guards leading the calisthenics. Good-looking women in leotards with torture machines for the backsliders. He'd make millions.

Every day he'd been scratching a short line into the wall with a chip of the stone he had found on the floor, trying to keep track of the time. There was a revolution coming, and while it didn't look as if he'd be there to see it, he'd at least know when it was happening. One of the major events in the world's history was about to occur and he going to miss it. Superman from the future screws up.

February the 27th would be the big day. He wasn't exactly sure of the date, but he thought the 27th would be soon. He tried to recall what had happened to the fortress of Peter and Paul during the Revolution, but he couldn't remember.

More and more his thinking stayed on his present existence. Like a man blinded late in life, aware that his visual memories had faded away, he found his memories of his own time fading. The terms he thought of himself within were those of Russia in 1917.

His physical situation did not change. He was always hungry, always cold, always dirty. And while he never got used to this, never was not constantly aware of it, he found that the emphasis of it gradually shifted until it was not the central part of his life. Discomfort, real and painful though it was, was not the worst thing in the world. Dying was worse. And if you were not dying, things were never as bad as they could be.

Somewhere in his brain he had turned a corner. It was as if his body had decided to take over from his intellect. Questions of the past and the future were still constant but on a more everyday level, a matter of existence rather than interest. He found a new life in himself. Prison was terrible, but the pain was a constant reminder that he was alive. In his own present he had never been really hurt. Now he realized he'd also never been really alive.

He sat on the floor. The light in this cell was brighter than in his first cell. The days seemed longer. He had found a new wonder down near the floor, a picture that had been painfully etched into the wall, incredibly detailed. It was a landscape with birch trees, a river, hills rolling into the distance that led off into the imagination. The beauty of it was so evident that no occupant of the cell had destroyed the integrity by writing anywhere near it. At first he had missed it, thinking it only a space of random scratches. Then the light of late afternoon sun had thrown shadows into the scratches and revealed the picture.

He had once read that when Monet died his studio was

found to be empty of paintings. Years later art historians had gone back in and found that the walls themselves, long panels of canvas, were paintings. Impressionism at its highest; pale, light-filled renderings of water and lilies that, because they were unlike work that had been seen before, had not even existed for those who first saw them. The art had been revealed only by time.

This work is no less, he thought, touching the cuts, tracing the branches of a birch tree, feeling the light wind that shook the leaves. The medium is stone, imprisonment, the artist lost, the audience a succession of men all doomed to some degree, but the work was no less art because of it; it was alive, giving life.

The door was pushed violently in, slamming against the wall. He rolled up from a sitting position and braced himself. He had a glimpse of two men holding a third, flinging the third into the cell.

The door was slammed shut. Alex waited in a crouch, listening to the footsteps recede beyond the door. In the quiet he heard his own breath and the rasp from the man on the floor.

He touched the rough wool of the overcoat. He rolled the man faceup. The face was bloody, but the eyes were open. Blood had drawn deltas and floodplains in the deep wrinkles that fanned out from the corners of the eyes.

"You . . ." The old man, Vassili, looked up at him and smiled. He licked his lips and tried again. ".You . . . forgot . . . to return . . . my necktie."

Chapter 23

THE OLD MAN HAD FOUGHT THEM. FOR HIS TROUBLE THEY HAD knocked out his front teeth.

Alex picked him up, surprised at how light he was. He laid him gently on the extra bunk. He wet the tail of his shirt in the water jug and tried to clean the blood off Vassili's face.

"They came the day you went to the bank," the old man said. His words were slurred, broken like his lips, mouth.

"Don't try to talk." He could picture them; there would be two of them, beating up one old man. Big guys in greatcoats, goons. A wave of hate rippled over him.

"They went through your things. They asked questions. It was the goddamned *dvornik*; he must have told them. I knew he was no good."

"It's all right; don't worry about it. There was nothing there for them anyway."

He took off his suit coat and doubled it up under Vassili's head. It was dark now, the only light coming in through the cracks around the door. He could see the old man's face in the faint light. It looked crumpled, the mouth lost beneath the huge moustache. The eyes were open, though, shining.

"I never told them a goddamned thing about you. Told them I was railroad man, not afraid of them. Rest of the house quivering and shaking—yes, master; no, master—bunch of mice. Thought you were gone for good. *Dvornik's* wife wanted to rent your room to someone else, but I made her hold it. Then they came back today, said I had to go with them. I fought them. Two of them. Not afraid.''

The small inset door opened and Alex saw the bowl and bread slide onto the tray. "Wait a minute," he shouted as the door closed. No answer. "This man's hurt!" He stood shouting at the blank door. He heard the squeak of the food cart as it moved on down the hallway outside. What do they care? They're the ones that hurt him in the first place. He went back to the bunk. Vassili's eyes were closed, his breathing fast and ragged.

Alex collected the bowl of soup and the bread. He considered trying to wake Vassili to feed him the soup, then decided against it. If the old man was going to die, it wouldn't be from hunger. At least not yet.

He sat on his own bunk and slowly drank the soup. He put the bread inside his shirt. He'd save it for the morning. The old man would need it.

Vassili said they had come the day he went to the bank. It had only been around a month, but it seemed longer than that. So much and so little had happened in that month.

Vassili was right; it must have been the *dvornik* who turned him in. It was too fast for them to have gotten on to him any other way. A man with no luggage, no visible means of support, a foreigner, rents a room. Why not turn him in? For this maybe the police would pay? Everyone else seemed to think he was a spy, so why blame the poor doorman?

There was nothing in his room; blue jeans, sneakers, a shirt—odd clothing but not illegal or even suspicious. What did they want with Vassili? Did they suspect him of something simply because he was his friend? Could they be that paranoid?

Something nagged at him, something he was forgetting.

Was it the Englishman? The demonstration? That took place after they were at the house looking for him, or at best at the same time. They couldn't have taken either of those events into their reasoning.

The old man muttered in his sleep. Alex went over and checked him. His breathing had slowed. He adjusted the rolled-up suit coat. He straightened Vassili's coat, buttoned it

175

all the way to the throat. It was a warm coat; the old man wouldn't freeze.

Alex went back to his bunk, put on the topcoat that they had returned to him after his trip to the hospital, wrapped himself in his blanket, and sat down. He drew his legs up and leaned against the wall. He couldn't understand. What did they want with the old man? His stomach growled. "Shut up," Alex said.

His stomach still complained, but it was mostly a formality, a reminder of past days.

It was as if the prison were rendering him, melting away layers of inconsequential concerns along with layers of body fat. Physical comfort was paramount, even though he had not been conscious of it, in his former life; now it no longer mattered. Back in the present he had never been really cold, really sick, or really endangered, and he had taken that to be the normal state of affairs for himself and the rest of the world. And it was true, at least for his own thin slice of life. Intellectually he knew that most people—people outside his small privileged class, poor people, people in third world countries, countries at war, other people—were cold, sick, and in deep trouble most of the time; but knowing a thing and being something are two entirely different planes of existence. They cannot be compared, no matter how sincere and honest the effort. A white man cannot know what it is to be black, a free man a slave, a healthy man what it is to die. You can think you know, read about it, see it, but you cannot *know*.

Prison had taken away his comfort; prison had hurt him. But it had not killed him. Neitzsche: "That which does not kill me, helps me." He hated it, the prison and the pain, but he was beginning to understand elemental concepts that had been hidden from him, hidden behind a protective membrane of objects, comfort, civilization, pale philosophies, politics, and pleasure. He had been swathed in it, this membrane, wrapped like a tuna sandwich in a vending machine. But some people escape. Here it might be Lenin—surely Rasputin. He remembered Rasputin struggling to his feet on the ice, tearing at the sheet, his eyes shouting the words into the cold night: "I am alive; I am alive." And now he, Alex, had made the first cuts in the membrane and felt the breath of life enter his body.

It gave him strength, this breath. His essence was stripped to the bone, but what was left behind was hard, elemental, real. He thought more clearly, hated more easily, lived on a vastly more simple scale, but he felt himself whole, compact, prepared for the first time in his life. Prison was the pressure that squeezed carbon into crystalline hardness. Gave it its cutting edge. He would cut the membrane, strip it from him.

He lay down on his wooden shelf and immediately slept.

In the morning he broke up the extra loaf of bread and soaked it in the bowl of broth. He then fed the small, soft pieces to Vassili. The old man seemed better, insisting that he was all right. After he had eaten, he actually did seem better. His face was beginning to blotch purple with bruises. The blood had dried in the wrinkles that fanned out from the corners of his eyes. The skin there looked like maps of the river Nile, deltas delicately traced from the pages of a child's schoolbook.

"This is nothing," Vassili said, sitting on the edge of the bunk. "Once I fell off the train. We were making a joke and I slipped. Some joke." He laughed as he remembered. "Broken arm"—he gestured to his arm and to his chest—"collarbone. Bruises everywhere. They never let me forget that one." The old man stretched, raising his fists to his shoulders, wincing. "These are some accommodations," he said, waving at the bunk and around the cell. "They have kept you here the whole time?"

"Most of it. My first cell was just like it, only smaller. I guess you get used to it after a while."

"You can get used to anything after a while. But what do they want from you? How long will they keep you here?"

Alex shrugged. He had learned that the question was one that had no usefulness.

"What's going on outside, Vassili? What's happening in town?"

"Things are worse. There are strikes almost every day now. I have been reading the papers at the library; it is the same everywhere. Our glorious allies were in town for talks. We are told we must stiffen our resolve. Nothing is changed; it is impossible to tell who is winning the war.

177

"The Duma is to reassemble at the end of this month. Fat old Rodzianko has finally come out in favor of liberalizing the government, but there is little hope that the Tsar will do anything." He looked at Alex who nodded for him to continue. He glanced around; the walls have ears. He went on anyway.

"The Tsar," he laughed, "has done nothing for months. It is incredible. Everyone knows that there is trouble, probably revolution, coming and coming soon. Everybody except our Tsar. How is it that I, Vassili Vassiliovitch, ex-railroad man, no one special, can see the trouble that is almost on us, see it like a storm coming on a hot summer day, and our Tsar is blind?"

"Perhaps he wants to see nothing," Alex offered. Vassili had hit upon one of the historical questions of the time.

"Perhaps. Though it is difficult to believe. There are two new groups in the Duma," he went on. "The Progressives and the Mezhrayonka. Both are of the left, although the Progressives are not as left as the others. Both promise us change. Will it ever happen?" He shook his head.

"It will happen," Alex said. Vassili looked at him with raised eyebrows. Alex nodded. "There will be a great change. Soon."

"Good," Vassili said. "I will be very happy to see it."

The door of the cell slammed open, startling them.

"Balfour."

He stood up and stretched. Straightened his clothes. "My interrogator would like to speak with me," he said to Vassili. "If lunch comes before I return, please go ahead without me."

Vassili nodded. He smiled, then stopped as his lips cracked.

"What do you want with him?" Alex demanded.

"I thought you might be lonely," Litenov said, his face impassive, as usual. "Don't you appreciate the company?"

"Not here. Not now. Not when you had to beat the man to get him here. Let him go; he knows nothing."

"What is there to know, Mr. Balfour?"

"Nothing. We've been over this ground a hundred times."

"He will go free when you begin to tell me the truth."

There. That was Vassili's purpose. A hostage. Litenov had

178

moved the interrogation process to the next level. He had
tried the basic method, had applied pressure directly to the
source. Nothing had come of it except the object, Alex, had
gotten sick and had a holiday in the hospital. The pressure
had been withstood, the pain controlled. Litenov understood
that the next level was pressure applied to others, as long as
there is a link. We can control ourselves, but we cannot give
another our will, strength, purpose, when there is no reason
for them to have it. To watch the pain of another is to
experience the doubling of pain, our own compounded by
theirs.

Unless one can convince the giver of pain that it will not
work.

"He's an old man who lives in the same building with me.
I've known him for a few weeks. The only thing he knows is
a lot of old railroad stories. Using him this way is stupid."

"If that is the case, if you care nothing for this man, then
his incarceration, and anything else that may happen, should
bother you very little. He is a small man, caught in the cogs
of a large machine. He is of no importance."

And that, Alex thought, is why you upper-class Russians
are about to get the shit kicked out of you.

"Because he means nothing to me personally doesn't mean
I don't care about him. In America we call such people
innocent bystanders. He has no part in this; it's cruel to keep
him here."

Litenov looked at Alex and laughed. For the first time his
face showed an emotion that looked genuine. "Cruel?" he
asked. "You think this is cruel?" He shook his head. He
waved his hand, a gesture that wiped away his laughter, the
entire subject. The way one waves away a fly.

"You test my patience, Mr. Balfour. I am tempted to
show you what cruelty truly is. You are like a child. You
think you understand, that you have answers, but they are the
answers of a little boy. You have no depth. Your purpose is
not to explain cruelty to me; your job is to answer my
questions."

"Soon I won't have to answer to anything."

"Yes?" Litenov's mouth tightened. "And why is that?
What do you propose to do about it?"

"I don't need to do anything; it's about to be done for me."

The raised eyebrow. The superior look, the air of scorn, was like a match to a fuse.

Suddenly it didn't seem to matter. The tiptoeing around, trying to be careful not to say anything that might change the orderly progression of events. Why bother? Time was not progressive; that was a conception invented by historians. It was elemental. Chaos. He was small, a piece of grit in the machine; he could change nothing.

"All right, here it is. In a matter of weeks all the little insignificant people like the old man back in my cell are going to get together and throw you pompous assholes out of office." The image of Litenov being marched away at bayonet point came to him like a Socialist propaganda poster. A fine image. "The Okhrana, all the ineffectual ministers and heads of government who have been bleeding your people dry, are going to get removed right along with the Tsar."

"The Tsar? Remove the Tsar? Maybe you are insane, Mr. Balfour, as has been suggested by my superiors. There has been a Romanov on the throne for the last three hundred years. You do not sweep away the Tsar like a pile of dead leaves."

"That's what you think. The Tsar will go."

"Go where? You are a fool."

"Go. Overthrown."

"You're not going to tell me that these lower-class revolutionaries are going to kill the Tsar. It would never happen. Russians love their Tsar like a father. You are insane."

"Am I?" But he hesitated. With the hesitation came an easing of the anger, a return to his senses.

"When will all this happen?"

Alex didn't respond.

"All right, enough of this. You have information; I want to know where you got it. You talk of revolution, but you've been here only a short time. You spend the day with the Englishman from the Merchants Bank, why is that? Why would they be so interested in you? You attend demonstrations with the workers, why? Why, Mr. Balfour? Rest assured that we are done with the easy way. Now you get Litenov, and if you thought that what has gone before was difficult, you are mistaken. I am real, Mr. Balfour; I am the sword, the whip, the gun.'' His voice went soft. He licked his full lips. There was no smile, no frown, no look of power, only the flat eyes, the intensity of an insect. ''I will not be denied.''

Wolverines. The thought jumped into Alex's head. As a child he was always reading stories about wolverines, animals that, though small, would take on anything in the forest. Take it on, kill it, tear it to shreds, and then piss on it. No one he had ever talked to had ever actually seen a wolverine, but they were legend. And now he was sitting across the desk from one.

''For the last time. Tell me,'' Litenov demanded.

''I can't. There's nothing to tell.'' He had decided a long time ago that he gained nothing by thinking up elaborate lies. I was at the bank opening a checking account. Of course you were.

''You won't tell me. You could, but you won't.''

He shrugged. ''Have it your way. Can't, won't; it's the same thing in the end. I've been telling you the truth all along.''

''You have told me fairy stories.''

Alex shrugged again.

''If you will not talk, then I must kill the old man.''

The idea of it splashed over Alex like the jug of cold water. They couldn't; it wasn't worth it. And yet the cold seeped into his skin. It was shooting a rabbit with a bazooka; the means and the end were in different categories.

''That's ridiculous, Litenov. What good would that do? The proper threat at this point is that you'll kill me, not the innocent bystander. You're getting the script wrong.''

Now it was Litenov's turn to shrug. ''Have it your way, Mr. Balfour. The threat remains. The old man. Then I will kill you. You see, you must tell me the truth. There is no other choice.''

For two days Vassili had sung him songs of the railroad, told stories. He'd traveled most of the rail system in his years; now he took Alex along on the trips.

''Through Siberia twice, when I was a young man. All the way to the end, to Vladivostok. Saw the Chinamen. Twice. Once in the summer, once in the winter.

"Siberia is beautiful; nothing as far as you can see except the tracks ahead, flat lands to the side, the sky so large you cannot see it all in one day. And the forests. The trees are so tall you cannot see the tops on cloudy days."

And Paul Bunyan and Babe the blue ox live right down the road, Alex thought. The old man had a hundred stories.

The two of them sat on their respective bunks, singing and laughing like two demented lifers, imprisoned so long that their world was reduced to one room to be transcended only by stories of past lives and loony songs from childhood.

Chapter 24

THEY HAD TAKEN VASSILI AWAY. THEY GAVE ALEX A SHOWER. The two events pulled at Alex's mind, worry and pleasure, vying for his attention like two insistent lovers, yanking him from the ecstasy of lukewarm water to the doubts of apprehension.

They had washed him in the hospital, but since then no one had paid any attention to his requests for a bath. He cleaned himself as best he could with the cold water in the stone jug. He could no longer tell how awful he must smell, having become used to the odors of his own unclean body, damp concrete, and the foul waste hole in the corner. When he was taken to the interrogation room, he would sometimes be sickened by the smell of cologne on Litenov. The Russians themselves did not often bathe, trusting the strong scent of perfumes to cover any offending odors. He supposed that bad as the cologne was, it was better than what he was giving off.

Vassili had left with a joke and a smile, a schoolboy being sent down the hall for a reprimanding from the principal. Alex didn't know where they were taking the old man, but after Litenov's threats he was afraid that it would not be for a friendly interrogation.

Taking Vassili away was done, Alex was sure, not to intimidate Vassili but to torture Alex.

He undressed in a small, cold room that opened onto another that had three pipes coming out of the wall at head height. The two guards stood at the door of the first room watching, silent as ever.

One of the men turned a handle and water began to trickle from the nearest of the pipes. Alex put his hand into it and found it lukewarm. He stepped beneath the water and felt it flow onto his face, an almost forgotten feeling that rivaled any memory he could summon. The water was real; memories were pale dreams. He cupped his hands and splashed water onto his face, his head. Beside him a guard grunted and handed him a sliver of soap, careful not to get his arm wet. Alex took the soap and worked it into a thin lather, turning his body so the water ran over him. He felt the thin stream cutting through decades of desert dust, carving channels through cracked and dried arroyos, cascading luxuriously over his head and body. . . .

"Enough." The trickle of water ended. The guard handed him a thin towel. It was the first word that the guard had spoken that Alex could remember. Breakthrough, he thought; soon we'll be pals. He dried and then painfully pulled on his ragged clothes, the contrast of before shower and after making it obvious how filthy the clothing really was. But he felt better than he had in weeks.

Vassili. He'd almost forgotten the old man. The pleasure of the shower had crowded out everything for just a moment. Alex thought of his bath at home, of the hours he had spent lying there, never aware what fortune there was in a bathtub full of water. Home. For a second he longed for it, felt it well up in him like tears. Molly. Loneliness hit him, an unexpected blow. He turned his head away from the guards. It washed over him, then receded. He pushed it all back down beneath the present, concentrating on the sound of his footsteps as he shuffled along between the guards. This was reality; this was truth; this was life. There is no past.

As he was escorted into his cell, he was disturbed by an anomaly. The guard had not closed the door. Alex looked at the man standing there, puzzled by this breach of the standard routine.

"The window," the guard said with no emotion. Not a command or a question. A statement. The door closed.

Alex found himself trying to find the trick in it. The window was above his head. To look out of it, you had to haul yourself up by the bars and hang there suspended. He'd done that early on and found nothing but an empty courtyard surrounded by a high wall and the cold gray sky of Russian winter. It was not a cheery sight. Certainly not worth hanging in midair for. But where was the trick?

What the hell. What could they do, poke him in the eye when he got up there? Come dashing in and tickle him while he hung from the bars? He would look out the window.

He reached up and got a good hold and pulled himself up. He was surprised at how easily he did it, as if the weeks on prison fare and push-ups had indeed done their job. The Prison Workout system really works. You too can become fit and healthy on a diet of cabbage and interrogation.

There was a line of men in the courtyard. Policemen or soldiers or guards in heavy blue greatcoats. They were facing away from him. The sky was overcast, a solid sheet of tattletale gray. The men were standing in a ragged line, holding long rifles. He was close enough to see their breath in the cold air as they stamped their feet and blew on their hands. His arms began to tremble. He dropped lightly to the floor.

Seeing so many people all at once was a shock. He'd grown used to never seeing more than two people at once.

What the hell was going on?

He looked around the cell for something to stand on. He got his blanket, Vassili's blanket, and took off his coat. He folded all of these into small squares and put them on the floor beneath the window. He got the heavy clay water jug and put it on the folded blankets. Carefully, he climbed up on this unsteady tower. By holding on to the bars, he could just see out without stretching. The line of men was less ragged. Another man, probably an officer, stood off to the side. Alex looked closely, the rigid stance was familiar. Litenov.

Firing squad. Litenov. He felt his legs weaken. Who was it for? Would they come for him?

Vassili.

Two guards entered his field of view from the left, Vassili stumbling along between them. Alex saw the scene as if it

185

were a series of geometry exercises. The heavy, broad line of men with rifles; Litenov a dot to the right side; the slow, intersecting dotted line of Vassili and his guards, arcing across the background to come to rest against the far wall.

Alex was like a man blind from birth who suddenly regains his sight. Show him a bus and he wouldn't understand what it was until he touched it. He knew what was happening, but his brain would not accept it, would not process the information. He had been blinded by his imprisonment. Now he could see; they were allowing him to see, and he did not want to.

They had taken off the old man's coat. They left him standing alone against the far wall. Alex was close enough to see the old man shiver with the cold. They were not far away. He could have thrown a rock and hit the far wall. He could have shouted at the men if there was no wall between. Stop. No.

Vassili tried to stand at attention, but spasms of trembling shook him and twisted him to the side.

Alex felt the rush of shock and fear as it exploded in his mind. They're going to shoot him. They're going to shoot him.

There was no sound. The glass of the window was so old, so thick, that it grayed out most of the color, rendering the scene into black and white like a scratchy old documentary movie. He thought wildly of what he'd read about Russian executions. Dostoyevsksi had been treated to one of the Okhrana's specialties, the mock execution. The bullets would be blanks. The prisoner/condemned would dissolve into compliancy at the sound of the guns, ready to tell all. I'll tell, I'll tell. It's not worth it, whatever it is you're going to do.

"No," he said aloud. His voice croaked, sounding odd and uninflected in the silence of the cell. "No."

There was no one to hear him. He was alone with the men in the courtyard, the men in the scratchy old film. But he could not end this, could not simply walk out.

One of the guards approached Vassili with a black cloth. The old man drew himself up and stopped trembling. He shook his head once and the guard moved away.

The line of men picked up their rifles and aimed. Alex

watched the old man, standing as tall as he ever could. Was he looking at Alex? Could he see his face behind the thick glass, a pale smear with featureless eyes, a mouth that was a simple hole, wordless, silent, afraid. . . . Could he see the face that was the cause of all of this, the face that was his death? His friend?

The crack of the guns was muffled by the glass. Smoke flew up. Vassili dropped to the ground. Alex could see the roses bloom on the old man's white shirt. The arms moved back and forth across the snow, once, like a child making a snow angel, then stopped.

For a long moment no one moved. Alex tore his eyes away from the small heap of his friend.

Litenov. Litenov was facing him. Alex could see the death's head smile, feel the man looking at him, watching the window of the cell, knowing that Alex was there at the other end of his gaze, watching. Litenov raised his arm, saluted.

Alex turned and slid down the wall. The jug overturned; he did not hear it. He sat in the puddle of cold water; he did not feel it.

Chapter 25

THREE DAYS LATER HE WAS BACK IN THE ROOM. THE SINGLE BULB with the shallow green metal shade was lowered back down the way it had been during the first session. He was slumped in the chair, staring at the pool of light on the wooden desk. They'd opened the door; he'd come in and sat without looking at anything. He was programmed by the room, the walk down the stone halls, the two who came for him. He waited without thinking. There was no room for thinking, the time past for thinking; there was nothing left but to act. The prison had gone too far, had squeezed too hard; the crystal was shattered. They had killed Vassili.

He heard someone stir in the corner of the room. He looked up, saw the shadowy figure of a man there. Because there were no windows, the darkness beyond the glaring light was deep, the contrast between the two extremes making the irises of his eyes expand and contract in an attempt to accommodate. He stared at the light on the desk.

"You bastards," Alex said. His voice was flat.

The figure stirred. Alex could hear breathing. The man was watching him. He didn't care. They'd get to the point soon enough. He'd had time to plan it. He would do it when Litenov sat down. When the man's guard was down, he'd kill him. Across the desk, hands around the throat. If he moved fast enough, he'd have time. Those outside would hesitate. They were not men who initiated action; they were men who took orders. They would not act quickly. They would not be in time.

He heard Litenov pull out the chair and sit. He moved his own legs into position and leaned forward. The light, the light.

The uniform was gone. This man—he knew now it was not Litenov—was wearing a suit. He did not move like Litenov, did not sit like Litenov, did not hold himself rigid like Litenov. The shadowy chin, cheeks, lit from the bottom up by the reflection of the light, like a madman in an old horror movie, were not Litenov's.

The head, the man, leaned forward into the light. The same mass of silver hair. It was not Litenov.

It was his father.

"Alex, you're a fool."

"And you're dead."

His father snorted and sat back in his chair. His face was lost again in the gloom. "This goddamn light," his father said, standing. He pulled the light up as high as he could reach and tied a knot in the cord. "Russians have an overinflated sense of drama. You see that light trick everywhere." He sat back down.

"You're dead," Alex said again. He felt as if he were caught in some sort of brain warp. He'd come into the room ready to kill a man, and here he was, talking to his dead father.

"Obviously I'm not dead. I know it must be a shock to you, but things will work out more quickly if you just accept it. After all, you're sitting in a prison in a time quite a few years before you were even born. If you can accept that, then you can stretch your imagination a little further and accept the fact that I'm not dead."

"All right, you're not dead. . . ."

"Very good."

Alex recognized, remembered, the sarcasm. He made an effort to damp down all the conflicting messages and questions that were rocketing around his brain. The time lines were now so tangled there was no question of patiently unraveling them, at least not right now. "So if you're not dead, what are you doing here?"

His father smiled the lazy, superior smile that he remembered so well. In photographs it always came off as kind and benevolent. The camera always lies.

"I could ask you the same question."

"And we could go around like this all day. Look"—Alex shifted forward in his chair—"let's not take up where we left off fifteen years ago. I've got a lot of questions that you've got the answers to. Let's start off with the fact that you're not dead. What happened in that airplane? The coast guard found the pieces of the plane but never the bodies." A wild hope sprang into his head. "Mother? Is she alive?"

Alex's father shook his head. "First of all, I'm not going to answer all of your questions, but if you're a good boy, we'll see how much information you get. No, your mother isn't alive. I shifted back while we were out over the ocean." He shrugged. "I didn't mean to, but you must know that it isn't something you can control. At least I couldn't then. I have to assume she must have gone down with the plane." His dry, matter-of-fact tone of voice showed no overt concern.

"You bastard."

His father rolled his eyes and looked at the ceiling. "Really, Alex, I wasn't all that happy about it either. Try to get a hold on yourself."

Memory. He had been a little boy; he couldn't remember how old, but no more than six. He'd stepped into a hornet's nest in the front yard of their house in Connecticut. He'd been stung a number of times. He ran into the house; his father was the only one home. His father had run cold water on his legs, the stings, and comforted him with those very words. Really, Alex, try to get a hold on yourself.

Only this time the words didn't hurt. He suddenly realized that he no longer had any reason to obey, listen to, or even put up with this man. He was an adult. He was free.

His father had died . . . disappeared . . . before Alex could reject his authority as a normal process of growing up. But now, after his shift into this past, his time in the prison, his sickness, and Vassili, his adolescent anger against his father had disappeared along with the ring of fat around his

190

middle. There was much he needed to know that only this man across the table could tell him. He needed information; he would get it.

"All right," Alex said. "How long have you been here? I mean in Russia, in this time."

"A lot longer than you have. It's a wonderful time, isn't it? At least it is if you position yourself correctly."

The contempt was implied but obvious.

"You mean if one has positioned oneself on the correct side of the table." Alex gestured at the piece of furniture between them.

His father nodded. "You are in the prison; I run the prison. The distinction is clear."

"You run it?"

"In a manner of speaking. Let's say that I'm the advisor to the man who runs it, the head of the Okhrana. I've found, and here's a piece of advice that's so true and so old that it's become a cliche, that it is always smarter to position yourself behind those in power rather than taking the power for yourself. It's much easier to direct the man who directs policy than to shoulder the entire burden. That way, when things come apart, as things naturally tend to do, the responsibility rests with someone else."

"So you're responsible for me being here?"

"Not directly." Smile. "As a matter of fact, I've only recently become aware that you were here. I've been out of town. I thought you might turn up, though. I've been expecting you for some time."

"Why?"

"We met once before. Recently. Don't you remember?" He said it smugly.

"No." Alex thought back, but too much had happened. Besides, he knew it was a little game his father was playing.

"Aren't you even going to guess?"

"No."

He was rewarded with a look of mild disappointment. Get used to it, Father.

"Rasputin," his father prodded. "The night he was murdered. I was there; you looked right at me."

Alex remembered. The man they had called Charonsky. He showed up outside after the shooting. Stood out of the light and stared at him. He remembered a feeling of cold recognition, not really knowing who the man was but that somewhere he had known him. He'd been dressed all in black, his face almost buried behind coat, muffler, and hat.

"Yes. I remember."

His father nodded. "That was not a particularly good night." He sighed theatrically. "Yussapov is a fool. Normally I have nothing against homosexuality, but that man goes beyond all bounds of good taste. Well, he's far enough away now. Unfortunately, his distance from Petrograd is what's going to save his life in the near future."

"When the Revolution comes."

"Yes, when the Revolution comes. Actually it's virtually upon us, isn't it?"

"You know it is. Tell me something," Alex prodded, "you said you were expecting me. Why?"

"I paid more attention to your growing up than you give me credit for. I understood your childhood dreams, even though your mother didn't. You see, I recognized them for what they really were. No one else would have."

"You were able to do this"—he gestured around them— "even then?"

"How do you think I wrote those marvelous books?" His smile was meant to be self-deprecating, but it came out self-important.

Of course. He should have realized it. The only excuse he could think of was that he was so close to the facts that he hadn't made the connection. The forest for the trees.

"Did Mother know?" He thought about it. "Or Surrey?"

"Your mother didn't, I'm sure of that. Surrey?" He shrugged his shoulders. "Surrey knew.

"Would you like some lunch?" his father asked.

Alex thought about it, expecting his stomach to shout out its assent. He was extremely reluctant to accept anything until he found out what was going on, but on the other hand . . . Prison had reduced him to questioning all acts of kindness, but it had also taught him to do anything you had to do to make yourself stronger.

"Yes."

His father got up from the table and went to the door. Alex took the opportunity to study the man as he gave instructions to the guard outside. His father's Russian was just as good as his own and it hadn't been one of the languages he knew. The ability to speak and understand must be part of the time-shift effect.

Physically, he looked much the same as he remembered him. Tall, good posture, a few pounds heavier, and more flush in the cheeks, but it only made him look healthy, even though it was probably a by-product of a too rich diet and too much alcohol. The same mane of silver movie-star hair. The news photographers always loved that hair. The man was definitely older, but he looked in excellent shape. The black suit he wore—he'd always favored black—was beautifully cut, obviously tailored. Wherever he had spent the intervening years, he had used them to good advantage. At least personally.

"Have you been in Russia all this time? I mean since you disappeared?"

His father sat back down.

"No." No explanation.

Alex let it go. It didn't really matter; what was important was what happened now.

Except for one thing.

"Vassili," Alex said. "My friend. Did you have anything to do with him being shot?" It had been three days. He still felt the muffled sound of the shot, saw the old man crumple to the ground.

For the first time Alex saw his father hesitate. "The old man. No, I had nothing to do with it."

"At least not directly," Alex interjected.

His father looked at him intently. "I got back to Petrograd several days ago. When I went over the files, I found that you were here. And that they'd put the old man in with you. They thought you'd break after they killed the old man. Then they would kill you."

"But what did they want?" It was something that Alex had never been able to figure out.

His father sighed. "Earlier on I called you a fool, Alex. I spoke harshly, but sometimes I wonder . . . Well, anyway, just look at it. You show up in a country that's involved in a major war with no papers of any kind, no money, no contacts, nothing. Then you have a meeting with the president of

193

one of the major banking firms in the city. Can you follow me so far?''

"Even I worked it out to that point. But why the heavy treatment? I can see them questioning me, but why the water treatment; why kill Vassili? It was too much of a reaction. It just doesn't make any sense?''

"First of all, Alex, don't expect things to make any sense. It's the first mistake you made and you're continuing to make it. It's the professional historian in you. But then you always were a methodical child.

"Secondly . . .'' He opened the drawer on his side of the table and took out Alex's file. He opened it up and lifted the stack of papers. And took out the child's notebook Alex wrote in when he had first arrived. He held it up, waited silently.

Alex suppressed a groan. Stupid. He'd forgotten all about it. The notes he'd put down, trying to come up with a piece of information to sell. He'd never considered that someone else might see them. There were a lot of things he hadn't considered. Because of them a man was dead.

"Never underestimate anyone. Just because you have information that others don't have doesn't make you any smarter than the people you are dealing with. As soon as I got back and found you were here, I had Litenov transferred. He understood that you possessed information that could be valuable. In the notebook were several predictions that came true: Mata Hari and the Zimmerman telegram. It followed that if he could break you, he could get other information just as valuable. He killed the old man to frighten you, to get you to talk. The old man was nothing to him, a bug to be stepped on.'' He shook his head pityingly. "You're still a child, Alex. Don't play with the adults until you grow up. You're dangerous.''

Alex didn't let it touch him. Besides, there was truth in it. The door opened and one of the guards brought in a tray with food.

It made sense. He'd been stupid; there were extenuating circumstances, but it had been his own fault. And a man had died because of it. Litenov had killed Vassili, but he himself had set it in motion.

The food steamed. As usual, his stomach had no conscience, no shame. He was hungry; the nearness of real food made his head swim.

Vassili, he prayed to himself, if you're out there, hear this: I take responsibility. I will avenge this death the best way I can. I am sorry.

There was nothing else in him, nothing else he could do. He accepted the death of the old man. He would carry it for the rest of his life.

He found the food to be the original ingredients of his standard prison meal. The soup was rich and thick, chunks of fish floating among the thickets of cabbage. Cabbage; he loved cabbage, food of the gods. The broth was hot, by far the hottest physical thing he'd touched since he'd been imprisoned. His senses expanded under the bombardment; steam from the bowl of soup brought tears to his eyes, the complex tastes conjuring up images and colors. He was the blind man after the operation, the deaf man made to hear.

He looked at his father. The man was watching him with a look of disgust. Alex put down the now empty bowl. He wiped his face on his sleeve.

"Incarceration seems to have robbed you of your manners," his father said.

Alex almost laughed. His father was looking at him with disgust. So what? At one time such a look would have twisted him into an uncertain knot. Now it was too small a thing to bother with. There was no danger in it. It was dismissed.

"Would you like more to eat?" his father asked, not really concerned. "Perhaps you're still hungry?"

Alex laughed. "I've been hungry for the last month. That was enough. For now." His stomach protested that decision, but Alex ignored it.

"What do you want with me?" Alex asked.

His father looked puzzled. "Want with you? What do you mean?"

Alex waved his hand. "Let's cut the bullshit, Father. You were never interested in my welfare in the past, why would you be now? You need me for something; otherwise you wouldn't have had me brought here." He held up his hand. "Don't embarrass us both by denying it. You said that you run this place, that you were expecting me. Here I am. Now, what do you want?''

His father studied him. Alex could see a reassessment taking place. His father's expressions had never been particularly guarded; the man had never cared what people thought enough to hide what he was thinking. Now he was having to come to decisions that were being forced on him. It was not a position he was used to or cared for.

"Cut the bullshit," his father repeated. "Charming expression. All right." He leaned forward, resting his arms on the desk. He had assumed his sincere expression.

"I'm going to offer you a deal, Alex."

"One that I can't refuse?"

His father looked puzzled.

"Go on," Alex said. "Just a line from a movie you wouldn't have seen."

His father nodded. "Yes. A deal that any sane man would not refuse. "I'm offering you Russia." He spread his arms. "As big a slice of it as you want. We're going to change things, change the course of history. You know what's going to happen. In a few short years this country is going to be under the control of one of the greatest tyrants that ever lived. The people will be ground down, subjugated to the will of the state. Once the Communists get set up here, they'll export their brand of terrorism all over the world. You know that. This is a chance to stop it before it ever gets started. Think of what it would mean."

"And we'll be the dictators?" Alex asked. "You'll be the big dictator and I'll be the vice-dictator? Kings, emperors, monarchs?"

"Don't act like a fool," his father said, irritated. "And don't mistake me for one either. I've already told you, the wise man stands behind the throne. He doesn't sit in it when he can get someone else to do that part. We stay in the background, manipulate events. We can change things."

Alex could see it. That was the bad part. The Revolution itself was not the problem; it was what would happen after. His father was right; Stalin was a monster. Stop the Bolsheviks, stop Lenin, stop Stalin; who knows what might happen?

No. And that's the problem: Who knows what might happen. Who's to say that it might not be worse? This was a point he had decided when it all began. Change nothing. History was not something to be tinkered with like a broken lawnmower. Besides which, the vision of his father as the power behind the throne was not a comforting one.

"What makes you think that you can change things?" Alex asked. That was probably the first question that needed to be cleared up. "You've been gone a long time; is that what you've been doing? Running around the world manipulating events for fun and profit?"

"Do I hear a note of disapproval in your voice? 'How sharper than a serpent's tooth it is to have a thankless child.' Speaking of profit, how are my books doing? Or did you give away all the money you must have inherited?"

Alex felt himself flush. He could see the triumph in his father's eyes, aware that he had made a hit.

"Ahh," his father said, "it looks as if you didn't give away the money. It was a tidy sum, wasn't it, Alex?"

"Yes," Alex said stiffly. "The books still sell; you needn't worry about your reputation. Charles Ames Balfour still lives in the minds of college students everywhere. Your books are on the required reading list."

His father nodded happily. "Now let us return to my proposal. Oh, by the way, back in your time, do you have someone waiting for you? Are you married? Family?"

It was Alex's turn to be puzzled. Where was the danger here? "I'm not married. Never have been." He could see no harm in it. "There is someone there." He wouldn't say her name. Molly. He didn't want his father to have any additional weapons.

His father nodded again. "Good, good. Now, as to the proposal. I'll need help, Alex. It's going to be a big job."

"Changing the course of history would be," Alex said sarcastically.

His father ignored the sarcasm or didn't notice it. "Your part in it can be as big as you want. Since you seem to be such a moral human being, you can do it for the good of Russians now and in the future. The millions murdered by Stalin will not die."

"You never answered my question. How do you know you can change things?"

"How do you know you can't? Our simply being here has

197

got to be changing things. All we're doing is increasing the size of the change."

"I'll say. Stopping the Bolsheviks is quite an undertaking. But why don't you find someone from this time to help you? Why bother with me? Why would you even think I'd want to help you?"

His father looked vaguely uncomfortable.

"There are difficulties," his father said vaguely. After a moment he decided to expand on it. "One of the problems is that working with people of their own time is difficult. It's possible to profit from things that will happen. Prediction, especially when it's accurate, is always a precious commodity. But a certain difficulty arises when you directly try to influence events using the principals involved. It's as if they're trapped by their particular time, unable to do anything out of synch. You can suggest, but short of the most violent methods, as I said, it is difficult."

"And you, of course, are above violent methods."

His father's gaze did not waver. "Not at all. In fact, I'm sure that we're going to have to be prepared to go the limit. If it bothers you, you can remember the millions who'll be saved by our actions."

"It does bother me," Alex said.

His father made a placating gesture. "That's nothing to worry about yet. I have other plans for you. You'll not be killing people; you'll be saving them. That should appeal to you."

He decided to play it out. Knowing what his father had in mind would be more useful than simply refusing outright. Besides, his first priority was getting out of prison. He would go along with things at least that far.

"All right, I'll bite. What do you have planned for me? What's my part in all of it?"

"Simple, my dear Alex." His father smiled. "You're going to rescue the Tsar."

Chapter 26

THE DOOR OF THE CELL SLAMMED OPEN. ALEX ROLLED OFF THE bunk onto the floor and came up in a crouch. He could hear men running, shouting, the jangle of heavy keys, doors being thrown open. A figure appeared in the open doorway.

The man was holding a rifle. His heavy greatcoat was tightly belted, making the coat flare at the bottom. He was wearing a black sheepskin hat. He was not a guard.

The man glanced up and down the hall. Other men ran by.

"Quickly, comrade. Gather your possessions together."

"What's going on?" Alex asked.

The man smiled and drew himself up. "You are free. The workers have occupied the prison. Long live the Revolution!"

The man turned at a shout from the end of the hall. He glanced once at Alex, then ran off. The sounds of men moved further away.

Alex looked around the cell. Gather his possessions together? He was wearing his possessions. He stepped to the door and looked up and down the hall. The doors to the other cells were open. He saw no other prisoners. It seemed that the cavalry had arrived.

It was the day after his father had sent him back to his cell to mull over the plan. Alex had remained carefully noncommitted. Not that he was going to throw in his lot with his father and his mad scheme. The man sounded like a lunatic movie scientist: "Join me! Together we will rule the World." Sound track: insane laughter.

But it had to be played correctly. He had no doubt that his father would leave him right where he was if he refused to go along with the plan. Or worse.

But history had taken a hand. The Revolution was upon them. And it seemed that the prison was an early victory.

He walked out into the hall, resisting the urge to look around one more time. It was like leaving a motel: Have we left anything? Check all the drawers.

Alex walked down the long passageways, heading generally in the direction of the sound of activity. Another man, actually more a boy, rushed by, carrying a rifle. He looked like a high-school student suddenly assigned the task of carrying a very heavy rifle. He was taking his job seriously. He did not even glance at Alex.

He came to the administration area of the prison. There were men milling about, obviously prisoners. Some of them had goofy smiles glued to their faces; some looked worried; some just sat on the floor, leaning against the wall. None of them looked normal. He wondered how he looked?

"Excuse me," he said to one of the smilers, "what's the procedure? How do we get out?"

"Long live the Revolution!" the man said to him in a stagey voice. He glanced around, but no one was paying any attention to them. "There are men you need to see first," he said in a more normal tone. "They've taken over the old offices. They ask you some questions and then they turn you loose. At least that's what I've been told."

"Where are these men?"

The man waved down the hall. "In the old offices." He pulled Alex to one side and lowered his voice. "Call them comrade. And say things like 'Long Live the Revolution.' They like that. And for god's sake, tell them you're in here for political crimes." Prison advice. Us against everybody else. There are, in the end, two types of people: us and them. Stick together.

"Why aren't you getting out of here?" Alex asked. He

looked around at all the other men just sitting against the walls. Why were all of them just hanging around?

"I will, I will," the man said quickly. "We all will." The loony smile was back in place. "Just getting my story ready. Got to have a story."

Alex realized that the prisoners were afraid to leave. Bad as it was, the prison was at least familiar. Why jump into something new? There are worse things than a stone cell and two crummy meals a day.

Alex pushed past the men and glanced through the first doorway. A ransacked office; file cabinets torn open, a desk toppled. The next office was in the process of being pillaged. Two men with guns were turning over the furniture and laughing. They looked briefly at Alex and went back to their work.

He eventually found the offices where saner-looking prisoners were being processed out by vaguely official-looking men. Alex got in a line that shuffled slowly forward. When it was his turn, he walked into the office and sat in a chair just like the one he had sat in for all his interrogations. But the man behind the desk was not an interrogator. It was not his father.

It was Maxwell Surrey.

After the initial shock, his brain began to put an explanation together. He knew that Surrey had been in Russia during the Revolution. He'd never talked much about it and this was probably why. Good historians were not supposed to take part in historical events.

He sat in the chair while Surrey got out fresh paper and began writing. Alex hadn't been one hundred percent sure until he spoke. He was so young. College age, smooth-faced, fresh-looking, with high color in his cheeks. The difference between this Surrey and the one he'd seen a few months ago was amazing. But the similarities were even more astounding. It was the difference between the dried-out locust shell left on the trunk of a tree and the vigorous buzzing insect perched among the leaves, totally different and at the same time hauntingly alike. The features were all there, the curly bush of hair, the sad eyes that in youth were simply large. The old Surrey was an echo of this one, a dried-out version, the skin of the snake, shed and left behind.

201

"Name?" Surrey asked.

Hey, you know me, Alex wanted to shout.

"Alexander Balfour."

Surrey looked at him curiously. "A foreigner. What nationality?"

"American." Alex saw Surrey's eyes light up.

"Hey, so am I." He held out his hand. They shook. "I'm doing graduate work here. Russian history."

Alex laughed. "This is graduate work?" he asked, gesturing to the walls around them.

Surrey smiled and then looked serious. "This revolution was inevitable. I couldn't just stand by and watch; you have to be involved."

"Isn't that violating the historian's creed of objectivity?" It gave him pleasure to tweak this young, eager Surrey.

Surrey waved the question away. "Those days are over, at least for me. I think it's an historian's duty to involve himself in the culture. That way you have a real basis to study it."

Good God, he's young, Alex thought.

Surrey got back to business. "Length of incarceration?"

"Six weeks, two months? I'm not sure."

Surrey looked at him sympathetically and nodded. "Nature of crime?"

"Political. I was brought in by the Okhrana. Never really arrested. They've been interrogating me, but nothing ever came of it. I'm also an historian. I'm here researching a book." The lie came easily. He'd told it enough times to make it convincing. At least on the surface. "They thought I was a spy of some sort."

Surrey nodded. "They thought everyone was a spy. But those days are over now. The People are in control. Or at least they will be soon. There are still some hold-outs, but they can't stop us." He wrote some information on the sheet of paper in front of him.

"I guess that's everything," Surrey said. "We're trying to keep some sort of records, but there isn't time for much. You can go now."

Alex sat for a moment, unsure exactly where he would go.

"Look," Surrey said, sensing the problem. "You don't

have to worry about them picking you up again. They're on the run; they really are. Is there anything they took from you that you need to get back? There's not much hope of finding things, but we can try."

Alex tried to remember the day they had brought him in. "They took my papers and my money. All of it." Might as well take care of the lack of papers problem right now.

Surrey smiled. "The money's no problem." He opened one of the drawers and took out a wad of rubles. He tossed them on the desk. "Money is the one thing they seem to have a surplus of around here. They robbed everyone they brought in. Help yourself. Courtesy of the Revolution. The papers?" He shrugged. "They're probably here somewhere, but there's no time to look."

Alex picked up the money and stuffed it into his pockets. He needed new clothes, food, all the necessities he'd been deprived of. All Power to the People, he thought.

"Anything I should know about the outside before I go?" he asked.

Surrey frowned. "Just watch yourself. There's not much shooting yet, but there probably will be. A lot of soldiers are on our side, but there's always the Cossacks. Look, I've got an idea. Why don't you meet me this evening. I've got a lot to do here, but I'm not going to miss things just for some clerical work. Go to the Duma"—he stopped, seeing the blank look on Alex's face—"The Tauride Palace; we've taken it over. Wait in the reception hall right inside. I'll try to be there around eight." He stopped, looking a bit embarrassed. "I haven't talked to another American in weeks. You get so you need to speak English, see someone from home. You understand?"

Alex nodded. "Yeah, I understand. I'll meet you there."

The solid glare of the light stopped him. He blinked away tears. It was like walking into a solid mass, a glassy whiteness reflecting from the snow. It felt as if he'd just walked out of the movies after a month-long matinee.

He stood beyond the prison walls in his old overcoat, waiting for his eyes to adjust. He had an overpowering urge to take off running, but he pushed it back. The only guards at the gates were young revolutionaries who watched him nervously as he waited, as if they were afraid he was going to turn and demand that they throw down their rifles and surrender. Not exactly seasoned troops.

The trams were running. The snow had been cleaned from the tracks. One clanged by, bright red, and stopped further down the street. Destinations were posted on boards that hung from the sides.

Finland Station. Why not? A place to start.

The pawnbroker answered the door the same way he had the first time Alex had come, peering anxiously around the edge of the partial opening. He recognized Alex, or at least he nodded his head as if he did, and let him in.

"Size 7¼ hat, one overcoat, one shirt, pants, and pair of shoes. Right?" His eyes widened as he looked Alex over. "And you're still wearing them? Pardon me, sir, but have you even removed them since you left that night? Sorry, that is none of my business."

"One watch, one extremely intricate pocketknife. You still have them?" He was aware of what he looked like. And smelled like. And felt like. First things first.

The pawnbroker nodded. "Of course, who would I sell them to? The Provisional Government? The Workers and Military Committee?" A sudden look of fear crossed over the man's face. "No offense? You are a revolutionary?" He gestured toward Alex. "Long Live the Revolution?" He said it in such a tentative manner that Alex had to laugh.

"Don't worry; I just came for my knife and my watch. And I need some other things. A decent pair of boots. Underwear if you've got it. A heavier coat."

The pawnbroker nodded, bobbing his head as he figured costs and sizes in his head. He scuttled out of the room and down the long hall.

There was a mirror on the wall. Alex hesitated, suddenly afraid, then shrugged and walked over to it.

The difference was staggering. He had to touch his face to make sure it was him. Who else would it be?

Some old fart with a beard. A wino in a greasy, once white shirt. A hippy with long, tangled hair. Man of the mountain. Old man Balfour. He turned away.

"How did you recognize me?" Alex asked as the pawnbroker bustled back into the room, his arms full.

"You? I didn't. I recognized the clothing. My inventory is up here." He tapped his head and winked. "The goods I never forget. People, yes; the goods, no. Here." He handed Alex the pile of clothes. "Try these on. They'll fit, of course; the pawnbroker never forgets a size. But try them on for your own satisfaction." He wrinkled his nose unconsciously. "Pants, shirts? You don't need?"

"I have others," Alex said shortly. He stripped off his filthy overcoat and dropped it on the floor. He kicked off his shoes.

The clothes fit. Just like the man said. He left his old ones behind, still on the floor. He slipped the watch and the knife into his pocket. He gave the pawnbroker a batch of rubles. The old man took them eagerly, but there was a sadness in his tone of voice as he let Alex out the door.

"The knife," he began, "I had hoped . . ."

"Yeah, I know," Alex said. He remembered the greed he'd seen in the pawnbroker's eyes when he'd pawned it. When was that? Long, long ago. "But it's a special knife."

"I agree," the pawnbroker said.

"No, not that way. Special to me. It's got a lot of sentimental value."

The pawnbroker shrugged and nodded. Sentimental value he had never understood. Rubles he understood.

The *dvornik* tried to block his way.

"Hey! Where do you think you're going?" the man demanded. He had both hands on his hips. He stood in the center of the hallway inside the door.

"To my room," Alex said, staring at the man. This was the guy who had turned him in to the police.

"Alex Balfour," Alex said. "You remember?" The man moved hesitantly out of the way. "The room's still there, isn't it? You didn't get rid of my stuff, did you?"

"No, no. The room is still there. I'll have my wife bring your things. You have money for the rent? You're behind."

Alex leveled the stare again and saw the man shrink back. He pulled a couple of rubles out of his pocket and dropped them on the floor. "I want a hot bath. Tea after." He mounted the stairs. Around him he could feel doors to various rooms being cracked as the occupants peeked out at the commotion. He didn't look around.

The tub was made of tin. The sort of tub you'd see a cowboy taking a bath in. He had to sit with his knees up. He blinked back tears of joy as he eased down further. He felt the hot water lap at his chin. He had never in his entire life felt anything like this. Once, in college, he'd gone to bed with two women at the same time. That had been great, one of life's treasured memories. It didn't hold a candle to this.

He stood before the mirror in his room, examining his body. It was changed, thinner than it had ever been before, muscles sharply defined where once there had been a civilized layer of fat. He was angular, stripped down, reduced to only those parts necessary to keep the unit functioning.

There was a knock at the door. He pulled on his new overcoat to cover his nakedness.

"Come in."

The landlady couldn't take her eyes off him as she handed him his bundle of clothes. She set the teapot on the table. "I ironed your shirt," she said.

All of a sudden I'm getting respect. He nodded, taking the bundle from her. The shirt on top was still warm from the iron.

"I want a pair of scissors." She gave a tiny curtsey and bobbed her head. "And I want you to pack up everything in Vassili Vassiliovitch's room. Bring it here."

Her eyes widened. "Vassili Vassiliovitch?" she asked. "He won't be coming . . ."

"Back. That's right. He's dead."

"But . . . we didn't know. I mean, if he's really gone, do his things belong to you? Surely you can see . . ."

He waved a hand to shut her up, tired of the quick greed he saw in her eyes. "I don't want to hear it," he said, his voice flat and uncompromising. "Bring it. I'll give you money; just do it. Now leave me alone." He stopped her as she opened the door. "Wake me at six o'clock. Bring me something to eat then." He turned away, dismissing her.

He pulled on his new underwear, which turned out to be a pair of long johns. He wondered if jockey shorts had been invented yet. Evidently not in Russia. He put on his own shirt and his blue jeans. They were too big for him now, but the familiar feel of the denim and the soft worn cotton was wonderful. He held off for another few minutes, savoring the feel of cleanliness as he sipped his tea. He never knew that being clean had its own feel, as if his skin had been stripped of a layer of cells and dirt that kept the air out. He could feel the touch of the clothing on every inch of his body, the nerves alive and suddenly sensitive after a month's enforced hibernation.

He put down the teacup and lay on the bed. It squeaked under him. The softness of the mattress was amazing. It gathered around him, holding him lightly, giving when he moved, clinging and yet yielding. He sighed. He remembered the two naked girls in his bed. That was nothing.

He slept.

Chapter 27

IN THE EIGHTEENTH CENTURY, CATHERINE THE GREAT PRESENTED the Tauride Palace to her favorite, Prince Potemkin. The huge old palace possessed two wings. Under the Tsar Nicholas, the two wings had evolved into the meeting rooms of the main elements of the government. One was the chamber where the Duma met, presided and watched over by a huge full-length portrait of Nicholas himself; the other, known as the Catherine Hall, was used as the budget committee room of the Duma. This building, these two rooms, were to become the heart and mind of the Revolution.

It was dark by the time Alex arrived at the palace. The large square in front was filled with soldiers and workers. Groups would form and grow, then break up and reform, constantly moving, a colony of cells multiplying and replicating. Fires, built haphazardly and fueled with broken-up carts and piles of papers liberated from various government buildings, flickered brightly, throwing odd shadows and highlights against the moving screen of men and the high portico of the palace. Messengers from inside fed the crowd the news from those hammering out the policies of the new government.

Alex made his way through the mass of men to the entrance. Inside the columned portico he was confronted by a guard with the now standard rifle with fixed bayonet and a red arm band. He could see into the rotunda beyond, where scores of soldiers and others stood in only slightly smaller accumulations than the men outside.

"I'm sorry, comrade," the guard said, "only those on official business allowed."

Alex glanced around as much of the room as he could see, but Surrey wasn't in evidence. If he had to wait outside, they'd never find each other.

"All Power to the People," Alex said, raising his fist in a black-power salute. "We Shall Overcome," he added. The guard hesitated. Alex suppressed a wild urge to break into a few verses of the song to establish his credentials.

"State your business," the guard said.

"I am a member of the American Delegation. We are meeting here to discuss consolidation between your workers' party and our own. We are speaking of the International, comrade; there can be no delays."

The guard still hesitated, but the words sounded right; Alex could see the vacillation in the man's eyes. He almost threw in another raised fist and a Right On, but he decided not to push his luck.

The man finally nodded and stepped back to let him pass. "Long Live the Revolution," the guard said.

"Right on."

He marched past the man, the words singing in his head, Powuuh to the People, powuuh to the people; right on. Oh, yeahhh.

He stood in the center of the crowd, looking around for Surrey. He felt like a stranger at someone else's cocktail party. All he needed was a drink in his hand. He hung around the edges of several of the groups, listening to the rumors generate and fly around the room like baby birds testing their wings.

"They say the Empress and the royal family have all been murdered. . . ."

"The Tsar has pulled the army back from the front and is marching on us. They will be here in two days. . . ."

"Protopopov has been killed. . . ."

"Kornilov has shot himself. . . ."

"The Tsar is coming. . . ."

"Alex!"

Someone shook his arm. Surrey.

"What a madhouse," Surrey said, pulling him to the side of the room. "You'll never believe what's going on upstairs.

"The Duma has taken over and formed a Provisional Government." A couple of men nearby glanced at them, listening to hear if Surrey had anything new. He lowered his voice. "Fat old Rodzianko is the chairman; the rest of the Progressive Bloc is behind him. The Mensheviks didn't want any part of it, so they and the Social Democrats and the Social Revolutionaries put out a call to the factories and the soldiers for representatives. They're all upstairs now. They've taken over the Catherine Hall and are having nothing to do with the Provisional Government. They call themselves the Executive Committee of the Soviet. The Ex Com. God, what a paper I'm going to write about all of this." He kept glancing around the room, searching for new faces. "Maybe we could collaborate on something," he went on. "Maybe do a book."

Alex almost laughed. That would be a switch. Alex Balfour, the son, writes a book with Maxwell Surrey, who later becomes Charles Balfour's editor and the son's teacher.

"Maybe," he agreed mildly. "Can we go watch some of the meeting?"

"Sure," Surrey said. "The trick here is to act like you belong wherever you're going. Nobody knows what anybody else is doing. There's absolutely no one in charge of anything. Whenever a problem comes up, they form a committee to take care of it."

"I noticed that security was a little confused. I invented an American Delegation."

"Great. Now there's two of us in the delegation. We can form a couple of committees. Let's go."

Alex followed him to the wide marble staircase that went to the second floor.

"American Delegation," Surrey said to the two guards at the bottom of the steps. "Make way for the American Delegation."

The guards saluted and stepped aside. They marched up the stairs in step, trying to look important. No one paid any attention.

Alex decided that the Ex Com would be more interesting than the Duma. There would have been some fascination in watching the minions of the old Imperial government stumble through the last stages of decay, but the Ex Com was to become the real power. At least until the Bolsheviks and Lenin took control.

The Catherine Hall looked much like the United States Senate in Washington. Individual desks laid out in a semicircle around a raised stage where the chairman and other officials sat.

Here the seventy-five or so committee members, most still wearing their heavy coats, lounged at various desks, some with their feet up, most of them smoking and putting the butts out on the marble floor. Rifles leaned casually against desks and walls. Scattered around the room were groups of other men talking and arguing.

A group of soldiers in the back of the room squatted around a small fire they had built on the floor. They seemed to be brewing tea.

The air was filled with cigarette smoke. The noise level made normal conversation almost impossible. A soldier with his hat pushed back on his head was reading from a sheet of paper.

"Also joining their Volinsk Regiment comrades in our glorious revolution are the following units: The Preobrazhensky Regiment and the Litovsky Regiment." After each name, those of the crowd who were listening would cheer. "The Semenovsky, the Ismailovsky, and also the Oranienbaum machine-gun regiment. The Petrogradsky Regiment, the Sixth Engineer Battalion, and the First Reserve Infantry Regiment. This last Regiment has taken the added precaution of executing all of its officers." This got the loudest cheer. "No news yet on the Cossacks, except that they have remained neutral. At this point approximately 60,000 of the soldiers on duty in Petrograd have joined the Revolution." Even the tea-brewers stopped their talking to cheer this news.

It sounded a lot like election night coverage of any major national election. Except here, as in all classic revolutions, the participants were voting with bullets rather than ballots.

"What about the Bolsheviks?" Alex asked Surrey. He had to shout to be heard above the din.

Surrey shook his head. "There are none," he shouted

211

back. "Or at least not many. There never have been. All the leaders are in exile. Have you heard of Lenin?"

Alex nodded. Yes, indeed.

"He's the leader. He's in Switzerland."

"How about Stalin?" Alex shouted.

"Never heard of him," Surrey said with a shrug.

Alex recognized a tall, thin man at the front of the room. Karensky. The man of the hour. He was talking to two others. Soon Karensky would take control of both the Ex Com and the Duma.

"Comrades," Karensky pleaded, holding both hands in the air, trying to get the attention of the men. "Comrades, we have a proclamation that needs your attention. It has been decided that we must arm at least ten percent of the workers to replace the police. There are many arrests to be made." The crowd began to pay attention. There was a spattering of applause at the mention of arrests. "The Red guards have responded heroically but we must bolster the ranks. It is only a matter of time until the Tsar sends his generals to attack. Now the workers must take up the gun to keep order and to arrest the autocrats."

"Where are these arms to come from?" a man near the back of the room shouted to the speaker. "Should we ask the Tsar to supply them?" There was general laughter.

"We will ask the Tsar for nothing!" The laughter stopped. "Never again. We will seize the rifles. We need men to attack the Armory. There are plenty of guns for us there. We will expropriate them."

"I'll go!" a man in a soldier's uniform shouted, jumping to his feet. "The men of my regiment and any others who care to join us will do the job. Who's with me?" He looked around the room. He was answered with a chorus of assent. He jammed his hat on his head and stomped out of the room without looking back. Many of the others gathered up their gear and followed along.

"Well," Surrey said, smiling at Alex, "shall we join the Revolution?"

Alex could feel his pulse begin to speed up. "What the hell, I never attacked an armory before."

They followed the others out of the room.

The Liteiny Bridge had long been the focal point of the

workers' demonstrations. It led directly into the heart of Petrograd from the Vyborg Distirct, the industrial center of the town and where most of the workers lived. Consequently, huge crowds of people swept back and forth across the bridge, responding to rumors and realities as they gathered at whatever target had been selected for takeover. Few of them were armed, but often simply the sheer size of the crowds was enough to convince those defending the takeover site that it was definitely not worth it. After the defenders filed out and were led away, the crowds would rush in and light fires.

As they crossed the bridge, riding in one of a number of commandeered trams, Alex could see the flames. The night sky glowed a dull orange.

"Police stations and the Law buildings," Surrey said. "I don't imagine you're sorry to see them go."

"I was taken in by the Okhrana, not by the police. But you're right, more than six weeks in the Fortress has not endeared me to the power structure."

"The ex-power structure. Things are going to be different when this is over. There'll be real justice, equality."

It was difficult at times for Alex to keep in mind that none of these people were aware of what was going to happen. Except his father. He wondered briefly what had happened to him. And his mad plan for saving the Tsar. He felt around for some concern over his father, but he couldn't come up with any.

"How old are you, Max," he asked.

Surrey looked hard at him, trying to figure out the reason for the question. "Twenty-one," he answered. "I know I'm young compared to someone your age, but I've been here long enough to understand what's going on."

Someone my age? Ah, youth, Alex thought. He understood that Surrey probably saw him as something of a father figure, but it was hard to acknowledge it. The tram bell clanged. They slowed to work their way through a crowd of men carrying red banners and flags. The evening air was unseasonably warm. It was as if the fires and the excitement had generated enough heat to warm up the city. "Do you really think it can work? And if it does, last?" Alex asked.

213

"Of course. The Tsar will fight, but the army has had it. The soldiers are on our side, not his."

"I'll grant you that; what I mean is, do you think that the ideals will last? That power will remain in the hands of those who can fairly govern? Just because the people are able to seize power, does that automatically mean they are equipped to dispense justice? You're a historian; you must know the usual course of events after successful revolutions."

"But the ideas are so simple," Surrey said, frowning. "Justice and equality. How can you screw that up?"

Alex would have laughed if Surrey hadn't looked so earnest. Screw it up? It was going to end up more screwed up than this young man could ever imagine. For the first time he felt the burden of knowing, envied the conviction he saw in the other's eyes, the innocence of his question. Justice and Equality? He thought of Stalin, the Gulags, the future. He turned away without answering.

The bell clanged again and the tram ground to a halt. Across the wide street was the Arsenal. High, thick walls; elongated slits for the defenders to shoot from; a massive wooden door.

They walked to the cluster of men who stood directly across from the building. Alex wondered why the larger groups were remaining fairly far away until the barely heard crack of a rifle from the Arsenal answered his question. No one bothered to duck. Revolutionary macho.

The man who had led them out of the Ex Com meeting was at the center of the group.

"We talked to them on the telephone," the man was saying. "As near as we can tell, there's no one in there but a few officers and some Cadets. But they say they're not coming out."

"So let them stay," another man said. "This is an arsenal, right? The weak point is certainly not the front door. I could walk to Siberia and back before we could knock down the door. The weak point is the roof. Arsenals are designed to have little in the way of structure as far as the roof is concerned."

Surrey looked at Alex and raised his eyebrows in question.

"It's that way in case the place blows up," Alex said.

"It's traditional design. The explosion goes straight up rather than sideways."

"So why not drop a few shells through the roof and blow the whole bunch of them to Vladivostok?" someone asked.

"The idea," the man from the Ex Com explained patiently, "is not to blow up the building, it's to seize the contents. We're after rifles, not dead Cadets."

"The weak point," Surrey said loudly, "is not the door or the roof; it's the people inside." Another shot from the building froze the group as the bullet ricocheted off a nearby parapet. "They're already worried," Surrey went on. "You just need to scare them a little bit more."

"We could shoot at the door," one of the soldiers suggested.

"Grenades," another said. "Make a lot of noise. Boom."

"That's the idea," Surrey said. "Plant a few grenades under the door. Just to show them we're serious."

Alex felt like grabbing Surrey by the collar and dragging him away. He knew that Surrey would live; he was there in the future, but he still didn't want him getting hurt.

"Give me the grenades; I'll do it," Surrey offered.

Alex felt his heart sink. He could see Surrey's eyes shining with excitement. When you're twenty-one, the possibility of dying is extremely remote.

"Think of it as a contribution from the American Delegation to the Revolution," Surrey added.

"Give the American comrade the grenades and show him how to use them," the leader ordered. There was a shuffling in position as a soldier shouldered his way over to Surrey. The crowd thinned a bit. Alex watched as the soldier explained that all you had to do was twist the handle of the grenade a full revolution and then get the hell away from it. You had ten seconds until it blew up.

"Okay, okay, I got it," Surrey was saying. Alex could see him breathing heavily, his face a little unsure now that the actual job was on him. But determined to go ahead with it.

Was it possible that Surrey could die? What would happen then? The man was inextricably tied up in his own life. If he were not part of it, there would certainly be drastic changes. Surrey gave him an ironic look and started running toward the Arsenal before Alex could try to stop him.

Several shots came from the building. Chips of paving stone puffed up near Surrey as he ran. The defenders were decidedly more accurate at closer ranges.

Surrey made the safety of the door. The building projected out several feet around the door, making a sheltered area that could not be attacked from the rifles at the window. Serious design flaw, Alex thought. Come on, Max; drop the grenades and get back here.

"What's the American doing?" someone asked in disbelief as Surrey puttered around in the doorway.

"Come on, come on," another man muttered.

Alex watched as Surrey examined the door. All those inside had to do was open the door and shoot him. They knew he was there. But then, of course, the door would be open, something they were trying to avoid. Stalemate.

Surrey turned and looked at them, then went back to his examination.

"Jesus Christ," Alex said to no one in particular and started running. He heard the shots but couldn't tell how close they were. He was panting heavily when he ran up against the heavy door. He looked over at Surrey who was watching him with a small grin.

"What the hell are you doing?" Alex demanded.

"Look here," Surrey said, pulling him to the side of the door. Unconsciously he lowered his voice. "There's a regular-sized door in the big doors. And a little hatch in the smaller door."

Alex looked where Surrey traced the outline of a small hatch like the one in the door in his prison cell.

"So?" He was getting a little anxious. The thought that he could get killed without changing anything suddenly occurred to him.

"The smaller doors must have been put in so they wouldn't have to open the big ones every time someone came in. The little hatch would be to identify whoever was outside." Surrey said.

"If we can get them to open the little door, we can drop the grenade inside. That's bound to have a bigger effect than just leaning them up against the outside here."

"How the hell are you going to get them to open the door?"

216

Surrey shrugged. "Let's just knock on it. They've got to be curious as to what's going on out here. Who knows, maybe they'll open it for a peek. They can always shoot us if they want. But if we time it right, it might work."

Alex sighed and looked back at the crowd of men across the street. They were waving their arms in come-here motions, but they were too far away to be heard.

"Okay," Alex said. It would be quicker to just try it than to stand around and argue. "Give me two of the grenades to put out here. You knock on the door. I'll wait fifteen seconds then twist the handles. If they haven't opened up by then, you drop your grenade and we'll get the hell out. If by any chance they do open it up, drop yours inside and run." He didn't think it would work, but it wouldn't hurt to try. Maybe it wouldn't hurt to try.

Surrey nodded and handed him the two grenades. They positioned themselves.

Alex flinched as Surrey knocked on the door with his grenade. The kid was crazy. This was a side to Surrey he'd never seen.

Nothing.

Surrey knocked again. Alex was at ten and counting.

Fifteen. Surrey saw him nod. Alex turned both of the handles and propped the grenades against the door. Surrey knocked again.

"No, Jesus Christ," Alex hissed. "Get the hell out of here."

He grabbed Surrey's coat and started to pull him away.

The little door made a small scraping noise. Surrey twisted the handle. Alex was breathing like a racehorse. He could feel his heart pounding.

The door opened six inches and Surrey dropped the grenade inside.

Alex grabbed his arm and pulled him to the side of the building just as the two grenades outside went off. The shock knocked them down, deafening them. They felt rather than heard the third thump. Alex looked up and saw the men from across the street, rifles raised, running toward them. Smoke billowed from the doorway.

The small door was lying in the street where it had been blown off. Surrey rolled over and smiled at him.

"I guess the weak point was not the door but the door within the door."

Alex stood up slowly and checked himself for injuries.

"The weak point was not the door but whoever opened the damn thing. It's hard to believe anyone would be that stupid."

Surrey stood and dusted himself off. "I've been here almost a year," he said, "and one of the constants I've found is the unfailing curiosity of the Russian male. They can't help it; it's part of their famous nature. Like their capacity to shoulder any burden their government piles onto them. Their infinite sadness. Drunkenness."

"National attributes." Alex leaned against the wall and looked at Surrey to see if he was kidding him. He couldn't tell. Surrey's face was covered with soot and dirt. He looked like Al Jolson in blackface.

"You don't know a couple choruses of the song 'Mammy' do you?" Alex asked.

"Huh?"

"Nothing," Alex said, pushing away from the wall. "Let's get on with the Revolution."

Chapter 28

HE WENT INTO HIS ROOM AND LEANED THE LONG RIFLE AGAINST THE wall. The *dvornik* had come to the door cursing when Alex had banged to be let in. Everyone was in bed; this was no time to be out; the rules of the establishment, etc. etc.

The *dvornik* shut up when he saw the rifle.

Alex didn't bother turning on the light. The electricity had been turned off all over the city. The Revolution had taken over the power stations. Service would be resumed in the morning. Maybe.

They would get the electricity back on if they could find someone to run the power station. Workers, soldiers, and bureaucrats all over the city were abandoning their posts. When the revolutionaries had charged into the Armory, they had found the defenders to be eight boys, their ages fourteen to seventeen years, one with semi-serious wounds to the buttocks, sustained while running away from Surrey's dropped grenade. The boy had opened the small door thinking that the only person who would knock would be their much prayed-for reinforcements. So much for Surrey's romantic theory on the irrepressible curiosity of the Russian male.

He sat on the bed in the dark and took off his overcoat. The coat stank of smoke. After the rifles and ammunition had been removed from the Arsenal, several buildings had been set on fire by overzealous revolutionaries. Alex and Max had stayed to help put out the flames. The likelihood of an explosion from overlooked ordinance was high, but Alex had reached a plateau of physical and psychic invulnerability.

They'd made him take the rifle and some ammunition. He hadn't wanted it, felt stupid dragging it around. He had visions of accidentally shooting someone. But they had insisted. It had become a strange sort of social ritual. If you were a revolutionary, you carried a gun. Refusing was a social and political gaffe, like turning down an Eskimo's wife. He took the rifle.

He decided to light the kerosene lamp and try to clean up in the basin of water on the nightstand. He was almost afraid to look in the mirror. Between the explosion and the smoky fire he probably looked like Elmer Fudd after his own gun had gone off in his face. Take that, wabbit.

He lit the lamp.

"Good evening, Alex."

He whirled around, almost knocking over the lamp. His father was smiling at him from the overstuffed chair.

"I see you've been out playing with the other little boys. Shot any autocrats this evening?"

Alex kept his mouth shut until his heart slowed.

"Not yet," Alex said when he had control. "But then, the night's not over. How about yourself? Imprisoned any innocent bystanders? Put anyone up in front of the firing squad? I guess not. You guys have been voted out of office, haven't you?"

"Ah, gay repartee in the midst of the cataclysm. Thrust and parry, the very essence of civilization."

"Jesus Christ. Look, I'm tired. Don't you have better things to do?"

"Such as?"

"Such as flee for your life. Don't you remember? They're shooting guys like you."

"Yes, I remember my history. Believe me, I have prepared adequately for the present circumstances. I'll be gone by morning."

"Good."

A mock frown. "But, Alex, surely you wanted to have the opportunity to say good-bye to your father. Besides, we

220

never had an opportunity to discuss the proposition I made you. I still intend to go ahead with my end of it and I assumed you would go along. I need you, Alex. I don't have to have you, but it would make things easier for me.''

"What do you need me for?'' He rubbed his hand over his face. The night was beginning to catch up with him. Why was his father so persistent? He went to the basin of water and splashed some on his face. He dried himself with his thin towel.

"I already answered that question back in the Fortress. I need an assistant who is aware of all the nuances. You're new here; your history is fresh in your mind.'' He frowned. "You'll find that the longer you remain here, the more difficult it is to predict events. Mentally one tends to go native, as it were. The details get lost. Have you experienced what I'm talking about?''

Alex didn't answer. He had, in prison, but why admit it?

"Can you move back and forth at will?'' Alex asked. He would not give anything away, but he would trade.

His father sighed. He shrugged his shoulders. For the first time Alex realized that his father was dressed like an ordinary Russian. A disguise. Except his father's worker's outfit looked as if it had been tailored on Saville Row. No scratchy woolens or baggy pants for Dad.

"Yes, I can shift when I so desire,'' his father said.

Alex wondered if he were lying. He thought of his own headaches, never knowing when it would happen. Would he get better at it?

"Will you tell me how to do it?'' Alex asked bluntly.

His father laughed. "Really, Alex, you won't even answer my simplest questions and yet you expect me to give away all my secrets. No, I won't teach you how to do it. Perhaps if you join me in my proposition, I'll relent but until I know that you're really with me, there's no hope of it.

"I can teach you many things, Alex. Throw in your lot with me and we'll work together. This is a gift we have; don't waste it. All things will come to you, in time.''

Alex didn't smile at the pale play on words. "Just sign on the dotted line? Enlist? What's my job? Ah, yes, all I have to do is rescue the Tsar and all the other Romanovs out from under the noses of the entire Red army.''

His father waved in irritation. He reached in his blouse pocket and took out a thin flask.

"Brandy?" he asked, taking off the cap and handing it to Alex.

Alex took the flask. It was warm from his father's body. The thought repelled him, but at the same time the fumes drifting up from the opened flask drew his lips like the pull of an adulterer's kiss. It had been months since he had tasted any alcohol. He drank. The warm liquid seemed to burst into his mouth. He stifled a cough. It was wonderful. He handed it back to his father. He regretted the drink already, aware that it was the first step on the road to acceptance. He could take nothing.

"It won't be all that difficult," his father said. "As you know, the general rule around here is a state of modified chaos. I'll be leaving to go east where the White armies will soon be forming. I'll need to be in control, or at least I'll need to control someone who will be in control. History shows that the Whites almost won anyway. What they lacked was a real leader, someone they could rally behind, a spiritual figurehead. These people have had their Tsar for three hundred years. They're lost without their 'little father.' The Reds will have Lenin soon enough. We need the Tsar. With him alive we can win."

"And if I refuse?"

His father reached into his pocket and drew forth a pistol. He pointed it at Alex's midsection.

"Perhaps then I will kill you."

Alex made himself laugh. It was not easy. "What good will that do? I certainly can't help you if I'm dead."

"No. But you certainly can't harm me if you are." His father had assumed a look of peevish irritation. "A few days ago you charmingly suggested that we 'cut the bullshit.' " He carefully switched the gun and the flask in his hands and took a long drink, his eyes never leaving Alex's.

"It's been seventeen years I've been gone, Alex. I've forgotten you and your world long ago. I've learned to live"—he reflected for a moment—"to prosper in whatever time I'm in. You don't get what I've had by being squeamish."

Alex nodded. "You're right about one thing; killing your own son is definitely not being squeamish."

His father shrugged again and took another drink from the flask.

"Save your outrage; I'm beyond it, believe me. Now for the last time, are you with me or not?"

His first impulse was to just agree to it and then get away as soon as possible. But somehow he doubted that his father was stupid enough to let him get away. He would have some way to ensure his cooperation.

"Give me another drink," he said, reaching for the flask. His father lifted it to him. Alex grabbed the hand with the gun and held it against the arm of the chair. His father struggled for a second, but it was over before it had hardly begun. He cried out as Alex twisted the gun back against his fingers, forcing him to let go of it.

"You should never drink with your gun hand," Alex said, not bothering to keep the contempt out of his voice. "It makes you clumsy." He felt no victory in it. He wondered if his father was drunk. He couldn't tell, but then he never could.

For the first time his father appeared unsure. He looked smaller. His eyes were shifting back and forth from Alex to the door of the room.

The problem, Alex thought, is that a rat cannot understand that others do not share their own ratlike motivations. If my father is prepared to kill me, he will expect that I could just as easily kill him. This is to my advantage.

"Now, Father, let us have some answers. It is really true that you can direct your time movement?"

"Yes. I already told you so." His father's voice was petulant.

"You already told me, but you didn't have the force of truth aimed at your gut at the time. Can you teach me how to do it?"

"Maybe."

"No bullshit now."

"I don't know. Maybe I can. It's not that simple, not like throwing a switch and saying 'presto, I'm back in time.' "

Alex nodded. He didn't think that it would be simple; the whole process was too subjective for that.

"How far back have you gone?" Alex asked. He tried to picture his father watching a dinosaur.

"About a hundred years was the farthest. No cavemen stuff, if that's what you're getting at. It took a long time fo⁻ me to be able to direct it. I still don't understand why I'm— pardon me, we're—able to do it. I've often thought that it might not just be me. Now that you're here, it looks even more like others may be able to do it. Unless it's strictly genetic, inherent only in our family."

Alex thought about it, the possibility that there were other time shifters. His head hurt. He wiped his face again, suddenly feeling the weight of the last few days pressing down on him. He focused his attention on his father.

"I still want to know why you need me," Alex said. "No more lies." Now he was the interrogator.

"I've already answered that several times."

Alex cocked the pistol.

"All right, all right. I told you in the prison. You can only work with people in a limited way. You can take advantage of things, but you can't have people here change things. There's some built-in mechanism that makes them unable to do it. Change has to come from outside, from us. We're not part of their history, so only we can affect it. I need help; it's too much for one man."

"And taking advantage isn't enough for you? You have to actually change things?" Tired, tired. Head hurts.

His father stood up so suddenly that Alex almost pulled the trigger. He stepped back.

"Of course I have to change it. Why else are we here?" His father looked around the room as if it were full of people who would back him up. He stared at Alex. "You of all people know what's going to happen. Is what I'm suggesting so terrible? How do you know? Who appointed you guardian of the past?"

"Who appointed you God?" Alex snarled. It was too much. The pain. His father began to smile.

"Not so much fun, is it, Alex? Not now, anyway. Say hello to everyone for me. Tell them all about your adventures, about all the fun you've been having. What? They won't believe you?" He laughed. "I forgot, you can't tell them; they'll think you're mad. That's not much fun, is it? Keeping it to yourself, never being able to tell, no one believing." He waved. "Even your mother didn't believe me." He looked sad. "Though maybe she did at the end."

Alex dropped the gun. He could see through his hand.

The room tilted, began to swirl.

The last thing he saw was his father laughing, head thrown back. There was no sound, only the pain in his head.

Laughing.

Chapter 29

MOLLY WAS SITTING CURLED UP IN ALEX'S ARMCHAIR. THE TV WAS on, the sound turned down to a murmur, the drapes pulled against the streetlight outside. The living room was dark; a cave, lit only by the warm glow of the color television. She liked it this way. It had an ersatz coziness that almost passed for the real thing. She watched the television the way one would watch the moving flames of a campfire.

She'd brought over most of the things she needed, only going home to pick up more clothing. She slept here, ate here. She'd moved in with Alex, only Alex wasn't here.

Until now.

She saw the movement, felt a change in the still air of the room. The figure was shadowy at first, a rippling smudge of darkness that filled in over a few seconds. He was standing in the center of the room. She jammed her hand into her mouth to keep from screaming, watching as he stumbled and caught himself.

He was gaunt, bearded, with long, tangled hair. Blue jeans and work shirt; heavy, rough boots. His eyes were shining like the eyes of a holy man on the road to nirvana. Alex.

"Molly," he said, his voice rough, unnatural-sounding even to his own ears. The air was different here. Thicker. It stank. He put his hand to his forehead, pressing at the pain

226

that throbbed but had begun to recede. His mouth was dry. His head felt feverish. He had shifted, he knew that, knew it from the moment he'd seen the look of surprise and then the laughter on his father's face. Laugh, clown, laugh; the comedy is definitely not finished.

He had felt the conflict rise in him with the head pain; loss, gain, regret, hate, anger, relief, fear, uncertainty. He felt the rent like a wound.

He saw her begin to scream and catch herself.

"It's all right, Molly; it's me. Don't be afraid." He took a step toward her and saw her shrink back into the chair. He stopped.

"Alex?"

"Yes."

"Good God," she said, shaking her head. She stood up but did not approach. He could see the fear in her eyes. He walked to the floor lamp and turned it on.

He stepped back so the light was on his face. She said nothing, only stared.

He went to the small bathroom beneath the stairs. He drew in his breath as he snapped on the bright light over the mirror and looked at himself.

He was filthy. His face was marginally clean where he'd rinsed it with water, but the rest of him was covered with the dirt and smoke from the explosion and fire. The cleaner center of his face looked as if he had put on flesh-colored makeup, a pinkish island in a gray sea.

He touched his hair and his beard. Both were curly and matted. His cheeks were gaunt, cut by stern creases at both corners of his mouth. His eyes were flat and hard, distant, someone else's eyes. Was this person inside me all the time? Is there one like this inside everyone, waiting to surface when the outer covering is peeled away until it is not born, but revealed, shorn of the membrane? He felt her hand on his shoulder. He turned to her and saw that the fear was gone. Almost gone.

"Upstairs," she said. "I'll draw your bath."

He was floating. His eyes were closed. He slid forward and felt the water close over his head. Total immersion. I am bathed clean, Lord. I am new; I am saved. He surfaced.

227

Breathed the steam. Slid back down again and stayed until his brain told him to come up for air. He felt no need for it; he could stay forever, sleep in the wet heat, remain wrapped in the bosom of the deep. He surfaced, opened his eyes.

Molly sat on the edge of the toilet, watching him. He felt a surge of love, elemental, as if he had regressed to a level so primitive that all outside stimuli were reduced to the same intensity—touch, the feel of the water, love, the woman in the room with him.

He sat up and shook his head.

She dried him off. He shaved off the beard. She took him to bed. He lay on his back, stared at the ceiling. She touched him. His body was hard. She ran her hand down his stomach.

He turned to her and she had to keep from flinching from his holy man's eyes. He looked at her naked body. She remembered the first time he had looked at her in this room, in the mirror, looked at her with love.

This was different. If there was love, it was buried beneath need, eclipsed by a force that bore down upon her and carried her away. It was simple, or rather elemental, an act that had little to do with tenderness or caring or pleasure or any of the other tangential aspects that are part of making love. This was the pure essence, instinct. Need. And in the need, she found, entwined, hidden, love.

He had fallen asleep. She lay beneath him and listened to him breathe until she had to move. Although he was much thinner, his weight seemed more concentrated. She rolled him over, straining to move him. He slept on, unaware. She watched him. Occasionally she would put her hand on his chest to feel his heartbeat. He did not move.

Then he was watching her when she awoke. The bedroom was gray with early morning light. His eyes had changed. The holy man was gone.

"Good morning," she said.

He touched her cheek. Smiled.

"Which is the dream?" he asked.

He ate four eggs and a half a pound of bacon.

"There is no sauerkraut in the house, is there?" he asked.

228

"No." She looked at him, puzzled. She was frying more bacon. "I could go out and get some if you want it."

"No, no," he said quickly. "I'd just as soon never see another cabbage or cabbage product for the rest of my life. I just wanted to be sure that the house was cabbage-free."

"Hmmm," she said, turning off the gas. "I think I'm through playing cook for you. Maybe it's time you told me about it."

He put down his fork and looked at his now empty plate. "It'll take a while," he said.

She shrugged. "It's Saturday; we've got all weekend. There's plenty of food in the house."

He watched her wash her hands and dry them on the dish towel. She had pulled her long red hair back into a ponytail. The color of it still amazed him. He kept wanting to touch it.

"More coffee?" he asked. She picked up the pot and poured him a cup.

"I came through into a snowdrift very near a large railroad station." He took a drink of the coffee. It was hot and strong, the first he'd had in months. "It was cold. I had no coat. It was very strange. . . ."

Chapter 30

IT WAS AFTERNOON.

They walked; he talked.

The stuffineess of the house had begun to close in around him; so many things, objects, machines. He couldn't stop touching them, running his fingers along the edges, finding surprises: Did the knobs of the faucets always have those flowers engraved into the metal? When was the last time he had actually used his automatic orange juice squeezer? He was constantly distracted, so they went for a walk.

Outside, for a while, it was even worse. The sudden shift from winter to late summer; the freedom from heavy, usually damp, wool; the women wearing tank tops and tiny shorts; the streets crowded with laughing people; all of it vied for his attention—look at me, look at me—pulling him away from his story. They sat on a bench in Washington Square and he finished it. He soft-pedaled the bad parts, but he tried to tell her everything.

She told him about Surrey. It had been a stroke. The old man was alive, barely, in a coma. He hovered over death like a hummingbird over a flower. He had not spoken a word since the attack. Probably wouldn't. There was no real hope.

"Damn, I don't want him to die; he's the last link I

have—he's my family. I need to know if he knew me from then but kept it a secret all these years."

"He's very old."

"I know it, but that never seems to be much comfort when someone you love dies." He pushed it into the back of his mind. He would deal with the pain of it when it was time. "If Surrey knew all along that the little boy Alex would grow up to meet him as a young man in Russia," he went on, "then that means that time is cyclical, recurring. If he didn't know me from his own youth, then that means that my trip into the past has occurred only one time. Right now."

"It's all so complicated," Molly said, watching a man without a shirt selling drugs to a man in a three-piece suit.

He tried to explain it. It wasn't that it was so complicated, exactly; the problem was that it was so convoluted. Twisting and turning on itself like a live Mobious strip. It was a problem that was best not thought about directly but looked at obliquely, out of the corner of the eye.

"Try to think of it the way you think about particle physics," he began.

She laughed. "Oh, all right. That's a subject I dwell on quite a bit."

He looked at the sky. "That's the trouble with women; they never think about particle physics. No. Really." He went on, serious now, "Up until a few years ago we were taught that the universe was made up of atoms that were made up of little balls called nuclei, with other little balls, protons and neutrons, orbiting around like the planets orbit the sun. Very tidy. Then things got a lot more complicated as they started really taking the atom apart. You had particles that exhibited very unusual characteristics; quarks, gluons, and others that wouldn't fit into the little balls orbiting other little balls theory. If you thought about it in those terms, you were unable to even think about it. Understand?"

She laughed again. "No."

He was beginning to look frazzled. "See, they used the word smear to describe what the particles did in relation to the nucleus. Some of the particles exhibited characteristics that were called charm. Then they discovered antimatter and found that it moved backwards in time." He stopped for a moment. "Hmm. I wonder . . ."

231

"If I get your point, you're trying to say that the old ways of thinking don't apply in these new situations. That one needs a new vocabulary to understand what's happening."

"Exactly. And we don't have any sort of a vocabulary yet to explain the time shifting. Now, if time is cyclical, then that means that it can't be changed. It is the same as it always was and always will be, endlessly repeating. If it isn't cyclical, that means that it can be altered. In that case my father becomes a very real danger. If he succeeds in making a major change, then everything that comes after will be transformed. The 'right now' that you and I are experiencing will be different."

She frowned. "All right, let me try to get this straight. Say your father saves the Tsar and Russia remains a monarchy. Do you mean that some other course of events could have happened, or will happen? Like Germany might win World War II and all of a sudden we'll be sitting here in the park and the policemen will be speaking German? Flags with swastikas will be out in front of Rockefeller Center? That sort of thing?"

"Well, that's a little extreme; I don't think that would happen. And then again, the change might be for the better. You can't really say, and that's the problem. There's no way of knowing, so worrying about what will happen is not really useful. I think the point is that because of all the unknowns, the only safe thing to do is try and ensure that nothing will happen. That no change will occur.

"You know, Alex, this is an insane conversation we're having. What if someone overhears us?"

"This is New York, Molly."

"You're right." She looked around the square as if to reassure herself. Grown men were skateboarding; derelicts danced and begged; solemn children played chess with old men.

"So the obvious question is," she went on, "what do you do about your father? If anything?"

"I have to go back. I have to stop him. He's going to change things, no matter what. I think he's doing it just to see what will happen, to see if he can do it. It's not a matter of getting rich or being powerful; it's just that he has an opportunity, so he's going to take it. I don't know what did

232

it, maybe being back there all this time, but something has driven him over the edge. He's dangerous."

She turned on the bench so that she was facing him. She touched the crease in his cheek at the corner of his mouth. "If being back there has done that to him, what's it going to do to you?"

He grilled hamburgers in his small fenced-in backyard. They ate them with thick slabs of fresh tomato. Molly made potato salad with green onion dressing.

"Exactly how long have I been gone?" The tomato was wonderful. He remembered sitting in his prison cell, dreaming about tomatoes.

"Six and a half weeks," she said. "Exactly."

He nodded. "It sound like the same amount of time I was back there. That makes sense. Time runs at the same speed, here or there."

"It seemed like a lot longer."

"I'm glad that you didn't run off with someone else. Beyond the obvious reasons, there's something that keeps telling me that you're important, that you're part of this somehow." He shook his head. "Anyway, what's gone on in your life since I left? All we've talked about has been what's happened to me."

She shrugged. "The usual, except for poor Surrey. Writing about corrupt landlords, subway muggings, and a sniper at Penn Station, your standard New York stories."

It was getting dark. She smacked at a mosquito. "Let's go in," she said, standing. "We redheads are too delicate to get bitten by bugs. It mars our flawless skin."

"Do you have to go back?" she asked. They were lying naked on top of the sheets after having made love. "I've been trying not to ask that question," she added.

"It's the obvious one to ask," he said, rolling over and looking at her. She was lying on her back, staring at the ceiling. "And the answer is yes, I have to go back. I don't even know how not to go back. I still don't have any control over it."

"How do you know, assuming that you do disappear into thin air again, that you'll end up where you want to be?"

"I've thought about that, but the question that really bothers me is how do I know *when* I'll end up? What if I go back and end up in Cleveland on August the ninth, 1843?"

"Or Davenport, Iowa, 1947," she offered. "In other words, nowhere in particular. I hadn't thought about that."

"Believe me, I have." He put his hand lightly on her flat belly. "But so far it's remained consistent. Even in the dreams I've advanced rather than skipped around. It's all been fairly logical, if you can say that any of it is logical."

"Aside from all that"—she rolled over to face him, her long red hair fanned out on her pillow like some underwater frond—"tell me something honestly. If you had a choice, if going back was something you had conscious control over, would you do it?"

"Yes."

"I knew that, of course. But tell me why."

He thought about it. Not the reasons why he would do it, but how to explain it. If you put it in terms of "saving the world," you sounded like a made-for-TV movie, and if you confessed to it as pure adventure, you sounded childish. And yet both of these extremes were factors. Besides, he felt responsible in that it was his father that was trying to do the damage.

"I'll go because I choose to do so. Even though I can't control the actual shift, once I'm back there I do have options. I can go along with my father; I can simply divorce myself and sit back and watch what happens; or I can actively involve myself by trying to keep him from influencing events. I suppose you could give me the argument that my choices are only seemingly choices, that I actually have no free will and that any action I choose to take has already been decided by some outside force, by God, Time, the Overlords, whatever. That's a possibility, of course, but to choose to do nothing because of it is an easy out, a weakness."

"God forbid that the new improved Alexander Balfour should appear weak."

"Not appear weak—I don't care about that—but be weak. Yes, I do care about that. One thing I've learned"—for a moment the sight of Vassili standing against the wall, the muffled sound of the shots, the cold gray stone of his cell, swirled around him—"is that we are responsible for things.

234

For ourselves, other people, events. That inaction can be as destructive as out-and-out evil. That our lives here''—he gestured around the room—''are essentially inactive. That most of us are content to work within our world in terms that are defined only by externals. That I had become, or had always been, that sort of person, not by choice but simply by circumstance.''

He sat up on the bed. The dim light from the window accentuated the lean intensity of his face.

''I know all of this sounds a little messianic, but I've been given this gift. Maybe I inherited it from my father or maybe I got it some other way, but the point is I can't reject it. I can't just say no, it's too much trouble; I'd rather stay here and be with my wonderful woman and teach my classes and spend my money. Even though that would be more fun, easier, and a lot more comfortable, I can't do it. It's as if I'd suddenly found a talent—say, I could paint really well or play the violin—and I rejected it because it was too much trouble to practice or stretch the canvases or just do the work. I have an obligation to do what I am able to do. I owe it. I don't know to whom or to what, but it's a debt. It's not something you turn down.''

''Fate? Destiny?'' She tried to pronounce the words without irony.

''Yes, maybe,'' he answered stubbornly. ''I know those words are cliches, but they've become so because people use them as excuses, not reasons. I'm not embarrassed by words like that. Maybe a few months ago I would have been, but not now. Hope. Courage. Destiny. If you use those words or talk about larger, more concrete values, most people get embarrassed and try to find another conversation to get into. I think the reason we get embarrassed is because although we sense the rightness of these concepts, we're afraid that we can't live up to them. That we'll fail.'' He took her hand. ''I think I've learned that the failure isn't tied to the end result, the success or failure of the actual deed, but that we choose to attempt the deed at all.''

''And you choose to do so.''

''Yes.''

She sighed and pulled herself up to sit across from him. ''And I have to sit around waiting and wondering if you're dead and if you're coming back and all the other fears that women have when men go away. Doing my stupid little job while you're out slaying dragons and getting to act noble."

"If it was you instead of me, what would you do?"

She thought about it. "We're the same age, Alex, thirty-five years old. Five years ago I would have done it for sure, gone back without even questioning it. Maybe I'm not as convinced as you are of your father's ability to alter the past. What I know is that when you go back, you're taking a very real chance that by being gone you will alter our present, our future. Us. And I don't think I'd be willing to take that chance. Maybe it's some basic difference in men and women. I don't know. I do know that you would rather have me say I'd chuck it all and go, but that's too easy and it wouldn't be true. I can't help you that way, not with a lie. You'll go and I'll wait. I'll wait because I love you. That's my choice."

Chapter 31

"SO ANYWAY, MAX, WHEN YOU WERE FARTING AROUND AT THE door instead of putting the damn grenades down, I thought I was going to have heart failure."

Alex got up out of his chair to look down through the oxygen tent. Through the plastic, Surrey looked as if he were lying at the bottom of a very shallow, very clear stream. The old man was breathing slowly but evenly, laying as still as if he were totally paralyzed. Maybe he was; no one here at the hospital seemed to know. He's in a deep coma, they said. Christ, that was obvious.

"Why didn't you tell me you were a hero of the Revolution? It would have made a great story while I was growing up. One thing I've got to know, Max, was I with you? Was I there? I know it sounds like a crazy question, but I need to know, Max."

Nothing. He felt like a fool talking to the old man, but after sitting quietly for a half hour with nothing to do but watch him breathe, he'd just started talking. There was no one around; the only witnesses were the bank of machinery that kept track of Max's heartbeat and other vital signs.

He leaned forward so he could see the old man's face. As still as death. Only the thin birdlike chest moving slightly under the tucked sheets. "I need to know, Max."

Surrey's eyes opened.

Alex lunged to his feet, trying to find the nurse's call button and keep his eyes on Surrey's face. "That's the boy, Max; come out of it. Don't let it take you down; you can do it." He was starting to sweat. He found himself straining to infuse his own strength into the old man.

Surrey didn't move, lay staring straight up through the tent at the ceiling.

"Blink, Max, if you can hear me; blink if you can understand what I'm saying. Give me a sign, goddamnit; something."

Nothing. The faint hiss of the oxygen leaking into the tent.

"What's going on here?" A nurse pushed through the door, professionally taking in the bank of machinery in one sweep.

"He opened his eyes," Alex said, standing up straight, beckoning the nurse to the bedside. She moved over to the bed and looked down through the tent.

Surrey's eyes were closed.

"They were open," Alex insisted. Don't do this to me, Max. "For at least two or three minutes."

The nurse checked the setting of the machines. "There's no change," she said, indicating the rows of dials, the cathode-ray blip of the heartbeat.

"But his eyes were open," he said again.

The nurse shrugged her shoulders. "It doesn't mean anything; sometimes that happens. He's just the same; there's no change in the patient's condition." She pulled taut an invisible crease in the sheet that covered Surrey, straightened the plastic tent, glanced over the machines again, and left the room.

Alex sat back down in the chair, his heart pumping as if he'd just run the hundred-yard dash. "It doesn't mean anything, Max," he said very quietly, sitting back in the chair, staring up at the ceiling. "It's not a sign of anything."

Surrey opened his eyes.

"You're different," Molly said.

She was on the couch, sipping a cup of tea, watching him. He was in his chair, reading one more in a series of histories of the Romanovs. The reading was so constant it was no longer a matter of interrupting him.

The books were everywhere, in all the rooms, piled on shelves and counters, most of them open to where he'd left off. He'd read them depending on what room he was in at the time; bathroom, kitchen, bedroom. They had become an almost seamless background to their lives, part of the furniture to be moved or lived around, a great scattering of information that Alex ingested almost by osmosis. He'd been at it a week.

He looked up at her. She was wearing jeans and a light flannel shirt with the sleeves rolled up. The evenings had begun to cool as summer faded. She wore a pair of his white socks and had her feet tucked up under her. He put the book aside and moved to the other end of the couch. She stretched out her feet for him to rub.

"Different how?" he asked. He felt her toes flex under his fingers.

"I don't mean any of this as criticism; it isn't. Just observation." She thought about it, trying to put it into words. "You're harder. And at the same time you're much more open than you were before. It's a curious combination. Not unappealing," she assured, "not by a long shot."

"I guess it's a part of all of it, the going back, what happened there, the way I feel about things."

"But it's not just mental."

"You tend to lose weight in prison," he said, glancing down at himself. "One of the few benefits if you're overweight. Actually, prisoners are usually healthier than the general population. The same effect is seen in monks. The food is bland but not as bad for you as what we get on the outside. No alcohol. Most prisoners look ten years younger than their actual ages." Sometimes he'd catch himself thinking he was back in the cell. Thinking in terms of we, prisoners, and you, the rest of humanity.

"But it's not just the weight either," she went on. "It's a combination of things. When you came back, that first night, when we made love"—she stopped and corrected herself—"no, when we had sex, it was different than any other time. More . . . brutal, but at the same time more exciting, on a

239

purely physical level. Usually you're more cerebral in your lovemaking.''

"Sorry." His voice was gruff.

"Don't get huffy. I loved it. I'm not sure I want it as a steady diet, but then, and since then, it's been a part of the way you relate to me. And everything around you. It's not just the sex; it's everything. You don't even want to cook anymore.''

"I'm still not getting the point.''

"All right, wait a minute; let me think about it." She set her empty teacup on the floor and sat up, tucking her legs into a lotus position. She pulled her long hair back with both hands.

"When I was a new reporter," she began, "after I left New York, one of my first out-of-town assignments was to cover the Indianpolis 500. Not as the primary reporter, you understand, but to supply, as the editor put it, 'a girl's point of view.' I was supposed to rove around down in the pits with all the racers and mechanics and put in the human interest stuff.''

"From a girl's point of view," he said.

"Right. No interruptions.

"Actually, I thought it was great. The noise—it's incredible up close—the smell of the fuel, everybody working as hard as they can to get this very small car out on the track so it can go very fast. Everything is concentrated, measured in seconds and tenths of seconds.

"The race had been going on for a couple of hours and I was down in the pits and I heard this yelling from the next group over. Kind of a high-pitched shout, a man, obviously in some sort of trouble. Nobody else where I was noticed it. Their attention was all on their car. But just below the constant roar from the speedway was this keening sound.''

She was there. The pupils of her eyes were wide and unfocused.

"I went into the next pit area. The mechanics, the other people who had business there, were backing towards me. I ran up and pushed through. A man was in the center of the pits, rolling around on the concrete, beating at himself, screaming. Another man ran up and tried to roll him onto his back, but the first man was fighting him. It was as if he'd gone mad, as if he were fighting some invisible demon.

240

"Then the second man started screaming and jumping around. 'Fire!' he started yelling, 'I'm on fire.' Then they seemed, the others in the crowd, to understand. They got fire extinguishers and began spraying the two men. But no one would go close to them. They just kept spraying them until they were both unconscious. Only then did the ambulance guys load them up and take them away."

She came back. "They were on fire," she said, "but you couldn't see it. Evidently the sort of fuel they use for those cars burns without a visible flame. The first man had spilled some on him as he was refueling the car. Somehow it caught fire. When the second man touched him, he got it on himself. Then he was burning. Only you couldn't see it."

"It sounds terrible," he said.

She nodded. "It was. One of the men died later. See, the horrible part was that you couldn't actually see what was killing them. There was this terrible thing going on, but you didn't know what was causing it. It was invisible, but it could destroy."

They sat quietly until he had to ask it.

"You started the story implying that there was a point that had to do with our present condition."

She looked at him. "Yes," she nodded. "The point is, it's like you're on fire. I can't see it, but you're burning. It's changed you, the fire; you've been hurt, but you're bound and determined to go on with it anyway. There's nothing I can do to help you. I can't put it out."

"Except this won't kill me," he interjected.

She just looked at him.

241

Chapter 32

HE SHIFTED TWO DAYS LATER.

He came through into a small fenced-in backyard behind a wooden house in a row of identical wooden houses. It was evening, just going to dusk. He came through crouched down next to a cow. He was wearing Rasputin's overcoat. The cow, chewing its cud, looked at him with mild interest. It mooed.

The temperature was in the low eighties.

He began to sweat.

He stood slowly, trying to see if anyone had noticed a heavily coated man suddenly appear out of thin air.

It had happened in the middle of the night. The night he found the name. His name.

He had been reading the xerox of the original report that Molly had gotten from the Hoover Institute. The "black bag" report that the two Englishmen had found. She had given it to him so long ago that he had almost forgotten about it.

It was a report by a royalist investigator assigned to look into the murder of the Tsar and his family. At this point the White forces were still fighting and in many areas controlling large areas of the country. This investigator's job, and the job of several more who came after him, was to collect and present the evidence that would show the country and the world that the Bolsheviks had slaughtered the entire family in a manner so brutal as to place them beyond the sympathy of people everywhere.

Most of it was known; lists of those involved, depositions taken from servants who worked for the royal family, physical evidence, and conclusions. The investigator was not especially talented and most of the evidence had appeared in other investigations. Except Alex's name.

At the end, among a long list of those people questioned by the investigator, he found it. It jumped off the page at him the way a familiar name can suddenly appear isolated in a page of print; the name of a past lover, a dead friend. Your own name in an unexpected place. He hadn't shown it to Molly; it was too much to try to explain when he didn't know what it meant or how it could have been placed there. But it had a power; he felt it tug at him, pull him. A link. It was proof. The first anomaly that he was sure of; the first clear evidence that the past was vulnerable.

He had been lying on the bed, thinking about it. Molly was asleep; he didn't wake her, thinking it might be a false alarm, a normal headache. He slipped out of bed and pulled on his jeans and a shirt, his boots. He went into the living room as the beat in his head pulsed, little flickering lights swirling at the corners of his eyes, and found the heavy topcoat, put it on. He was determined not to end up in snow again without a coat.

The sable collar tickled his neck.

He slipped off the coat and looked around for a place to stash it. A man wearing a winter overcoat in what was obviously the middle of summer was going to look very odd.

Behind the cow there was a rough shed that held tools and hay. He pushed the coat behind the hay bales and went back into the yard.

The cow farted.

"Easy there, nice cow," Alex said quietly, patting the cow's dusty flank. "Were you aware that seventy-five per cent of the methane in the atmosphere is a product of the world's cow farts?"

The cow mooed again, louder.

243

Alex winced. "No? It doesn't really matter. How the hell do I get out of here?" The cow looked at the gate in the fence. "Good cow." He patted her once more, opened the gate, and stepped out onto the quiet street.

He was on a back street, unpaved, flanked on each side by rows of unpretentious houses. A merchant/working-class neighborhood. He walked in the direction that looked as if it might lead to the main part of the city. He assumed he was in Petrograd; at least it looked like it, felt like it.

After a half an hour he had made it to the river. Petrograd is built on a series of islands, cut by canals and rivers. By walking towards open spaces he knew he would eventually find a river. The river would take him to the center of the city. He stopped a young man and found that he was on Vasilievsky Island. The date was the tenth of July, 1918. It was sixteen months after he had left. He leaned against the marble parapet and stared out over the Neva, trying to sort the history out in his mind. He was shocked at the amount of time that had passed. Evidently he was moved to a particular time with no real relation to the period he had last left, or no relation that he could discern. The question now was, was he too late?

By now the Bolsheviks would be in control of the government. The Red Guards would have become the Red Army. The White forces, the collection of monarchists, officers of the Tsar's armies, and more moderate revolutionaries, would be fighting back, attacking the Bolsheviks all over Russia. But the Bolsheviks held the center of the country, the supply lines, the core.

He glanced at two soldiers with rifles who seemed to be patrolling the quay. They were wearing a uniform he'd never seen before, dun-colored jackets and pants with red piping. Red tabs on the collars.

He considered his options. His old rooming house was out. They'd long since have turned his room over to someone else and sold his few belongings. Besides which they would probably turn him over to the Reds as soon as he made an appearance. A simple change of administration would not be enough to alter their old habits.

The problem, as usual, was time. Or in this case, lack of it. The date, July 10, decided it.

244

On July 17, according to established history, the Tsar and his entire family would be murdered. According to his father's plan, the Tsar would be rescued by the Whites and restored as the legitimate ruler of Russia.

He had one week and he needed help.

Surrey.

He tried to remember where Surrey said he lived. Somewhere in the University district. Surrey was a student; that's where students lived.

An old gentleman, formally dressed in a three-piece suit and homburg, approached along the quay. He was walking three large German shepherd dogs. He looked so out of place in his suit and grave manner Alex decided that he was safe to approach, an island of neutrality in the city's sea of possible dangers. Even the dogs looked vaguely distracted, hardly interested in sniffing along the parapet.

"Excuse me," Alex said, turning to face the old gentleman, "but can you direct me to the University?"

The man stopped, clucking to the dogs who immediately sat. He studied Alex for a moment, as if cataloguing this stranger who had stopped him.

"Of course," the man said gravely. "You're quite near. If you walk further on down the quay, you will come to the Academy of Science; turn to the left and two blocks will put you on the grounds of the University."

Alex thanked the man and turned back toward the river, but the dogs and the man stayed beside him.

"Now you must excuse me," the man said in the same measured tones, "my name is Pavlov, Ivan Petrovitch. I realize I'm being forward, but could you tell me your national origin? Your Russian is excellent, but I sense that you are a foreigner."

"I'm an American," Alex said. He felt a thread of nervousness. The man was being a little more curious than he liked.

"Odd," the man said. "I would have thought you were from somewhere further away. I mean, well, I guess I'm not sure what to I do mean. I'm a scientist and I enjoy guessing the origins of foreigners, something of a game with me. I would have guessed American, but you seem much more distant to me." The man's brow was creased into a frown.

"No," Alex said. "Sorry."

Finally, sensing Alex's discomfort, the man tipped his hat and clucked again to the dogs. They stood in unison and waited patiently. The man lifted the leash and the dogs moved off actually in step with one another.

Alex watched the man's back as he and the marvelously trained dogs walked away. He was relieved; the man was too observant.

He had just turned left when it hit him. Pavlov? Dogs? He mentally kicked himself. His first real in-the-flesh celebrity that he had actually had a conversation with and he had missed it. What could he have done? Ask for his autograph?

He walked on. He felt in his pockets, taking inventory. He had his rubles from his time before and his trusty Swiss army knife. He'd prepared the jeans he had on and left them by the bed so they were the ones he'd put on, fireman style, if he shifted in the night. It had worked. He felt pleasure in this, a plan that had actually been conceived and then executed. A small victory.

"You mean the foreigner, the Englishman who fights for the Revolution," the student said. He was one of a group of young men Alex had decided to ask.

"He lives there," he added, pointing at an old dormitory building, "on the top floor. Everyone here knows the Englishman."

Alex nodded his thanks and walked to the dormitory. Surrey, it seemed, was famous. They had been a little confused about his national origins; Russians tended to think anyone who spoke English was an Englishman, but he was sure he had the right man. Maxwell Surrey, Hero of the Revolution.

Surrey opened the door at the first knock.

He glanced up and down the hall and pulled Alex inside.

"You shaved off your beard," Surrey said.

He looked tired. He'd aged sixteen months, but it looked more like five years. The fresh-faced college-boy look was gone.

"I thought you were dead," Surrey said, gesturing to one of the two chairs in the room. It looked like any standard

246

dormitory room. Small bed, two chairs, a desk. A gas ring instead of the more modern hot plate. Alex sat down.

"Not dead," Alex said, "I had to get out. The police were waiting for me back at my room that night. The embassy got me out. There was no way to let you know."

"I checked at the embassy," Surrey said, frowning. "They said they had never heard of you."

Alex shrugged, trying to look unruffled. Amazing the way a small lie can quickly start to pile up on you. "As you remember, it was a rather confused few days. I only recently was able to work my way back in. But what about you? You seem to be rather famous—One Who Fights for the Revolution. A group of students downstairs knew immediately which way to point me when I asked for you."

Surrey put a kettle of water on the ring and lit the burner with a match. "Most of that comes from the night we raided the arsenal," he said. A small smile showed, more in his eyes than on his lips. "It's become something of a local legend. The night the two crazy Englishmen blew up the arsenal. You see, you're part of it, like it or not."

That was not so good. Becoming legend, no matter how small, was not exactly the way to keep out of history.

"But you seemed to have gone on to greater triumphs," Alex said.

Surrey shrugged. "A lot was happening; I just went along with it. Once you commit yourself to something like this, it just seems to carry you along. So it carried me along." He took the bubbling teapot off the burner and poured them two cups of tea. He handed one of the heavy, chipped cups to Alex and sat down in the chair opposite him. He leaned forward, elbows on his knees, and sipped at the tea.

"It started out so well," Surrey said. He gave a small laugh and shook his head. "It seems like a long time ago. As I said, I just got caught up in it. I never meant to, historical objectivity and all that, but it happened anyway. It seemed the right thing to do. Overthrowing the tyrant, freeing the people from the yoke of slavery . . . all the slogans; it just felt right." He trailed off into silence.

"But now it's changed," Alex prompted. It was no great mystery. The glorious Revolution of the People had become the Dictatorship of the Proletariat. One of history's harsh lessons; revolutions tend to sacrifice idealism and equality shortly after victory. Along with anyone who doesn't go along with the party line. And realization of this lesson does a lot to disillusion young men, make them grow up, see the cold reality that had been obscured by the heat of passion.

"I do a lot of translating for them," Surrey said. "They trust me." He stopped and amended that. "At least as much as they trust anyone. My credentials were good"—he smiled at the memory—"you and I took care of that when we opened up the armory. Lenin sees me as someone who will be useful when the revolution spreads to England and America. I'm to be a player in the English Workers Revolution. Crazy, huh? But that's the way he thinks. To him, Russia is just where it starts. He doesn't really care about Russia in particular; he never has. He cares about his glorious worldwide revolution. People, countries, none of it matters except as part of the master plan.

"You know, he once told me that he never expected the revolution to begin here, that he had been sure that it would start in Switzerland." He laughed. "Can you believe that? He said that Switzerland was the perfect country for revolution because every citizen was issued a rifle for civil defense on their eighteenth birthday. An armed citizenry is the prerequisite for revolution. Can you see the fat burghers shooting their leaders and setting up a socialist state?" He shook his head. "Lenin sees it that way. He says the English or the the Americans are next. This revolution is just the match that sets the fire. The man's insane."

"Not insane," Alex said, "just consumed."

"Maybe," Surrey nodded. "Besides all of that, he's a brilliant politician. When they took over, the Bolsheviks, I thought it might work out. Kerensky couldn't make it work; the army was falling apart; the peasants weren't getting what they wanted; there was even less to eat than under the Tsar. For a while it looked as if the Bolsheviks might have the determination to set it straight. It's turned out that they had the determination and nothing more. Or rather nothing more than Lenin's genius. They planned everything perfectly. At 2:00 A.M., exactly, October the 26th, they moved into the Winter Palace and took over. Secured the bridges, the railroads, the telegraphs, all of it. That was it. Perfectly timed, perfectly choreographed." He shook his head.

"But you're working for them?" Alex asked.

"Yes. I translate English into Russian and Russian into English. At first I thought most of it made sense. Now I don't."

"You said they were determined," Alex said.

"That's right," Surrey said grimly. "Determined to shoot anyone who questions anything they say. Trotsky's not too bad, but Stalin. You've heard of Stalin? Didn't you mention him to me once?" Alex nodded. "They sent him to the Volga to organize the grain supplies to the cities. Controller of Food Supplies. He has his own little army that spends its time shooting anyone who even looks as if he might object to having his grain confiscated. He and Trotsky are always at each other's throats while Lenin tries to keep the peace. Meanwhile the bodies pile up in the streets." He drained the last of his tea and looked at Alex. "I can't be part of it much longer."

"What are you going to do?"

"Get out, I guess. Go back to the States. I hate it, though. It feels like I'm running away. But I can't take the killing; I just can't stand by and watch it."

"Tell me something," Alex said. He'd made up his mind to go ahead with it. It was tampering, but by now his only recourse was to assume that he was supposed to tamper with things.

"Do you know where the Tsar is right now?"

"Why?" Surrey asked, with a look of interest.

"Tell me first; then I'll tell you why." Alex said.

"He's in Ekaterinburg. That's in the Urals. They were in Tobolsk, but the Bolsheviks thought they might escape from there, so they moved them further east. It's supposed to be a secret, but I'm the guy who translates the documents. Besides, a lot of people know."

"Is there a chance they might escape?" Alex asked. The question was more than academic to him.

Surrey snorted. "There are more plots to free the Romanovs than there are rats in the sewers around here. Everybody who was anybody under the old regime and who's still alive has a plan."

"Any chances of success?"

"Probably not. Unless one of the White armies takes over the entire area where they're being held. Which is a possibility, except they'd be moved out before that can happen. There's no organization, no real leaders. That's why the Reds intend to keep the Tsar and the whole family under lock and key. So there will be no real leaders. Later on there will be a show trial for the Tsar, Trotsky for the prosecution. And then he'll be found guilty and the royal family will be imprisoned for the rest of their lives. Or worse."

"Why don't they just kill them now?" Alex asked.

Surrey looked genuinely shocked. "They'd never do that. Even the Bolsheviks wouldn't do it. They're looking for approval from the rest of the world; what would the rest of the world think if they murdered the whole family in cold blood? To say nothing of the English. The Tsar is the cousin of their king. There are negotiations under way to have all of them shipped to England. That may happen if they decide against the trial. Look, if the Bolsheviks killed the family, they'd have the English, and probably the Americans, down on their necks, and they can't afford that right now. They've enough problems just trying to beat down the Whites and the rest of the counterrevolutionaries."

Alex was up against his usual problem; how much could he tell and be believed?

"Think of it this way," he said. "You said that the Whites have a good chance of taking over the area where the family is being kept."

"It's almost a certainty," Surrey said. "They'll be moved before it happens, though."

"All right, but what if there's no time to move them? What if everything gets screwed up?—The telegraph lines are down; the Whites are shelling the town; there are no orders from Lenin as to what to do. Everything is falling apart. Now, pretend that you're the commander in charge of the prisoners. If the family falls into enemy hands, the entire course of the war could be changed, almost certainly would be changed. And the fault would be yours. You would be responsible for the possible failure of the greatest revolution of all time. On the other hand, what real value does the family have? A show trial that everyone in the world knows the verdict of before it even begins? A bargaining chip with the English, who don't really seem to want to be involved. Whoever takes the family is going to have years of problems, political, economic, moral. At this point they're a liability to say the least. A potential disaster just because they exist. The destruction of the Revolution over a handful of people? Think about it. You're in charge: What do you do?''

Alex was leaning toward Surrey, close enough to watch the realization dawn.

"Kill them," Surrey said in a small voice.

"Exactly," Alex said. "There are no other choices."

Surrey rubbed his face and sighed. "I guess it doesn't really matter, just a few more bodies on the pile."

"But it sticks in your craw, doesn't it? I mean, it's one thing to see it after it's over, but it's another to know it's going to happen and then stand by and let it." Memory: Vassili standing in front of the firing squad. It is not enough to be uninvolved.

"Sure it does," Surrey said.

"Okay. Here's the Tsar and his family, held by the Reds who are probably going to kill them. Here are the Whites who are advancing on the town where they are being kept, bound and determined to capture them back so they'll have a figurehead again, someone to lead them all back to the same place this country was before the Revolution. All of this action centered on a man and his family who at this point would rather be out of the whole business, a man who was too small and ordinary for the job in the first place, who already failed once and should be allowed to sink into obscurity. Instead, he and his wife and five children are all about to be killed.''

"All right, I get the point; the Bolsheviks will probably kill them, and yes, it does seem, to put it mildly, unfair. I told you I was sick of all the killing. If they do this, it will be the end as far as I'm concerned.''

"But wouldn't you like to do something about it?" Alex insisted.

Surrey's eyes narrowed. "Of course. Wouldn't you?"

Alex nodded. Surrey sat back in the kitchen chair. They looked at each other and smiled.

"Just what do you propose, Mr. Balfour? You want to ride off on our horses and rescue the bunch of them?"

Alex gave it a count of three to stretch it out. Surrey's smile got broader.

"That's exactly what I want to do. Only I think it would be better if we took the train."

Chapter 33

BEFORE THE REVOLUTION THE SMOLNEY INSTITUTE WAS AN UPPER-class girls' school. During the Revolution the buildings were seized and turned into the headquarters of the Bolshevik party. A year and a half later the same buildings were already beginning to take on the aura of legend, reminders of the party's early triumphs and victories, reminders of a time before the icebergs of everyday government had begun to score and rend the bottom of the newly commissioned ship of state.

Since the October Revolution the Bolshevik workers had spread themselves out and into the Petrograd buildings that handled the day-to-day government work. A necessary step in the Revolution. But some of the leaders—the political architects Lenin, Trotsky, Mhartov—still kept offices in the old building. There was a sense of safety there, a faint whiff of nostalgia, the smell of burning autocracy lingering in the hallways. The comfort of simple wooden desks in plain straightforward offices. A proletarian sort of place, or at least proletarian once the taint of upper-class education had been scoured away by the carbol of working-class determination.

The Institute was where Surrey worked. Office 2-C. Right down the hall from Comrade Lenin.

The lounging guards at the gates of the Institute did little more than glance at Alex and Surrey as they came through.

At the door to the main building they were perfunctorily questioned, but it was obvious that everyone knew Surrey and accepted his responsibility for Alex.

The long gray halls of the building were filled with women carrying sheaves of documents and knots of men walking and talking. Surrey told him that most of the documents that funneled through the Institute offices were concerned with the foreign aspects of the government. The building and its workers had become, in effect, the Bolshevik State Department.

Gone was the rough atmosphere of the early days, the soldiers loitering in the halls, rifles stacked in all the offices. The place looked like what it was, or had become; a government office.

Surrey's desk was covered with official-looking documents with notes scribbled into the margins in red ink. The Bolsheviks were very big on red ink. He introduced Alex to his fellow workers as a comrade from England come to help with the work of translating. Alex sat at the desk, which was wedged behind a bank of wooden filing cabinets, while Surrey went off on another errand. He left Alex with a stack of copies of letters that had been exchanged with the English ambassador in Ekaterinburg. The British embassy in Ekaterinburg was located directly across the street from the Ipatyev house, known formally as the House of Special Purpose, where the Tsar and his family were being held. The British ambassador had become the key diplomat in the negotiations concerning the release of the Tsar.

Most of the correspondence outlined various plans for the acceptance of the royal family by the English. The language was tedious and obtuse, officially circumventing any real commitment by either party; a formal dance between two partners who detested each other but were forced by convention and need into a polite turn around the floor before getting down to business. For the Bolsheviks, used to simply shooting those whom they disliked, this sort of diplomacy was extremely difficult. It was like expecting a testy Doberman Pinscher to relinquish his genetic inheritance and ask nicely before chewing off an intruder's arm.

After two hours of leafing through endless pages Alex saw Surrey's return as a release almost as heartfelt as his deliverance from the Fortress of Peter and Paul.

Surrey smiled at his officemates as he led Alex into the hall. No one smiled back: Bolsheviks were serious workers.

"I think I've got all the documents we'll need," he whispered. "Travel passes in both our names, letters of intent from the Party, rail priority passes. I've got a girlfriend in the travel section. She gave me the blanks and I typed them up myself."

"Wasn't that a little risky?" Alex asked.

Surrey shrugged and smiled.

"Maybe, but we won't be around to get into trouble for it. If we pull this off, neither of us will be coming back here. If we don't pull it off, it won't matter much one way or the other."

They leaned together as they walked, talking in low voices. They looked just like the other groups of men walking arm in arm. Plotters, Alex thought; they all look like men who are conspiring against, for, or about something. The Revolution has spawned a generation of lean and hungry men.

He stopped. Through a series of doors he saw a man sitting at a desk. The prematurely bald head was unmistakable.

People are usually surprised when they actually meet others they have only seen in pictures. It isn't that they look different from their pictures, but so much like them. Here was Lenin, scribbling away at his desk, very much alive.

Surrey pulled on his arm, but Alex shook him off. Lenin looked up.

The cold eyes narrowed, looking at him from under the inverted V's of the familiar eyebrows. The features were all hard angles and lines—eyebrows, goatee, thin slash of a mouth—all of it topped by the only real curve, that curious bulging dome of forehead. It was the sort of head that he used to see in science fiction magazines when he was a kid, illustrating what the people in the far future would look like: short, stumpy bodies; atrophied arms and legs; bulging heads. The point was obvious; they were smarter than we were, so their heads had to be big to hold all those brains.

The eyes. Little. Cold. Terrifying. Get in my way, the eyes said, and I will kill you.

"You." Lenin nodded at him.

Alex stood, feet nailed to the floor, transfixed. He felt like a baby bird staring over the edge of the nest into the eyes of a

255

marauding snake. Who me? I'm sorry, I didn't do anything. I confess. Don't hurt me. You're wanted in the principal's office.

Surrey interposed himself. He glanced once at Alex and walked into Lenin's office. Alex lifted his frightened feet and followed.

"Comrade Lenin," Surrey said, "I'd like to present a comrade from England. He's here to help in the translation department."

"Alex Balfour," Alex said, stepping forward and holding out his hand.

Lenin glanced at the hand and then shook it. His hand-shake was cool and limp. "I wasn't aware that any help had been wequested." High, reedy voice.

"The order came direct from Comrade Trotsky and the War Department. I suggested Comrade Balfour."

Lenin just looked at them. "Then he is your wesponsibil-ity, Suwwey."

Wait a minute, Alex thought. Suwwey? He can't say his R's correctly. This man, Lenin, prime architect of the great-est revolution in history and he sounds like Elmer Fudd? Suwwey????

"Yes, comrade, I take full responsibility." Surrey glanced over at Alex and his eyes widened. "If that's all, we must get back to work," he said quickly.

Lenin nodded. He was frowning at Alex.

Surrey had him by the arm and was leading him out of the office.

"Jesus Christ, Alex," he whispered, "are you crazy?" They were in the hall, moving rapidly toward the outside door. "Wipe that goddamn smile off your face. You want to get us killed?"

"I can't believe it," Alex said. "The guy's got a handshake that's as limp as a dead frog and he can't say his R's. Amazing."

"And I've got a pocketful of forged travel passes and a crazy friend who's about to laugh in the Old Man's face." He pushed open the door. "I couldn't believe it when I saw that goofy smile on your face. No one smiles at Lenin."

Alex shook his head. "Amazing."

*   *   *

The train was packed with soldiers, old men and women, children and their parents, lone businessmen in suits, peasants with massive bundles—all of them crowded into compartments and aisles, brought to equality by the new regime and the scarcity of travel space.

Or at least equality until Surrey threw a rock into the pond by showing his priority rail pass. Two soldiers were kicked out of a compartment to make room for the traveling officials. Alex and Surrey sat down; the soldiers, grumbling, stood in the hallway outside the compartment.

"Those are the dog-deputies," Surrey said, indicating the two civilian trainmen who had uprooted the soldiers. *"Sobatcie."*

"Dogs? They're called dogs?" Alex asked. The men were dressed in blue uniforms with the familiar red collar tabs.

"It's the acronym for Soldier and Workmen Deputies. Dog-deputies. Except don't call them that to their faces. They rule the railroads now."

"I noticed. Don't you feel a little twinge of Bolshevik guilt about kicking the soldiers out of these seats? Not quite in the revolutionary spirit is it? Equality, fraternity, and all that."

"Well, you saw that they got to complain about it. Under the Tsar they wouldn't have considered raising their voices. Under Lenin they can complain all they want. Besides, they understand that we're two officials traveling on important business. We need our rest so we can do our job well."

"Bullshit. What they understand is if they complain too much, Comrade Lenin's dog-deputies will take them out and have them shot."

"Yes," Surrey said, giving him a wicked smile, "they understand that, too."

He pulled out the passes and handed one to Alex. "You'd better keep that in case we get separated. Note the signature."

Alex looked closely at the small cardboard square. Lenin.

"I practiced at my desk until I got it perfect. I felt like the giddy schoolgirl writing my lover's name in my notebook," Surrey said. "Actually, I'm authorized to sign his name on the lesser documents."

"Well, it should get us through any trouble we run into."

"Oh, yes, as long as it's Bolshevik trouble. If we run into White trouble, it will probably get us killed."

257

Surrey said it with so little concern that Alex turned in his seat to look at him. Now that they had actually started, Surrey had relaxed back into his former self. It had been the difficulty of moral choices that had aged the young Surrey. Now that they had made their choice, he had happily reverted. Alex understood that this was the natural condition of youth; resiliency, a rubber-band simplicity. It was something you lost as you got older. And wiser.

Surrey trusted him to figure out the angles and direct the action. Alex hoped that he would be able to come up with something before they needed it. He would hate to get Surrey killed. He would hate to get himself killed. It was all so complicated. Work on the plan, he told himself; get the big picture and let the details fall where they may.

Dawn. Alex saw the famous domes of Moscow from the train windows as they sat in the station. The five hundred miles from Petersburg had passed in the night. When they were back on the move again, the character of the Russian land began to change. The softer, civilized look of the birch and pine woods and cultivated fields began to thin and flatten. The peasant houses, often decorated with intricate curlicues of carved trim and painted various pastel shades of blue and red, gave way to two-story and then single-story thatch-roofed huts. Surrey explained that inside the huts, the design of which had not changed in centuries, there was usually only one room. The primary piece of furniture was a huge tiled stove that was cooked in during the day. At night, during the winter, the whole family slept on top of the stove. The family's domesticated animals—cows, chickens, goats—usually slept in the same room with the people. In the summer the animals were kept outside.

Surrey turned out to be a fund of information. The socially accepted Russian method for young men and women to be alone together was to go on long healthful hikes in the country. Surrey had spent a lot of time walking in the country. He pointed out and named the flowers that blurred by outside the train windows: cosmos, Queen Anne's lace, camomile, swan flower, purple Ivan's tea. Alex was amazed that he knew the names of so many.

"Knowledge acquired through many walks in the woods,"

Surrey said with a laugh. "It's the principal enjoyment of Bolshevik youth. No decadent opera, no bourgeois ballet dancing. The simple pleasures of nature."

Alex thought of those simple pleasures. Molly. The train rolled on.

The civilians on the train began to give way to the military. The businessmen had all disembarked in Moscow and most of the peasants got off at small railway stations that merited stops so brief the train barely seemed to cease moving. Fat old ladies in *babushkas* leapt from the still moving train, first throwing down cages of live chickens, always seeming to land and stay upright. A continuing stream of soldiers took their place.

The passengers had time, at the larger stations where supplies were loaded and engines changed, to scramble off and crawl under the carriages of neighboring trains to buy food from the trackside vendors. The famine that was rife on the streets of Petrograd had not touched the outlying stops. You could buy boiled potatoes and raw carrots, turnips, radishes, onions, and tomatoes. Various fruits; raspberries, plums, and gooseberries, and at one stop, scrawny boiled chickens. The currency was either old rubles or Bolshevik script, depending on the varying degrees of patriotism of the sellers. Surrey had a supply of both, which they made good use of. They ate whatever was for sale, washing it down with the strong tea that was continually brewing in the smoking samovar at the end of the carriage.

Surrey said that keeping the train rolling was a priority of the Bolsheviks, a matter of honor, even though it was continually being hijacked by the White forces in the Urals. Then, as the Whites ran it back west, it would be hijacked by the Bolsheviks, and in this way the Trans-Siberian Express continued to make its famous run, with more than a few casualties and decidedly not on schedule.

Late the second day, two hours after stopping in Vyatka, the train ground to a halt in the middle of nowhere. Immediately the four soldiers in their compartment took down their rifles, which were stowed in the overhead luggage rack. No one thought that the Whites could be so far west, but the stop was definitely unscheduled. Alex opened the window and leaned out. The land stretched flat, dotted with a few trees, toward the horizon. The day was hot and cloudless, the sky huge like a western American sky, a glaring blue bowl inverted over the still, empty plain.

Getting onto the train, one car in front of theirs, were four women.

"Relax," Alex said to the soldiers, who were the same age as most of his students back in New York, "the engineer has stopped to pick up his girlfriends. Four women."

They nodded to him but held on to their rifles.

The train pulled out again.

The door of the compartment was thrown open.

"Greetings, comrades."

A woman, tall, dressed in a bright peasant skirt and blouse, stood in the doorway. Behind her Alex could see several other women setting down parcels and baggage in the corridor. "I am told there are Officials of the People in this car."

The four soldiers and Alex and Surrey stared at the woman. She was so robust and healthy she looked to be the living embodiment of the ubiquitous Bolshevik posters of Mother Russia: strong arms burnt red from toiling under the sun, bright blond hair under a blue print kerchief. Woman: able to harvest the crops and tend the wounded, mother of future regiments of Red Army soldiers, backbone of the revolutionary movement. "I am Ekaterina Nicolaevna Kovalevsky," the woman said.

It finally occurred to Alex that she was referring to them. Officials of the People: upper-echelon Bolsheviks.

Surrey came to his senses first. "What can we do for you, Ekaterina Nicolaevna?" Surrey asked, nodding to Alex to include him. He was using a voice Alex had not heard before. Alex supposed that Surrey thought that he sounded official, serious.

The woman looked over the four young soldiers who were staring up in awe. She looked as if she could pick up any two of them in her arms without much effort.

"Brothers," she said, nodding to the soldiers, "I am going to ask you to relinquish your seats." She held up a hand to forestall the inevitable complaint. "Yes, I understand that men and women are now equal, that you have as much right to the seats as we do. I not only understand it, but I wholeheartedly endorse that right. But as you can see"—she gestured to the woman behind her—"we have been traveling on foot for many hours. We have come from a small village where we have been teaching the peasants, without any recompense beyond room and board, I might add, and are on our way to the Perm District for reassignment. We too are soldiers in the war against counterrevolution. We need to confer with these officials here"—she gestured at Alex and Surrey—"so that we might coordinate our activities. If it were not for the Party and its business, I would not ask you to give up your seats. Unfortunately, these matters come before considerations of mere personal comfort. I'm sure you understand." She paused. The six men stared up at her, mesmerized by her speech. The four soldiers looked like baby birds waiting to be fed.

"The seats, comrades!" she thundered.

The four soldiers stood as one, banging their rifles together as they jumped up. She smiled broadly. They looked around their seats, gathering up their belongings. The woman stepped back into the corridor as the four soldiers sheepishly filed out, dragging their packs.

The train had picked up speed until it was rocketing along again, swaying with the movement that they had come to accept as the natural way of the world after two days of travel.

The woman stepped back into the compartment, still smiling, and, with no visible effort, threw a heavy valise onto the overhead rack. She dropped down into the seat beside Alex.

"Ah," she sighed, "that is much better." She looked them both over. "And now, comrades, may we join you?"

Chapter 34

"NARODNIKS," SURREY SAID AS HE CHEWED A CHUNK OF COARSE bread. He was showing off his Russian history. "Nineteenth century populists. They felt that they had a mission to carry education to the common people, the *narod,* so these people could pull themselves out of the muck. In our country we call it pulling oneself up by one's bootstraps. The Narodniks were patriots, but of course the Tsar and the ruling classes had no desire for the peasants to be anything but peasants." He swallowed his bread and smiled like a little boy waiting to be commended.

"Narodniks?" Katya snorted. They had agreed to use the familiar forms of the names of the women and the first names of the men. She was tearing off another chunk of the bread for one of her girls. The bread came apart with an audible ripping sound. She glared at Surrey. "The *narodniks* were upper-class do-gooders. They were fools; self-important, deluded fools. The peasant doesn't need to know how to read and write and add, at least not yet. The peasant needs political education. He needs to know how to organize his village into a working unit, how to feed his fellow workers, how to root out the counterrevolutionaries among us, how to shoot anyone who stands in the way of the Revolution. He needs education, yes. Political education. Then,

and only then, can the more subtle forms of knowledge be disseminated."

Surrey looked chastened. "Of course, Katya, I did not mean . . ."

She waved him into silence. "I understand, Maxwell, that you did not mean to denigrate the Party. You are a student, and students get carried away with their own knowledge. But you are also an official in our Party and, as such, above reproach as to your political motives. High officials. Might I see your cards again?"

Surrey had showed them their travel passes after they had all sat down and exchanged names.

Alex handed his travel pass to the woman. She sighed as she looked at it. "Signed by Lenin himself," she said. "Truly an honor. I have seen him, of course, but never close up, only from the audience. Someday . . ." The word drifted off, but the meaning was clear. Lenin was her hero.

She told them she was twenty-eight years old. As long as politics weren't mentioned, she could carry on a normal conversation. She radiated good will, filling the compartment with confidence and competence and a healthy sexuality like a fine, if earthy, perfume. Eau de good-nature, Alex thought. Spicy, musky, the smell of strong thighs and salt-of-the-earth goodness.

She had taken over the compartment. The three other women had dragged in their myriad bundles and bags. Alex and Surrey had helped them stow everything up above and under the seats. Katerina had directed the placement from her seat. Then she had told the girls where to sit.

"Elena," she directed the youngest of them, a pretty girl with a bad sunburn and bright blue eyes, "you sit next to Maxwell. You two are the youngest and can talk whatever nonsense young people talk. I will sit with Alex and we will talk as adults. As the oldest we will sit together."

"Galina Maximovna and Avdotia, take the end seats. Try to sleep; you are tired after our journey. We have walked many *versts*," she explained to Alex, "for the village was far from the railway. We left before dawn and stopped to rest only one time."

They were all dressed in some variation of peasant attire. Simple skirts and blouses, but clean and well made. All of them were pretty, but Katya and Elena were the prettiest. Alex was glad Katya chose to sit next to him, even if she made the choice because of age differences. Him older than Surrey? If she only knew. Still, he felt like he'd been chosen first for the softball team.

"Now, tell us why officials from Petrograd are traveling so far from home," Katya asked. "You, to come so far, must have important business."

Surrey waved his hand deprecatingly. "A simple fact-gathering mission, Katya. Merely part of the everyday workings of the government."

Surrey had snapped back from his ideological mistake about the *narodniks*. The constant searching for error on the part of the Bolsheviks was beyond Alex. Surrey, though, seemed to have developed the knack for it, almost like learning some odd half-language, like Esperanto or Pidgin English. Alex was happy to let Surrey do most of the talking.

"Yes, but what facts are you gathering?" Katya went on. "That is the question." She leaned forward toward Max. "Would it by any chance have anything to do with the former Tsar and his family?"

Alex felt his heart lurch and a quick glance at Max showed the other man was also surprised. The whereabouts of the Tsar was not supposed to be general knowledge.

Surrey narrowed his eyes in approved Bolshevik style. "And what would you know about the Tsar and his family, Ekaterina Nicholaevna?"

For the first time the woman seemed to lose some of her self-possession.

"Only that they are being held at Ekaterinburg, Comrade Surrey. Everyone knows that they are there."

"Everyone does not know that they are there," Surrey said, his voice thin and hard. Alex wondered where he had learned to put the threat in his voice like that. With the narrowed eyes and the thin, hard words he looked and sounded truly dangerous. "And it would be wise for you to forget that you know it," he added.

"Of course, Comrade Surrey," Katya said.

"Where do you come from?" Alex broke in, changing the subject. "I mean originally."

Katya looked at him gratefully and began to chatter about

their various backgrounds. All of them were from middle-to lower-class families and had had sympathy for the Revolution from the very beginning. Their present assignment was one that they had not sought in particular but that they all thought would lead to higher projects within the political reeducation ministry.

The day progressed into evening, the weather cooling both outside and in the small compartment. During the hot days they had to keep the windows open, but the rush of air that resulted brought in a load of dust and coal smoke that left a fine layer of dirt over everything in the compartment. In the evening they could leave the window only slightly cracked and still be comfortable. In the night the temperature fell even further and necessitated the use of light blankets.

Katya spoke mostly to Alex. Elena, the girl beside Surrey, kept Max occupied with a steady stream of gossip. Several times Katya asked Alex quietly about their trip, but Alex put her off, not resorting to Surrey's hard-line attitude but at the same time letting her know that he was not going to discuss it. Eventually she gave up and stuck to safer topics like the scenery blurring by outside.

The flat vistas had given way to high mountains in the distance, the Urals, beyond which, Alex knew, was the true immensity of Siberia. They all watched the mountains grow as the train raced on, fixing on the peaks as a visual relief from the flatlands. Katya told them that the peasants who lived on the flat plains found the sight of all that land stretching from horizon to horizon comforting.

"Perm District," Katya said, nodding at the distant mountains. "Tomorrow we will be in Ekaterinburg."

Perm. Alex thought of Tolstoy and the novel *Resurrection*. Tolstoy's prostitute marching into exile with the political prisoners, setting out from Perm. The convoys of prisoners, before the trans-Siberian railroad, marched, wearing only government issue slippers that wore away quickly until they were barefoot. Fifteen to twenty miles per day, resting every third day. A thousand miles. Five-pound fetters around their ankles. Shuffling along into history. Eventually they would ride in bare boxcars. The later prisoners would arrive more quickly, but they would all end up in the same places.

Night came. The compartment cooled and they had to bring out the light blankets. The conversation trailed off until they slept.

Alex woke. A hand was stroking him. The compartment was dark. The hand unbuttoned his pants and sought him.

Molly. No, this was not Molly. This was no simple dream.

Katya's head was on his shoulder, her breath heavy on his neck. She moved against him. Alex held himself still, as if sleeping, sorting through the conflicts. Beyond her breathing he heard the light snores of the two women in the far seats and, above the snores, the light, soft moans from Surrey and the girl Elena as they moved, barely discernible, beneath their own blanket.

He felt Katya's heavy breasts pressed against his arm, warm and soft beneath the thin material of her blouse. He was free now and she stroked him. He moved his hand to her hip and felt her move even closer to him. He tried to think of Molly and how he loved her, but that had nothing to do with this; it was too far away, too abstract to weigh against the night, the rocking of the train, the clatter from the tracks, and the breathing and the light moans and the feel of this woman as she pulled him to her, moved over him, and then down onto him. He arched quietly into her with a shudder that shook them both. She covered his mouth with hers and smothered the sounds of pleasure.

The train raced toward the mountains, invisible in the dark.

Chapter 35

Alex heard a faint shot, a faraway pop, hardly more noise than a man cracking his knuckles. The train began to slow. The wheels locked. The long piercing shriek of iron wheels dragging against iron rail filled the air, blocking out the shouts and screams of the passengers. The cars accordioned, slamming together in succession, giant dominos falling one against the next in a staggering slow motion.

They had gone through the town of Perm at daybreak. Alex slumped in the seat. Katya slept lightly in the curve of his arm. A wisp of her blond hair tickled his nose. Surrey and Elena were in approximately the same position. Alex watched the others sleep, like fresh little children, no guilt there. He wished he could say the same. What was going on; what had happened? Why did it feel so good to have this woman tucked under his arm?

They began to stir. For a bit there were embarrassed smiles and downcast eyes, faint blushes on healthy Russian cheeks, but the business of cleaning up and getting tea took precedent.

Then the shots. The train braking. Flailing arms and legs. Tumbling against the wall, falling to the floor.

Alex pushed Elena off him and rolled up on the seat. He stood up and got a quick look out the window. A line of soldiers lying on the ground, firing at the front of the train. A puff of smoke from the line of rifles. He flinched back down as a bullet went into the ceiling, spraying dust into the compartment. They were no longer firing only at the front of the train.

They lay in a pile on the floor, pressed together, listening to the answering shots from the soldiers on the train. After what seemed like a long time but was probably only a matter of minutes, the shooting from the train trickled off and ended. There were a few more shots from the outside and then silence. Their position began to get painful.

Alex pulled himself up again and looked over the windowsill. Men with rifles were walking beside the train. The sounds of compartment doors being flung open came from the front of the car. Everybody got up and dusted themselves off, staying back from the window.

Their compartment door slid back. A very large soldier with a huge handlebar mustache stood in the doorway.

"This train has been appropriated by the Volunteer Army of Russia," the soldier said, glancing around the car at them. "There will be a delay while we unload your military supplies. After this is completed, you will be allowed to continue on your way. In the meantime, any papers of identification must be presented for inspection by our officials." The door was shut and another soldier took up a position in the corridor outside.

"Get rid of the passes," Surrey hissed. "You women, anything you have that identifies you as a Bolshevik must be hidden."

"Whites, I assume?" Alex asked.

"Volunteer Army is one of the names they use," Surrey said, going through his wallet. "Give me your card," he said to Alex, glancing at the guard in the hall.

Alex handed him the card and Surrey slipped everything between the back of the seat and the wall of the compartment.

"Here's the story," he said in a low voice to Alex. "I'm a mining student going to Ekaterinburg to study their operations. You're a fur dealer from Finland. Tell them the Bolsheviks took your papers in Petrograd and won't return them until after your trip." He looked at the women.

"We have hidden our papers," Katya said in a low voice. "We will be four women traveling to visit relatives in

268

Ekaterinburg. Because of the Bolsheviks we have left Petrograd. You do not know us; we only met on this train.''

"True enough," Alex said. "Keep it simple and we should be all right. They don't have time to really question us. I thought this area was all Red-controlled?" he said to Surrey.

Surrey shrugged. "It's supposed to be, but individual raids aren't all that unusual.''

The door slammed open again. "Papers!" a man demanded. He was tall, fair-haired, clean-shaven, and wore a uniform from the Tsarist regime.

They told their stories. The man seemed not to care. He kept glancing from them to the activity going on outside the car. He passed quickly over the others and then pointed at Alex. "You," he said. "What is your business?"

Alex told him the story again. The man watched him closely. There was a minute of dead air as Alex finished and the man scrutinized him. "Outside," the man said.

They all began to stand, but he waved them down. "Just him," he said, pointing at Alex. Surrey began to protest, but the man silenced him with a look of contempt. "Quiet. You do not wish to go where he is going. You will remain here in this compartment until the train is allowed to continue."

Alex stood up and pulled his pack from the overhead rack. The man looked at the pack as if he was going to tell him to put it back, but then motioned Alex to follow. As soon as the man's back was turned, Alex bent and whispered "British embassy" to Surrey, who nodded. The four women were staring at him. He gave the best smile he could come up with to Katya and followed the officer.

Outside, men ran up and down the length of the train, supervising and loading supplies onto the backs of a string of mules. Alex stopped for a moment and breathed in the fresh, clean air. It was still cool from the night and the fields around them were lush with brown grain waving in the light wind. The hills and mountains beyond were a bright green in the morning sun. It all had a faintly unrealistic, schizophrenic feel; train robbing and killing were activities of the night, not possible on so glorious a day.

"No stopping!" the officer commanded, waving his arm at Alex.

Beside the tracks they had laid out the bodies of the

soldiers who had tried to defend the train. Among the twenty or so bodies Alex recognized the four young men who had been in the compartment with them. They looked very young and very dead. Pale; expressions of surprise on their faces. Me? No, not me. It isn't time yet. There must be some mistake.

He was pushed into a lineup with other men approximately his own age. He put his bag on the ground and waited with the rest.

"Just like boot camp," he said to the man next to him. The man, dressed in a suit and looking like a Finnish fur dealer, looked at him as if he were mad. Alex smiled and shrugged.

He had no idea what was going on, but he found he wasn't particularly afraid. The brightness of the sky was all wrong for death, the fresh, clean air filled him with something more like hope than despair. If they were going to kill him, they could have done it more easily back where they had the other bodies lined up.

There were approximately twenty-five men in the row, all around the same age and general build. At the other end of the line Alex saw two men ride up on horses and dismount. Now he understood.

The two men began to walk slowly down the line, inspecting faces of the men. When they got to Alex, they stopped.

"Hello, Father," Alex said. "Looking for anyone in particular?"

Alex's father glanced at the officer with him then back to Alex.

"My name is Charonsky and I am a colonel. You will address me as such," his father said. He turned to the officer with him. "This is the man I've been looking for. I suggest we get the rest of them back on the train and get out of here. We're too exposed."

The officer nodded. "I agree," he said. He turned to a soldier behind him. "You," he barked, "get these men back on the train. Tell the lieutenant to drag the bodies off into the ditch. Get the train moving if all of the supplies are unloaded. Burn what we can't carry." The soldier started off, but the officer stopped him. "And have any of their soldiers shot. We can't take any prisoners." The soldier nodded and ran off toward the train.

The officer turned back to the men who were still lined up beside Alex. "Go!" the officer shouted. "Back on the train. Be glad that we did not shoot you. The Volunteer Army is merciful; we do not kill civilians. Unlike the Bolshevik scum. Tell them that in Ekaterinburg. Tell them also that we are coming soon."

The line of men broke and ran for the train. From the other side of the line of cars he could hear the sound of shots as the last of the Bolshevik soldiers were killed.

"Oh, yes, the White Army is truly just," Alex said at the sound of the shots. They were standing alone now. He imagined the scene behind the train, the two lines of men, those with rifles and those who were dying.

His father looked at him. "Still the bleeding heart, eh, Alex? What would you have them do? We've got a hard ride over the mountains with a string of loaded-down mules. The entire area is in the hands of the Reds and you'd have us drag along a bunch of prisoners who are going to take any opportunity to escape. Should we just turn them loose so they can shoot us later when we meet them again? What would you do if *you* were giving the orders?"

Alex remained silent.

"That's what I thought," his father said, turning away, assuming Alex's silence to be assent. Alex picked up his pack and followed him. Let him think what he wants.

In the background the train built up steam and began to pull away. He watched it pass as he walked along the tracks. He looked at the windows until he saw them, Surrey and Katya. They floated slowly by, their faces pale, hands pressed against the window. Surrey looked like one of the boys in the ditch nearby. Only alive, thank God.

He rode one of the small shaggy horses. The regular soldiers walked, most leading mules and carrying rifles. The officers rode. Several scouts ranged ahead, up into the hills, making sure the way was clear. No one talked much, including Alex. Whatever was going to happen would happen, no matter how many questions he asked. He was a prisoner of sorts; at least he understood that he wouldn't be allowed to leave. He rode between his father and an officer who wore the insignia of the Tsar's own guards.

They trailed through the fields of grain and up the low foothills. The forest marked the real beginning of the mountains. Tall, long-needled pines. The temperature dropped under the trees and the men seemed to relax a little. They began to talk among themselves. The only sounds were the murmurs of the men, the clank of bits and harness among the animals, the liquid notes of a wood thrush.

"I was beginning to think you weren't coming," his father said.

Alex glanced at him. He looked as clean and well preserved as he had back in Petersburg. He rode his horse naturally, held himself ramrod straight. His uniform was military but with no distinct bias, no obvious signs of allegiance. But of course that's the way it would be.

"What made you so sure I would?" Alex asked, watching the woods in front of them.

His father laughed. A false, brittle sound. "Curiosity, as much as anything else. You're here, in this time; how could you stay away from one of history's great mysteries? Besides, we're about to change the course of things to come; I didn't think you'd really want to miss out. How could you?"

Nothing had changed. His father still didn't understand. Would never understand.

Alex shrugged. He would appear to remain neutral as long as possible.

"Our moment is soon to arrive," his father went on. "If the execution is to happen the way it's written in the books, then it happens soon. But you know that, don't you?" His father stared at him, looking for some reaction. He kept his eyes straight ahead.

His father smiled at Alex's silence. "At any rate, we hadn't formalized our deal. In fact, as I remember, you were threatening to shoot me the last time we were together. What a good son. It seemed less than the usual assertion of loyalty, so I thought I would keep an eye out for you. There are very few ways into this area; I simply watched the most obvious, though I'll admit to a bit of luck. We hit every other train or so and I was lucky you were on this one.

"What makes you think I'm any more likely to work with you now than I was before?"

"You were on that train, for one. If you weren't going to try something, why were you there? If you hadn't shown up, things would have taken the course that history says they took. I can't do the job; my face is too well-known to too many people. Ekaterinburg is swarming with Bolsheviks, many of them former officials under the Tsar. Those of us that have the brains for the job are all too well known. Those that aren't"—he gestured at the soldiers walking—"haven't the brains or the vision for it. Besides, as I explained once before, they don't seem to have the ability to change the course of things." He leaned forward in the saddle, into Alex's field of view. He smiled. "So it's up to you, my son. With a little help from me."

Alex did not turn his head. His father laughed.

The campfire crackled, snapping sparks into the updraft. They floated up under the high ceiling of trees and sky. He and his father sat to one side, isolated from the three other officers, talking in low tones that did not carry over the flames. The regular troops were gathered around a larger fire in the center of the small clearing. The officers had argued among themselves over the advisibility of having campfires, but it was decided that the men were tired and needed hot food.

They had eaten a heavy wheat gruel from battered tin plates. There was strong tea in mugs. The combination sat on the gut, giving off warmth and the heavy feeling of satiety.

"Not that I doubt your allegiance to either me or the counterrevolution, as our Bolshevik friends refer to our efforts, but I have arranged for you to take along a little help on your adventure." His father was sitting on a small folding chair. Alex had dragged up a log.

"Four of my men will go into Ekaterinburg with you. They have not been told what their mission is, only that they are to do whatever you say. You'll need the help."

Alex stared into the fire. This is not help, these are my guards. Their purpose is to make sure I do what I'm supposed to do and then bring me back.

273

"They'll do what I tell them?"

"Of course. Within reason." His father was watching him, eyes glittering with the reflected flames.

"What if I tell them to get lost?"

His father shrugged. "They won't obey. They have my instructions, which are to stay with you."

"And to bring me and whomever we collect back to you after it's all over."

"Of course. I'm perfectly aware that you're capable of doing the job or not doing it and then disappearing. Even though you aren't aware of it, your options are severely limited. There really isn't anywhere to hide, even in this immense country. There are very few roads, very few railroads. A man on the run usually dies in this wilderness. That's why the Tsars have always used this land as a prison.

"You will leave us tomorrow," his father went on. "You and the four soldiers. They are strong; they have weapons."

His father was sitting higher than the others around the fire, brightly lit from the flames. His father took the bullet in the right leg.

Once, in college, Alex was riding in a car at night with two other friends. He had been facing forward, looking out the front windshield, when he was suddenly aware that the left front tire of the car was three feet in front of the left headlight. He saw it a second before the car slammed to the pavement and slewed in a great circle, ending up in the ditch on the side of the highway. Only then did his mind make the connection: The wheel has come off the car I am riding in. Comprehension following perception. A very odd feeling.

His father was looking at him. The right leg of his father's pants puffed outward and then indented into a small hole. Alex saw it happen, then heard the report of a shot and at the same time saw his father knocked backwards off his chair. By the time he heard the shot his brain had made the linkup. He rolled off the log he was sitting on.

He tried to scrunch his body down into the dirt behind the log. His father was lying to his right, moving weakly, like a dying crab on the beach, like a smashed, not quite dead spider. The chair was upset, lying on the ground, giving the

274

whole scene the appearance of some sort of clumsy comedy. Other shots rattled away back in the forest.

Alex watched one of the officers frantically kicking at the fire, trying to put it out. The man took a bullet in the chest and went down onto the burning coals. He made no sound.

Alex started to crawl to the darkness of the forest at the edge of the clearing. Time to get the hell out of here.

"Alex, help me." His father.

Alex pressed his face onto the dirt and listened to the shots. There were sounds of firing from their own position as the White soldiers found their weapons and got organized. Basic self-preservation screamed inside him to get out of the clearing. An overriding layer of civilization that he heartily wished would go away forced him to crawl back to his father. He rolled the wounded man onto his side and with a small amount of shame stationed himself so that any bullets would have to go through his father before they got to him.

"Don't leave me here," his father whispered harshly. There was real fear in his eyes. His careful hair was mussed, giving him a lopsided drunken look.

Alex could smell the burning flesh and cloth from where the man lay across the campfire. He had achieved his purpose, though; the flames were out. The clearing was now lit only by muzzle flashes and the dim light from the swath of stars far above.

"You're only shot in the leg," Alex said. "Hardly a mortal wound. As you used to say to me, Father, get hold of yourself."

"No, no," his father insisted, still in the same urgent whisper, "there are no doctors, no medicine. It'll get infected; there'll be blood poisoning; I'll die. You've got to get me out of here."

Alex looked at the face only inches from his own. He thought of the time his father had held a gun on him, threatened him with one thing or another, told him how he was sending four men with him to make sure he came back; Christ; he thought back over a whole lifetime of major and minor indignities, thought about it and then turned around and began to belly-crawl away.

"No, no, no." The whisper; the whine of a mosquito in the night.

If he was really hurt, I would get him out, Alex said to himself as he crawled away. He gritted his teeth until his father's voice was covered by the sound of shots. Alex still heard it, though, heard it in his head where it was loudest. He got into the trees and stood up. The blood whirled in his head, making him lean against a trunk for a moment.

The two soldiers guarding the horses were standing close together, looking into the night toward the sound of the firing.

"You two," Alex commanded in his best Russian-officer voice. "Get in there and help those men. Now!"

The two soldiers glanced wildly around, finally locating Alex's shadowy figure. They hesitated, then started off at a ragged trot.

Alex untied one of the horses. Using the tether as a harness, he guided the horse into the darkness.

Chapter 36

ALEX WALKED ALONG THE SIDE OF THE DUSTY STREET. IT WAS hot, mid-morning. The streets in Russian towns were astonishingly wide, reflections of the endless steppes. Simple, hard-packed dirt that became deep dust in the summer and a morass of knee-deep mud between summer and winter, winter and summer. In the winter the dirt froze hard and the roads were only then truly usable.

As soon as he got into the actual town of Ekaterinburg, the traffic began to pick up and he did not feel quite so isolated. Safety in numbers. He was dirty and tired and hungry, and he still hadn't come up with anything clever in the way of a plan.

He stood on a street corner and looked down into the main part of town. The name would be changed to Sverdlovsk after the Revolution; Francis Gary Powers would be shot down here, and there would be a mysterious nuclear explosion in the 1950's in the mountains nearby. But right now it looked like a provincial Russian town, known for its mining and fur business. Wide streets, a scattering of horse-drawn vehicles, the minarets and domes of the ever-present churches. Low hills covered with sunburnt prairie grass lay beyond the town.

He stood for a moment, remembering the long night he'd just been through.

He had wandered around in the dark on his horse for several hours before deciding that there was too much chance of running into a patrol from either the Whites or the Reds to keep that up. He couldn't tell where he was going anyway.

He had tied the horse to a tree and curled up at the base of another and finally dozed off, waking at every forest sound. He'd started out again at dawn.

Shortly afterward he'd come across a set of train tracks that he knew must eventually take him into Ekaterinburg, there being only one set of east-west tracks for several thousand miles.

He'd walked the tracks, first leading the horse and then riding. He'd circled a village that was too small to be Ekaterinburg, and when he'd finally come across a road with a large town in the distance, he had dismounted and turned the horse loose. He had no idea if the horse could be recognized as the property of the White Army, but he could not take the chance.

He'd come to a large lake. He'd stopped and washed, allowing himself the luxury of lying in the early morning sun to dry. When he began to doze, he'd forced himself up, dressed, and got back on the road.

The sky was a high bright blue and he'd felt very alone, like a bug caught under the dome of a bell jar. The dust from the road puffed up at each step, making a small sound that was quite distinct in the vast silence around him. Where were the birds? The wind? There was only the tiny bug Alex.

He entered town as part of a small procession of peasants heading in with produce and goods tied to horses and to themselves. He was greeted courteously and with curiosity. He nodded, smiled, returned the greetings.

He crossed a second set of railroad tracks. He walked by a factory, the Denilov Dye Works. The air was thick with the smell of rotten eggs: sulphur, used in many of the dyes. The nameless road became Glavnaya Street. There were houses now, the wide streets bounded by two-story, mostly wooden and sometimes brick buildings housing several businesses in each.

He stopped in front of a large wooden building and bought

a pie from an old man with a tray set up on a folding stand. The pie was triangle-shaped, filled with potatoes and peas, and covered with a fine layer of dust. He munched on it as he stood and read the signs on the front of the building: Moscow Peoples Bank; Anchor Insurance Company; the Ekaterinburg Union of Savings and Credit Societies; the editorial offices of *Ural Economy*, which seemed to be a newspaper devoted to business. He finished off his pie and thought vaguely about dysentery and food poisoning. That would be an ignominious way to end it all.

The streets were filling up now. There were no sidewalks, only a narrow walkway between the hitching posts and the flat fronts of the buildings. One walked in the streets, keeping an eye out for runaway carriages.

At the corner of Voznesensky Avenue he turned left and looked down the long street. From where he was standing he could see the building that must be the British Consulate. And beyond, almost out of sight behind a heavy wooden fence, the Ipatyev house, House of Special Purpose, present home of Tsar Nicholas II and his family. He crossed the street and began to walk down it, aware that his heart rate had moved up a notch and his bowels had begun to tighten.

He stopped to admire an icon-covered screen in front of the Orthodox church directly across the street from the British Consulate. Representations of Christ, the Virgin, St. Nicholas—all competed for space among the elaborately carved fretwork. He kept his face absolutely neutral as Maxwell Surrey joined him.

"Beautiful, isn't it?" Surrey said. "A fine example of Russian craft."

"Yes," Alex said. "A little too baroque for my tastes, but I'm sure it does the job."

"Admirably," Surrey said. "I thought they'd taken you out to be shot. I've been waiting here since we got in."

"I'm glad you did. Shall we walk?" He was very glad to see Surrey, but shouting and pounding each other on the back seemed to be a bad idea.

They turned and walked slowly down the street. "We'll go to the railroad station," Alex said. "Pay close attention to the house behind the wooden stockade on our immediate left. Don't stare at it."

279

Outside the wooden stockade were two Red Guards who seemed primarily interested in the younger women who passed them on their side of the street. Alex could hear them shouting greetings to the women.

"Am I to assume that behind that wall is the object of our adventure?" Surrey asked.

Alex nodded.

"I guess we'll storm the wall, swarm over the top, and blast all the guards inside. Then we'll load everyone into our vehicles and drive them to our hideout in the hills."

"Do I detect a note of sarcasm in your voice? Is this the same Maxwell Surrey, Hero of the Revolution, who stormed the armory in St. Petersburg, armed with only his wits and a few hand grenades?"

"At least I had the hand grenades. Here, all I've got are my wits, and they're not going to get me behind that fence."

"Oh ye of little faith. We have something better than hand grenades. We have . . . ." He stopped and faced Surrey. "We have knowledge. We know what's going to happen and when it's going to happen. And that, my friend, shall make them free."

Surrey just looked at him. "Wonderful, you've gone insane. That should help a lot."

"Forget it," Alex said. "From now on, especially when we get inside the embassy, just pretend that you know what I'm talking about. I'll explain later."

Surrey nodded.

Getting into the British Consulate proved easier than Alex thought it would be. The consul, Edmund Preston, explained that being as far out of the mainstream as Ekaterinburg was insured that any English speakers, even Americans, were welcome.

"Sir William sends his regards," the consul said. "He assumed since he never saw you again that you were dead. He gives you high marks and says I'm to listen to your proposal. I have full discretion, mind you, to take you up or turn you down. It's not necessary for me to check with the home office again. It's my decision." He paused to let the message sink in and then went on. "He refers to you as his fortune-teller; why is that?"

"I'm very good at predicting events," Alex said.

As soon as they had gotten in to see the consul, he had caught the man's attention by asking him to check with Sir William Smith-Carrendon at the Merchants Bank in Petrograd. Then he and Max had walked around town for two hours while Alex prayed that Sir William and the bank were still in residence, that the telegraph lines were working and that Sir William would vouch for him. His prayers had been answered. There was a God, no matter what Comrade Lenin said.

"I'm going to make some predictions for you. If you think about them, they're only common sense, things that I'm sure you've already thought of. What I do, primarily, is supply timetables." Close enough to the truth, Alex thought. Or at least as close as I can go.

"The negotiations for the release of the Tsar are proceeding very slowly, am I right?" Alex asked.

The consul raised his eyebrows, a gesture that neither accepted nor rejected the question. A diplomat's gesture. "Well, as you know, communications are always difficult. . . ."

Alex waved the obfuscation away. "True, but I notice that you just got through to Petrograd in a fairly short time. No, the reason the negotiations are proceeding slowly is that no one really knows what to do. Also, no one wants the responsibility of the Tsar and his family. I am aware that your king publicly decries the whole imprisonment and asks for the return of the family, but I also know in private he is being difficult about the whole thing."

No answer; raised eyebrows.

"There's no shame in it; any government would be wary. As long as the Bolsheviks remain in power, the Tsar will be the symbolic and probably real focal point of efforts to overthrow them. Does England want to become the headquarters of this resistance? And the Bolsheviks, how long will they be able to stand having the uncertainty of trying to hold on to the prisoners without losing them to the Whites?"

This time he got a definite head nod. "And I suppose you have an answer for all of these difficult questions?" the consul asked.

"Yes." He certainly had everyone's attention. Surrey watched him with a mixture of anticipation and disbelief. The consul showed only disbelief.

281

"The thing to do is get them out alive and then hide them. Forever. The key is to simply remove the Tsar from the equation. If he disappears, you have satisfied your consciences on humanitarian grounds. Then let the Reds say whatever they want to say. Of course you deprive the Whites of their figurehead, but you can't intercede to the point of turning him over to them and putting yourself directly on their side anyway. It wouldn't be diplomatic." He said the last with more than a touch of sarcasm because of its truth. These people were caught between so many rocks and hard places that any real, recognizable choice and direction was impossible. What he was offering was possible because it was anonymous and protected their anonymity. A way out of their dilemma.

"We get them out. All you do is find a place for them to go where they'll never be noticed again. It's a big world; you ought to be able to find somewhere. After all, you're English."

"And you are Americans. Tell me, what does your country get out of this?"

It had never occurred to Alex that this question would come up. The reason it didn't occur was because he wasn't thinking like a diplomat. These men thought in terms of countries not individuals. The consul assumed they were working for their own government and as such would be attempting to implement that government's policy. The trick in all of this was in realizing that most people tend to think that others carry the same motivations that they themselves do. Diplomats saw only diplomatic motives in the more complicated actions of others. Saving the Tsar and his entire family from a fairly horrible death simply for the sake of sparing them was beyond the realm of most of these people. Not because they were insensitive—they weren't—but because their motives didn't allow extraneous information to enter their equations.

"First of all," he said, improvising, "if England takes them, the United States won't have to. Surely you're aware that our government is also negotiating a release?" He had no idea if that was true, but either way it didn't matter. The consul would accept it as true. "After all," Alex went on, "they are related to your king. We would take them because it's expected of us, but we don't want them any more than

282

you do. At least politically. Morally, though, we consider the alternative of their deaths to be unacceptable."

"That leaves us with you two heading up the operation?" the consul asked. He swiveled his chair slightly as he looked at both of them. "Two American secret agents. All right then, I'll listen to your plan, but I don't know how you think you can succeed when others have failed. By my count alone there have been at least four separate attempts to get them out. They've all come to nothing, of course, but the people were here and involved."

"What people?" Surrey interjected. Up till then he had let Alex do all the talking.

"Monarchists. Friends of the royal family. All quite ineffective. But you can rest assured that right now there are plots being hatched somewhere in this town to try to get them out. None of the attempts have actually been put into action, thank God; these people have no real idea how to go about it, but who knows what will happen next. After all, here you are."

"Yes, here we are," Alex said, "and with your help we'll get them out." With your help and my knowledge of what's going to happen, when it's going to happen, he thought. And a lot of luck.

"Just what exactly do you need?" the consul asked. His tone was still politely neutral, promising nothing.

"We'll need weapons for the two of us; pistols, grenades if you've got them." He glanced at Surrey and saw a small smile there. "We'll need the guns by tomorrow. Provisions for a two-week journey for both of us and the whole family. At the other end we need a way to get them out of the country, a ship standing by. And trucks, lorries, to transport them in. We'll also need to stay here, all of us, for eight days. We'll have to be hidden."

"And that's all?" The raised eyebrows again, the words spoken with famous British understatement.

"That should do it," Alex said. He added a smile for politeness' sake.

"Absolutely impossible," the consul said.

283

Chapter 37

IT WAS NIGHT. ALEX AND MAX SAT IN A SMALL GROVE OF BIRCH trees. Alex could smell the small lake nearby, the dank odor of low water.

They had carefully worked their way into the trees, keeping to the shadows. It wasn't likely that they would be seen. Ekaterinburg was too provincial a town to have streetlights and there wasn't much in the way of a moon. Most of the town had by now gone to sleep. Soon they would move up the low hill in front of them so they could watch the house.

"What do you plan on doing when you grow up, Max?" Alex asked. He kept his voice pitched low and quiet. The sound of their voices was absorbed by the vegetation around them. He figured they would wait another hour or so. Got to pass the time.

Alex could hear Surrey shift his position.

"Christ, I don't know. Maybe I'll become a soldier of fortune, make a career out of rescuing deposed monarchs in distress."

Alex toyed with the idea of actually telling Surrey what he would be in later life, knowing all along that he couldn't tell him.

"Actually"—Surrey's voice had lost its bantering tone—"I

guess I'll just become a boring historian and vegetate at some university. All that seems pretty far away right now. . . . Alex, I realize this is a little late to be asking, but do you really think we're going to be able to pull this off? You're always saying to cut the bullshit, so . . . This is not the British consul who wants to know; this is Max Surrey, Hero of the Revolution.''

"Yeah, I think we're going to pull it off.''

Alex felt rather than saw the man beside him shake his head. Every once in a while he realized just how innocent Surrey was. He hadn't been tempered the way he had, by prison, the petty torture, sickness, Vassili's death. Most of all, he didn't have the luxury of knowing pretty much what was going to happen. Surrey was operating on pure nerve, which took more guts than Alex had invested. It was time to give Max a little more information; he owed it to him. There was still always the possibility that either of them or both of them were going to get killed trying to pull this off. There were no guarantees, no way that Alex could prove that the time lines would stay solid.

"Max, I'm aware that you thought I was doing some heavy bullshitting in there with Preston, telling him I was going to make some predictions. I know it sounds crazy, but I do know what's going to happen up there in that house tomorrow night, or what's probably going to happen. Most of it's common sense, things that anyone can figure out.''

"All right, just what is going to happen up there?''

Crickets. In the distance a train whistle. The air was cooler, giving up the heat of the day slowly but perceptibly. Alex reached back and touched the smooth trunk of the tree he was leaning against.

"Sometime tomorrow night, in the early morning, the Tsar, his wife and five children and three family attendants will be awakened by the head of the guards. They will be told to dress and go to a room on the first floor. That room, if there were no hill and no fence, would be straight ahead of us from where we are sitting.''

He kept his voice flat, talking quietly. "The Tsar will carry his son Alexis. When they are all in the room, he will ask for chairs. Three chairs will be brought: one for the Tsar, one for the boy, and one for the Tsarina. These three will sit.

285

It is a small room and will be quite crowded after the guards push in. I don't know how many guards there will be, maybe just a few, maybe as many as eleven.

"The head guard, a Captain Yurovsky, will then read a short statement from the Bolshevik committee, a sentence of death. He will then shoot the Tsar. The other guards will open fire into the rest of the family and servants.

"After the first volley they will find that the boy, Alexis, is not dead. Yurovsky will shoot him several more times. They will then find that Anastasia is not dead. They will bayonet her until she shows no more signs of life."

Alex looked up at the stars and drew a deep breath.

"How can you know that?" Surrey asked. "That isn't just common sense, things that anyone can figure out. You can't really know that's what's going to happen." Alex could hear the exasperation in Surrey's voice. "I'm serious, Alex."

"Believe me, I'm just as serious about this as you are. You're going to have to take all of this on faith. I know it's a lot to ask, but I can't explain it."

"You mean you won't explain it. People always say *can't* when they mean *won't*." Surrey's voice was bitter.

"All right, if you want it that way, yes. In the long run, it doesn't affect what we're trying to do. Think about it. We've gone over all of this before. The Bolsheviks have got to do something about the family. The whole area is ringed by the Whites, getting closer every day. They can't take the chance; they've got to kill them."

"Maybe," Surrey said grudgingly. "But the whole family? All the servants? Just shoot them? Herd them into one room and blast away?"

Alex let a little of his own anger show. "What do you expect? Some sanitary little execution, just a little business between gentlemen; sorry, Nicholas, but you understand? Bang, you're dead. Grow up. Besides not being stupid, you're not blind. You know the Bolsheviks have committed atrocities that make this pale by comparison."

"But that was during the first days of the Revolution," Surrey protested.

"You told me to cut the bullshit; now it's your turn."

Both of them sat in silence. Alex knew that Surrey was nursing a very complicated set of conflicting emotions, but there wasn't much he could do about it. The man would have to work it out for himself. There was a time when he would have argued and tried to persuade, but that time was over. Either Surrey was with him or he'd do it alone. He was not even sure why he was doing it, but he wasn't going to give it up now. A man's got to do what a man's got to do, quoth the immortal John Wayne.

"Maybe you're right," Surrey said after a minute of silence. "At least about the killing part. I'd like to know the whole story, but I guess you're entitled to your own business." From his voice Alex could tell Surrey was looking at him. "But promise me this. I'll go along with what you say if you'll explain all of it after it's over."

"I'll say this much," Alex said, "I guarantee that one day you'll understand everything."

After another wait Surrey said, "I guess that will have to do. But if I'm going to be the official historian of this caper, I need all the information I can get."

Alex was glad that Surrey had moved it back away from the edge. "Forget it," Alex said. "Nobody is going to be writing any of this up. I realize that it would make a great doctoral dissertation, but if we pull it off, it has to remain a secret."

"You're taking all the fun out of it."

"That's right. Now I'm going to make it even less fun. I think it's time we gave this a dry run. What we're now going to do is crawl up that hill to the fence, scout things out, and then make our way back to the embassy."

The night was as dark as it was going to get. The crickets were still chirping away.

He remembered a story he had heard about Vietnam. He and the rest of the antiwar movement people had thought it just one more example of the inept military mind. Army intelligence had come up with the scheme. They had dumped a long load of tiny radio receivers down strategic lengths of the Ho Chi Minh trail. The animal warfare specialists had decided to apply the knowledge that crickets stop chirping when there is movement nearby. By tuning in the frequency of the receivers they would be able to tell by the succession of silence when the Viet Cong were using the trail. It hadn't worked: The theory may have been correct, but the humidity killed the receivers before the plan went operational.

Alex stood up slowly and worked his legs to get the circulation going. The crickets fell silent. Maybe it hadn't been such a dumb idea after all.

The low hill in front of them held scattered trees and wide patches of tall grass that showed a deep gray under the dim starlight. They would move into the patches of deeper shadow beneath the trees until they were near the stockade. There was a clear area between the last of the trees and the fence, but they'd just have to chance it. Alex was pretty sure that most, if not all, the guarding was going on inside the house and around the front toward the street.

"Okay, let's go," he said to Surrey. "Keep it quiet from here on out."

Alex assumed that the silence from Surrey was the other man's way of keeping it quiet from here on out. He grinned to himself, took a deep breath, and started up the hill in a low crouch.

He was amazed at how much brighter the open spaces felt once he was out in them. He knew his clothes blended in well, but he still felt exposed. He moved in a low crouch at a fast walk. Slow enough to control the noise of moving. The only sound was the light swish of tall grass.

The last small stand of trees was thirty yards from the high fence. Between the trees and the fence was a rough track just flat enough to allow trucks to negotiate. He assumed that meant a gate in the fence on this side, something he'd been hoping for. Otherwise they were going to have to dismantle part of the fence. Or climb over it or dig under it. Or knock on the front door.

He felt Surrey beside him as he crouched in the shadow of the trees and looked out. The house was hidden from view by their low angle and the fence. There was no sound other than natural ones. No one was in sight. He left the safety of the shadows and trotted over to the fence.

He flattened himself against the palings, though it probably didn't do him much good. There was no shadow, nothing to hide behind or in or under. He heard Surrey behind him, turned to look at him, saw his face pale in the dim light. He wondered if his own face was as pale and ghostlike as

Surrey's, wondered if the pallor was a consequence of starlight or fear.

He forced himself to ease off the fence and to slow his breathing. He felt hideously exposed and vulnerable, truly a soft bug in peril of being seen. Seen and squashed. He gave Surrey an attempt at a smile and saw the other man at least nod in acknowledgement. His mouth was dry and cottony. His bowels were cold and loose.

He felt the wooden fence, running his hands along the rough-hewn boards. There were wide cracks between the palings. From where they were he saw nothing through the fence, only more darkness. He moved slowly down the fence toward the opposite end. It was a very long walk.

At the other corner they found the gate. Through an opening he could see light from several of the rooms. There was enough light from the house to show a small inner yard between fence and house. There was a door into the room on the first floor, where tomorrow night he would have to go. The lighted windows were on the second floor. A man sat at a desk, a soldier. Alex felt his skin crawl as the man glanced out the window into the dark.

Surrey's hand touched his shoulder. He kept himself from flinching at the light touch. Surrey pointed to a chain inside the fence where the gate was locked. On the inside. Alex nodded, turned, checked the area behind them. Nothing. He took a deep breath and started back.

At the bottom of the hill, among the birches, he stopped and leaned against a tree. He heard Surrey move up beside him, breathing heavily.

"Nothing to it," Surrey said softly.

Alex laughed nervously as he waited for the tension to ease.

"Right," he whispered. "Now it's back to the consulate without being shot and we've done a fair night's work."

"Right," Surrey said. "I do have a few questions, though. Couple of things that might prove a bit sticky."

"Later," Alex said. "Nothing to worry about beyond a few guards and a ten-foot fence that's locked on the inside. A couple of minor points to be worked out. Nothing serious."

Chapter 38

"Two Browning pistols, ammunition, and some suspect dynamite? This is it?" Alex picked up one of the pistols. The blueing was worn off the barrel and the handle was scratched. "Does this thing really work?" he asked.

Preston, the consul, stood by the table where the guns lay. "Mr. Balfour," he said carefully, with just a touch of humor, "I am a diplomat, not a secret agent. I have never fired a weapon in my life. I haven't the slightest idea whether any of this"—he gestured to the table—"will function properly. If you would like to give up the whole idea, I, for one, would certainly understand. We can always fall back on diplomacy as our means to the end. I do have some expertise in that particular field."

Alex waved the idea away. "There's no time, Preston. It's got to be done right away." He stood frowning down at the weapons.

"Ah, yes, I forgot," Preston said, "your famous timetables."

Alex gave him a hard look, trying to see if the man was serious. He couldn't tell. The Englishman was too accomplished a diplomat to broadcast his feelings. "Did you get the rest of the stuff?" Alex asked.

The consul looked toward the ceiling of the room, as if

reading from a list printed there. "I have informed the consulate chef to begin stockpiling supplies for additional guests. I have invented a delegation from Britain that is due to arrive shortly, as any sudden increase in our supply needs will be suspect. I have inquired about the availability of transport and, regrettably, there is none. In Ekaterinburg the primary means of getting around is still the horse and buggy. Any motorized vehicles belong to the military. As to evacuation at the other end, I have begun inquiries through the foreign office as to what will be available at the various exit ports. That will take some time."

"All right," Alex said, "keep working on it." Preston was doing everything that he could, Alex knew that. Alex had appealed to the man's more vulnerable sense of decency and fair play. Always the way to an Englishman's heart. As long as Alex could pull it off without embarrassing the English government, he would get as much help as they could give.

A basement storeroom had been cleaned out for their use. Most Russian homes had no basements, as the ground was usually frozen year-round. But there was no permafrost at Ekaterinburg, so basements were a possibility. It was perfect as far as Alex was concerned. Your normal Russian soldier was not going to look for a basement because he had no experience of them. Alex hoped there would be no Russian soldiers of any color, Red or White, looking for them in the embassy, but it was always a possibility.

He and Surrey had made it back to the embassy with no problem. They had gotten onto the grounds through an old door into the garden that Alex had found earlier in the evening. It had been nailed shut, unused for years, but the two of them had pried it open. They would use it again the next night.

"If there's nothing else this evening, Mr. Balfour, it's quite late and . . ."

After Preston had gone, he and Surrey pulled out a pile of canvas tents that had been in storage and put blankets over them. They made reasonable beds, better than a night in the forest, better than a prison cot.

"A few minor points," Surrey said as he lay on his makeshift bed. It was cooler in the basement than in the

291

consulate upstairs. "First of all, how are we going to get through the locked fence? Second, where are all the guards going to be when we blast our way in there; and third, I'm not actually certain that I'm going to be able to shoot anyone in cold blood."

Alex sat on his bed and pulled off his boots. He wondered when he was going to get some fresh clothing. By the time he had gotten out of prison he was used to his unwashed smell. Then he'd gone home and enjoyed the luxury of a daily bath. Now he was back with his aging socks and his equally aging underwear.

"Very good question. First, the gate will be open because they're going to have to have some sort of trucks there to take the bodies away. Remember, there are a lot of people going to be shot, or at least the Bolsheviks are planning on shooting a lot of people.

"Secondly, the guards will either be in the room doing the actual shooting or will be somewhere else where they will have been instructed to pay no attention to any gunfire from the house. That's the beauty of the plan. If they're going to shoot a lot of people, there's going to be a lot of shooting. Under the circumstances anyone in the area who might make trouble will have been told to pay no attention to it. So if we go in blasting, as you so colorfully put it, no one is going to come running to see what's up."

He lay back on the bed and looked at the ceiling. There was one dim bare bulb burning from a cord hanging in the corner. The room smelled musty, although it was dry. On the wall was a tattered Union Jack and a framed steel etching of King George V.

"As far as shooting anyone, I can't help you with that one."

When they went into that room, there were going to be a lot of guns around and the likelihood of shooting and getting shot was high. They had surprise on their side, which would help. If he could do it, he wanted to very quickly convince the guards that it was in their own best interest to simply drop their guns and allow themselves to be tied up. He was pretty sure that no one who knew what was going on would be checking up on the progress of the massacre for a good long time. Perhaps not until morning, by which time they could be assumed to be fairly far away. Even though they would be hiding right here in the consulate basement.

But if he had to shoot someone to protect himself, then so be it. Molly had been right; he was changed. But this was a changed world, a place where being passive or fair or logical meant being dead.

"Look, Max, this is going to sound sort of simplistic, but think of it this way: If you've got to shoot someone to keep from being shot, then what's the difference? The alternative is a death in any event. It might as well not be yours."

Alex stood up and turned out the light. He found his makeshift bed in the dark and stretched out. Tomorrow he would know how it really came out. History? What was history?

Tomorrow he would know.

Chapter 39

THE NIGHT WAS CLOUDY. HIGH, THIN CLOUDS THAT VEILED THE STARS and the scant moon. The light was bare, a faint grayness that lay on the landscape. Alex and Surrey waited in the same copse of birch trees in the same hollows that their bodies had made the night before.

The air was dead still. No crickets.

Alex could feel the weight of it pressing down on him, squeezing his stomach into a hard knot.

"Now?" Surrey whispered. The heavy, still air muffled the question.

Surrey felt it, too; the pressure. It made him feel better to know that Surrey was as tight as he was. They had been lying without speaking for an hour. There was no real way to be exact as far as timing went. He had it figured as close as he possibly could. Now all they needed was some luck. Do it.

There was no cowardice or bravery, only action or inaction. You either did it or you didn't. Simple. Then why was it so hard to breathe?"

He stood.

"Now," he said softly in Surrey's direction. The word released them. He started into the first open area in a low crouch. He was glad they had done this the night before. It would not do to fall into a gopher hole and break his ankle,

294

knock his head against a tree, step into a ditch. Such mistakes undermine the confidence of the troops.

He moved from cover to cover, working his way up the hill, zigzagging into the protection of the shadows, crossing the open areas quickly and fluidly. Just like he'd read in books, seen in the movies. Take advantage of the terrain. Surrey moved behind him; Alex could feel him there, shadowing him.

They came into the last large grouping of trees beyond which they could clearly see the fence. Alex held out his hand and felt Surrey run into it. He drew the other man down beside him and pointed toward the fence. There was a very large dark object between the trees and the fence. They both stared at it for a minute until Surrey pulled him close and whispered, "Truck." The large black object solidified into a truck-shaped shadow for Alex. He nodded, wondering if the truck had a driver, a man who was now sitting in the cab, laughing at them, watching them as they ran up the hill looking like two boy commandos on a make-believe raid.

Alex moved through the last trees very slowly. He stopped at the edge where the dark gave way to the gray. The expanse of fence and the open area between the trees and the house seemed lighter than the open areas he'd already crossed. Perhaps the clouds had thinned or his eyes were used to the dark or his nerves were tightened to a higher pitch. Perhaps.

Nothing from the house or the truck. No lights, no sounds.

He glanced around, more to let Surrey know that it was time to move again than to actually see anything. They had to check the truck; there was no way around it. He put his hand to the ground to lever himself up and yahaaaa . . . his hand pushed down into warm, cloth-covered flesh. He clamped down on his mental scream. A body. Behind him Surrey grunted softly as he ran into him. Neither of them said anything as Alex got his breathing back under control.

Alex reached back for Surrey with one hand and stretched forward with the other.

Cloth. Buttons. Arms. A face. He shuddered as his fingers sank into a warm wetness where the man's neck had been slashed. He wiped his hand on the grass and crept backwards, pulling Surrey along with him.

"There's a dead guy in the grass," he whispered. It

sounded ridiculous. Surrey's shoulder seemed to tighten under his hand. Neither of them said anything.

"Do not move," a low voice behind them commanded.

Alex felt his heart turn over and a spurt of adrenaline hit his veins.

"Move back under the trees very slowly. Do not turn around; I will tell you when to stop. I have a gun and I will kill you if you try to escape."

There was nothing to do but to do it. They moved slowly backwards until they were well into the trees. He did not think; there was not enough information. He simply kept his mind open and waited for a chance.

"That is far enough. Turn around."

He turned. He could see the outline of Surrey beside him. In front, two figures, felt, more than seen.

"And now, very quickly and with no lies you will tell me what you are doing here."

He knew the voice. Where? Somewhere in the corner of his mind he felt the velvet touch of a hand in the night. The soft hiss of breath in his ear.

The train. Ekaterina Nicolaevna.

"Katya?" he said. The form in front of him went very still.

A long silence. "Move to the other side of the trees," the voice said. "Away from the house. Quietly."

They walked to the far side of the copse, hands outstretched to push away unseen branches.

"Down."

Alex and Surrey crouched at the edge of the shadows. He felt like a Vietnamese prisoner. Just then the clouds moved away from the moon and the night brightened as if a curtain had been raised. First one, then another, the crickets began to chirp.

Katya knelt beside them. She was holding a pistol pointed in their direction.

"Elena," Surrey said softly as the other woman knelt down.

"Yes," Katya said. "And now I must know what two officials of the Bolshevik party are doing here in the dark."

"Who's the dead guy?" Alex asked.

Katya shook her head. "He was in the truck. I had to kill

him. Now, no more questions. Answers. What are you doing here?"

"Probably the same thing you are," Alex said. He saw her arm rise and felt the cold, hard barrel of the pistol press against the side of his head. It was a very curious sensation, having a woman you had made love to put a gun against your head. For a moment he contemplated trying for the pistol or pulling out his own. Then he contemplated the dead body with the slashed throat lying up in the tall grass.

"We aren't Bolsheviks," Surrey said. "It doesn't matter," he said to Alex, "they aren't either. You're not, are you?" he asked the two women. "All that on the train was an act, wasn't it? The traveling political unit preaching the message of the Revolution to the peasants."

"I will tell you one more time," Katya said. Her voice was stretched thin, impatient, nervous. "You will answer my questions or I will do to you what I did to that guard." Her hand moved to the neck of her blouse. She held up an open knife. The blade caught the moonlight. "Now tell me. What are you doing here?"

"We're here to get the family out," Alex said. Surrey was right; there was no reason not to tell the truth. The two women weren't any more Bolsheviks than they were. From the minute they had met they had all been pretending to be one thing when they all were the other.

"Look," he said, suddenly realizing that they were wasting time. He had no firm idea when the action was due to begin, but if they were late, a lot of people were going to end up dead that might be saved. "We've got to get back up there and see what's going on. I'll give it to you straight. We're going to get them out and it has to be tonight, right now, or they're all done for."

"Why tonight?" Katya said suspiciously. "How do you know it must be tonight?"

"There's no time for talking. Christ, we've got to get on with it. You've got to trust us." Alex felt her take the gun away from his head. Relief. "The Whites have the area surrounded; the Bolsheviks are confused, I know," he answered. "There's no time to go into it. It has to be now."

An unexpected breeze blew down on them from the direction of the house. He heard something. Talking? The sound

297

of a door opening. He held out his hand and stood up, straining to hear. Crickets. Goddamned crickets. Voices?

He watched Katya while he listened. Even in the pale light he could see her make her decision. Trust. She nodded.

"That is why we are here," she said. "To try and rescue them."

"Women?" Surrey asked.

Alex almost laughed out loud at Surrey's question. His straining to hear what was going on up the hill and the surrealistic aspects of the conversation they were having had pushed to the edge of some sort of anxiety-madness. Inside his head a little voice was screaming, Fuck it, just go!

"Yes, women," Katya said, fiercely. "We have cossack blood. The two that were with us were afraid and would not come, but we are not afraid."

Alex held up his hand again and made a shushing noise. Voices again. He could swear he heard talking from the house.

Shots.

No, no, no. . . .

A ragged volley. Four or five shots. Screams. All muted. Far away, not so far away. Distant, then clearer as the light breeze shifted towards them and picked up in strength.

He felt a great rage swell up in him. The voice wailed in his head. No, goddamnit, no; not yet, not yet! Ah, Christ, all this and he'd fucked up. He forgot the others, turned, ran up the hill, pushing through the small trees, branches slapping at his face, hearing the screams and the shots. He pulled his pistol out as he ran, not bothering to be quiet, cursing under his breath. Single shots popped, muffled and yet clear and distinct in his brain.

Each shot a death.

Without thinking, he hit the fence gate with his shoulder and threw it open. Unlocked. Luck. He ran across the small inside yard and hit the door to the downstairs room. The door smashed open. He stumbled inside.

Thick smoke. Screams. Bodies. Pale, shocked faces turning toward him. People standing, moving, lying.

His brain swept it in, moving ten times faster than his body. He suddenly understood why movies often portrayed action scenes in slow motion. Things didn't move slower;

your brain just worked faster. A series of close-cropped freeze-frames.

A scene from a madhouse; a staggering, swirling horror that showed on the faces of the men and women crammed into the small room.

Soldiers, men in uniform, six of them, all with pistols pointed at the family, several not even aware that he had come through the door, firing at the group on the other side of the room. The looks on their faces were like fifteenth century etchings: greed, lust, fear.

But the faces of those being shot were the faces of the damned. One of the daughters stood with eyes squeezed shut as she awaited the bullet that knocked her down; another ran back and forth, screaming, the look of terror on her face straight from Dante, her mouth torn in a scream, her wild eyes flashing from wall to ceiling to wall, afraid to rest on those who quickly shot her; an older man, fat, sobbing, dropped to his knees and raised his hands in prayer. All of it taking only seconds to see, to die.

The air was thick with the gunsmoke, like the smoke from a hundred cigar-smoking conventioneers. It wreathed the scene, giving it an added touch of evil. Alex watched, frozen, as one of the soldiers shot a woman who clutched a pillow to her chest, saw the man pull the trigger, the gun leap, the woman thrown back and down.

Five feet away a man pointed his gun down to the floor where a little boy lay twisting. The Tsarevich, heir to the now non-existent throne, already shot; Alex could hear his high little-boy's wail distinct from the other screams, saw his little-boy's body leap as the bullet slammed into him. Alex saw his own pistol lift and center on the man as another shot hit the boy.

The side of the man's head disintegrated as Alex's bullet hit him. The body twisted in the air, turned slowly, fell. He felt an elation grow in his breast, felt the fear, the noise, the adrenaline, as the heat smoke anger hate pain boiled up in him and spilled over, burst out, freeing him from any rational thought, any moral whining, any consequences beyond stopping the man from shooting the little boy again. He was a child again; his father was teaching him; he heard the voice, understood now that the voice in his head was the voice of his father: Raise, point, shoot, *feel it; you are the hand of God!*

He shot the man another time as the body hit the floor. There was no thought now, only a great screaming relief, an unbearable need followed by the joy of release. The membrane tore; he pulled away the last shreds, struggled out, climbed free of his past, the future, born anew.

The sound was overwhelming, constant; shots from everywhere as all of them simply fired their guns, an ear-stunning roar. Beneath it Alex seemed to hear, to feel, a great thrumming noise like some giant chord struck deep in the earth's bowels as the room trembled around him.

The guns were pointed at him. He threw himself sideways, feeling a tug on his right arm, rolled, looked back to see Surrey and the two women behind him, watched Elena take a bullet in the chest, crumple. Katya did not flinch, stood with both hands on her pistol firing at the soldiers, her blond hair bright in the smoky room, flame spurting from the end of her gun, strong arms jerking with the recoil. A mad, mythic vision that even in that horrible place, in that split second, stirred in him and filled him, flowed, pumped into his body a harsh, hot love. Madness. He was alive with it. He shot another soldier, rolled to his right, steadying his pistol as he came up into a kneeling position.

The soldiers died. Trying to reload their pistols. Trying to hide behind each other. Crowding back against the wall. Shouting. Going down, the last of them, falling into each other in a strange dance, puppets jerked about and thrown into a pile on the ground.

Into the center of them, roaring like a wounded bull, came the Tsar. His face white with rage, eyes bulging, arms outstretched as he leapt on the soldiers, pulling the last one down. The firing stopped as men scrambled on the floor.

Alex dropped his pistol and pushed into the knot of twisting, gasping men and dead bodies. There was blood everywhere; the men were slick with it.

"Surrey!" he shouted, seeing the other man jump in beside him. He smashed a hand under his boot, saw a gun fall away, kicked the man in the head with his other foot. Surrey was on top of the only other moving soldier, pounding the man's head, over and over, into the floor. Alex grabbed Surrey's shoulders and pulled him away.

The only sound was the retching moan from the Tsar as he turned from the pile of unmoving soldiers and crawled to the bodies of his family and servants. He was on his hands and knees, eyes glazed with horror, crawling from one to the other, touching their faces, looking into their dead eyes. He got to his wife, pulled her bloody head into his lap as he rocked back and forth, trying to smooth the hair from her face.

Katya was kneeling by the body of her friend Elena. "Dead," she said to Alex. Surrey pulled himself to his feet. Alex saw him wince, then saw the stain of bright blood on the man's side.

"You're hit," Alex said, helping Surrey up.

"So are you," Surrey said, wincing.

Alex looked at his upper arm where Surrey was pointing. Then he felt a dull throb, saw the blood through the tear in his shirt. He had not felt it until that moment.

Katya stood and walked over to the soldiers lying on the floor. She seemed untouched. Her loose khaki pants and military shirt seemed strangely clean, in that room of blood. Her skin was pale with bright spots of color at the cheeks. Alex watched her kneel briefly, then stand and point her pistol.

"No," Alex said, too late, as she shot twice, killing the last two.

"She was my friend," she said simply, turning from the bodies. "We must see to the others."

Alex nodded, realizing that he had no idea how long it would be before those on the outside who knew what was happening came to investigate.

He set up a fallen chair and pushed Surrey down into it. He looked at the wound quickly. Surrey was pale but seemed strong enough for the moment.

He and Katya checked each of the bodies of the royal family.

Counting servants, there had been eleven. They checked all of them, straightening splayed limbs, looking for any signs of life. Beneath two of her sisters they found one of the daughters alive, unhurt, trembling. She screamed when they touched her, pulling back. Katya gathered her in her arms and pulled her to her feet, stroking her hair, holding her.

Alex checked the others quickly, feeling his resolve, his will, beginning to fade with the last of the adrenaline. There were none alive, only the girl and the Tsar.

"Let's get out of here," Alex said, helping Surrey up.

"I'm all right," Surrey said. He didn't look all right. He was pale, his lips a thin, bloodless line.

Alex went to the Tsar and helped him to his feet. The Tsar just looked at him. There was an emptiness behind the eyes.

"Jenny," the girl said, pointing to the floor. She bent down and picked up a stuffed toy dog. "Jenny," she said, stroking the pale brown fur.

"No," Alex said to Katya, following the woman's glance to her friend's body. "We can't take her with us. I'll take Surrey; you get the Tsar."

He looked around the room. The memory of it would never leave him. The sight, the stink of seventeen dead bodies, the smoke, the sick smell of the blood. It was there forever.

"Move," he said. "Now."

They went.

Chapter 40

SURREY WAS DEAD. SHE HUNG UP THE PHONE VERY CAREFULLY, turned, pulled Alex's terry cloth robe tight around her and went into the living room. She sat on the edge of the sofa and tried to think. There must be something she should do, some action that would help, some piece of business that would organize the loss she felt, channel it, label it so she could call it up or put it away at will. Nothing.

Alex should know. What could she do, call him on the time-phone? Hello, Alex, sorry to tell you this, but back here in the present your friend and surrogate father, Maxwell Surrey, has died. When you finish up your business there, please hurry home; we need you.

She picked up a magazine and looked at the cover and then put it down. She fiddled with the hem of the bathrobe where it needed to be resewn.

She had been to see him in the hospital. There was no point to it; he never came out of his coma, but it made her feel better. He was part of her lifeline to Alex, part of the rope that connected them. Now the strands were beginning to unravel. She could feel it begin to slip. If it gave way, she knew he would not come back. She could feel it.

So the loss was compounded, the loss of the funny old man that she saw with love through Alex's eyes added to the possible loss of Alex, gone forever into wherever he was, the past.

She went to the window and opened the curtains. Dawn. She leaned against the wall and stared out. It would be another beautiful day. In the time Alex had been gone fall had come, breaking the heat and humidity, bringing a crispness that made even New York seem fresh. If you used your imagination, you could come up with the smoky memory of burning leaves.

She had gone to a party the day before. A man had come to her and asked if she was alone. Yes. Did she live in the city? Yes. Did she live with someone? Yes. Yes and no. Maybe. Who the hell knew? The man had wandered off, confused. No more than she. But she would wait. Because there was nothing else she could do and besides she loved him. It seemed, now, as if she had always loved him. And so she would wait, and meanwhile the old man had died, the poor old man.

She leaned forward and touched her nose to the window. She had cleaned all the windows in the house. The glass was cool. Her breath fogged a circle that threw a haze over the street outside. A beautiful day, Alex. What are you doing? Are you going to parties? Come home, Alex; it's a beautiful day.

"Alex," she said softly. It sounded foolish in the dead air of the living room, early in the morning, a word floated out into an empty room. Words, spoken words, only exist if there is someone to hear them. Does the falling tree make a sound if there is no one to hear? Yes, but what difference does it make?

She got up, went to the kitchen, put on water for coffee.

Chapter 41

"I'M SORRY," PRESTON SAID, "BUT THERE ARE NO DOCTORS. AT any rate there are no doctors we can use. It's out of the question."

Alex winced as Katya pulled the wrapping on his arm tighter. The wound was straight across the large muscle on the outside of his upper right arm. The bullet had furrowed a channel through the meat of the muscle but had missed the bone. He turned his head away from the odor of raw flesh, gunsmoke that still clung to his clothing, the stink of his own sweat.

"There's got to be a doctor," Alex insisted. "I'll be all right, but Surrey and the Tsar need help."

"You've got to realize the situation," Preston went on. He was standing stiffly, almost at attention. His fair English skin was flushed and he kept glancing away from Alex to the others around the room. They had made it back to the embassy and into the basement room without being seen. "By now the Bolsheviks have discovered that things have gone wrong. They'll be all over the town looking for the Tsar. And whoever got him out and killed their men. And that's aside from the fact that they're simply are no doctors. They all left when the Bolsheviks took over. There's nothing for it; I'm afraid you've got to go it alone. Good God, man, stop looking at me like that. Don't you think I'd help if I could?''

Alex tried to think. The pain in his arm kept taking over, demanding his attention.

The basement room looked like a primitive hospital after a major battle. Which in fact it was. Surrey was flat on his back on a pile of canvas, watching them silently. His face was white with shock and loss of blood. The bullet that hit him had entered on the right side of his abdomen and had gone straight through.

The Tsar was also lying down. He had been hit four times, but, miraculously, only superficially. In the end, perhaps the soldiers had been unable to aim directly at their divinely appointed Little Father. Tatiana, the Tsar's daughter, sat in the corner, clutching her stuffed dog to her breast, saying nothing, watching her father, listening to his loud, ragged breathing. Katya moved silently between all of them, tying up the wounds, trying to stop the bleeding.

The blood. The room was thick with the smell of it. Stale air, sweat, dirt, the musty canvas, and blood. Always the blood.

"All right," Katya said, turning to them, "there is no doctor. To worry about it any longer is useless. We must be realistic. What can we do?''

Alex shook his head to clear it. The movement set up a new ache in his arm.

He tried to remember his basic first aid. He'd read about men wounded in Vietnam, but there they had sulfa packs, penicillin, pressure bandages. What had his father said back in the forest? Infection. That was the real danger. Bullets carried bits of torn clothing into wounds, bits of dirt, bacteria that would culture almost immediately. If unchecked, the blood would poison and they would all die. If he was lucky, he might only lose his arm.

Infection. Sulfa packs. Penicillin. Sulphur. . . . The smell of rotten eggs. It flickered at the edge of his brain. The dye factory.

"There's a dye factory out on the edge of town; I saw it on my way in," Alex said. Preston nodded. "Send someone there. Get me sulphur, a couple of pounds of it, as pure as they've got. They use it in the dyes." Preston just stared at him, uncomprehending. "Just do it! Don't think; just do what I say." Preston hesitated, then nodded and started for the ladder out of the basement. "Wait," Alex stopped him. "We also need more clean cloth for bandages, lots of it. Boil the cloth. And hot water. And alcohol."

"Right," Preston said. "I'll see to it immediately."

He worked on Surrey first. He knew he should have seen to the Tsar, but friendship won out over royalty. He washed the wound with the hot water, clearing away the dried blood so he could see the damage.

The entry hole was clean and still seeping blood; the exit wound looked worse. He felt better when he could find nothing to indicate that any of the internal organs had been hit. Not that he really knew what to look for. He washed the ragged edges of the wound with the alcohol. He remembered reading somewhere that it was a mistake to dump an antiseptic into the wound, that it killed the body's bacteria-fighters rather than the invading bacteria. He felt Surrey holding himself rigid against the pain.

"This is where it starts to get bad," Alex said.

"Jesus Christ," Surrey rasped, "I already thought it was bad."

"That was just the preliminary. It gets worse."

"Just do it."

"I need two strips of sterilized cloth. One inch by six inches." He indicated to Katya the size he needed.

She tore off the strips and immersed them into the water. She picked them out with the point of a knife she had also boiled and passed them to Alex.

"Hold his legs," he said to Preston, who had been crouched beside him. Alex glanced at the consul. The man looked a little pale. He was trying hard, but they had left this part out at diplomat school.

"Take his shoulders," he said to Katya.

Still using the knife, he dropped the strip of cloth into a pile of sulphur he had spread out on a tray. The bright yellow powder stuck to the wet cloth. As carefully as he could, he pushed one end of the strip down into the wound. He had to get it in deep. He felt the sweat break out on his forehead as

307

he probed the wound. Surrey strained against the two who held him.

"I need to get the strips all the way in," he said, talking to cover his tension. He wasn't sure where he'd picked up the information, but he was pretty sure it was right. "The wound has to heal from the inside out; otherwise there's the chance it will heal over on the surface and fester on the inside. The cloth strips act as drains. They'll keep the wound open to the air. We'll pull the drains out as it heals."

He carefully rolled Surrey's stiff body on its side. He pushed the cloth drain into the back wound. He sprinkled more sulphur onto the surface of the wounds and applied clean wads of cloth to the front and back. Katya helped him wrap the torso with strips of cloth. They had Surrey on his back when they heard the man faint.

"Drag him out of the way," Alex said, looking over at Preston stretched out on the floor. The consul's face was pale but still composed. He even fainted with a stiff upper lip.

"You okay?" he asked Surrey. Max's eyes were bright with tears, but he forced a tiny grin and nodded. "Get some water into him," he said to Katya. "It doesn't look like the bullet went through the stomach or the intestine, so the water shouldn't hurt him."

He couldn't tell if the Tsar was conscious or unconscious. His eyes were open but totally unresponsive. He lay on his back, staring at the ceiling. Alex tried a few questions but received no response.

"Okay," he said to Katya, "more clean cloth and water. We won't need the drains, just bandages to pull the wounds closed."

There was a lot of blood, but once they got that cleaned up, it didn't look so bad. He'd been hit four times, in the arm twice, in the neck and side. All wounds like Alex's, ragged cuts rather than holes. They dusted everything with the sulphur and bandaged them. The Tsar didn't even quiver. He seemed to be gone, somewhere outside the room, away from the death and the blood. Alex left the wrapping of the last bandages to Katya. He was suddenly dizzy.

"You're next," she said, looking at him with a frown of concern. He was sitting on the floor, feeling terrible. It was all beginning to catch up with him. Maybe he wasn't cut out for the active life. Freedom fighter. Doctor. Christ, the sulphur was just a guess; maybe he was guessing wrong. Maybe straight sulphur, if that's what this was, was poisonous in large quantities.

He gestured to his own wound. "It doesn't need any drains. Just clean out the trench, dump in the sulphur, and tie it up."

He clenched his teeth against the pain. He kept his head turned away from the wound. He'd put up with it, but he didn't have to watch it. The thought of the raw wound brought the dizziness back. Tough guy. Faints at the sight of his own blood. He stayed with it while she tied him up. Wouldn't do to show weakness in front of the Amazon. The Valkyrie. Got to be tough, like a cossack.

He kept himself upright while Katya washed Tatiana's face and pushed her down on the makeshift bed. The girl tried to smile her thanks. She seemed to be coming out of the catatonia that still held the Tsar. She clutched the stuffed dog tight in her arms.

Alex didn't argue when Katya made him stretch out on the pile of canvas. The consul had dragged himself upstairs.

He heard her switch out the light and carefully make her way back. The sounds of breathing from the others seemed louder in the darkness. She lay down next to him, slid close until the length of her body was pressed to his. She very carefully put her arm around him. He lay in the dark staring at nothing, feeling his arm throb, expecting a night of pain and worry. Her hand settled lightly on his shoulder, directly over the pain. Her body was warm and soft against his. He was surprised to feel himself falling asleep.

Chapter 42

ALEX WAITED FOR THE WORST. THE EDGES OF THE FLESH AROUND all of their wounds turned pink then red, an indicator that there was at least a local infection. But none of them developed dangerous temperatures or chills, no overt signs of septicemia. It could have come on them in a matter of hours. He waited for it.

The Tsar stayed in his own private world, inaccessible to all of them, even Tatiana. They fed him his meals, which he took but never asked for. He asked for nothing. He sat, lay down, ate on command, but his mind was far away.

Tatiana lost her horror of that night, or at least buried it, and became their primary source of medical care. She had worked as a volunteer in hospitals with her sisters and mother during the years before the Bolshevik takeover. The First World War had supplied her with countless gunshot wounds to learn from. She kept the dressings clean and fresh, washed out the wounds, and fed those that couldn't feed themselves. She and Alex had a long procedural argument over the use of disinfectant in the actual wound, she taking the position that it was necessary. Alex remained adamant, telling her that the sulphur would do the job better. She grumbled but went along with it, accepting his judgment.

After several days they all began to call her Tanya. She

concentrated most of her attention on Surrey. At first Alex thought it was odd that she didn't spend her time with her father, but as he watched he began to realize that she didn't really consider this wounded man, the Tsar, to be the same man who had been her father, Emperor of all Russia and husband to Alexandra.

"He has lost her, my mother, so he has lost everything," she explained to Alex. "She was first in his life, before even Russia. Everything he did was for her. He loved us all, and his country, but he loved her more. Everyone who was close to him knew his feelings for her and accepted them. They could not have changed them in any case. He will not die; he is a very strong man, but he may never live in our world. Perhaps it is better this way."

So she gravitated to Surrey; they were both twenty-one years old and he was her rescuer. In the few short days her attitude toward Surrey progressed from practical concern to something more. She became very proprietary about his care and he, Surrey, did nothing to dissuade her.

They tried to organize their room, but it still looked like a recreation of some primitive attempt at a hospital. Straight out of the Middle Ages. It stank of sulphur, dirty bodies, and blood. They were afraid go upstairs to the consulate to bathe because of the constant threat of a Bolshevik search. They used a chamber pot behind a pinned-up blanket for a toilet and washed in the few gallons of water that were hauled downstairs by the consul.

At night Alex would lie on his bed of piled canvas, listening to the varied breathing in the small room, monitoring the state of his charges. The Tsar's breathing was heavy, labored but even. Katya, beside him, slept quietly, her breath light on his cheek. Tanya slept so quietly she made no sound at all. Surrey sometimes moaned, but Alex didn't mention it to him. Surrey had a large painful hole in his side. He was allowed to moan in his sleep.

He lay there listening, checking them off one by one; Tsar, Tatiana, Surrey, and Katya. Only after he was satisfied they were all settled could he sleep. They had become his responsibility. As in the old Chinese tradition, he had rescued them and now their lives were his responsibility. He liked the feeling. It worried him, but it filled a place inside him that, although he had never noticed it before, had been empty.

After five days with no major medical problems Alex began to let himself relax a little. And as soon as he did he found himself seeing the little room much the same way he had seen his prison cell. His arm was healing; aside from being very stiff and very sore he could use it. Otherwise he was healthy. His body began to ache to move around, breathe fresh air, do something besides sit around all day.

"What's the general situation?" Alex asked, standing at the foot of the ladder that led out of the basement. He met there with Preston at least once a day.

"The Whites are getting very close," Preston said. "Their airplanes are flying over every day. They're making the Bolsheviks extremely nervous."

"What about the Tsar and the family?"

"Of course they've mounted an extensive search. No announcement as yet about the killings. They've covered the town looking for him, but they're keeping quiet about the reason for the search. I've had a man watching the house. They took all the bodies away the same night you were there. They took them to an abandoned mine called the Four Brothers, several miles from here. Chopped them up, poured acid on them, and burned them. Dumped what little was left down the mineshaft."

Alex glanced around to see if any of the others had heard. Not the sort of thing you wanted to hear about your family. Tanya was talking to Surrey. The Tsar was leaning against the far wall, staring at nothing. Katya was busy ladling out the stew that Preston had brought.

The disposal of the bodies was just like in the book Molly had given him that first day they had had lunch together. *The File on the Tsar*. Except the Bolsheviks were a couple of bodies short. The two authors of the book hadn't been right in their conclusions, as Alex had thought back when he had first read it, but they had been right in their basic premise: the family of the Tsar had not entirely perished.

"They'll be pulling out soon," Alex said, almost to himself. "They'll have to make some sort of an announcement."

312

He looked at Preston. "They'll have to announce that they've executed the whole family. They can't admit that they've lost any of them, especially the Tsar. They'll continue the hunt, but the Whites are going to have them on the run for a while." He thought about it for a minute. "I'll bet the local Bolsheviks haven't reported the loss. I'll bet they're not going to say anything about it until they get him back. If the Central Committee or Lenin knew that they had misplaced the most important prisoner in their short history, they'd be lined up and shot by nightfall.

"If we can hold another few days, we'll be all right," Alex went on. "The Whites will be here by then. The Tsar will be all right, though I don't think he'll ever be much use to anyone again. I still want a real doctor to look at Surrey."

Preston cleared his throat. "I'm afraid the doctor part of it is out in any case. I've had very precise instructions from the foreign office on this. The Whites are not to know that we've got him." He nodded at the Tsar. "They feel it's just as important to keep it from the Whites as the Reds.

"There's still a war on and our people are trying to convince the Reds to come back in with them," he went on defensively. "We're trying to maintain friendly relations, as much as that is possible. If the Whites get hold of Nicholas and anyone ever puts it together that we helped them, we'll be finished as far as diplomacy goes. They're really quite firm about this. They're willing to supply you transport out of here, but only on those conditions."

"They'll take us out and then hide the two of them forever," Alex said, more to himself than to Preston. That was all right with him. In fact, it was what he'd planned all along. That way there would be no time discrepancies. Or at least none that he could think of. To do otherwise was to do what his father wanted. It meant no doctor for Surrey, but for now he would go along with it. If Surrey took a turn for the worse, then he'd find a doctor and they would just have to lump it.

"I think it would be safe to have you come upstairs, one at a time, of course, tomorrow. Stretch your legs a little. Get a proper bath. We'll keep a close watch."

Alex nodded. A bath.

*   *   *

After the others fell asleep, Katya had rubbed lightly against him in the dark, her quick, sure hands running coolly along his body.

They had all had a bath. The exercise and the bath had tired everyone out. Everyone except Katya. She and Tanya had hung blankets around all of their sleeping mats. She had pulled theirs to the farthest corner of the room.

"A new game," she had whispered to him, "a game; we call it wounded soldier. A true cossack is never wounded beyond the capability of love. Only death brings inability. You are to lie very still; you are wounded. If you move, you will hurt yourself. If you move or make any noise, I will stop the game." Then she made love to him. He did not move. He found it excruciatingly pleasurable. He forgot the pain in his arm. Forgot the claustrophobia. Forgot everything except the feel of her body as she settled lightly down onto him, moving slowly, very slowly.

But afterwards he still could not sleep. He felt Katya's light breath on his cheek. She never had trouble sleeping. She was constantly cheerful, happy, and extremely competent. The more he was around her, the more he realized he was falling in love with her. In a very curious way.

It had begun with the sound of guns, when he had gone down, rolled, turned and saw her wreathed in smoke. She stood like some avenging goddess meting out death to the doomed. It was the stuff of fantasy. But it was real.

Katya's history, whispered in the night: Katya, the only child of a Cossack officer whose hereditary job was to guard the Tsar. She knew the royal family because of her father's connection, had even played with the girls when they were small, though Tatiana didn't remember her. Her father had raised her in many of the traditions he would have raised a son. Cossack traditions. When she was old enough, she had joined the women's regiment, the Death Battalion. They had been assigned to guard the Winter Palace against the Bolsheviks. They had failed, their officers capitulating without firing a shot. She had fled, in a fury, to where her father was hiding, biding his time while trying to raise an army to fight the Reds. It had been he who gave her the task of the rescue.

The act on the train had been part of it. The three other women with her then had been in the battalion with her, though only Elena, who had died, had been another daughter of a Cossack. The loud Katya who had ordered the soldiers around was not the real Katya. The real Katya was quiet, absolutely loyal, skillful, and very well trained in the military arts. Women warriors. Valkyries.

She was beautiful and strong. She accepted his judgments on all matters. She did not argue or complain. She cared for him with a kind of fierce love that was part of her tradition. Good God, how could he not love her?

"*Ya vass lublu,*" she whispered in the night. I love you. For her, it was all very simple.

Chapter 43

Surrey looked at him over the rim of the bowl of hot broth he was drinking. "Christ, I'm sick of meat broth. When I was a kid, we used to call this stuff mouse breath."

Alex laughed. "Mouse breath? Why was that?"

Surrey shrugged and then winced. "Ouch." He touched his bandaged side lightly. He was much better, but sudden movements still hurt. "I can't remember why we called it that. I suppose it was because it smells like what a mouse's breath smells like. Whatever that smells like." He started to shrug again and then caught himself. He put the empty bowl on the bedside table. The light in the room was bright. Through the open window they could hear the sounds of traffic, both horse-drawn and occasionally motorized, in the streets outside.

They had all moved upstairs. The Bolsheviks had been gone for three days. The Whites had moved in and occupied the town but had kept their distance from the British Consulate. They had opened formal negotiations with the consul for aid from Britain. There would be no searches or questions. They did not want to upset the English.

The Tsar was also doing well. At least physically. His wounds had healed over and he had been up and moving around for several days. He fed himself and dressed himself,

316

but that was all he did. He spent his days sitting in a chair, staring out a window. His only desire seemed to be to sit in the sun when he could. He floated somewhere far away in a corner of his mind where his wife was not dead. He would function, after a fashion, but he would not participate.

They had shaved off his beard and mustache. The transformation was astonishing. Without the royal facial hair he looked quite ordinary.

They had also cut Tanya's hair. She had not complained about it after Surrey told her that she must cut it to disguise herself. By now she and her little stuffed dog were inseparable from Surrey. Surrey accepted the compliment with sheepish good humor.

"What do we do next?" Surrey asked. There was a faint smile on his face. "I'm getting as sick of sitting in bed as I am of eating mouse breath. Starting today I want real food and I'm going to get out of bed."

What next indeed, Alex thought. He scratched at his arm. The wound no longer hurt much, but it itched. He seemed to remember that that meant it was healing.

He'd thought about it, the what-next question. There was no putting it off. It was time to get the Tsar and Tatiana out.

"What we do next," he said to Surrey, "is get the two of them out of here."

Surrey nodded. "When?"

"Soon. There's just one problem."

"Good, we can handle one problem. I was thinking it might be a bit more difficult than that." Surrey's smile was now back to its former glory. It gave Alex a surprising amount of peace to see it back in place.

"The problem is, we're going to have to split up."

The smile was replaced by a frown. "Why? What's the point of it? We've worked pretty well together up till now."

"It's not that," Alex said. "That goes without saying." He knew that his plan was going to disappoint Surrey. They had formed a bond, part father-son, part friendship—a complicated but strong friendship built up through respect and shared danger. It would be difficult to break that bond.

"We're going to take them out in two different directions. You have to trust me on this, but I think it's the only really safe way. If we split up, we have twice the chance that we'll

317

get at least one of them out. Together, we run the risk of all being hauled in if we're caught."

"Well," Surrey said, shaking his head, "there's no real arguing with logic that simple. Except that with the two of us together we'll have twice the ability to get ourselves out of any trouble that comes up."

The part that Alex couldn't tell him was that the direction he was going to take was the trail right into a trap. If his father wasn't dead, he would be waiting and he would be waiting on the only logical escape route. The train run to the coast, Vladivostok. And he had to do it. There was one piece of business with his father that had to be taken care of. He had to make sure of one small change so that all of it would happen the way it had just happened. He had decided that his, Alex's, name on the list of names in the report was the element that had drawn him back into the past. He had to make sure that element was put in place. But allowing Surrey to come in contact with his father was unacceptable.

He would appeal to Surrey on another level. "You're going to take out Tatiana; I'll take the Tsar." For the first time since the rescue the two of them would be off by themselves.

"You're sure we can't all go together?" Surrey sighed at Alex's nod. "Okay. I've trusted everything you've said so far. How do I do it?"

"Tomorrow we'll go over it. Now you should rest. Get back your strength, Maxwell; you're going to be needing it in the very near future."

The two of them stood in the map room with Preston. One whole wall was covered with a map of Russia. Alex was amazed at the lack of information on the map. Most of it east of the Urals was blank, painted a dull tan color with a few tracks of blue where rivers were supposed to be.

The main features were the railroads, though even they were rare. There was one line from west to east, one set of tracks that crossed the great tan emptiness.

"It's quite impossible to predict the delays with any accuracy," Preston said. "It could be a bit dicey."

Yes, indeed, Alex thought. Typical British understatement. A bit dicey. Preston had turned out to be loyal, considerate, and helpful, but sometimes his English phlegm and his

318

diplomacy-first attitude wore a little thin. Yes, crossing four thousand miles of some of the most difficult terrain in the world with history's most wanted man might be a little tough.

"Quite interesting, actually," Preston babbled on, pointing at a large lake two-thirds of the way across the map. "Lake Baikal. You'll see the tracks drop down and go around the southern end of the lake. In the winter they simply lay track right across the ice and cut directly over. Rather unnerving, I'm told, what with the weight of the locomotives. Beautiful country, though. In its own way."

Surrey rolled his eyes at Preston's digressions and smiled. "So what's the plan, Alex. Splitting up is going to be difficult, seeing that there's only one railroad. Do you go first and then I follow or vice versa?"

Alex pondered the map for a moment. "No, I'm the one who's taking the long route. You're going back the way we came." He glanced at Surrey and saw his brow wrinkle with a second's worth of worry.

"All right," Surrey said slowly. "But isn't that dangerous?"

"Not for a Hero of the Revolution. Actually, you'll be going more north than west." He tapped the map at Ekaterinburg and traced a railway line to the northwest, all the way to the coast.

"Archangel," Alex said. "If you get there, you'll be safe."

Preston was nodding his head and bouncing slightly on the balls of his feet. "Hmm, yes, interesting, interesting."

"The Allies," Alex continued, "particularly the Americans, have been landing men and supplies at Archangel ever since the Bolsheviks signed a peace treaty with the Germans. The Allies, or rather the former Allies, are still publicly pretending to work with the Reds, but secretly they're fighting them. Or at least helping the Whites fight them." He waited for Preston's contradiction.

"I say . . ." Preston began.

Alex waved him quiet. "Don't bother; I know you're supposed to deny all this, secrecy and all that."

"But how . . ." he began and then stopped with a sigh. "Right, I know; you just know these things." He shook his head.

"Anyway," Alex went back to Surrey, "there are British ships at Archangel; you can get out that way. It might be a little rough from Perm"—he touched a town designation on the map, then another—"to Vologda, but there's no real way of knowing who's in control anywhere. Once you get north you'll find Americans, French, Italians, and Whites you can ask for help if you have to. Of course you'll have to keep the identity of your traveling partner quiet, but I don't think you'll have much trouble there."

Surrey nodded and studied the map.

"If I may make a suggestion," Preston said, clearing his throat. Alex nodded. "Rather than going to Vologda, which I'm sure would be quite dangerous, if you take the train north to Kotlas, you can pick up transport on the Dvina River. The river flows directly into Archangel."

Alex studied the map. "He's right," he said to Surrey. "It's a better route. Thanks, Preston."

"We'll work out your timetable so the proper authorities can be informed. And of course I'll have to report this to my masters in London."

"All right," Alex agreed, "that about takes care of it."

"Ah, it sounds so simple," Surrey said with a smile.

"The plan is simple, that's true," Alex agreed. "The reason is there are so few options."

Surrey nodded. "And when does all of this begin?" he asked. Alex wondered if he heard at least a tiny bit of anxiety in the question.

"You'll have to decide yourself when you'll be able to travel. You shouldn't go until you're satisfied that your wound is healed."

"And you?" Surrey asked.

"I leave tomorrow."

Chapter 44

"I WILL COME WITH YOU," KATYA HAD SAID. HE HAD THOUGHT about it long and hard, tried to view the problem dispassionately. Impossible to do. He wanted her to come. What he was going to do with her when they got to the other end, wherever the other end was, would be decided then. For now, it was Alex, Katya, and the Tsar.

Alex was amazed at the efficiency of the Russian railway system. Even though the Whites had chased off the Reds only a few days before, the trains were running pretty much on schedule. No one questioned the man the consul sent to pick up their tickets. Three tickets to Vladivostok, straight through to the end of the line. The train would leave at ten A.M.

They said their good-byes at the consulate. Tatiana cried, but the tears seemed to be more for the past than the present. Nicholas did not seem to be aware that he was saying goodbye to the last of his children. If everything worked correctly, they would never see each other again.

Alex pulled Tatiana to the side and spoke to her in a low voice.

"I don't know what's going to happen, Tanya, but when you get out of the country, the English are going to look after you."

She broke in on him. "No! Maxwell will help me; he has said so. I will not leave him." Her jaw was set in a stubborn line.

"All right," Alex said, "Surrey will take care of you, but the English are responsible for you. There will be money matters, questions of where you're going to live, things of that nature. Now, we don't have much time, and I can't really explain it, but I'm going to give you some written instructions to help you in the future. You're not to show them to anyone, do you understand?" Her eyes were very serious. She nodded. "Good." He handed her a small, folded square of paper and patted her hand. He had made out the list the night before.

She embraced him, quickly, like a little girl. "Thank you, Alex." She stepped back and glanced at her father. "For everything."

"I'm sorry it couldn't have been more," he said.

She nodded, gave him a small smile, and turned to say good-bye to Katya.

Alex went over Surrey's plans with him one more time, but there was little to add. It would be up to Surrey to get them through.

"I'll find you at Princeton," Alex said. Surrey intended to go back to graduate school when he made it back to the United States. Alex felt guilty at what he assumed was a lie. He didn't think he'd stay in the past long enough to meet Surrey anywhere. He felt the loss. The man had become a good friend; they had done things that no other men had ever done. Added was the complication of their future life, the line that tied them together, doubling back from past to present, back again. The train whistle blew.

Alex had two weeks to make the journey; Preston promised them a British vessel at the other end for that period of time but not beyond. Normally it was a six-day journey. The problem, aside from the more mundane problems of the civil war, was his father, waiting somewhere along the line like a spider waiting for the foolish bug to tumble into the web. Alex: foolish bug. But a bug that was heading for the web with wide-open eyes. He had no choice; he had to find his father.

The train, three days later, at the southernmost tip of Lake

Baikla, in the mountains where the tamarack pines had just begun to turn from green to gold, slid slowly to a stop. The bug had tumbled to the spider.

Alex gently moved a dozing Katya from under his arm, sat up and looked out the window. Lining the track was a contingent of mounted men, wild-looking men, rifles strapped to their backs, atop small, shaggy ponies. His first response was to laugh at the little horses: Americans are used to tall, fine-boned horses; these long-haired beasts looked like children's mounts, rejects from some itinerant carnival pony ride. But Katya was awake now and the look on her face knocked the laugh right out of him. Then she said the word that had been said thousands of times by thousands of Russians with the same stark inflection that had never lost its power, had never become a cliche, was never a laughing matter.

"Cossacks."

Alex felt a moment of dread well up in him, catching him unexpectedly, bringing a tingling feeling of panic. He found himself searching the corners of the compartment for some place to hide or a back door he could disappear through.

Katya was looking at him, waiting for him to tell her what he wanted her to do. Responsibility. It grounded him. He had two people to take care of; he would take care of them. He had no time to sit around and think about it, to try and look up the answer in a book or to dwell on the best possible way to go about it. He would act. There was no other choice; fear, uncertainty, was not an option. No other choice; not a bad definition of bravery.

"Listen to me," he said to her, turning away from the window to face her, speaking quickly. The Tsar, sitting in the corner, paid no attention. "These people are looking for me," he said. "Stay with me; don't let anyone separate us. If we get in serious trouble, though, and I tell you to get out, to run, do what I say. You must do what I say. Do you understand? You're to take Nicholas and get away."

Katya's eyes were locked onto his. She didn't argue. She understood orders.

The door to the compartment slammed back. "Outside!" a

323

rough Cossack bellowed. He was tall and dangerous-looking, with a thick moustache and high, prominent cheekbones, a Mongolian slant to his eyes. There were bandoleers strapped across his chest and a curved silver knife at his waist. His clothes were tattered, torn at the elbows and knees. He carefully appraised Katya and the Tsar. "All of you, outside. No luggage. Outside."

They joined the line of passengers shuffling toward the doors at the end of the train. There was little talk, only nervous glances that never connected. Alex had a sudden vision of all of them shuffling off toward the ovens, clutching their little bars of soap made of stone.

Outside, Alex looked down the line for someone in command. Most of the riders had dismounted and were parading along the line of passengers, inspecting the women and the clothing of the men as if they were in some strange market where the goods were displayed on the employees. This was the first test of their disguise of the Tsar. Alex waited for the shout of recognition. One of them reached out and laid a filthy hand on Katya's cheek. He turned and said something to a comrade, who laughed. Alex felt a rush of rage, but the tiny shake of Katya's head and the warning look in her eyes stopped him. She was right; it was not the time or the place for chivalry.

Alex saw a slightly cleaner man who wore his belted tunic and bloused pants as if it were a uniform. He was appraising the passengers from atop his horse.

"*Ataman*," Alex shouted at him. He had no idea what the power structure among the Cossacks might be. He had used their word for leader. The man looked at him, his attention caught by this rare event, a passenger who had the temerity to speak out. Alex stepped forward. The man kicked his horse and moved nearer.

"I am not *Ataman*," he said, his voice surprisingly benign. "We are Ussuri Cossacks, our *ataman* is Ivan Pavlovich Kalyokov. "What do you want?"

"My name is Alexander Balfour. If you have a man named Charonsky with you, he is looking for me." He motioned to where Katya and Nicholas had moved up beside him. "We are traveling together; if Charonsky is with you, he will want to see us."

Some of the other Cossacks were looking at the man on the horse. This small exchange had stopped the general milling about for the moment.

"Shall I kill him?" one of the Cossacks asked.

The horseman glanced at the man and then back to Alex. He still did not speak. Alex couldn't tell if the man were making up his mind or simply caught up in his observations of Alex, a strange and lower form of life. The tension began to stretch, but Alex did nothing to break the silence. He remembered a bit of political wisdom he had once heard somewhere: The one who speaks last loses.

"Follow me," the man said at last, turning his horse and moving down the tracks toward the front of the train. He did not look back to see if they were following.

They walked along the tracks. The train was on their left. The rail bed itself had been carved out of the solid granite of the mountain, leaving very little room for much more than a wide shoulder. Beyond this shoulder, on the right, the mountain plunged down a densely forested incline to a canyon, threading the center of which was a mountain stream. The woods were mostly pine, but the heavy humidity gave it the feel of a more tropical climate. In contrast, the high peaks in the distance were already dusted with the coming winter's first snows.

The passengers were lined up against the high carriages of the train. The line of Cossacks stood carelessly on the lip of the roadbed, inches away from the edge of the canyon. There was enough room to thread their way between these two lines, though Alex saw the flanks of the horse in front of him touching some of the men as it brushed by. He felt as if he were walking down a row of hostile Indians who were preparing to beat him with sticks. The passengers watched them with barely concealed expressions of fear and sick satisfaction. As if Alex, Katya, and Nicholas were being led off to some horrible fate that they, at least for the moment, had escaped.

The late afternoon sun had slipped behind the crest of the mountain, casting the scene into shadow. The air was cool and damp, touched by the mist from the stream below. The train curved around a long horseshoe turn, car after car of waiting passengers. Alex guessed that there were at least three hundred men, women, and children strung out along the tracks, standing silently, watching the Cossacks laugh and smoke.

They marched all the way to the front of the train. There, facing the locomotive, was the Cossacks' train. It was short, only a few cars long, as heavy and squat as a small dinosaur, plated with thick slabs of concrete with metal sheathing. There was a large gun mounted on the front, projecting forward like a horn on a rhinoceros. A handwritten sign over the large central headlamp gave the train's name: The Merciless. Atop the cars behind the locomotive were machine guns mounted at the front and the rear. There were no real windows in the cars, only barred slits.

They walked along beside this train, past the first three cars, and then the rider in front of them pulled up and dismounted.

"Wait," he said. He did not seem worried that they were going to run away.

Alex thought of it, looked down the track ahead of them, then gave it up. He had not come all this way, straight into the spider's web, to then run away.

The Cossack leaned out of the door at the end of the train and motioned for them to enter.

The first thing that hit them was the smell. The light was too dim to see much of anything. It was the sweetish stink of rotting flesh mixed with sweat and dirt. Alex focused on the pale bedclothes at the far end of the car. He stepped closer.

"Ahh, the prodigal son returns," his father said from the bed. He leaned over and pulled a small shade away from the slit window. The outside light made it possible to see. His father was lying on a narrow bed, elevated by several large pillows, covered with sheets that were rumpled and sweat-stained.

He looked very old. He had a week's growth of beard that had come in white, grizzled-looking rather than distinguished. The silver wings of hair were tousled and matted. The face was greasy and lined. But the eyes, the eyes glittered like tiny miners' lamps, feverish. The look of an animal trapped in a small cage.

326

Alex moved to the side of the bed and looked down. His father smiled up at him as if daring Alex to feel sorry for him. The stink was stronger.

"Boil water," Alex said to the Cossack who had come in with them. He made it a command rather than a suggestion. "Boil whatever clean cloth you can find. And I mean clean. Get it from one of the passengers if you don't have any of your own." The Cossack didn't move, looked at Alex's father.

"Charonsky?" the Cossack asked.

His father nodded. The man turned and left.

Alex reached down and pulled back the sheet. The stench of rot wafted up. Alex looked at the dirty wrapping on the swollen leg. "Looks like you've got a real problem here," he said in a tight voice. He had to swallow to keep from throwing up. "See if you can get these rags off him," he said to Katya. He reached over and picked up the vodka bottle from the bed. "Soak them off with this."

He stepped back as Katya moved to the side of the bed. He stood at the end and watched as she worked. His father stared at him.

"Well, where are they?"

"Who?" Alex asked.

"*Pfah*," his father grunted as Katya soaked the bandages in vodka. "You know very well who. The Tsar. The rest of them."

"It didn't work. I couldn't get them out; they were all killed. The Bolsheviks issued a statement; for once it was true."

"Nothing they say is true. We had men in Ekaterinburg. There was a search that went on for days after the killings. The messages to Petersburg were ambiguous. The Central Committee was not informed of the search."

Alex glanced at Katya. She peeled the last layer of binding off the wound. She turned away from the pus-weeping hole. His father didn't seem to notice. It was then that Alex realized just how drunk his father must be. To lie there with his leg rotting away, he would have to be very drunk.

"It's too late, Alex," Katya said.

For the first time his father looked at her. "Who is this woman?"

327

For a second Alex thought about it. Just let it go. Let the leg kill him. It wouldn't be his fault, would it? Yes.

"Listen," Alex said to his father, "are you too drunk to understand?" His father laughed at him. Alex felt an old fury building in him. "They're going to have to cut it off. The leg. We'll clean it out, but it won't be enough. I've got something in my pack to put on it when they do it. Sulphur." He leaned down closer. "Do you understand?"

His father was still smiling.

"Oh, yes, Alex. I understand. I understand everything."

Chapter 45

KATYA HAD FINISHED CLEANING THE WOUND. ONE OF THE COS-sacks had brought the hot water and the clean cloth. She dumped in some of the sulphur and wrapped the leg with the cloth. It wouldn't work; Alex knew it was too late for the sulphur to stop the infection. It was a wonder that he wasn't already dead. His father watched Katya work, occasionally taking a long pull on the vodka bottle. He was on a plateau of drunkenness that didn't seem to get any worse. He drank to maintain his position on the plateau. Katya stood up and moved away.

"Thank you, my dear," his father said in a courtly voice. Then his eyes narrowed. He had finally spotted Nicholas, standing in the shadows at the end of the car. "Ahhhhh," he said, drawing the word out. "And who is this? Step forward there, friend."

Before Alex could intervene, Nicholas walked to the side of the bed. He did what he was told to do.

"Take off your hat, friend."

Nicholas removed his worker's-style hat. The same type of hat that Lenin wore.

"Yes. Very clever." He looked at Alex. "Very good. Very clever. Maybe you're not so stupid after all." He nodded to himself. "Yes."

"He's not right," Alex said. "Not right in the head. He can't help you. He can't help anyone now."

"Don't be a fool. I can see that he's 'not right,' as you put it. Oh, well, it doesn't really matter. Actually, it's probably for the best. We'll just prop him up and let someone else give the speeches. Say something like he's taken a vow of silence until Russia is free of her enemies. Should work out rather well." He nodded to himself again.

There was no sense in going up against him now. Let him make his plans, Alex thought. I'll get him out; you'll never use him. I didn't come this far to turn him over to you; I came for other reasons.

Alex leaned over and raised the shade on another window. The light was fading outside. He stiffened as he heard the first shots. There were screams, then more shots. He looked at his father.

"What are they doing?" Alex asked.

"They're killing them; what do you think they're doing," his father answered petulantly.

Christ. These people are mad. "Why? What's the point of it?" Alex asked, his voice rising with the level of firing from outside. "Can't you stop them?"

His father laughed. "You fool. What's the point of it? There is no point; they're simply killing. These are Cossacks; Kalyokov's Cossacks. They kill because they've always killed. It's the nature of the beast." He stopped as Alex turned away. "You'll get used to it, Alex. You'll see."

Alex went to the door of the car and slipped out onto the platform. The light around him had faded to a sort of twilight, a shadow-effect of the high mountains and the thick forest. The sky itself was still bright. Alex could see down the length of the train to the first curve. There were several small campfires. The shooting had stopped. The passengers were still lined up against the train, some standing, some squatting. The Cossacks moved among them.

A Cossack, laughing, grabbed a woman who was slumped down clutching a little boy. The Cossack tore the boy from the woman and threw him to the ground, where he lay, stunned. The woman reached for the boy, but the Cossack caught her arm and pulled her against him. He pulled her head back by the hair and kissed her. There was applause,

330

shouts of encouragement came from several others standing nearby. The Cossack began to tear at the woman's clothes.

She twisted away from him, almost freeing herself. As he pulled her back, she swung around and raked his face with her nails. Alex thought he could see the tracks of blood down the man's cheeks. The man bellowed with the pain and in one quick movement picked the woman up and held her over his head. One of the men watching began a chant—*Akhulgo, Akhulgo, Akhulgo*. The word made no sense to Alex. The chant was picked up by others, *Akhulgo*. Everyone watched the Cossack with the woman held high. She was rigid with fear. The Cossack turned, took one step, and threw the woman into the chasm. She screamed, a long scream, suddenly cut off as she hit the side of the cliff. There was silence as everyone strained to hear. Then, from far away, the tiny sound, a quick, faint swatch of sound, as the body crashed through the branches of the small trees that lined the creek at the bottom of the ravine. Alex almost expected to feel the ground quiver, to hear a thud when she hit.

The man who had thrown her leaned over and looked down. Then he turned and picked the boy up, and with a contemptuous toss, like a man throwing away a piece of litter, an empty cigarette package, he threw the boy over. The others watched and then cheered. They passed the man a bottle. He lifted it and drank.

It spread along the line. The chant. Others took up the game of throwing passengers into the ravine. They would lift them high and throw them, watching as the bodies bounced off the sides of the mountain and smashed through the trees at the bottom. Curiously, very few of the passengers ran or fought. A few of the men resisted, but for the most part, men, women, and children, holding themselves rigid, praying, screaming, or silent, allowed themselves to be lifted and thrown.

The shouts, screams, laughter, chanting, all of it coalesced into a sort of new sound, a single human voice that had no analogue. Alex watched, unable to move, unable to look away, hearing, seeing that amalgam of sound and sight that seemed not to be simply heard and seen but felt, until it sang in his blood, became a part of his being. A Goyaesque nightmare of writhing bodies, firelight, the sudden flick of humans into space as they dropped—some like stones curled into themselves; some with arms outstretched, like flightless birds; all doomed souls—into the pit.

And he watched, like some dumb passerby rubbernecking at an auto accident—where's the blood? anybody hurt?—sick with the knowledge not of the horror—yes, the horror, but not just that—the horror and the fact that he could not look away.

He wrenched himself back. He pushed the door open and stumbled inside. He was breathing heavily. At the end of the car Nicholas and Katya stood by the bed. They were staring at him, stilled into a sort of Pieta, frozen in the pale, thin light leaking in through the slit windows. The sounds from outside were muffled, indistinct.

"They're throwing the people over the cliff," he said, his voice harsh in the sudden quiet. "They are throwing them over." He felt stupid, as if his tongue were too heavy, his brain slow and thick.

His father snorted. "*Akhulgo*, yes?"

Alex nodded.

"One of their favorites," his father said. He looked at Katya. "This one knows, don't you?" Katya nodded. "Cossack?" Katya nodded again. "Tell him, tell your friend about this great tradition."

Katya's face was pale. She moved away from the bedside and turned to Alex. She recited it, like a schoolchild. "Akhulgo is a place, a town in the Caucasus. Part of our history; the story is told to the children." Alex glanced at his father. He was smiling. He obviously knew the story. "In 1837 the Russian army besieged the town. It's very high, up in the mountains, high walls. Cossack women fought alongside the men. When the defenders ran out of ammunition, they threw rocks on the army below. When they ran out of rocks, the men threw themselves off the walls onto the bayonets. When there were no more men," she looked at Alex and away, "the women threw their children, alive. When there were no more children, they threw themselves."

The sounds from outside had died away.

"It's sort of a tradition with them," his father said. "When the circumstances permit, as in this place, they like to do a

332

bit of a reenactment. They don't even see it as particularly brutal.''

"There were three hundred of them out there!" Alex shouted. How could they, all of them, talk about it this way? Katya wouldn't look at him.

"Now, now," his father said. "No need to get upset."

He sank down into a chair. Yes, they were all mad. He, included. He sat, unable to do anything more than stare straight ahead.

Katya pulled the Tsar to the sofa and both of them sat. His father upended the bottle and finished it. He dropped it onto the floor. It rolled a half turn and stopped. No one spoke. There was an exhausted quality to the silence, as if it had at last been too much for all of them. From outside came singing. Alex felt disgust for everything Russian. These were the romantic horsemen of the steppes? The magnificent fighters who would die rather than lose their great freedom? He listened to the mangled words and discordant renditions of sad Russian songs from the drunken men around their campfires and felt nothing but loathing. A single shot from outside pulled him back to another time, drew him back to the room in which the Tsar's family, the soldiers, had died. And who was he, he thought; yes, civilized man, Alex the Good. Another shot from outside.

He could still feel the fierce heat of the close-quarter fire fight, see the man's head burst as he shot him, feel the joy—yes, joy—swell up in him as he fell to his knees and fired his gun into the men who were trying to kill him, and in that moment knew that the seed of whatever strange flower it was that bloomed outside in them was in him as well. Was in all men. There was a line from Dostoyevski, a line that floated up in his mind. "I maintain that the best of men may become coarsened and degraded, by force of habit, to the level of beast." Lines written in a Siberian forced labor camp.

Oh, yes; oh, yes.

Chapter 46

SHADOWS ROSE AND FELL ON THE WALLS OF THE COACH. THE MAN standing in the doorway held the swinging lantern high as he peered inside. Alex turned and looked at the man, one of the Cossacks, one side of his face lit, the other in deep shadow.

Alex looked at his father, sitting erect in the bed, eyes glinting, reflecting the single point of light from the lantern. How long had his father been sitting there in the dark, watching?

"Charonsky," the Cossack said. "I have brought soup."

"Put it down," his father said. "We'll take care of it."

The man hesitated. "Do you need . . ."

"Put it down!" Alex's father shouted. "I need nothing! Go away."

The man nodded, put the heavy pot of soup on the floor, turned.

"Wait," his father said. "Leave the lantern."

The man nodded again and put the lantern next to the pot of soup.

"The dishes are in the cabinet next to the table," he said to Katya. She and Nicholas were still sitting on the short couch. Nicholas seemed to be asleep. It was hard to tell.

"I'm hungry," his father said. He ran his hand lightly

334

over his sheet-covered leg. "It feels better; what did you do to it?"

Katya was silent. She rose and went to get the dishes for the soup.

"I cleaned it and put in the yellow powder, sulphur," she finally said. "It's still bad. You will lose the leg."

That's it, Katya, Alex thought, break it to him gently. He got up and picked the lantern up off the floor. There was a hanger for it by the door.

"Yes, well, you've already mentioned that possibility," his father said. "Light the one down here," he said to Alex, motioning to an unlit lantern by the bed.

Alex lit the other lantern. The flame quivered, flared, then held as Alex closed the chimney.

His father took the bowl of soup Katya handed him and put it on his lap. He picked up the spoon and began eating. "It's cold," he said, "as usual. I think I am getting tired of living with these animals."

"Why do you?" Alex asked, eating his own soup. Katya gently woke Nicholas and gave him a bowl.

"Because they are slightly better than the other animals." His father had switched to English. He glanced at Katya, but she had made no sign that she understood. "How can you even ask? You know what's going to happen. Can you deny that the prospect in the next fifty years is a good one? That is, if we let history take its course. Have you overlooked the little matter of Josef Stalin?"

"From what I've seen of your side, it would probably be just as bad. Your friends outside are hardly models of good behavior and fair play."

His father was eating hungrily. He seemed none the worse for all the vodka he had drunk.

"Russians," his father said. "They only understand violence, suffering. '*Sobaka Palku Luibuit.*' An old Russian saying. 'The Dog loves his lash.' What they did out there today"—he waved his spoon in the general direction of the Cossacks outside—"that's nothing new. I don't even need to see it to know. Kalyokov, the *ataman*, is the biggest animal of them all. 'Ah, Charonsky,' he says to me in all seriousness, 'I cannot sleep at night if I have not killed during the day.' You've seen the name on the front of this train?" Alex nodded. "The Merciless. The other armored trains have names just as charming: The Destroyer, The Terrible, The Master, The Horrible. Ten machine guns to each train, two three-inch guns, a couple of one-pounders. They roll these things into a town and blast away."

"Winning the hearts and minds of the people," Alex mumbled to himself.

"What's that?" his father asked, frowning.

"Nothing," Alex said. He wondered what his father knew of the Vietnam war. Was it possible to travel forward to the time after the plane crash, in effect, his future?

"Kalyokov," his father went on disgustedly. "Let me tell you about Kalyokov. An Austrian orchestra was playing at the *Chaska Chai*; they didn't know any Cossack tunes, so what does Kalyokov do? Kills them, of course, right in the middle of the concert. He and his men go up on the stage and shoot them all. As far as I know, the bodies are still there on stage.

"Then there were the Red Cross workers. If he hadn't killed them, I would have had decent medical help for this." He gestured to his leg. "But he decided that he needed the Red Cross money and supplies, so he killed all three of them, two men and a woman. After he raped the woman. So now there are no Red Cross workers. They see nothing beyond the absolute present. Not one minute into the future. Their long-range planning is limited to telling someone else to cook dinner." He put the empty bowl and the spoon on the small table beside his bed. "I'm sick of it all."

Alex forced himself to eat his soup. He needed the strength, but it was cabbage, large chunks of cabbage floating among bits of meat that had probably once been one of the shaggy ponies.

"Why don't you move ahead to somewhere you can get your leg taken care of?" Alex asked. Perhaps putting it in these terms would get his father to give him some real information on the process of shifting.

"Move ahead? What if I do it and I come out somewhere where I can't get my leg fixed? What if I'm two years in the future and I'm sitting here on these train tracks? My leg is still going to be useless. What am I supposed to do, crawl to the nearest town? I can shift, but I can't do it with that sort of accuracy." He was watching Alex carefully. "Ah, I seem to have caught your interest."

"Just what is it," Alex began carefully, "that you want from me now? Why am I here? Aside from this"—he waved in the direction of the sofa where the Tsar sat, now awake, watching—"what is it you really want?"

His father smiled, ran his hands through his hair. He hesitated, then went ahead. "It's simple, son, I want to go back. I want to go home."

"You want to go back with me," Alex repeated, trying to make sense out of it. It was not an answer he could have guessed was coming. His father was right; it was simple. Too simple.

"The leg, Alex, I don't want to lose the leg. I could die here. I don't want these people working on me. They'll kill me."

Alex gestured to Katya and the Tsar. "And them? What about that part of it? I thought that's what you were interested in."

"We'll come back." His father's voice was a mixture of supplication and conciliation. "We'll put them somewhere, move up to your time and get the leg fixed, then we'll come back and finish our work here." His father's forehead was slick with sweat; his smile looked as if it were glued in place. The calm bestowed by the vodka was now gone.

It was the words; the words were all wrong. Son? His father had never called him son. Work? His father's work consisted of trying to manipulate history to his own advantage. Riches, power. Home? His father had no home; certainly it wasn't at Alex's house. The thought of it was grotesque. He and Dad together, kicking around the house, sitting down to dinner.

Evidently his father didn't see it that way. "The house you live in, wherever that is, was bought with my money, wasn't it?" The tone of voice had picked up a little edge of irritation. "That makes it my house, at least in part. Remember, I didn't die; I simply left. I can return and take up where I left off. You once told me my books were still popular; I'll write more—there's no shortage of material."

After years of abuse and neglect his father expected him to

say it was all okay and do him this little favor? What was he supposed to do anyway; why did he need him?

"It's certainly an interesting idea," Alex said, turning away and pacing as if he actually were considering it; easy now, slow, slow. "Tell me, how would we accomplish such a thing. And more to the point, if you want to go back, why don't you just go?" He had to keep his voice from cracking on his last words.

"Well," his father said, straightening out the sheets that covered him, "it's not quite that easy."

"No?" Alex asked.

His father wiped his face with the sheet. The effort of being reasonable was killing him.

"I don't pretend to know everything about the process," his father began, "but I've been at it a good many more years than you have, Alex. I've learned things that seem to be rules, or at least lines of resistance and connection.

"First of all, the whole thing, the time travel, seems a direct function of our minds and, as much as anything else, our desires." The incredulous look on Alex's face stopped him for a moment. "If you know more than I do about this, why don't you do the explaining," he said roughly. Alex shook his head and said nothing.

"By now I'm sure you've guessed that the books I wrote were renditions of my own experiences in the past." Alex nodded. "The first time it happened I was surprised and shocked, as I assume you were the first time it happened to you. But I accepted it pretty quickly." He couldn't keep the smugness out of his voice. "It seemed to work this way: If I was interested enough in a subject, immersed in it, I could sometimes induce the effect, project myself into the era I was studying. It helped me to go to the actual geographical area and involve myself with the people there. After a little experimenting I got the hang of it. As I said, it was a matter of wanting it badly enough."

"If you want it badly enough, it works? That's hard to believe."

"You're here, aren't you!" his father shouted, sitting forward. He winced at the pain. He made an effort to calm down. "It obviously works, doesn't it?" He wiped his face again and resumed in a quieter voice.

"It's seems to be hereditary. In fact there's some evidence that my own father might have known about it"—he waved it away—"but that's another story.

"I also think that other people can do it, but I'm not sure. Thousands of people disappear every year; they've got to be going somewhere.

"Anyway"—he leaned back on his pillows and looked straight ahead, no longer paying much attention to Alex—"it doesn't always work the way we want it to. Sometimes it just takes you, even though you don't expect it or want it."

"The plane crash?" Alex asked.

"The plane crash," his father said. "I had no idea it would happen. I'd been doing research on Iceland, had been thinking hard about it when it happened. Maybe it had something to do with the airplane, I don't know, I was just suddenly gone, a hundred years back on an island in the middle of the winter with only the clothes I was wearing. Fortunately, I didn't come through a thousand feet up in the air, which is where the plane was. And that was the end of going back to my own time. I haven't been back since. I can't get much closer than I am now; maybe a few years into this future, but that's it. That's one of the reasons you're here, why I hoped you'd come back. I knew you would someday, knew it for years. Those dreams you used to tell your mother, they were the beginnings; I recognized them. I had dreams like that when I was young. It was just a matter of time."

"Why," Alex said, changing the subject for a moment, "didn't you simply move forward a few years ago and see what you'd be doing now? So you could have avoided this." He gestured at the leg.

"You can't do that. You can't occupy the same space with yourself. I tried it a number of times."

"But you can move into the future?"

"Yes, I said so. A few years."

It was the answer Alex was hoping for, the reason he had allowed himself to be captured and taken to his father. By now he was convinced it was his name on the list found at the Hoover Institute that had triggered his return to this period. That it was this anomoly that was the stone thrown into the pond that created the ripple that disturbed the surface of his own time. He had to make sure his father found the report and inserted his name.

"What you have to do . . ."

His father's laugh stopped him. "Don't tell me what to do. Don't you see? *I* have to decide what it will be." He laughed again at the look of confusion on Alex's face. "You can't directly influence your own entry into this past, otherwise I could simply move further back and change things around so that I wouldn't be shot. Once a particular series of events has begun you have to play it out. Even I can't know what will happen in this future we are now creating."

Alex shook his head and tried to think it through. That meant that he hadn't had to see his father again. The bug had flown into the spider's web for no real reason. And now he was truly caught until he understood the answer to the last question, the same question he'd been asking all along.

"And me?" he asked. "What do you need me for?"

"I can't get back without you!" his father cried, his voice strangled with the confession, the truth.

"You have to have someone back where you leave from, an anchor, someone who cares enough about you to draw you back. Someone who wants you back. You have someone like that, don't you? Someone who thinks about you? I don't. Not since your mother died in the plane crash. Don't you see? Don't you understand? She was always there for me; she loved me. That's why I insisted that she always go along with me when I went back. She was my anchor, but she's gone. When that plane went down, I lost the only person who cared enough about me to pull me back. One time you accused me of not caring about her. You fool! Don't you see?" His voice was high, manic, cracking as it rose. "I have to get back; I could die here if I don't get medical help. I'm trapped, goddamnit; I'm trapped!"

340

Chapter 47

His father slumped back against the pillows. His sweat-slick face had lost all color. In the weak light from the lantern the sheets, his face, his hair, even his hands, seemed to have faded to the color of dust, the color of sick old men. His breathing was heavy and ragged.

"Do you understand?" he asked weakly, looking up.

"And how would we accomplish it?" Alex asked. He found himself untouched by both the rage and the weakness. If there was any pity left in him, it was not for his father. He had seen too much. He was beginning to understand the Tsar's retreat into catatonia. At this point all he wanted to do was get all the information he could get and escape.

A sliver of hope showed in his father's eyes. He mistook interest for acquiescence. "I'm sure we could do it." His voice was eager. "I've never tried it, but of course there hasn't been anyone else to try it with. You've noticed when we shift forward and back we still keep our clothes, our coats, coins, wallets, other objects in our pockets. Anything within a certain distance from our bodies gets carried along." He ran a hand through his silver hair again, a habit that was new to Alex.

"Since I can move more or less at will, at least backward and a little way into this present's future, I thought we'd wait until you begin to shift and then . . ." He stopped. He looked like he was going to choke on his words. "If we held on to each other, you see, close, then I think we would go through together. After all, I am your father. . . . I know we can do this thing. . . . We wouldn't even have to wait; I could try to push us forward. . . ." He stopped himself before he began to plead. The look in Alex's eyes must have been clear.

The image was more than Alex could bear. The thought of he and his father, clutched in an embrace, trying to shift into Alex's own future brought the soup he had just eaten right to the edge of being spewn onto the floor. He turned his head away. He couldn't look at him, couldn't speak to him.

His father saw it and pushed forward the only card that had interested Alex from the beginning. Information.

"Now wait a minute. . . . Listen, this is important. There are three ways to shift," his father said, talking quickly.

Desperation energized him. Alex could feel the man's need; it was like a charge of static electricity in the room. He had risen above his weakness. As a child Alex and his friends had caught huge bumblebees and put them in glass jars. You could feel the power of the bees as they knocked against the sides of the glass jars, feel it as a tingling buzz in the palms of your hands, feel the trapped energy as it battered itself, over and over; small, pure bundles of need, barely contained. He could feel his father batting against the sides of the glass jar.

"First of all," his father went on, "after a certain amount of time has passed, you always snap back to your present, as long as you have your anchor. It's as if you're on an elastic tether that can only stretch so far until it pulls you back. That's the way I used to get back to you and your mother on my trips." He spoke eagerly, then sadly. "But now my tether is broken, without someone to anchor me I can't get back; I'm stuck. I can go a few years into the future, towards getting back to my own time, but nothing more than that."

"You said there were three ways," Alex prodded. Get it and get out.

"The next way is if you're physically removed from any real interaction within the time frame. If you're not really part of anything, not really participating, the hold on wherever you are just gets weaker until you slip back to the present. The bad part is that you never know how long it's going to take, but the less you interact, the faster it happens.''

"A corollary of the 'desire' theory you told me about earlier," Alex said. "If you *don't* want it enough, divorce yourself, you shift back to your present where your ties are stronger?" His father nodded. "And the third? So far the shifting has all been passive, uncontrolled. It can't all be like that.''

"You're right, it can't.'' Some of the old intransigence came back into his father's eyes. "You expect me to just give that away? No, Alex. Take me back. Hold me. I'll do the rest. But you have to help. You have to want it. I can't make you do it; we have to do it together.'' Now he was pleading.

Alex turned away again. That image: he and his father locked in an embrace. He walked to the end of the car, trying to puzzle it out. But why not? Beyond the disgust, the years of anger, why not? The sudden offer of return shimmered like a pool of sweet water. Drink it. Bathe in it. Just go back. What difference would it really make?

Maybe he was supposed to take him back. He caught himself running his hand through his hair, an unconscious imitation of his father. Maybe that was his purpose in all of this, to get his father, the wild card, out of play. Take him back where he could be watched, where he could be kept from playing God. What would he do, put him in some sort of jail? How would he stop him from shifting when he couldn't even stop himself? It wouldn't work. The only way to stop his father was to kill him.

"Alex," his father called from the other end of the car, "think about it. We could live like kings. I was a fool to do nothing with it before, back when I was writing. I made money, but nothing really big. Think about it." There was a pause. "I could die here," he added weakly.

What would they do? Live together in his house? He and Molly and Dad? Would they take little jaunts into the past and place bets on horses they knew were going to win, screw around with things just so they could see how they turned out? No. He didn't want to have anything to do with his father. Whether or not his father died was a function of his own actions. The guilt was not his, Alex's. He didn't want to be around him, have him anywhere near him. And he didn't have to. It was his choice. Kill him? No. Let him die? Maybe.

Take him back? Not a chance.

Katya slipped under his arm. She looked into his eyes. "We must go," she whispered. The sound of her words surprised him. She was speaking Russian. He and his father had been speaking English all along. He nodded.

His father looked back and forth between the two of them. "You and this woman? . . ." he asked. "She means something to you?"

"Means something to me?" he asked, puzzled. "Yes. Why do you care?"

"Why do I care?" He laughed an odd, dismayed laugh. "You still don't understand? I told you, you can only get back if you have some need, someone there who you want to get back to, who wants you back. If you do this"—he waved his hand at Katya—"you threaten that. If this becomes stronger, you'll never leave. I'll never leave. Don't you want to go back? Get rid of her!"

Katya looked at Alex, trying to puzzle out his father's foreign words. Get rid of her? Not go back? Molly? He tried to put it together, make sense of it. Not now, not this. He felt something break inside him, some frail dam that had been holding him back. It was enough. There had been too much information. Too much talk, too many offers; too much, too much. Now it was time to act. And there was his father, lying there, nagging at him, the source of the pain, the cause.

"Get . . ." his father began. Alex reached down and firmly put his hand over his father's mouth. No more. No more talk.

"Katya," he said, pressing down, feeling his father struggle then lie still. "There may be a man guarding the door outside. If there is, remove him. Do you understand?"

She gave him a small smile. "Yes, Alex. I will do it. It is time to be gone." She turned and went down the length of the car.

"And you," Alex said, looking down at the face under his hand. "We're getting out. I'm not taking you back. Now or

344

ever. I'm not leaving you the Tsar. You made this filthy bed of yours; now you can lie in it. I'm right on the edge of having Katya do to you what she's doing to the guard outside. I couldn't, I'll admit it. But she's quite capable of it.'' He felt his father's mouth move under his hand. It took a second for him to realize what it was. The man was smiling. Smiling.

Katya appeared back at his side. "It is done.''

"Get Nicholas. Go to the end of this train; wait for me there.''

He watched as she took Nicholas by the hand and led him away. "Now,'' he said, leaning close to his father, "I'm going to take my hand away so you can tell me what you find so amusing. Don't bother to shout; no one will hear.'' He took away his hand. His father was still smiling.

"Don't you see?'' his father said in a cracked whisper. "You can't kill me. You need me. If I'm not around, who'll do whatever it is that brings you back to this time in the beginning? I'm supposed to do something, remember?'' His father gave a little giggle. The report. He was right. His father had to get the report, insert his, Alex's, name in it, and take the black bag with the report to the Hoover Institute so that the whole ponderous machine would begin to turn. His facked licked his lips and went on. "Wheels within wheels. Just when you think you understand, it turns again. You'll never win, Alex. You can run, but I'll catch you. I don't care about the Tsar or any of that now. I care about you. I'll catch you and put you in a cage, and when you have been in the cage long enough, you'll beg me to let you take me back. You'll learn to want it. You'll never leave this time while that woman's around. You can't kill me. In fact, you'd better pray that my leg doesn't kill me. They may take it off, but it won't finish me. You'll leave me that pouch of sulphur to make sure of it. I'll get better. Then I'll catch you. I'll send those men outside; they'll find you and they will bring you to me.'' He laughed weakly. "Yes, you'll learn to love your old dad. You'll do what Daddy says.''

Alex stared at him.

He took a strip of cloth from the pile of bandages Katya had made. He worked quickly now. He had no idea how long he would have before his father was discovered. He forced

345

his father's mouth open, pressed the gag into it and tied it at the back. He took another strip of cloth and tied his hands.

He stood back and looked down at the trussed-up figure. Honour thy father. This man had never been his father. He would leave him the sulphur. His father was right about that. He couldn't kill him or let him die. The rest of it, time would tell.

He put the package of yellow powder on the nightstand. His father was watching him. Was he still smiling?

Alex dropped lightly off the platform onto the gravel beside the tracks. The stone was cool beneath his hands. The air was clean with the smell of fresh pine.

Chapter 48

KATYA WATCHED ALEX DROP TO THE GROUND. SHE BENT OVER A man lying on the ground. She stood up and took Alex's hand. He felt the solid heaviness of a pistol, a weight that always seemed greater than the object would warrant. The gun was still warm from the man's body. Two other heavy objects: grenades; he recognized their feel from his attack on the arsenal. He put them in his pack.

She bent back down again, searched for a moment, then found her knife lodged between two ribs in the general vicinity of the man's heart. Right where she had left it. Alex heard her grunt slightly with the effort of pulling it out. There was a slight snick as it clicked against a button as she wiped it off on the man's shirt. He wondered where she kept that knife. He'd never seen her actually take it out or put it away. It simply appeared when she needed it.

Down the length of the train were low campfires and around them the shapes of men, most of them lying down.

"They are all drunk," Katya whispered. "I left Nicholas at the end of the train. I came back to see if there was a pistol. This one"—she nudged the body on the ground with her foot—"was unhappy because he had been assigned to guard the old man in there. He could not get drunk with the rest of them. He could not join in the killing or the raping of the passengers. He was very happy to see me. Now he is dead.''

It was a small tale, but Katya's dispassionate rendition had a way of adding a certain chill. Having her as a lover sometimes made him feel like a male black widow spider approaching the female. He somehow expected to reach for the warm softness of her breast and come up with the hard sharpness of the knife she used so effectively. It lent a certain tang to the experience. He understood why the male black widow took the chance.

"Let's go," he said. The only way out was along the tracks. They could go back the way the train had come or forward the way they had been going. Back meant several hundred miles to the nearest town. Forward meant an unknown distance to possible help. The unknown won: Of two evils you choose the one you know least about.

Once they got beyond the train, the darkness became complete. There were no campfires. Only the pale moon reflecting faintly from the double strip of metal rails.

It was cold. They had no coats, only the clothes they were wearing when they had been taken off the train. They shuffled forward slowly, trying to stay on the ties without really being able to see where their feet were going. On the left the track bed was so close to the wall of the mountain that there was no room to walk off the tracks on that side. To the right there was more room, but there was also the great drop-off that ended in the ravine. They could hear the rush of water far below. In the darkness it sounded closer than he remembered. He tried walking on the right, and while it was physically easier, the strain of waiting to slip over the edge was too much. Back on the tracks. Three ducks in a row; Alex leading Katya leading Nicholas, who stumbled along like their idiot child.

After they got used to the placement, they were able to lengthen their strides so they were skipping every other tie. This required them all to stay in step. The occasional misstep by any one of them broke the balance of all of them. Alex thought, after the third time they had all fallen, that they must look like some family of yokels practicing a simple-minded circus act. After two hours, though, they had it down.

They stopped twice to rest before he knew they'd have to stop to get some sleep. He decided that it had been at least four hours since they left the train. His pocket watch had long since quit running. He'd lost the habit of winding it while it was at the pawnbroker's. Now he estimated time the same way most of the people around him did. When it was dark, it was night; when it was light, it was day. Only the railroad made finer distinctions.

With any sort of luck it would be well into the next day before the Cossacks got moving and found his father. They had a four-hour start on them and could keep it up. But they had to rest. The unnatural rhythms of walking the ties had tired them. In the daylight they'd be able to move much faster. He'd give it till dawn, which he estimated to be in a couple of hours.

He found a natural hollow in the rock wall on their left. He arranged the others in a sitting position and squeezed in beside Katya. It was uncomfortable, but it would keep their body heat where they needed it. Katya moved up against his side, pulling his arm around her. She sighed and seemed to doze off immediately.

Get rid of her, his father had said. Or you're stuck here. He turned his head; his lips touched her hair. No. There were worse fates than being here with this woman. So be it.

What woke him? The light? The sky was just beginning to gray into predawn. Pain? Every muscle in his body seemed stiff and cold. A sound?

He extricated himself from Katya and crawled the few feet to the railroad track. He touched the cold iron rail. Did he feel something? He put his ear to the rail, listening, the way Indians were supposed to. It made his ear cold. He heard nothing.

He stood up and stretched, painfully. Katya was moving, but Nicholas slept on. He walked a few feet down the track and found a small trickle of water on the rock face, a tiny spring that sank into the ground at the base of the tracks. He pressed his hands against the rock and wiped the cold water across his face. He knelt and cupped his hands at the base until he had enough for a mouthful.

There. A sound. A squeal. Almost like the cry of an

animal. Almost, but not quite. From up the mountain. A faraway sound. Sensed more than heard. The train, you dumb shit. They're backing the train down the mountain. They had found his father and now they were coming. They had not had the luck he was counting on. That squeal was the sound of the brakes as they backed it down. They would be coming slowly, yes, but faster than they could travel. Trains don't get tired and have to stop and rest.

"Katya, get him up," he said. "Right now." She heard the urgency in his voice, saw it in his face. She shook Nicholas and began to pull him to his feet.

Run? How long could they stay ahead? They were still on the mountain; could they beat the train to the bottom? Would they find a place to hide if they did beat it to the bottom? Option: Stay and fight. Laughable. One pistol and two grenades. Katya and her trusty knife. Option: He stays and delays; they go ahead. Possible.

He could catch up later.

He led them to the trickle of water. Nicholas pressed his lips to the rock face and sucked at the moisture.

"Listen to me," he said to Katya. "There's only one way. They're coming. You can hear it; they're backing the train down." He stopped. She tilted her head and listened. The faraway screech.

"We can run," she said. "It's daylight. We can see; we can stay ahead."

"No, it won't work. We've got to split up."

"No," she shook her head. "I will stay with you."

He took both her hands. "We've got to get him away. If we don't . . ." How to explain it to her? If we don't, the future, my future, will be changed? "We have to get him out, you know that. None of them can have him; we can't let that man back in the train get him. We can't let the Bolsheviks have him. It's too big, Katya; it's worth more than the two of us." Christ, where are the violins? She just stared at him, her jaw set.

"What would your father say, Katya? Would he take the chance of letting any of them get him? Or would he get him to freedom? Why did he send you in the first place; why did you come?" She looked away.

"We could kill him," she said stubbornly. "That way

none of them could have him. Would he even care?'' They both looked at Nicholas. He was standing watching them. Push him over the cliff? Alex thought. Stab him? Then what was it all for? What was the point of the whole thing? It had its own weight now, its own momentum. He would finish it.

"No, It's up to you now. I can hold them, maybe all day, maybe longer. It's me they really want. I'll join you later; I'll get away.''

"You'll die here,'' she said, turning away from him. She faced down the tracks, down the mountain. "I will never see you again.''

"No,'' he said, "I won't die.'' He put his arms around her, unable to say any more, unable to lie. How did he know what would happen? The future. He knew nothing. She leaned her head back against his cheek. "Go,'' he whispered, pushing her gently away. "Run.''

She took Nicholas by the hand and started down the tracks. The mother and the big idiot boy. She turned once and looked back at him. He made no sign, no gesture. She turned away again and began to run, disappearing around the shoulder of the mountain.

How does a man fight a trainful of Cossacks? First of all you get rid of the train. He got one of the grenades out of his pack and sat down to study it. Grenade: Spanish for pomegranate, meaning having grains. All right, Professor Balfour, now that you've used your fun fact, what else do you know? The device was activated by twisting the handle. That action would trigger a fuse of some type which gave the bearer ten seconds, more or less, to get rid of it before it went off.

He studied the tracks. The rail bed was built up on a pile of gravel. The heavy ties seemed to be pinned to the bedrock below the gravel. Your old-time train robber would pry up the rails so the train would either have to stop or derail. Very effective, except he had no pry bar. It was painful to think of using the grenades; he had little enough to defend himself with, but he saw he was going to have to sacrifice at least one of them.

He dug a shallow hole beneath the right-hand rail. He

351

jammed the grenade, carefully, under the rail. The handle projected out to his right.

He considered trying to prime the grenade so it would go off from the pressure of the train. That was possible, but it left a large likelihood that if he did, he would be sending the whole train, with his father inside, over the edge of the ravine. Since he had already found himself incapable of patricide, he dismissed the idea. Even if he blew the tracks up before the train got to them, there was a chance it could derail if it didn't see the track damage and stop in time. And any derailment could be extremely serious under the conditions.

He would have to wait until the train was close enough to where he would blow the tracks so they would understand that something was going on and have men watching for trouble. And at the same time he couldn't wait until it was so close that they could catch him if they moved quickly. He remembered the officer on his horse. They wouldn't have enough horses for all of the men—the train wasn't long enough—but they would have enough of the shaggy little horses to catch a man on foot.

So he waited, listening to the screech of brakes as the train descended. After a half an hour or so he decided the moment had come, more because he was getting extremely anxious to be gone rather than because he thought it was the optimum time.

He put his pack on and tightened the straps so it wouldn't bounce around while he was running. He bent down, twisted the handle as far as it would go, turned, and took off down the tracks, running along the right side of the railbed.

It was a very long ten seconds. He made it around a bend in the tracks so he was in no danger of being hit by shrapnel. He was beginning to worry that it wasn't going to go off when there was a sharp bang and a tiny tremor beneath his feet. He considered going back to make sure that the track had really blown but couldn't bring himself to do it. He was running easily, away from trouble, down the mountain. He couldn't go back.

He ran. After a half an hour of steady downhill going the pitch of the roadbed seemed to begin to level off. In the now full sunlight he rounded a long gentle curve around the bulk of the mountain and came onto a long, open vista that stretched away down the last of the mountain and off into a wide valley. He slowed to a walk, breathing heavily. In the distance, down the valley, he could see the glint of a large body of water. Lake Baikal. He stopped, put his hands on his knees, and tried to catch his breath.

He stood up and looked down the line of the tracks, sweeping the length of them until he found it. Far away, crossing a bridge that spanned the stream that eventually ended in the lake, two tiny figures. Two miles away? Three miles? More?

He turned and walked back up the tracks the way he had come. He rounded the shoulder of the mountain and left the sunlight, entering a swath of shadow that seemed far chillier than it had before he had felt the warmth of sun. He walked up the track for a minute, then stopped, leaning against the rock wall. He closed his eyes, slowed his breathing even more, and listened.

The stream, rushing water: Ignore. Birds, the soft whisper of a breeze, the buzzing of insects: Ignore. He turned his head slightly. Separate the sounds; catalogue them and push them into the background. Listen for the unknown. There. A faint clink. Memory: the ride with his father and the Cossacks into the hills. The sound of bits, stirrups, metal against metal. Horses. Small, shaggy horses trained to negotiate treacherous mountain paths. How far behind? Not far enough. Moving how fast? Fast enough.

He walked back to the dividing line where sunlight met shadow and stood, half in, half out. He could not see Katya and Nicholas; they had moved on. If he ran, he might catch them. And then the men on the horses might catch all of them together. He turned and went back into the shadow.

He went to the smooth rock face, placed his hands flat against the wall, felt the cold granite under his fingers. The only way out was up. He lay his cheek against the stone. There were no other choices.

He felt along the rock face, looking for natural formations, trying to get the feel of the stone. It was granite, blasted out of the mountain by the engineers as they cut the roadway through the mountains around the southern end of the lake. The cut was rough and raw, geologically young, still holding the burrs and small outcroppings that would be smoothed by the wind and rain to come. There was no place better than any other, at least no place he could see. The cut would rise straight up until the natural slope of the mountain would lean away and he could hide in the trees. Anyone who came after him would either have to follow where he had gone or go around, if there was an around.

He reached up, found a small ledge for his fingers, and hoisted himself onto the face.

A few years before, he had learned the rudiments of rock climbing from a friend. They had gone out a few times, but the friend had moved away and he hadn't been interested enough to continue on his own. Now he wished he'd been interested.

He knew that one of the most important things was to keep his body away from the surface of the rock, that he would have better balance that way. But his body was already screaming that it wanted to hug the face, sucker-on as close as it could. And he was only three feet off the ground.

The first moves were easy, rock ledges for both hands and feet. He reached a six-inch ledge and stopped to rest. He looked down and saw that he had climbed the grand distance of approximately fifteen feet. Wonderful. His arms were already tired, his fingers raw from the scraping of the granite. In the distance he heard voices. He reached, found a hold, and pulled.

Four more moves and he had to stop again and try to dry off his hands. He was sweating so much he was losing his grip. His arms ached and he had scraped his right knee through his pants. He definitely heard voices, the sound of horses. Sound traveled well in the mountains. How well?

He concentrated on the rock, shutting out all other considerations. He established a rhythm: Reach, pull, push, rest. Again. Over and over. He was moving well, the muscles now resigned to the job, his confidence restored as his body remembered the few tricks and handholds he had learned from his friend.

He reached up and found . . . nothing. Flatness. He ran his palms back and forth and felt only a vague change of pitch, nothing he could utilize. He looked up, searched the face for a handhold. Nothing. He was standing on a small three-inch ledge. It faded away immediately on his right. He began inching to his left, forcing himself to keep his body away from the rock face. Five feet to his left the ledge ended abruptly. He ran his left hand up and over and found nothing helpful. He began to hyperventilate. He stopped searching, closed his eyes, and forced himself to breathe more slowly.

He looked up to see how much further he had to go. The movement threw him off balance and he felt himself begin to slip. He leaned forward, overcompensated, and hit the rock with his face. He squeezed his eyes shut and waited for his boots to come off the ledge. He steadied. He gasped. Sobbed. Caught himself, forced himself to calm down. He had not fallen. He was alive. He opened his eyes. Slowed his breathing. Very carefully, looked down.

Five men on horses. Already by him. They had missed him.

No! If they passed him, what was the point? He had to stop them from reaching Katya and Nicholas.

"Cossack dogs!" he shouted at the rock in front of him. The effort almost threw him off backwards again. Immediately he heard a muffled response and then silence. In the back of his mind he tried to formulate a few more curses but couldn't come up with anything. He figured "Cossack dogs" had done the job. Crude, childish, but effective. Their attention had been caught.

He leaned as far left as he could and stretched his hand upward. His cheek pressed against the rock. Sweat stung his eyes. His fingers inched along, pulling the rest of his hand, feeling their way like blind inchworms over the grainy rock. Forget the men below; forget everything but the rock. His arm was stretched until it felt as if the socket at his shoulder had begun to separate. The whole left side of his body began to tremble with the exertion. The instep of his left foot began to tighten into a cramp.

His hand touched a bump in the rock.

It was rounded and about an inch wide and projected out a quarter of an inch. If he committed himself completely in a sliding move to the left, he thought he could get his fingers over it.

If he used the projection, it was going to pull him all the way off the ledge. Once committed, he would not be able to get back. If there were no footholds over there, he was done. He could hang on for a few seconds, maybe even a minute,

355

then he would drop off straight down. Surprise, you Cossack dogs, look out below.

His brain reviewed the options. As usual, it came down to accepting the option that he knew the least about because there might be more there than in the options he was clear about. He turned off his conscious faculties and let instinct sort it through, make the choices.

He pushed off the rock, up and to the left, catching the tiny nob as his feet came off the ledge.

He gasped as he pulled his left leg upward, scraping it over the rock, hearing the leather drag as it searched around for anything it could use to stand on. He forced his body away from the rock, using his elbows as the fulcrum to adjust his center of gravity as his other leg crept up. He was now splayed, froglike against the pale granite. His left leg dropped straight, giving up, allowing his right the last inch of upward movement. At the point of his farthest reach, his knee at waist level, he found it. A tiny projection, a pea-size irregularity that caught the sole of his boot. He leaned automatically to his right, using the projection, extending, even though he knew the end of the movement would push him off the foothold, but he did it anyway because this was his body working, not his timorous questioning, decision-making brain; he extended, reached up with his right hand and found the crack, found the deep, thin cleft that gave him purchase for one hand and then the other as he pulled himself up, and still moving, found the next crack, then a ledge, and pulled himself up on a really good ledge that must have been all of twelve inches wide. And lay gasping and trembling, his body shaking with fatigue and the shock of release, scrunched up flat against the cold rock wall.

The first shot came from below and he had the answer to one of the questions that was beginning to form. What's going on down below? The Cossacks must have gotten over their initial astonishment at seeing him, a big black June bug smack dab on a white stucco wall, just waiting for the blow of a rolled-up newspaper. Had gotten over their astonishment and no doubt profound amusement. Chips of rock dislodged by the bullet sprinkled down onto his face. He closed his eyes even tighter and thought about apologizing for calling them Cossack dogs. It probably wouldn't work. Now they were really angry.

Chapter 49

Cossacks have a reputation, passed down through the ages, for being very good at a number of pursuits. These include extreme cruelty, being brave while riding their little horses into the very jaws of death, beating peasants with their illegal knouts, raping women, and last but not least, throwing helpless prisoners over cliffs. But he had never heard of one that was anywhere near proficient at rock climbing. Especially after a night of heavy drinking and general mayhem.

They are also not known for their shooting ability. They are very good with their *kindjals*, their two-edged daggers, but with a rifle and over a certain amount of distance they are not terribly dangerous. But with time and practice they could improve and there was always the matter of luck. The next volley convinced him that he was going to have to start moving if he was going to stay alive.

He scrunched along, feeling his way with one hand, checking the rock face with the other. A few shots showed that they were following his progress. The ledge widened to the point where he could crawl along on his hands and knees without exposing himself. Ten feet further he found a rock climber's gift. A long, jagged cleft that split the rock face as far up as he could see. It was wide, body width where he was, probably wider up above. With any luck it would run all the way to the top.

He took a quick peek at the men below. There seemed to be around ten of them, all peering up at him. He got out his gun. He remembered the man—it seemed a long time ago—the Russian soldier who had died in the trench, the man who said the purpose of shooting was not necessarily to hit anything but more to let your enemies know you were alive. And still fighting.

He moved a few feet away from where he'd been, peered over the ledge, and fired off three shots. He had the satisfaction of watching the Cossacks scatter away up and down the tracks. He put his gun back in his pack, clutched his pack in his teeth, and squeezed into the open cleft.

The cleft stayed negotiable all the way to the top of the cliff. It took him two hours to climb it, moving crab-fashion up the sides, slowly and methodically, stopping only briefly for rest breaks. When he pulled himself out at the top, arms scraped from elbow to palm, legs trembling and cramping with the exertion, his body was only minutes away from total breakdown. He had not had much sleep the last few days, very little to eat, and the cliff had just consumed whatever resources had been left. He decided that it was safe to rest, that luck was with him, that for now he was safe, beyond the grasp of his father, Cossacks, Bolsheviks, or any manner of enemy. He crawled away from the edge of the cliff over several yards of loose scree, onto grass, real grass, warm in the sun, soft and fragrant. He stretched out on his back and looked at the blue sky, the high white piled clouds. Ten minutes, he said to himself, that's all I ask. Then I'll figure out what to do next. I promise.

He slept.

Hours passed. The rain woke him. Cold, fat drops that splashed onto his face. He groaned and rolled over, forcing himself into a sitting position. His muscles fought him. He got to his hands and knees, the pain holding him there while he stretched each arm, each leg, like an old arthritic dog waking on a cold winter day. He stood. For a second he thought he would fall, but the world held.

The sky was a uniform gray. He shivered.

He rotated each of his arms in a circle until the muscles stopped creaking, did a few deep knee bends, approached, very carefully, the edge of the cliff. The last few feet were negotiated on hands and knees.

He peered carefully over the edge. Shock hit him like a hard slap in the face. He stared dumbly down, trying to assimilate the information that was in front of him. Directly below, halfway up the rock face, was a Cossack. Clinging to the rock like a large cockroach. He had taken off his coat but had a rifle and a rope strapped to his back. Below him, scattered in a rough semi-circle, were the rest of them, watching their comrade and calling out suggestions.

He rolled back from the edge onto his back. He no longer felt the rain. Didn't these people ever give up? What did he have to do, kill every one of them? Yes, said the rain, said the rocks beneath him, said the trees further up the mountain, said the thick gray sky. Oh, yes, Alex, it never ends; once you start something, you have to play it out to the end; you just can't stop and say that's it, I quit, enough, home free. Finish it. You're not a little boy anymore; you are a grown man. This is not there: there it doesn't matter much; there the stakes are low; there all you can lose is your parking place or miss your meal or twist your ankle—here you can lose your life. Follow it to the end.

Once again the mental dam broke free beneath the push of too much pain, too much danger, too much anguish: frail barrier; unable to hold, the line crumbled.

He did it. He went back to where he had slept and got his pack. Took out the last grenade, went to the edge of the cliff, twisted the handle, and flipped it over without even looking. He stepped back. The explosion was curiously muffled, as if the rain, the sky, the cliff, had thrown the sound away, or absorbed it. He got down on one knee and looked over.

Below, at the bottom. Bodies, scattered; none moving. He looked a long time to make sure. He could see quite clearly. The man on the cliff was still there, looking up, looking up into Alex's eyes, holding on with both hands, looking up into his eyes with a hatred undiminished by intervening space. There was a great silence in the world.

He finished it.

A rock. The size of a basketball. He brought it to where

the man would be, looked over, rolled it to the edge. The man was hanging on with one hand, trying to pull his rifle around to the front. Alex pushed the rock over and watched it take the man, peel him off of the rock, flick him away, into the air, slam him into the pile of dead men at the bottom of the long, bloody cliff.

Alex turned, finished now, picked up his pack and walked up the mountain into the forest.

Sometime the rain stopped. Night came. He sat under a dripping pine tree, shivering uncontrollably. Sometime in the night he dozed, waking with a start every time cold water dripped down his neck. He curled up on the ground. Day finally came. He gathered up his pack and walked further into the woods.

He had very few choices left to make. Down the cliff was out of the question. Finding his way down the mountain without using the railroad tracks would take days. Katya was too far ahead to catch up with, or at least he hoped she was. He would go back. Home.

The two ways to return that his father had told him were, one, after a certain length of time had passed, you automatically went back as long as your anchor was there. Molly? Are you still waiting? And two, if you were not participating, if you had no interaction, the hold weakened. He heard his father's voice in his head: the bad part is, you never know how long it's going to take. All right, he would not participate. If it took too long, then he would die. Either way, he would be out of this.

He found a sheltered spot under a tall pine. The ground was thick with a bed of needles. He would wait.

He sat for two days until he could no longer sit. He lay down. He began to hallucinate. He welcomed the voices in his head, the faces; he was lonely, bored, cold, wet, afraid, tired hungry. Alone. He watched the past stretch out in front of him, watched himself groping along, a blind man in a maze.

He was no longer alone. They were with him: Molly, Katya, Max, his father, old Vassili, Lenin with his cobra's stare, the men he'd killed, the men, women, and children he'd seen killed. They spoke to him.

360

He learned many things. The knowledge filled him, seeped into all the emptiness that had been there before, made him whole. Now, Molly? I was too young the last time; you were there ahead of me; I did not understand. Now I understand.

Father? I did not choose you then when I was born; I do not choose you now.

Max, you are my friend, my father.

Katya. You were my dream.

I have failed, failed you one and all. What good did it do? No matter. The importance, the value, was in the doing, the act.

Small insects crawled over him.

He did not mind.

Chapter 50

HE WAS BACK IN THE PRISON INFIRMARY. HE WAITED, GAZING AT the white ceiling, for the nurse with the truncated-spire head-gear to hove into view. He had the same curious tunnel vision and the same dreamy feeling, neither here nor there. He supposed that sooner or later they'd put him in his cell, but he didn't care. Time passed pleasantly.

He was mentally humming a few bars of the "St. James Infirmary Blues" when Molly entered his field of vision and stared down at him. She looked worried. She was wearing the pale cream silk blouse that he liked.

Molly?

"Alex, are you in there?" Her voice came from far away, muffled, hollow.

He tried to speak. Nothing.

It's me, Molly, it's me; I'm in here!

She looked away from him and he heard her ask, "What have you got him on? His eyes are open, but he's still asleep."

No, I'm not, Molly; I'm awake, I'm awake.

A muffled response and then a doctor type looked down at him.

Hi, doc!

A bright light switched on, first into one eye, then the

other. There was some fussing around with one of his arms and then his leg. More muffled mutterings.

How come you guys are in prison, too? Where's the nurse with the big hat? Do I have to go back to my cell now? I feel so good. I think I'll go back to sleep.

He turned his head. Molly was asleep on a green plastic and metal-tubing chair beside the bed. It was a very ugly chair. She was wearing her soft bleached blue jeans and a light cotton sweater. Her red hair was tied back, but a strand had come loose and lay across her cheek. He could see it from where he lay, moving as she breathed, a twist of crimson against her pale skin.

The tunnel vision was gone. Beside the bed was an IV that trickled a clear liquid into his arm. He moved his head back and forth. He looked down at himself. He was covered by a sheet; his arms were free and both his feet seemed to be under there. He lifted one arm; there was his hand, just where it ought to be. He swallowed. He was thirsty.

Of course he wasn't back in a Russian prison cell; he was home, in New York, where he was supposed to be, except he was in a hospital room. At any rate, he had made it back to the present. He thought about the times his father had come back when Alex was a child, beat up, sometimes starving. Wasn't there a better way to work this?

"Hello," Molly said quietly. "Are you really awake?"

He turned and looked at her. He tried to speak, couldn't, cleared his throat, and then croaked a hello.

She got a glass of water from the nightstand and held it to his lips while he drank. "Hello," he said again, more clearly.

She took his hand. "That's it? Hello? You suddenly appear in the middle of the night, unconscious, virtually dead; you scare me half to death and all you can say is hello?"

She was trying to be sarcastic, but it wasn't working. Her voice wasn't up to it.

It seemed to fall into place as he looked up at her. She made it real. He thought of Katya, the dream, the past. He had loved Katya, but in the end he had failed her, left her, lost her. But there had been no other way, could have been no other outcome. Molly was the anchor; Molly was what mattered; Molly filled the spot deep inside that had been so empty for so long. It seemed so simple: The thing that had been missing all along was Molly. Oh, yes, so simple.

He watched a lone tear trickle down her cheek.

He squeezed her hand. "Ah, Molly, my love," he whispered.

Two days later he was off the IV and eating real food. Hospital scrambled eggs, a piece of toast. It was wonderful. "I almost achieved enlightenment there at the end," he said with his mouth full. He had told her only a little about what had happened. He had to promise her a minute-by-minute account in the near future. It was too much, too big, would take too long. It could wait. "For a while I understood everything. I could feel it inside me. I had all the answers to all the questions." He stopped for a moment and chewed his toast. "Unfortunately, I can't remember any of it. Just the feeling, just the knowing. Terrific, huh? Here I achieve nirvana and I can't remember the specifics."

"You almost achieved death there at the end," Molly said. She was sitting in the plastic chair with her legs pulled up. She was wearing the same blue jeans and silk shirt she had worn the first night she came to his house. It made him feel good to see her in these clothes; it gave him a sense of continuity.

"You were suffering from malnutrition, dehydration, and exposure when they brought you in. The doctor said you might have lasted another day or two, depending on the temperature wherever you were. You were under, here, in the hospital, sleeping or drugged for forty-eight hours. It might have been nirvana for you, but it wasn't for the rest of us."

"Sorry. But it was interesting. It was worth it. I didn't die. Which reminds me, has anyone said what's going to become of Surrey's stuff? All his books and notes and letters?"

Soon after he had regained consciousness, she had told him that Surrey had died. It had confused him for a few minutes; old Surrey, young Surrey, then and now, it had all been a jumble. After he got it sorted out, he realized that he hadn't been as affected by it as he thought he would be. To him, Surrey was still alive; he'd just left him a few weeks ago. Although the old man was gone, the young one was still out there; only he was in the past. It was a different way of looking at things, putting the continuum on a horizontal rather than a vertical plane. His dead father was really alive; his old friend Surrey was really dead and in some other time his young friend Surrey was still kicking around. The trick to keeping it straight was in not thinking about it too hard.

"No one's said anything about it as far as I know. Is it important?"

"I don't know. Maybe."

She shrugged. "Forget it for now. Just get well."

"I am well," he said. "Well enough, anyway. I'm getting out of here tomorrow. I'm bored and I have things to do."

"No, Alex, not yet. The doctor said you were badly hurt."

He waved both arms and wiggled his feet. "All better, see. Besides, as you know, I'm a Friedrich Nietzsche follower: 'That which hurts me but does not kill me makes me stronger.'"

She shook her head. "Then you must be very strong indeed."

He looked at her, serious now. "Oh yes, Molly. Very strong."

Chapter 51

IT WAS A COOL DAY. THEY WOULD HAVE A FIRE THAT NIGHT. HE smiled at the mailman and took the handful of letters. He closed the door, put the mail addressed to Molly on the hall table, and sat down in his chair. The only letter for him was in a thick manila envelope. He tore open the flap. Another sealed envelope inside with a cover letter.

"Dear Mr.Balfour: As lawyer for the estate of the late Maxwell Surrey I would appreciate your calling on me at your earliest convenience. In his will Mr. Surrey has listed you as his chief beneficiary and as such you will inherit the bulk of his estate as soon as various formalities are observed. There should be few complications as his instructions were very straightforward. I include here a letter that was found among his recent effects. Instructions appended to it charge me to forward it to you as soon as possible in the eventuality of his death. I have now done so. Again, please contact me at your earliest convenience. Sincerely, G.T. Hunt, Attorney-at-Law."

He opened the second envelope.

"My dear Alex: Forgive this melodramatic reaching out from the grave, but I feel I owe you several explanations. I am writing this a week after we had our grilled cheese luncheon at which I evaded most of your questions, for

366

which reasons you will by now be aware. With your recent disappearance I have assumed you have embarked upon your—or should I say, our—great adventure.

"I do not know how long I will live, but I am an extremely old man and it cannot be so very much longer. I go to the end with little reluctance. I am tired of baby food and infirmity. Besides, we had some times, did we not?

"The fact that you are reading this rather than hearing me say it to you means that I am, indeed, dead. And let me tell you that it gives a man a very odd feeling to write a line like that. But do not grieve for me; I have gone to my end willingly. When a man can no longer tie his own shoes, it is time to put away the books, clean up your desk, and go to join your ancestors.

"So, get on with it, Max, I'm sure you're saying, waiting for the old man to answer the questions, finish the story.

"Oddly enough, for a man of my percipience, it took me an astonishingly long time to figure out what was going on. I did not meet your father until twenty-five years after our adventure. By then I had made my own life, teaching, research, travel, history. That particular memory had faded into the half-life of youthful adventure. Except for one important exception, which I shall come to in a moment.

"At that time I came across an article by your father in one of the journals that indicated that he and I were pursuing a parallel course on some historical questions. It was a brilliant article; your father was an historian of great perception. Had he not become a popularizer, I am sure he would have had a distinguished career as a scholar. But fate plays us some funny tricks, and by *funny* I don't necessarily mean 'amusing.'

"I contacted your father. We corresponded; we met, and the rest, as they say, is history. Ho, ho. We became friends. I have always felt your surprise at this, my friendship with your father. Let me say that in the early days, before his great commercial success, your father was an admirable, amusing, stimulating man to be around. A man of great gifts. You cannot understand your mother's love for him: Had you known him back then, you would understand. What he became later, under the pressure of his fame, was in many ways inevitable and, for those who cared for him, forgivable. You, bearing much of the brunt of his oppression and distance, seeing nothing of the earlier man, will find it difficult, if not impossible, to forgive. But by now you will understand the terrible pressure that his unusual ability had placed upon him. For it is now upon you.''

Alex got up and went to the kitchen to fix himself a cup of the strong Russian tea he had searched for and come up with in New York's small enclave of expatriate Slavs, Little Odessa. He no longer cared for normal tea; it tasted weak to him. The house was quiet. Molly was out shopping. He held the warm cup between his hands, near his face, and inhaled the leathery steam.

He sat back down, balanced the cup on the arm of the chair.

"To me, at that time, your father was a young man. A brilliant young man with a future within the field. With a lovely wife. I helped him with his books, especially the first ones, as he struggled with all the problems of early success.

"Shortly after our meeting you were born. Even then I did not connect you, even though the names were the same, with the man I had fought beside years before. Coincidence. Who would have connected these events? It is easy to say now, looking back: Max, you were stupid; how could you have missed it? But I did. Only when you reached adolescence and began to actually look like the man I had known did it begin to fall into place. Your father's absolute realism in his books, your family's long absences, etc., etc. I asked your father, of course; *confronted* him would be a better word. He denied everything. What could I do? It was his business. And so we all lived, perched on the edge of knowing and not knowing and pretending not to know. Very precarious. I waited, Alex; I thought it through and came to the conclusion that I couldn't tell you anything about what would happen, or what had happened. But now, here it is, the rest of the story.

"The journey north with Tanya was something of an anticlimax. Once out of the Urals and north past Kirov the entire railway line was held by the Americans with assistance from the British. As soon as my citizenship was established, there were no more problems. When we arrived in Archangel, the British took us on board the warship that Preston had arranged for us and we were soon in England. I stayed in England for a year, working to extricate Tanya from the

368

entanglements of the British foreign office. They insisted that she be hidden away on some remote farm in the north to live out her days as a milkmaid, a plan that neither she nor I, obviously, approved. For by then, as you no doubt have guessed, she and I were lovers. What you surely could not guess was that we stayed that way throughout her life, ending only with her death on August sixteenth, nineteen sixty-two. A loss to which I have never become reconciled.

"Do you remember the little stuffed dog she dragged around with her everywhere? They were inseparable. Well, there was a reason for that. Inside the little dog she had a large selection of the Russian crown jewels. All the women in the family had jewelry sewn into their clothing, but Tanya had outdone the others with her little dog. Those jewels were to be the basis of the rather large fortune she amassed over the years and, ultimately, gave away to various Russian relief organizations. Which brings us to your clever list, which I have appended to the last page of this letter. A souvenir for you."

Alex flipped to the last page. Stapled to the top, the paper old and yellowed, was the list he had given Tanya. A very short list. The result of one art history class in undergraduate school. "For purposes of investment," he had written, "buy the work of the following painters: Monet, Degas, Renoir, Cezanne, Manet." He had assumed that the English would have supplied her with money. Those particular painters would be selling for very little at the time. And the value of their works would increase dramatically over the years. He flipped back.

"Yes, a very clever list. What you neglected to consider was that the work of these men did not appreciate in value for quite some time. Had Tanya to depend on them alone she would have quickly starved to death. Fortunately, the value of precious stones has always been high and constant."

Alex felt his cheeks flush. Long-distance embarrassment. He remembered making out the list and his frustration. Here he had been, in that position that everyone has wished himself at one time or another, back in the past with the knowledge of the future. How he had longed for a course in economics. Tell her to buy IBM? It wasn't even called IBM back then. Tell her to bet on a particular racehorse. What racehorse? Television? Computers? How does one explain such things in a note?

"What you might have done was warn us of the Depression. But once again the jewels saw us through that difficult time and back to prosperity. Tanya became quite an accomplished businesswoman, an investor in the stock market, with a sideline in what were to become the great masters of art. Thanks to you. Also, thanks to you, I have long been the possessor of a Picasso and two Monets that the outside world has never seen. These will become yours now that I am dead. Now that I am dead? Old as I am, the pen trembles at these words. Odd how we cling to even a worn-out life.

"At any rate, Tanya lived in one of our better residence hotels for her entire life. She was reclusive, never venturing out unless circumstances demanded it, but on the whole hers, and ours, was a satisfactory life.

"But what of the others? I remained in contact with Preston, the consul, for many years. He, as did I, assumed that you were dead. Katya, with her usual competence, delivered the Tsar to the English in Vladivostok. (Preston had by then decided that he should handle matters directly and had entrained to Vladivostok without difficulty.) Katya showed up only hours before the ship was to disembark. In a long letter to me, delivered through the embassy here in New York, Preston reported that you had been left behind at some point to man the barricades and that Katya had fought through alone. He attempted to convince her to go with him, but she insisted on staying behind. He had the distinct impression that she was going back to find you. It didn't surprise me. Even though I knew her so short a time, her qualities, loyalty among them, were obvious."

He put the letter down. Surprise? No. Just another casualty he had left strewn behind him. She went back for him.

His head hurt. Small lights began to twinkle in the corners of his eyes. He rubbed his face. He heard the door open.

Molly stood in the doorway, carrying a bag of groceries.

"Alex?" She put the groceries down. "What's wrong?"

He stood up, felt the world tilt.

She pulled off her jacket and dropped it on the floor. Went to him.

370

He looked down at her. Her face was worried. Molly. Such lovely red hair.

"Alex? You look so pale." She put her arms around him.

She was warm. A presence. Real. The world held. He held onto her.

She squeezed him and looked up. "Are you all right?"

He nodded. "Yes. It's just a letter. From Max. He wrote it before he died. His lawyer sent it. In a way it's like having him back again, talking to him. I'll be all right." He smiled to prove it.

She stepped back, looked at him up and down and decided he was telling the truth. "I'll put the groceries away," she said. "Why don't you start a fire?" He nodded and went back to the letter.

"I guess the last character in the play was Nicholas. He too survived and lived a long life. He was taken to England and lived out his years on a small farm in a remote spot on the English coast. The same plan they had envisioned for Tanya. He lived as a hired hand/boarder with a solid middle-class English farm family. Preston wrote me every few years, though there was little to report. Nicholas never spoke again, although towards the end he would write short notes to the family who kept him. They all grew to love him and he became something of a local character, the simpleminded, hard-working old bachelor. In his spare time he grew roses that were said to be quite extraordinary. He was known to the locals, with fondness, as 'Rose Nick.' If they only knew. He died at the age of eighty, quietly, in his sleep.

"And there it is, my friend. As I said before, we had some times. I leave you to it. Now it is I who have gone.

"Hah! But not quite yet! There are a few grilled cheese sandwiches left in me. Not many, but who knows? Perhaps we have met again?"

The letter was signed with Max's usual flourish. Down at the bottom was a postscript.

"I almost forgot. Nicholas did not go to his grave without recognition aside from his known past. It seems he developed two hybrid roses that entered the commercial marketplace. They can still be found in today's rose catalogues. One, ironically, a deep blood-red, named the Nicholas. The other, a pale white, very delicate, named for the love of his life, the Alexandra.''

Names. Alex slid the letter back into the envelope. He laid it carefully on the floor. The names of the past. He got up and went to the fireplace, bent down, and began arranging the logs. Max, Preston, Nicholas, Alexandra, Vasilli, Tatiana, Katya; and Molly. Always Molly.

He stuffed a newspaper under the logs. He lit a match, looked at the small flame. And now? Was the world really as bland as it felt, as thin as the tea that no longer satisfied him? Was there anything left for him here, anything other than Molly?

He lit the fire. And what had the world gained? Max and Tanya. Alex and, for a little while, Katya. And now, for the future, Molly. The Tsar of All Russia and two roses, one red, one white. Was it worth it?

Oh, yes; oh, yes.